THE WRATH OF
THE GREAT GUILDS

NPL F

Nashville Public Library | FOUNDATION

D1320138

PRAISE FOR THE PILLARS OF REALITY SERIES

"Campbell has created an interesting world... [he] has created his characters in such a meticulous way, I could not help but develop my own feelings for both of them. I have already gotten the second book and will be listening with anticipation."

—Audio Book Reviewer

"I loved *The Hidden Masters of Marandur*...The intense battle and action scenes are one of the places where Campbell's writing really shines. There are a lot of urban and epic fantasy novels that make me cringe when I read their battles, but Campbell's years of military experience help him write realistic battles."

—All Things Urban Fantasy

"I highly recommend this to fantasy lovers, especially if you enjoy reading about young protagonists coming into their own and fighting against a stronger force than themselves. The world building has been strengthened even further giving the reader more history. Along with the characters flight from their pursuers and search for knowledge allowing us to see more of the continent the pace is constant and had me finding excuses to continue the book."

—Not Yet Read

"*The Dragons of Dorcastle*... is the perfect mix of steampunk and fantasy... it has set the bar to high."

—The Arched Doorway

"Quite a bit of fun and I really enjoyed it. . .An excellent sequel and well worth the read!"

—Game Industry

"The Pillars of Reality series continues in THE ASSASSINS OF ALTIS to be a great action filled adventure. . .So many exciting things happen that I can hardly wait for the next book to be released."

—Not Yet Read

"The Pillars of Reality is a series that gets better and better with each new book. . .THE ASSASSINS OF ALTIS is a great addition to a great series and one I recommend to fantasy fans, especially if you like your fantasy with a touch of sci-fi."

—Bookaholic Cat

"Seriously, get this book (and the first two). This one went straight to my favorites shelf."

—Reanne Reads

"[Jack Campbell] took my expectations and completely blew them out of the water, proving yet again that he can seamlessly combine steampunk and epic fantasy into a truly fantastic story. . .I am looking forward to seeing just where Campbell goes with the story next, I'm not sure how I'm going to manage the wait for the next book in the series."

—The Arched Doorway

PRAISE FOR THE LOST FLEET SERIES

"It's the thrilling saga of a nearly-crushed force battling its way home from deep within enemy territory, laced with deadpan satire about modern warfare and neoliberal economics. Like Xenophon's Anabasis – with spaceships."

—The Guardian (UK)

"Black Jack is an excellent character, and this series is the best military SF I've read in some time."

—Wired Magazine

"If you're a fan of character, action, and conflict in a Military SF setting, you would probably be more than pleased by Campbell's offering."

—Tor.com

". . . a fun, quick read, full of action, compelling characters, and deeper issues. Exactly the type of story which attracts readers to military SF in the first place."

—SF Signal

"Rousing military-SF action... it should please many fans of old-fashioned hard SF. And it may be a good starting point for media SF fans looking to expand their SF reading beyond tie-in novels."

—SciFi.com

"Fascinating stuff ... this is military SF where the military and SF parts are both done right."

—SFX Magazine

THE WRATH OF
THE GREAT GUILDS

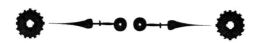

Pillars of Reality
Book Six

JACK CAMPBELL

Published by JABberwocky Literary Agency, Inc.

To my niece
Dr. Megan Meier

To S, as always

ACKNOWLEDGMENTS

I remain indebted to my agents, Joshua Bilmes and Eddie Schneider, for their long standing support, ever-inspired suggestions and assistance, as well as to Krystyna Lopez and Lisa Rodgers for their work on foreign sales and print editions. Thanks also to Catherine Asaro, Robert Chase, Carolyn Ives Gilman, J.G. (Huck) Huckenpohler, Simcha Kuritzky, Michael LaViolette, Aly Parsons, Bud Sparhawk and Constance A. Warner for their suggestions, comments and recommendations.

CHAPTER ONE

I WILL GO to Dorcastle."

She said it, knowing that the mightiest military force in history would soon attack that city.

She said it, knowing that the foremost target of the attackers would be her.

She said it, because she had to. Because the daughter of Jules had been prophesized to someday unite Mages, Mechanics, and the common people to save the world of Dematr. And, according to the Mages and the common people, Master Mechanic Mari of Caer Lyn was that daughter. They believed in her. They needed her. If she didn't do the job, no one else could.

But if she failed, if she died at Dorcastle at the hands of the Great Guilds and the Imperial legions aiding them, then the common people would remain in bondage and the world would soon sink into chaos.

No pressure.

* * *

Alain walked with Mari out into the earliest morning twilight, the sky to the east barely brighter than the night above and to the west. Behind them, the walls of Tiaesun loomed. Far to the north, the walls of Dorcastle awaited.

Mari's black hair and dark jacket had blended with the fading night, but now began to stand out against the growing light of dawn. Alain remembered the first time he had seen her, emerging from the dust raised by the destruction of the caravan with which they had been traveling. The only outward difference between now and that day about two years ago was that Mari carried one of the new rifles.

"What are you thinking?" Mari asked him in a hushed voice.

"I am thinking that this day we are wearing the same clothing as we did the day we met," Alain said. "You in your Mechanics jacket and I in my Mage robes. But though our appearance is nearly the same as it was then, both of us have changed, me much more than you. I have rejected much of what the Mage Guild once forced me to believe. I once again accept feelings, I once again believe that other people are real."

"Do you think I haven't changed much?" Mari scoffed, an edge of tension riding her voice. "Aside from me falling in love with a Mage, do you really think the eighteen-year-old woman you met the day the caravan was destroyed would have seriously considered riding to confront the Great Guilds and the Empire?"

"Yes," Alain said. "Because she would not leave behind anyone who needed her, not even a seventeen-year-old Mage such as I was."

"Maybe. But she was running for her life, trying to get away from people trying to kill her. This time I'm running toward people who want to kill me. And in the last couple of years I've learned a lot more about how it feels when people are trying to kill you." She stopped walking for a moment, breathing slowly, looking up at the sky. "I'm scared," she whispered.

Alain grasped her hand in his. "I will not let harm befall you."

"You're an amazing man with amazing abilities, my Mage, but even you can't promise that." Mari inhaled deeply, squeezed his hand, and began walking again over the rough grass outside the city. "I can't let anyone see how scared I am. I'll get the job done. No matter what. Help me do what I have to do, Alain."

"Always." Distressed by her fear, but not knowing what other comfort to offer, Alain followed Mari.

They had expected to find Major Sten from the Confederation, who had carried the word of the danger to Dorcastle, waiting to accompany them back north. Instead, a large group of people and an even larger herd of saddled horses stood by the road. In the growing light, Alain saw that most of the men and women waiting for them were cavalry, swords at their hips, metal cuirasses armoring their chests, and helms topped with short plumes that nodded in the faint breeze. The lances held by the cavalry troopers formed a small, bare forest pointing skyward.

"What's this?" Mari asked.

"An escort," answered Queen Sien of Tiae. Dressed similarly to the cavalry but wearing a gold band set with a large emerald on her forehead rather than an armored helm, Sien had blended in with the others in the pre-dawn murk.

"It's too many," Mari objected.

Sien came up to Mari and embraced her. "Not for my friend. Not for the daughter of Jules who we hope will free this world."

"Sien—"

"I owe you so much. Tiae owes you so much. My kingdom lives again because of what you helped make happen. Consider this a small return on that."

Alain looked over the cavalry. More than one hundred soldiers, their green uniforms new, their armor and helms old but shining, their sabers and lances sharp. The horses were a mix of breeds, but all strong and well seasoned. There were two mounts for every rider, and several wagons loaded with feed for their horses and provisions for the soldiers. From most places, the commitment would have been welcome but small. From Tiae, still recovering from decades of anarchy, it was an impressive and meaningful gift. "The company of these soldiers will be welcome to us," he said. "If even a hint that we ride north reaches the wrong ears, there will be dangers awaiting us before we reach Dorcastle."

"Some of them will protect you all the way to Dorcastle," Sien said. "And then remain to aid in the defense of the city."

Mari stared at her friend, and then at the cavalry again. "Do they know what's coming to attack Dorcastle? The Imperial legions and the full force of the Great Guilds?"

"They know," Sien said. "They are all volunteers. When the Kingdom of Tiae broke and fell into anarchy, it had no friends to come to its aid because it had never concerned itself with the needs of others. But now the kingdom is reborn, and perhaps wiser. We have little to offer, but we will send what we can to aid our neighbors to the north."

"The Queen of Tiae is wise," Alain said.

"The Queen of Tiae wishes she could send an army with you. But she will accompany you part of the way," Sien added. "I and the remaining cavalry will ride to Pacta Servanda."

"But the Syndari allies of the Great Guilds might hit other parts of Tiae—" Mari began.

Sien silenced Mari with a gesture, leaning close to her and Alain. "Breathe not a word to others outside us three. The oldest obligation of the royal family is tied to Pacta Servanda. It is known only to the family and their closest advisors. I know of it only because one of the kingdom's surviving advisors was able to tell me before he died. Pacta Servanda must not fall. I do not know why, but that is my duty as queen, and that is why I made what could have been the last stand of Tiae at that place."

"Why is this?" Alain asked. "Why is such an obligation placed on the rulers of Tiae? Pacta is only a modest-sized town."

"I don't know," Sien said. "But I know that with the crown comes the responsibility to defend Pacta. Let us waste no more time on this." She stepped back. "The daughter must ride to Dorcastle, and the Queen of Tiae must ride to Pacta Servanda."

"Neither the Syndaris nor the legions will know what hit them," Mari said, smiling, as Sien and Alain swung into their saddles.

Mari slid her new rifle into the leather scabbard hanging next to her saddle, then mounted the mare, sighing. "This is going to be a long, painful ride."

"With the Syndaris threatening shipping, we could not risk a journey north by sea," Alain said.

"I know. And there hasn't been time to get the steam locomotive tracks repaired and replaced in Tiae, and the trains in the Confederation will be under the control of the Mechanics Guild. None of that's going to make this ride any easier on my backside. Did all the couriers get off at midnight?" Mari looked at Sien, whose stallion was looking about excitedly, head held high.

"They did," Sien confirmed, patting her horse's neck to calm him. "To all cities along the coast of Tiae, and to the stronghold at Pacta Servanda, as well as to the Confederation and to your army south and east of us."

Mari looked to the southeast, where nothing could be seen but darkness building on darkness beneath the slowly paling sky. "The moment General Flyn hears of the danger to Dorcastle and Pacta he'll start countermarching back to Tiaesun and then north."

"I will see that Pacta holds. With your help, Dorcastle will too, until your army arrives," Sien said.

"Yes," Mari said. "Dorcastle will hold."

Alain, trained like all Mages to tell when others spoke lies, easily heard the worry under Mari's self-assured words. But the others listening heard and saw only her confidence as Mari waved a farewell and then flicked her reins, Alain and Sien keeping their horses close to hers, the cavalry escort following.

One of the cavalry rode up beside Alain, saluting him, Mari, and his queen. "Major Danel, commander of your escort by order of the Queen," he introduced himself. Danel was old for his rank, tough and wiry with scars on his face, a survivor of the decades of anarchy in Tiae.

"I could have chosen no better commander for the task," Sien said. "That he volunteered immediately speaks of his quality."

Mari nodded at Danel. "Major, why did you do so?"

"As well might I ask why you volunteered to go to Dorcastle, Lady," the major replied.

"There's only one me," Mari said. "But why did you and these others volunteer?"

"You may speak plainly," Sien told him. "Lady Mari and her Mage value straight words as much as I do."

Danel looked backwards for a moment, where his soldiers rode silently, only the sound of shod hooves on the road and the rattle of harness marking their presence. "I can't be certain of all of them. I know that for me and many others, there is not much left behind. My family was wiped out long ago."

"I'm sorry," Mari said.

"You would have been barely a child yourself when it happened, Lady," Danel said. "Even younger than Queen Sien was then. There was nothing you could have done to stop it. Many of the others also lost everything that mattered to them. Until the New Day began to dawn in Tiae. You, Lady—you and your Mage—have given us some things to fight for again. Freedom for everyone from the chains of the Great Guilds. A reborn kingdom, under a queen who is worthy of her rule. So, we will fight. We will fight in a foreign land so that those who have much more left to lose can stay close to their homes and defend Tiae."

"You do not worry about death?" Alain asked, surprised that a common person would feel that way. He kept his voice and expression free of emotion without even thinking about it. Even after two years with Mari he usually behaved in the manner in which Mage acolytes were brutally taught.

Major Danel rode quietly for a long moment before answering. "I have seen enough of death for it to be a familiar companion. I stopped fearing it long ago. And if, as some say, those who have died await us on the other side of the unseen door, then perhaps I would find welcome there. But even if that is not so, I want my death to matter, Sir Mage. I have fought to save my kingdom, and now I will fight to free the world."

"Those are good reasons," Mari said. "Thank you."

"What will that world be like, Lady? Will it be a world free from war?"

"I wish I could promise that. I can't. All I can promise is that when wars happen, they will be because the people and their leaders choose those fights, not because the Great Guilds are playing games with human pieces."

"Let us hope those people and leaders have wisdom," Danel said. He half-bowed in the saddle toward his queen. "As much wisdom as our own."

Sien nodded in reply. "Like yours, Major, my wisdom was born of pain. Perhaps we can build a world where there is more wisdom and less suffering."

Major Danel smiled, saluted once more, then fell back behind Mari, Alain, and Sien.

They rode through the growing light and heat of the day, stopping for only short breaks, changing to their spare mounts when the pace of the ride began to wear too heavily on their horses. They halted long after the sun had set. Alain, toughened as he was by his training as a Mage, nevertheless welcomed the too-brief rest. Mari, exhausted but already stiff and sore from the long ride as well as haunted by her worries, kept him awake for a while as she shifted restlessly in her sleep. Sien slept slightly apart from them. She had spent most of the day in silence, as if devoting all of her thoughts to the task ahead.

Before dawn, they rode onward.

* * *

Two days after leaving Tiaesun, following the path of the long-neglected Royal Road, they reached the spot where the new road from Pacta Servanda intersected it from the west. Two wagons and a string of fresh horses awaited them, as well as men and women who sprang to attention.

Captain Patila from Mari's army, standing by one of the wagons, saluted. "Your Majesty, Lady Mari, Sir Alain, it's good to see you."

"How goes the work at Pacta Servanda?" Sien asked.

"Well, Your Majesty. Colonel Sima and Lady Mechanic Alli are preparing a very warm welcome for the Syndaris. All were happy to hear that you will lead the defense of Pacta."

Sien nodded. "With commanders such as Colonel Sima and Lady Mechanic Alli, as well as fighters such as you, I have no fear of the outcome." She turned to Mari. "I should not linger here, with the Syndaris possibly to strike at any time. I wish I could ride to Dorcastle with you."

"If I'm going to make friends with queens," Mari said, "I have to accept that they have their own responsibilities. Alain and I will see you again once this is over."

"Of course," Queen Sien said, sounding as if she truly believed that would happen. "Remember, Mage Alain, you have promised to bring Mari back to me."

"I will," Alain said.

Sien gripped his arm. "The common people have long used the saying *a Mage's promise* to describe something worthless. But I know that from you a promise is more valuable than any jewel. Bring yourself back safe as well, my friend."

The cavalry had already sorted itself out, the sixty-one who would ride to Dorcastle separated from the forty who would ride with their queen to Pacta. Sien mounted again, looking down at Mari. "Fate chose a worthy champion in you. If the task can be done, I know you will do it."

"Thank you," Mari said. She and Alain watched Queen Sien lead her cavalry west along the new road. "I should be going to help hold Pacta," Mari commented to Alain.

"If it can be done," Alain said, deliberately evoking Sien's words, "then she will do it. You are needed elsewhere."

"*We* are needed elsewhere," Mari corrected him. "Can you tell me anything else about Pacta, Captain? I'm glad they could spare you long enough to bring us these fresh horses."

Patila smiled confidently. "Lady Mechanic Alli asked me to send you her regrets. She is busy fortifying and preparing her artillery to greet the Syndaris in the manner they deserve."

"How does Alli feel about the situation?" Mari asked wearily. She handed her tired horse over to the wranglers from Pacta, who were helping transfer saddles and other tack to the fresh mounts.

"She told me that if the Syndaris had hit us by surprise, it might have been ugly," Patila confessed. "But since the courier arrived with your warning and orders, Colonel Sima and Lady Alli have been reinforcing all of the seaward defenses and emplacing new ones. If the Syndaris come in great strength, we may be hard pressed. But I think we will hold them. Especially with Queen Sien at Pacta to lend heart to us. It surprised many of us to hear she was coming, but we were all happy at the news."

"I'm glad that Queen Sien is respected by everyone," Mari said.

"Second only to you and your Mage, Lady. You know that we of the Western Alliance, and those of the Confederation, regard nobility with great suspicion, but Queen Sien has the respect of us all."

"Good. Um…" Mari began awkwardly, "my parents and sister… and the other families at Pacta…"

"They are all being moved to safe locations well away from where we expect any fighting," Patila said. "Except for those who have volunteered to help defend Pacta, that is. Since they lack training, we're using them to guard places behind the front and to protect the other citizens."

"Are there many such volunteers?" Alain asked, curious.

"More than we can arm," Patila said, smiling. "By order of Lady Mari, Pacta is a place where all have a voice and a belief in what they work for. They want to fight to protect that."

"It's just common sense," Mari objected. "Help people realize that what they do matters, that their efforts count and that everyone needs to work together, and they'll work and fight better."

Patila shook her head. "Such sense is far from common."

"It shouldn't be." Mari, clearly seeking something else to talk about besides praise for her decisions, frowned at the wagons Patila had brought. "What is all this?"

Patila waved her hand toward the farther wagon. "Feed and rations for beasts and humans going on north. We thought you might need them. This one," she said, patting the side of the near wagon, "contains fifteen new A-1 rifles, ammunition for them, and three DKs."

"You can't afford to divert rifles from the defense of—" Mari began. "Wait. DKs? What's a DK?"

"Dragon killer," Patila explained with a grin. She indicated three long tubes in the wagon. Alain recognized the type of weapon that had saved him in the Northern Ramparts. "Only five have been finished. Lady Alli insisted that you get three of them."

Mari smiled, then grimaced. "Lady Alli is the best. But why did she send fifteen rifles? I told her to hold onto everything she needed to defend Pacta."

"She and Colonel Sima felt that we had sufficient firepower to send you the fifteen," Patila said. "We have enough rifles for everyone trained in their use, and Lady Alli is concerned about giving rifles to those who lack experience. She said she feared they would do more harm to our own side than to the enemy."

"Having seen Apprentices on their first day on the firing range, I know what Alli is thinking, but still…"

"I'm just following orders, Lady," Patila said.

"They could be important at Dorcastle," Alain said, having seen how much Mari wanted to accept the rifles but also that she feared weakening the defenses of Pacta Servanda. "From what I know of Alli, she would not have sent the rifles unless she was confident it was the right decision."

"Yeah," Mari agreed. "If Alli says she can spare them… You should have mentioned these when the queen was here, Captain."

"Lady Mechanic Alli said she would personally inform the queen when she arrived at Pacta," Patila said.

"All right. Major Danel?" Mari called to the commander of the Tiae cavalry. "How many of your people have ever fired a Mechanic rifle?"

Major Danel came to the wagon, gazing at the weapons in astonishment. Under the long rule of the world by the Mechanics Guild, the less-capable repeating rifles hand-built by the Guild had been so rare and expensive that an entire army might have only ten, with little ammunition for those. "These are intended for us? All of them?"

"All of them."

"Lady, few of my soldiers have ever used Mechanic weapons in battle, but your General Flyn arranged that we all receive some training while your army was at Tiaesun."

"You've got saddle scabbards for the rifles, too?" Mari asked Patila. "Of course. Alli wouldn't forget those. Get the rifles handed out to your best shots, Major. There's ammunition here, too."

Alain's attention was diverted as he saw a lanky young man making his way toward them from the horses. There was no sense of menace in the man, just nervousness, but Alain placed one hand on the knife under his robes and drew Captain Patila's attention to him.

"Hold on," Patila said, blocking the young man's path. "Why did you leave the horses?"

"I have a letter," the man said, stubbornness vying with anxiety at being confronted by the captain. "I have a letter I am supposed to deliver to Sir Mage Alain if I ever see him."

Patila held out her hand, and with a slight hesitation the man brought forth a folded piece of paper. She unfolded it, shook it out and looked it over, then passed the letter to Alain.

Alain, aware that Mari was watching curiously, looked at the letter and despite his Mage training had trouble controlling his reaction. "This is from Bara. Aunt Bara."

"You…you remember her?" the young man asked.

"I could not forget her, any more than I could forget my mother and father," Alain said.

"You have an aunt?" Mari demanded. "You never mentioned having an aunt."

"I did not think she would wish to acknowledge me since I became a Mage." He began reading.

Sir Mage Alain, you very likely do not remember me, but I am the older sister of your mother. Over two years ago I saw a

Mage visit the remembrance grounds in our village and stand before your parents' graves for a long time. I thought the Mage must be you, but I was afraid to go to him. Since then I have heard many things about the daughter, and about the Mage with her. They say his name is Alain. I can only hope that Mage is my long-lost nephew.

My eldest son Petr wants to join the daughter. I fear for his safety, but he is set on it. He is a good man, but so young yet in his mother's eyes. If you are Alain, please welcome your cousin Petr, and please look out for him for my sake.

If you are Lori's son, I know she would be very proud of you for helping the daughter and doing so many brave things. I never forgot you. I hope you have not forgotten us.

Alain had to pause when he finished, trying to deal with emotions he had long kept buried deeply. "Petr. You are the son of Aunt Bara."

Petr nodded, his face working with emotion. "Is it really you, Alain? We played sometimes, when we were little."

"I have memories of you," Alain said. "We were very young. You liked horses. I was frightened of them."

"You were a few years younger," Petr said. "The last time we saw each other was on your fifth birthday. Just a little guy." He held out a flat hand near his hip to mime Alain's height at the time.

"I remember. The Mages came for me soon after that. I held to the memories of that day even when the Mage elders demanded that we acolytes forget our former lives," Alain said.

Mari had taken the letter, read it, and now smiled at Petr. "Welcome, cousin."

Petr turned an awestricken look on her. "Lady...I...I...I'm not—"

"I'm married to Mage Alain. That makes us cousins," Mari said. "Thanks for helping to free the world. Please write your mother and tell her that Mage Alain was very happy to see you."

"Is...he?" Petr asked, eyeing Alain's unrevealing expression.

"I am," Alain said, trying his best to relax and show feeling. He knew his smiles often looked strained, but attempted one anyway.

"That's good. But…daughter…" Petr fumbled. "I wanted to be a soldier for you. When I got to Pacta they told me that people who were good with horses were needed more than people who were good with swords." He shrugged apologetically. "Not that I'm good with a sword."

"They told you the truth," Mari said. "Without good herders our cavalry and our wagons don't move. You and your skills are playing a very important part in defeating the Great Guilds. I'm sorry we can't stay to visit, but we have an important appointment in Dorcastle."

Alain, grateful that Mari was so smoothly welcoming and reassuring to Petr, fought his Mage training successfully enough to be able to reach out and grasp Petr's shoulder. "I am…happy to see you once more after so many years."

Mari had pulled out a sheet of paper and was quickly writing. "Captain Patila? I know you'll be very busy once you get back to Pacta, but I need to have this delivered to my parents."

"Of course, Lady. They'll be all right," Patila added.

"I'm sure they will be with defenders like you," Mari said. "Thank you." Mounting her new horse with a pained expression as her bottom met the saddle, Mari flashed another smile at Petr, though Alain could see the strain she hid behind it. "Look us up when we get back to Pacta."

Petr nodded to her, then to Alain with a wide smile, before turning and jogging back to the other wranglers.

Major Sten rode up, looking more haggard than the rest of the column but just as determined. "You said Colonel Sima is in command at Pacta Servanda?" he asked Patila.

"Yes, sir," Patila agreed. "He's the senior officer in the Army of the New Day at Pacta."

"Is there…" Sten paused, grimacing. "I don't know how to ask this. Sima is from the Confederation. I worked with him some years ago. From your accent, you must be from the Western Alliance. Do you work well with him?"

"Yes," Patila said. "Sima is a good commander. We've got officers from the Confederation, the Alliance, the Free Cities, and even a former Imperial. The soldiers and sailors are just as mixed a lot."

"And you work well together?" Sten extended his hand. "That is good to hear. We've grown too separate, haven't we? But the Army of the New Day shows that we can work side-by-side."

"The Great Guilds have tried to keep the commons separate," Mari said as Patila shook Sten's offered hand. "But we are all one people."

Patila looked a question at her. "Legend says the Mechanics came from the stars."

"We all came from the stars," Mari said.

Alain, seeing their astonished expressions, added a warning. "Do not yet speak of this to others. When the war is won, all shall know. Until then, there are those who must be protected."

"Yes, Sir Mage," Patila said, breaking her stare at Mari to salute Alain.

"Hold Pacta," Mari said to Patila as the column prepared to ride north again. "Queen Sien and I talked on the way up here. If you can't hold, I told her to blow up everything and fall back toward Tiaesun."

Alain cast a glance at Mari. Sien had firmly rejected the idea of abandoning Pacta Servanda no matter how bad the pressure got, even though Mari had insisted on it if retreat proved necessary. Having learned some wisdom about people, he had stayed out of the argument. The two women were equally determined to do as they thought best and unwilling to yield to the logic of the other. In this case, both were right in their positions. But he did not expect Sien to fall back.

"Sir Mechanic Lukas was supervising the placing of explosives when I left," Patila said, her face somber once more. "Some of those explosives will greet the Syndaris on the piers and the beaches when they arrive. Fear not, Lady. We will hold Pacta for you and for the queen of Tiae."

"Hold it for *you!*" Mari called as the column started north again, smaller now.

The forty cavalry were notable for their absence, but the loss of

Queen Sien felt harder to deal with, Alain thought. "What was in the note to your parents?" Alain asked Mari as they once more rode side by side.

She shrugged, as if pretending it was no big thing. "I wanted them to know I love them. Just in case I don't get another chance to tell them that." Mari looked at him. "And I told them that if you survive and I don't, I hope my parents will always consider you their son and that Kath will always think of you as a brother."

"My thanks." Alain shook his head. "But I will not survive without you."

"Don't talk like that."

Their mounts were fresh and frisky, posing some problems for men and women whose bodies were tired and sore. Major Danel led the column at a brisk enough pace to wear out the horses a little so they would be easier to handle, after which the familiar routine settled in once more. Ride for a while, dismount and walk for a while, mount up again, switch mounts, walk for a while, and so on until the sun was long past setting and the column finally halted for the darkest portion of the night.

They left the city of Minut far to the west as they rode, heading north toward the heart of the Bakre Confederation.

It was late in the afternoon of the next day when the weary column reached the border with the Confederation, where a narrow bridge spanned the broad river known here as the Glenca. The column was once again walking their horses, trudging along with footsore resolve, when the bridge came into sight.

Alain followed Mari and Major Sten as they walked their horses along the bridge to the Bakre Confederation side. There a stout barrier, a fortified guardhouse, and a small detachment of soldiers waited.

Sten, himself a Confederation officer, reached the barrier first. "Open up, Lieutenant," he told the commander of the border guards. "The daughter and her Mage are on their way to Dorcastle."

The lieutenant stared at Mari, then at Alain, then switched her gaze to the soldiers with Mari. "A courier passed this way earlier with the news. The daughter is welcome, and..." Her eyes avoided looking directly at Alain. "This is her Mage?"

"Yes," Mari said, her voice growing a little sharp at the lieutenant's reaction.

Alain understood it, though. To the world, Mages were objects of fear and loathing, a reputation earned by centuries of Mages taught to think of other people as mere shadows on the illusion of the world, shadows who could be mistreated or exploited without a second thought. "No ally of Lady Mari need have any fear of me," he told the lieutenant, doing his best to put feeling into the words.

"Yes, Sir Mage. Lady, it goes without saying that you and your Mage may enter the Confederation. But...these are foreign soldiers with you."

"From the army of Tiae," Major Sten said. "Sent by Queen Sien to escort the daughter safely to Dorcastle."

"And then to assist in the defense of the city," Mari added.

"They come to our aid?" the lieutenant asked, astounded. "I mean no offense, but I did not think it possible that Tiae could spare any soldiers to aid us."

"They cannot spare any," Sten said. "But still they send help."

"By order of their queen," Mari added. "Even though the Confederation did not presume to ask, Queen Sien sent what she could."

The lieutenant's eyes widened as they took in the rifles at the saddles of Mari and many of the soldiers. "This is an incredible gift. Open the barrier," she ordered her troops. "Konstan, ride to Denkerk and tell them the daughter, her Mage, and valiant soldiers of Tiae will be there this evening. Let our commander know that they will need fresh horses and spares for sixty-three riders."

As they walked past the lieutenant and onto the soil of the Confederation, Mari paused to smile at the lieutenant and her soldiers. "Thank you."

"Thank *you*, Lady," the lieutenant replied. "Soldiers! Salute!" She and her small force held their salutes as the soldiers of Tiae walked their horses past.

Alain saw the weary cavalry perk up at the gesture of respect. For nearly twenty years the Kingdom of Tiae had been broken, fallen into anarchy, its lands given over to the depredations of bandits and warlords fighting over the scraps of the once proud land. To be from Tiae was to be a refugee from a failed state. But now they received honors from those who would once have disdained them or viewed them with suspicion. Taught as a Mage that emotions meant nothing, Alain saw the impact of the salutes on the Tiae cavalry and realized once again that the teachings of the Mage Guild were false.

"You should uncase your colors," Major Sten advised Mari. "Let it be clear who rides north."

"Good advice," Major Danel of Tiae agreed. He passed the order back, and the two soldiers carrying the banners removed their protective sleeves so that the green and gold flag of Tiae waved over the column of riders beside Mari's blue and gold banner of the New Day.

They passed through a small village, the citizens gathering alongside the road to cheer and offer food and drink to the passing soldiers. But they had far to go yet to Dorcastle, so despite the lateness of the day and the sun sinking toward the horizon the column kept moving.

It was after sunset when they spotted Denkerk ahead, impossible to miss since the town had apparently lit every lantern, torch, and beacon the people could get their hands on. The town garrison—local militia forces rather than Confederation regulars—stood in ranks outside the town to greet the arriving cavalry and escort them into Denkerk.

Tables had been set up in the central square, loaded with food and drink. The horses were led off to be cared for by locals after the soldiers of Tiae removed personal items and their new rifles from the saddles.

"The mayor and the council await, Lady," the local commander told Mari, indicating the doorway to the grandest building on the square.

"Aren't we all eating out here?" Mari asked, looking around.

"Uh…yes, but…the daughter…special…"

Mari shook her head. "I need to eat with the others. Please ask the mayor and council to join us."

"Certainly, Lady!"

"What do you think is funny?" Mari asked Alain, standing next to him with a worn-out expression. He knew without asking that after all the riding she hurt too much to sit down again right away.

"Is funny the right word?" Alain asked, not surprised that Mari had seen feelings in him where others would have seen nothing. "I knew you would eat with the soldiers before you spoke."

"Yeah." She narrowed her eyes at him. "So?"

"It is who you are. I like who you are."

Mari smiled at him. "Good. Because you're stuck with who I am."

The next moment her attention was diverted to the town officials coming out to greet her. Alain watched, silent. No one sought to speak to him. Even though Alain wore the armband of the New Day, none of the commons here knew how to approach him. Certainly none of them showed any desire to speak to a Mage.

He rarely noticed these days the intangible thread that had connected him to Mari since he first developed feelings for her. There and not-there, the thread would stretch and fade with enough distance, but this close it offered Alain a connection, invisible to all others, with another person. He welcomed that more than usual.

Alain realized that he had become used to having around him people who welcomed his company. Friends. Once more among commons who saw Mages only as something to fear and avoid, he keenly felt the absence of friendly faces. If not for Mari being here he would be as one completely alone amidst the crowds.

Perhaps it was the melancholy brought on by that realization that triggered his erratic and unreliable foresight once more.

It had been nearly a year since he had seen the terrible vision of Mari at some future time, lying on a surface of fitted stone blocks, apparently near death. But now he saw the same vision, saw the blood upon her jacket, and had barely time to take in the horrible scene before the foresight faded and left him looking at Mari as she stood before him, doing her best to greet and reassure the local officials.

Alain kept his expression rigid despite the jolt of fear the vision brought. They were on their way to Dorcastle, to the great battle he had foreseen long before, and surely that was why he had once again seen Mari badly injured. Everything they had tried to avoid that battle had failed. If that awful fight at Dorcastle was where she was destined to be so badly hurt, could he change that? Or would his attempts to change it bring it about instead?

It did not matter. Nor did Mari's past, futile attempts to make him promise not to risk his own life to save hers. Alain looked at Mari, doing her exhausted best to present herself as the hero the commons needed, and knew that he could not endure this illusion of a world if the one thing, the one person, who made it real for him were to leave it. He would save Mari.

No matter the cost.

CHAPTER TWO

"IT'S TIME, LADY."

Mari, certain that she had closed her eyes just a few moments ago, looked up at the pre-dawn sky over Denkerk. She heard the nickering of horses being saddled and the movements of men and women preparing for another day of tough riding. It would have been much easier to feel sorry for herself if those others hadn't been experiencing the same misery.

"Are you all right?" Alain asked, sitting up beside her.

"You mean aside from my thighs and my butt? Sure," Mari said. "I was just wondering again if horses were designed as instruments of torture." She shoved herself up, grimacing at the pain of stiff and sore muscles. "How are you? You've been sort of moody."

Alain paused before answering. "I am concerned about you."

"Thanks, but it's not like this is the first time we have had to worry about people trying to kill me. And you." She would not let herself think about fear, now that they had come this far.

Mari made it to her feet, gritting her teeth against the hurt the movements generated. At least the discomfort distracted her from worrying about what would be waiting at Dorcastle.

Major Sten walked up—or perhaps *limped up* would have been a better description. This hard ride, coming on the heels of his swift ride south, must be very difficult for him to endure. Sten saluted Mari.

"Lady, the commander here tells me that there should be barges waiting at Danalee that we can ride downriver to Dorcastle."

"Barges?" Mari perked up at the news. "How about the horses?"

"There should be enough to carry all of them as well." Sten made a face. "A lot of barges should be coming upriver from Dorcastle. Evacuating the people of the city."

"Oh." The thought of all those people fleeing the city before the Imperials and the Great Guilds struck took the glow off the news. Mari rubbed her back and backside with both hands, trying to massage away some of the stiffness. The town had offered her and Alain a very nice bed inside a nice house, but she had felt obligated to sleep outside along with the Tiae cavalry. "Let's see how quickly we can get to Danalee."

One of the local militia officers came running up. "Lady? We're going to send a strong detachment along with you. Scouts have already started up the road to spot any danger before you reach it."

"Do you have warnings of danger along the road?" Alain asked, his voice reverting to that of an emotionless Mage.

Mari gave him a sharp glance to remind Alain how he was speaking and earned in return the tiny changes to his expression that passed for a sheepish look of apology.

The Confederation officer, who had probably never spoken to a Mage in his life, froze in mixed dread and indecision.

"You don't have anything to fear from my Mage," Mari told him.

Alain made an obvious effort to put more feeling into his voice. "I am sorry."

"Ah…that's…all right," the officer said, relaxing. "We had heard about the daughter's Mages but…it's hard to believe until you see it. Ah…your question, Sir Mage. No. We do not have anything specific. But we have already heard from towns up the road which have learned that the daughter is coming. The word is spreading fast. If the Great Guilds hear of it, they may attempt something."

Mari exhaled in exasperation as she pulled out her far-talker, thinking that surely this trip was already hard enough without worrying about her former co-workers gunning for her. The far-talker was one of the new models her workshops were building, smaller and better than those the Mechanics Guild depended on. But its range was still pretty limited. She squinted at the device in the dim light, switching the frequency to that usually employed by the Guild. "Let's see if anyone close enough to us is talking about it."

She knew that the locals were staring at the device. It was one of the technologies that the Mechanics Guild had kept secret from the common folk. "This is called a far-talker," Mari explained. "It lets people talk across long distances."

Something murmured faintly from the far-talker. Mari turned up the volume and held up the device to get better range.

"…on her…north?"

"…rumors…orders…Longfalls."

"Avoid…get back…"

"…what…Mages…?"

"…crazy…die…Dorcastle…"

Mari glared at the sky as the faint voices faded out. "There's something in the air that impacts the range of these devices. Something that changes with time of day and weather."

Major Sten spoke cautiously. "Could you tell what those voices meant?" From his attitude, he might have been speaking of the words of a mystic oracle.

"Not really." Had the Guild heard that she was moving north? The last bit, about someone crazy dying at Dorcastle, certainly sounded like the outcome the Guild expected for her. "Just fragments of sentences." She looked at Alain, who shook his head to indicate his foresight had provided no clues either, then replaced the far-talker in her jacket pocket. "Let's get going."

With fresh horses and spares for all the riders, they made good time again despite everyone's fatigue and soreness. As they moved up the road toward Danalee, the pain of riding alternating with the pain of walking, Mari had to force herself to perk up every time the column passed through a town or village. The people running out to see them—

to see her—wore the expressions of hope that always tore at her. Some of those watching cheered at the sight of her, others cried, and if not for the discouragements of Major Sten and the Confederation militia a long tail of eager volunteers would have joined the march to Dorcastle.

"Stay and protect your homes!" Mari called until her throat was sore, imagining those poorly armed and untrained volunteers encountering the fearsomely implacable Imperial legions. "My army will be coming this way in a few days!"

Early on the morning of the second day, as the column passed through a rolling countryside dotted with groves of trees and devoted mostly to pastureland, Alain said a single word whose emotionless intensity cut through the fatigue in everyone. "Stop."

Mari, jerked out of her own fog of weariness, looked from Alain to the road before them as she reached for the pistol under her jacket. "What is it?"

"Danger is ahead," Alain said, his eyes searching the road. "I sense two spells being used."

Major Sten exchanged glances with the commander of the Confederation militia. "The scouts up ahead haven't reported anything," the commander said, apparently more worried about contradicting Alain than by any dangers posed by the road.

"If the spells are those for concealment, then your scouts may already be dead," Alain said.

"What's beyond that low ridge ahead of us?" Mari asked.

The commander looked to his soldiers, one of whom spoke up. "The road curves, then enters a cut in the ridge." He paused, worry apparent. "It's called the Throat Cut, because when these areas were still being settled bandits would spring down onto travelers."

Alain stared intently. "There are Dark Mages. Two, I think, trying to hide their presence but failing. Something...they are not alone. Others there distract them." He pointed slightly to the right. "They are on that side of the road."

"They're waiting for us," Major Danel said. "I'll take Tiae's cavalry up the road as they expect."

"While we circle around and hit them from behind?" Major Sten said. "Lady Mari and her Mage can wait here—"

"No, we can't," Mari said before she could really think about it. "We won't sit here safely while others face danger. We'll ride with the main group."

"But, Lady—"

"You will want me there," Alain said, his Mage voice cutting off all debate. "Mari, there is a sense of familiarity to one of the Dark Mages. We have encountered that one before."

"Really?" Mari paused to think about the Dark Mages they had met in the last couple of years. "Let me get something from the wagon. Major Danel, your soldiers with rifles should prepare them. We might end up facing something that lances and swords can't cope with."

While the others stared at her as they took in her words, Mari rode back to the wagon and hefted out one of the dragon killers. She returned to the front of the column, the long tube of the DK balanced before her across the pommel of her saddle. "Any time you're ready," she told Major Sten and Major Danel.

Sten saluted, then led the Confederation militia cavalry off the road to the right, where scattered low trees and bushes offered cover for their movement. The group swung wide to come up behind the right side of the cut ahead.

Major Danel waited, the horses of the Tiae cavalry shifting restlessly at the inactivity, some of them looking ahead with their heads erect, ears up. "They sense something," Danel said.

Alain nodded. Mari could tell that he was readying himself to cast spells if needed. "Is there much power here?" she asked. Mages could sense the power they needed to help cast spells, but her every attempt to detect that power using Mechanic instruments had failed, leaving it a mystery to her.

He nodded again. "Enough. Unfortunately, that means enough for the Dark Mages as well."

Danel looked to the right, up ahead, to the right again, then gestured to Mari. "We should start, Lady."

"All right," Mari said. "Keep the pace we had before. Everyone stay alert, but don't look like you're expecting trouble." She realized having a dragon killer balanced in front of her didn't exactly look like no one was anticipating an attack, but odds were that none of their foes knew the tube represented a weapon.

Mari paused as Major Danel directed a half-dozen Tiae cavalry to positions ahead of them. Alain gave her one of his looks, the one that hoped she wouldn't argue with common-sense measures to limit her exposure. "All right," she repeated in a low voice to him, checking that her pistol was ready as well as the rifle in the scabbard next to her saddle. "Between the DK, the rifle, and my pistol, I'm a mobile arsenal."

Her words drew grins from the cavalry, relieved to hear the daughter joking about the coming fight as if she had no fear.

She realized that she really had become very good at faking it.

The column got back into motion, the horses walking ahead at a steady pace, snorting and staring as they picked up the nervousness of their riders. They crested the low ridge, giving a good view of the land sloping away before them, and not far down the road the cut that the Confederation rider had warned of. Brush grew alongside the road and up along the cut.

"Why wasn't that vegetation trimmed back?" Mari grumbled to Major Danel.

"You'll have to ask the Confederation," Danel said, his gaze searching the land ahead. "At a guess, they haven't worried about danger here for a long time, enough to have stopped taking such precautions. Lady, we can now see the road far enough in front of us that we should be able to spot the scouts. They're not in sight, which means trouble. We're fortunate your Mage is with us."

"I've often been fortunate to have him with me," Mari said. "I'm not sure how I survived before that."

The forwardmost riders were still about fifty lances from the near edge of the cut when Alain held his hand palm up before him and stiffened with concentration.

A spot amid the brush looking down on the cut erupted into flames.

A long moment later, another fire burst to life a little distance from the first.

Mari heard shouts of surprise as the ambushers found the tables turned on them. She held her reins tightly as hooves thundered from the right, where the Confederation cavalry was charging the rear of the ambush. She could hear battle cries and the clash of metal on metal.

Men and women armed with a variety of swords and crossbows leaped from the brush and into the road, fleeing the fires and the charge by the Confederation cavalry. Major Danel shouted a command and the Tiae cavalry leapt into motion, hitting the off-balance ambushers before they could gather their wits. Most tried to run, only to be speared by the lances of the cavalry before they got far.

In that moment, when victory seemed already won, Alain called out loudly. "Beware!"

Mari saw something appear at the far end of the cut, a large shape suddenly visible above the vegetation cloaking that area. "Get your people back here!" she yelled at Major Danel, dismounting and holding tightly to the dragon killer.

Danel was surprised by the command, but had been a soldier long enough not to ask questions when urgent orders were given. "Recall! Everyone back!"

Mari handed off the reins of her horse to the first cavalry to get back to her, standing in the center of the road as the soldiers rode quickly past on either side. Alain dismounted to stand beside her, his long Mage knife in his hand.

"There is more than one spell creature," Alain said to her. "I am certain from the feel of the spell that the other is not a dragon."

"Then we'll deal with the dragon first," Mari said, her heart pounding and her breath coming faster as she tried to sound and act calm. She prepared the dragon killer as a massive creature at least four times the height of a tall person stepped onto the road at the far end of the cut. "Make sure no one is right behind me!" she yelled to the cavalry.

The dragon glared down the road, fixing on the cavalry moving about to the rear of Mari, and with a dreadful roar came charging toward them, its massive tail held out behind it, its mighty hind legs pumping, the claws on its smaller forelegs extended, its mouth open enough to expose wicked teeth larger than daggers, the armored scales covering the beast glinting in the morning light.

Taking a deep breath, trying not to think about what would happen if she missed, Mari advanced one leg to steady her aim, balanced the dragon killer tube on her shoulder, and aimed through the sight on the weapon. Despite her fear, a small part of Mari noticed that Alli had improved the sight. She had forgotten how fast dragons could move when they were attacking.

This one had gotten far too close far too quickly, its armored chest filling her sight.

Mari squeezed the trigger, feeling the heat as the rocket inside the tube ignited with a roar that rivaled that of the dragon and sent a spray of fire out the back.

The rocket sprang out, crossing the distance to the oncoming dragon in an instant, leaving a trail of smoke to mark its path. The crash of the warhead going off filled the world, echoing back from the sides of the cut.

The dragon staggered as the rocket struck, first coming to a halt, then stumbling to one side. As the smoke of the explosion cleared, a massive wound could be seen in its chest. The spell creature wavered, then fell, hitting the ground hard enough to make rocks bounce.

Mari inhaled deeply again, standing up and dropping the empty and now useless tube, her body quivering with reaction.

"There is a Dark Mage down there who created that dragon," Alain told Major Danel. "That Mage must be killed before another spell can be cast."

"Yes, Sir Mage!" But before Danel could send his cavalry charging past the carcass of the dragon, another dread form appeared, shambling forward through the smoke drifting down into the cut from the still-burning vegetation along the ridge.

Shaped like a very broad and extremely tall person, the troll had skin whose hairiness and thickness exceeded that of a boar, and a face whose crude features resembled the work of an amateur attempting to sculpt something human. It moved much more slowly than the dragon, but with a merciless sense of indestructible menace.

Mari sighed, not liking what must be done next. She found trolls repellent, but also felt angry at their creators. The trolls themselves were tools used by the Mages who could create them, weapons that could not question their orders but could feel pain. "Major, dismount your soldiers with the new rifles. Send some of your cavalry with lances around the side of the cut and get the Dark Mages who created these spell creatures."

"Yes, Lady." Danel gave the orders, some of the cavalry racing off to the side while others came to stand beside Mari and Alain.

"Steady your weapons," Mari directed the soldiers. "Aim for the troll's eyes. That's its most vulnerable point. Space your shots. Take careful aim between each one. The troll is slow enough that with this many rifles we can kill it before it reaches us." Her voice, far steadier than she felt inside, reassured the soldiers who hefted their new weapons with renewed confidence.

Someone brought Mari her own rifle. She took the weapon, unwilling to leave to others a task that she knew had to be done.

"It knows nothing but killing," Alain said beside her. "It can do nothing else."

"I know," Mari said. "We have to stop it, because it can't stop itself. This will be a better world when Mages who can create trolls are gone from it."

The troll had reached the dragon's remains, slowing even more to make its ponderous way past the dragon's tail.

Mari brought her rifle to her shoulder, aiming, her sight on the troll's left eye, small and dark beneath a heavy brow ridge. She fired.

A ragged volley marked the soldiers firing as well.

The troll jerked from several hits, but kept coming. It shambled forward, a slow, large target for the rifles, its head jolting from the shots slamming into it.

There was something terrifying about the way the creature could absorb such punishment and keep advancing. Mari, who had already faced trolls, felt her own nerve wavering. She might have dropped back a short distance except for the knowledge that the Tiae soldiers were all looking to her to bolster their own resolve. She couldn't retreat without seriously rattling the soldiers beside her, so she stood firm despite her growing uneasiness.

A ball of intense heat appeared in the troll's face, causing it to reel, as Alain added his own powers to the fight.

The troll shook its head, its skin smoking, then stubbornly started forward again.

Mari stood her ground and kept shooting until the troll stopped less than three lances away, wavering, its crude face now a ruined mass. "Cease fire!" Mari yelled.

The sudden silence felt unreal. It was broken by an inarticulate grunt from the troll, which tried to move one broad foot forward but instead fell to lie unmoving.

"Is it dead?" Mari asked Alain in a low voice.

"It was never alive—" he began.

"I know!"

Alain walked forward until he was next to the troll, gazing down at it. "It has ceased," he said.

Mari saw horses coming toward them through the smoke, Tiae and Confederation cavalry mixed together. Major Sten, in the lead, saluted as his horse shied away from the remains of the dragon and the troll. "Two Dark Mages. We feared they would strike at us with their spells but they only used knives. We killed both."

"They were surprised by how quickly their spell creatures were destroyed," Alain said, "and having put so much strength into creating the creatures could not recover in time to save themselves."

A couple of men and one woman wearing the clothes of commons were brought forward at lance point. "Prisoners," Major Sten said.

Mari looked them over, spotting a familiar face. "That big man. Alain, he's one of the Dark Mechanics from Dorcastle."

The man glared at Mari and spat, oblivious to the tears running down his face. "My friends are dead. Are you happy?"

"No," Mari said. "They're dead because they wanted to kill me. I regret every death, but I'm getting tired of people who leave me no choice and then want me to feel guilty for what they did. Instead of attacking me, why didn't you help us overthrow the Great Guilds? You could have practiced the Mechanic arts in the open instead of hiding them from the Mechanics Guild."

"We wanted to make a lot of money, not practice arts, you blasted fool!" the man raged.

"Then blame your own greed, not me. What happened to the scouts?" Mari asked Sten.

"Killed," Sten said, his face an angry mask. "As your Mage guessed, the Dark Mages must have slain them. We found the bodies. Both died without drawing a weapon. They never had a chance."

The Confederation militia officer was just as mad as Sten. "I'll assign some of my people to bring the prisoners along behind us. We'll walk them to Dorcastle to help labor in defense of the city."

"Maybe we can use them as human shields when the Imperials attack," someone growled.

"No," Mari said. She did not think she had put a lot of force into the word, but everyone immediately stopped to listen. "The Great Guilds made themselves the only law, and the world has suffered for it. Use these prisoners as your laws demand, and no worse."

Major Sten nodded, his expression still grim. "The daughter has spoken."

Mari coughed as smoke swirled around her. "Let's get out of here." She turned away from the big man from Dorcastle, somehow knowing that she would never see him again. Mounting up as a soldier brought her mare, Mari rode past the destroyed spell creatures and dead ambushers, her horse shying away from the bodies. She kept telling herself that the tears in her eyes were only from the smoke.

Alain, riding beside her again, reached over to rest one hand on hers. "Are you all right?"

Mari grimaced. "The daughter feels horrible."

"How does Mari feel?"

"Like she has since the day she learned about the daughter thing, wishing that it was someone else's job, but knowing that it's hers." Mari blinked as they cleared the cut and the smoke, using one hand to rub away the moisture in her eyes. Up ahead in the distance she could see a low bank of smog that marked the location of Danalee, another step closer to Dorcastle.

* * *

They were still a short distance from the city, the slanting rays of the afternoon sun casting their shadows to their right as they trudged along, when one of the new scouts came riding back. "There's someone waiting up ahead. A Mechanic."

Mari massaged her tired eyes, then gazed ahead. "Is he wearing one of my armbands?" she asked, indicating the many-pointed golden star on a blue field on her own and Alain's forearms.

"No, Lady. There is an escort of militia from Danalee watching him. They say he came out of the city early this morning and has been waiting in that place along the road all day. He appears to be unarmed," the scout added.

"Why does he have a militia escort from Danalee?" Major Sten asked.

"They say orders have gone out, sir, to make sure no Mechanics are harmed unless the Mechanic is threatening someone. They're protecting him from anyone who might attack him. It's because of the peace of the daughter."

Major Sten and Major Danel turned questioning looks at Mari, who needed a moment to realize what "the peace of the daughter" meant. "Are you talking about me telling people that they are going to need Mechanics when the new day comes?" Mari asked. "Yes, I have been sending word around that making forbidden technology available to everyone won't do any good if the people who understand how to make and use that technology have been driven off or killed. Many Mechanics haven't joined me, but that doesn't mean they can't help a lot once victory has been won."

"Perhaps that's what this Mechanic wants to talk about," Major Sten suggested.

"Let's find out," Mari said. "Alain, come with me. The rest of you stop as soon as this Mechanic comes into sight."

Alain kept his eyes on the Mechanic as he came into view, but sensed no warnings of danger to Mari.

The Mechanic had been sitting alongside the main road where a small secondary road joined it, but stood up when he saw Mari riding toward him. He walked into the center of the road and stood still, his arms spread out and his empty hands clearly visible.

Well off to the side, twelve Confederation foot militia watched, their short swords in their scabbards. Smiles appeared when they saw Mari's banner flying above the approaching column, and a buzz of excited conversation began among them.

Mari rode within a few lance lengths of the Mechanic before dismounting. Alain waited until she was on her feet and watching the Mechanic before he also dismounted.

The Mechanic, an older man with the hands of someone who had used them in labor for many years, nodded to Mari. "I'm Master Mechanic Lo."

Mari nodded in reply. "I guess you know who I am. Lo of Danalee? Mechanic Alli has told me about you."

"Is that so?"

"Tough. Fair. Knows his job. That's what she said."

"Hmmph." Despite Lo's dismissive snort, Mari could see that he was pleased by the characterization. "How's Alli?"

"Doing great," Mari said. "Building the things she's dreamed of making."

"Like that?" Lo nodded toward the scabbard at Mari's saddle.

Mari eyed Lo appraisingly, then turned enough to draw out her rifle. She pulled out the magazine, made sure the chamber was empty, then handed the weapon to Lo. "You were a supervisor in one of the Guild's weapons workshops when Alli worked for you. What do you think?"

Lo took it, turning the rifle in his hands and examining the weapon carefully. "Not bad. Decent work. Some signs of haste in the construction of the parts. Semi-automatic? This is way ahead of Guild rifles."

"Commons made some of the parts and helped assemble the weapon," Mari said.

Lo paused, looking uncomfortable. "So what do the Mechanics do?"

"Design the weapons, make modifications, oversee the process."

"They're still in charge?"

"When it comes to making things, yes," Mari said. "It's what we're good at. Outside the workshops, the commons rule themselves."

Lo raised one skeptical eyebrow. "From what we've heard, you rule the commons."

"No," Mari said. "I command my army, and help decide priorities for construction and that only for as long as it takes to overthrow the Great Guilds."

"A year ago I would have said only a fool would speak of overthrowing the Mechanics Guild," Lo said. He looked at the rifle again. "But if you're making these…how many?"

"That's one of the latest," Mari said. "Check the serial number."

Lo squinted to read, both eyebrows rising this time. "How do you make enough ammunition?"

"Mass production."

"Blazes, girl, did you ever meet a rule you didn't want to break?"

Mari shook her head. "Safety rules are one thing I never break, but many of the other rules of the Mechanics Guild are all about the Senior Mechanics staying in control of everything and everybody."

This time Lo paused for a while before speaking again. "I'm here for two reasons. One is because I worry about Alli. She's a gifted Mechanic. I wasn't happy when I heard she had gone rogue with you, because I didn't want the Guild to lose her potential and I didn't want her to be hurt."

"The Guild saw her potential as a threat," Mari said.

"I won't argue that," Lo said. "I heard from someone in a position to know that Alli had been marked for arrest before she threw in with you. You likely saved her from being sent to the Guild's prison in Longfalls, for which I am grateful. But…"

"But?" Mari prodded.

"The other reason I wanted to see you in person is that…word came down to us that you were thought to be on your way to Dorcastle. You've probably already heard that the Senior Mechanics have ordered everyone to fort up inside their Guild Halls."

"I hadn't heard, but I expected it," Mari said. "Are you supposed to stay safe inside the Guild Halls until the Imperials come marching into town?"

"Yeah." Lo grimaced. "I spent a few years inside the Empire. I admit to not being thrilled at the idea of them running the commons here. But that's not why I snuck out. Even though it seems impossible that you'll survive, let alone win." He looked at the rifle he held again, then passed it back to Mari. "You've surprised a lot of people."

"You are worried, Sir Master Mechanic," Alain said.

Lo gave Alain a glance. "First time a Mage ever talked to me, and the first time I ever heard of one being polite to anybody. I won't try lying to you…Sir Mage. Of course I'm worried. I have a wife, and two sons, and a daughter. One of those sons recently married. The commons have been getting more dangerous. That was happening before you made a name for yourself, Mari, so unlike some I don't blame you for it. I think you're riding that tiger. But I don't want that tiger devouring my family."

"It won't," Mari said. "Have you seen the pamphlets that have been sent among the commons?"

"The Senior Mechanics have forbidden anyone to read them, so of course we have all read them." Lo studied Mari again. "The daughter tells all commons not to strike at Mechanics, not to retaliate, not to take revenge. 'The world needs Mechanics,'" he quoted. "I needed to look at you and see if you really meant that."

"I do," Mari said. "I've got the banned technology that the Guild has kept from everyone, and everyone is going to have access to it. But they won't be able to use that technology unless they have Mechanics who can understand it and build it. I know how much the commons hate their overlords. But I can convince them that most Mechanics are willing to just use their skills, not be rulers, and that we are going to need Mechanics. Then their own self-interest will ensure your family stays safe. I know that the leaders of the Bakre Confederation understand that."

"Will the commons really listen to you?"

Mari paused this time, knowing her discomfort was showing. "They wouldn't listen to Master Mechanic Mari. But they do listen to the daughter of Jules."

Lo gazed down at the road for a while, finally raising his eyes back to Mari. "A Mechanic is always supposed to make best use of the tools available. The daughter story is disdained by the Senior Mechanics, but anyone who listens to the commons knows how much it means to them. You know what's going to hit Dorcastle?"

"Yes," Mari said.

"But you're going anyway?"

"They need me."

Master Mechanic Lo nodded, his eyes judging her. "If you somehow win, many of your former Guild mates are going to need you. Mechanics like me and my family. I don't mind the prospect of working for myself instead of the Guild. I do mind the thought of being enslaved."

Mari shook her head. "I swear to you that I will not let that happen. If...I'm not around, and the Confederation treats you poorly, head south. Queen Sien of Tiae will take in you and your family and ensure you are treated fairly. She knows how important you can be to the future of the reborn kingdom."

"I wish I didn't have to depend on your word alone for that," Lo said. "No offense."

Mari smiled thinly. "Compared to some of the things the Senior Mechanics have said about me, that's nothing. You don't have to take my word for it. Master Mechanic Lukas and Professor S'san are in Tiae. So is Alli, who I know respects you. Send word to them. They'll tell you."

"I'll do that."

"Can you get back to the Guild Hall in Danalee safely?"

Lo paused, looking at Mari again. "Yes. These commons seem unusually worried about my welfare."

"Good." She raised her voice. "I want you to get back safely to your Guild Hall." Mari could see the Danalee militia had heard. "Go in peace, Master Mechanic."

"Thank you," Lo said. "I can't wish you luck, but you have my respect. Tell Alli not to get her butt shot off." He turned and walked steadily down the side road.

Mari hastened to where the Danalee militia were about to follow Lo.

"Make sure he gets back," Mari said to them, worried about Lo being alone in a country teeming with commons who hated their Mechanic overlords. "You will need Mechanics like him when the Great Guilds are overthrown. And keep yourselves safe, too. Don't," she added hastily as the militia members began to kneel.

"We have all heard of the peace of the daughter. He is a friend of yours?" one of the militia asked.

Mari hesitated, not certain whether to grant Lo that status but remembering Alli's stories about him. "Yes," she finally said. "And once this all over, and he is free of the iron grip of the Mechanics Guild, he can do a lot for Danalee. As a fellow citizen, not as an overlord."

"He's a *Mechanic*," one woman commented in acidic tones.

"So am I," Mari said. "Don't judge him by the way he looks. Judge him by what he does. Judge him by what he can do for all of you and your city once the Great Guilds have been overthrown."

She couldn't tell if she had convinced them, but the militia soldiers all saluted before hurrying off in the wake of Master Mechanic Lo.

"It is well that you did not have to attempt to convince them to trust in a Mage," Alain remarked.

She turned to see that Alain had followed her once the militia had left. Had there been a trace of sadness in his voice? "I'm sorry. Everybody is so happy to see me. I forget how they react to the sight of other Mechanics, and to Mages."

"You have made changes in Tiae," Alain said. "Others see me differently there."

"You miss it, don't you?"

"Yes. But I could not stay in Tiae without you."

She couldn't think of anything to say to that, so Mari just smiled at him. They walked back to the main road and rejoined the rest of the column.

The cavalry walked with their horses again until much closer to the city, then everyone remounted for the entry into town. As they had drawn closer to Danalee, the road passing outlying homes and businesses like stables, farms, and inns, Mari had noticed Alain becoming more tense. But he said nothing. "What's the matter?" she finally asked.

Alain shook his head slightly. "I do not know."

"Foresight?"

"No. At least, not in a form I have ever experienced it. Something feels wrong. I cannot explain it any more clearly than that."

Mari looked ahead, where growing crowds were lining the streets in anticipation of her arrival. "Wrong dangerous?"

"I do not know."

"Does it feel like Mechanic stuff?"

Alain paused. "It does not feel like anything." He glanced at Mari. "That is it. Not how it feels, but what I do not feel. Danalee has a large Mage Guild Hall. I should be catching traces of the minor spells being used by Mages and acolytes. I should be picking up signs of their presence. But I feel nothing. It is silent."

That sounded bad. "All of the Mages and acolytes in Danalee are completely hiding themselves from you?"

Alain shook his head again, distress becoming apparent to Mari. "No. Acolytes could not hide their presence, and the newer Mages should not have the skill to be impossible for me to spot. But there is no sense of any of them. Something is very wrong."

CHAPTER THREE

THE CHEERING CROWDS up ahead contrasted oddly with Alain's sudden sense of alarm. Mari had told him that she could tell when a city was alive by the presence of a low cloud of dust and smoke above it, a cloud created by the presence and the activities of the people in that city. Dead cities, like Marandur, had only clear, empty skies above them.

This was like that in Mage terms. A city such as Danalee would normally have many Mages and dozens of acolytes moving about and working spells, many so low-level and faint that Alain would be barely aware of them. Only nearby Mages and spells would normally force themselves into his awareness. But that background hum of Mages and their works was silent here, as silent as in the ruins of Marandur.

Even a Mage could be disturbed by such a thing.

Beside him, Mari turned to beckon Major Sten and Major Danel to ride close. "My Mage senses something wrong in Danalee," she said. "Something to do with Mages."

Sten gazed back, alarmed. "What should we do?"

"I must go to the Mage Guild Hall," Alain said.

"Not alone, you're not," Mari insisted.

"We can't go charging through the city," Sten said.

"And if you head off on your own," Major Danel said, "if the daughter isn't with us, people will notice."

"There is something wrong," Alain said, trying to put force into his voice.

Sten nodded quickly. "The Danalee militia and police up ahead are acting as greeters and crowd control. I'll ride up there fast and see if we can swing the procession near the Mage Guild Hall. Will that suffice, Sir Mage?"

"I do not know," Alain said. "But it will help."

Major Sten kicked his heels into his mount, urging the tired horse into a gallop. Alain watched Sten speak urgently with the militia officers, then trot back to salute him and Mari. "They are concerned to hear that there may be a threat to the city, and will lead our column so it passes close to the plaza surrounding the Mage Guild Hall. Once there, we will await your instructions."

The crowds here were very big, even taking into account the size of the city. An unusually large number of watchers were elderly or very young. The reason for that became apparent when Confederation dignitaries greeted Mari, one of them an old man who thanked her on behalf of himself and the others evacuated from Dorcastle. There were two cities' worth of children and older people in Danalee, its population very recently swelled by those fleeing the expected Imperial attack.

Despite his other concerns, Alain found himself wondering what would happen to those elderly and very young if the Imperials and the Great Guilds captured Dorcastle and continued south toward Danalee. Where would they flee next, their numbers swollen by those from Danalee also trying to escape the invaders?

As the column of cavalry wended its way down the center of streets lined with commons cheering themselves hoarse at the sight of Mari, Alain tried to remain focused on the increasingly disturbing silence where he should have felt the presence of Danalee's Mages and acolytes. Their progress felt painfully slow to Alain, even though he understood the need to avoid panicking the commons.

He was surprised when Major Sten rode close and nodded to their left. "The Mage Guild Hall lies over there, Sir Mage."

That was very wrong. He had never been so close to a Mage Guild Hall and so unable to sense anything marking its presence.

"What's the matter?" Mari asked Alain, her eyes searching the crowd for trouble.

"Even this close, I sense nothing," Alain said. "It is as if there are no Mages or acolytes in this city."

"We have not seen Mages leaving, Sir Mage," one of the local officers said, looking very nervous to be addressing Alain. "It would have been noticed. Some have arrived recently, a few days ago. It was unusual to see such a large group."

"A large group?" Alain asked, trying to keep feeling in his voice so that the locals would not be alarmed by his emotionless Mage voice.

"Twelve, Sir Mage."

"Twelve at once? And yet nothing from the Guild Hall. This worries me even more. I must go to the Hall and find out what is wrong there."

"Stop the column," Mari ordered. "Open a path through the crowd. My Mage and I need to see the Mage Guild Hall."

"But Lady—!" the highest ranking local official protested.

"There is something *wrong* at the Mage Guild Hall! Don't you think it's important to find out what?"

Major Sten spoke quickly. "Tell the people that the daughter, and her Mage, are going to confront the Mages here."

"Yes!" the official agreed, seizing on the suggestion. He turned to the other officials. "Spread the word to everyone that the daughter is going to confront the Mages in Danalee now." He hesitated, looking back at Mari. "How dangerous is this?"

"We do not know," Alain said. "That is why we must go find out."

The mood of the crowd grew fearful as the cavalry column swung to the left and began heading to the large plaza in the center of which rested the Mage Guild Hall. Police and militia clearing the path appeared as anxious as the other citizens. No one walked in that plaza by choice. Alain led the way as they rode toward the Mage Guild Hall, a forbidding-looking structure with only a few doors and narrow windows. Otherwise, the building presented solid, unadorned walls to the world that the Mages denied and regarded as an illusion.

Alain rode steadily, straining every sense for some indication of what was happening inside the Mage Guild Hall. For one brief moment he thought he felt a trace of something brush against his senses, then it was gone.

But in its wake, that something had left a sense of pain and loss.

No longer paying any attention to the others, Alain rode up close to the main door of the Guild Hall. He dismounted, barely aware of Mari following him, and walked quickly to the door. As he expected, it was barred on the inside. Alain pounded on the door, which should have resulted in the acolyte on duty opening it for him. But there was no response, and no sound from within.

Alain gathered his focus, gazing steadily at the door.

The world presented the illusion of a solid door. But with the help of the power available here Alain could, for a little while, overlay on that illusion a smaller illusion, one in which the door had an opening in it large enough for a person to walk through.

Creating this spell would advertise his presence clearly to any Mages in the Hall. But Alain felt increasingly sure that there were no other Mages here any longer.

The opening appeared. Barely noticing the gasps of fear from the crowds watching from a distance, Alain walked through the opening. He realized too late to warn her off that Mari was right on his heels, her pistol out and ready.

Once inside, Alain relaxed the spell so he could direct his attention elsewhere. The door appeared to be solid again behind them. He stood, straining his senses once more, as Mari swung up the two stout bars that had held the door closed from the inside. She opened the door, waving reassuringly to those waiting, then stood beside Alain. "Anything?" she whispered to him.

"No." The hallway he looked down was undecorated, plain walls and open doorways opening into rooms and other halls, and absolutely empty of any Mages. Silence would have been normal, because Mages so rarely spoke to each other, but there should have been other sounds, of Mages moving about and doing tasks. Here there was nothing.

"It feels deserted," Mari commented, looking around worriedly, her weapon held out before her.

Deserted. But a scent grown familiar and unwelcome came their way, riding the slow air currents inside the building. Alain knew that smell from battlefields. He broke into a run, heading for the large, open room where the acolytes would sleep on bare floors at night and eat bland meals during the day between harsh periods of training. He heard Mari following him, her Mechanic boots thudding on the floor and setting off echoes amid the unnatural silence.

Alain came to a stop at the entry of the room, shock warring with his Mage training to suppress emotions.

Boys and girls in the plain, thin robes of acolytes lay about the room. None of them moved. The stench of blood filled the air.

He walked slowly into the room, crouching beside a boy to study him closely. Blood pooled beneath the body. A slit on the boy's robe marked the place where a knife had gone in. Traces of surprise, fear, and pain still rested on the boy's features.

"Are they dead?" Mari asked in an appalled whisper.

"Yes."

"Wh☒ *Why?*"

"I do not know." Alain sat back on his heels, trying to deal with the terrible scene. "They died not long ago. Perhaps last night, perhaps this morning. I may have sensed the last trace of life leaving one of them as we approached this Hall. There is no Mage teaching that would explain this."

He studied the injury that had killed the boy. "This appears to be the work of a Mage knife."

Mari looked about with horrified eyes, her weapon held steady in both hands. "You've told me that Mages are taught that other people aren't real, just shadows on the illusion of the world. And that acolytes who err are punished very badly." It sounded accusing, though Alain knew that Mari did not mean it that way.

"Yes," Alain said, standing up even though it felt as if a heavy weight rested across his shoulders. "But acolytes are part of the illusion that must exist if the Mage Guild is to continue, because only if the Guild continues can the search for wisdom go on. Individual acolytes who fail, who break under the training, are killed by the elders. But not all of the acolytes. Not ever."

He turned and moved swiftly, heading for the offices of the elders. Mari followed. As they went, Alain caught glimpses of dead Mages lying in some of the rooms they passed. Some had fallen as if struck suddenly. Others seemed to have died in the act of fighting back. One dead Mage still held the knife which had failed to protect its owner.

Alain found the answer he sought in the main room which had served the elders. The bodies of nearly twenty of those elders lay on the floor or slumped over the table. "We have seen other elders dead in this Hall. Why so many here, more than should be in this Hall?" Alain asked, knowing that Mari could not provide an answer but needing to voice his question. "Were the twelve Mages who arrived yesterday all elders?"

But there was something else odd here. The room appeared to be just another vista of death, yet Alain felt something he could only think of as the absence of absence. He moved carefully about the room, looking closely at everything, finally spotting the figure of an elder sitting in one corner. Only a small amount of blood marked the front of the elder's robes, and his chest moved gently as breath came and went. The elder must be focusing every bit of his strength on remaining invisible to other Mages, doing it so effectively that it was indeed as if he was not there to Mage senses.

Alain gripped his long knife firmly as he stepped closer to the elder. Mari stood slightly to the side, her weapon aimed.

"Elder," Alain called in a low voice. No response. "Elder!" he tried again, using a louder and more commanding voice.

The breathing deepened, and after a long moment the elder's eyes opened and focused on Alain. He studied Alain silently, then looked over at Mari, who still had her pistol aimed at him.

Alain decided to speak in the way a Mage normally would to an elder. "This one has questions."

The elder blinked at Alain. "The young Mage wants to know why all here have passed into the next dream?" The elder might have been asking about a minor issue rather than a massacre.

"All but you, elder," Alain said.

"All but me." The elder breathed deeply, moving his hand to let his own knife fall. "It was a difficult spell, young Mage, to make the blade of the knife disappear just as it began to cut into me, and then pretend to withdraw at just the moment as it reappeared."

"You faked your death."

The elder waved a dismissive hand. "I made an illusion of my death. It was necessary."

"Why?" Alain pressed.

The elder looked at Mari again, then back to Alain. "These elders came. Twelve in number. They brought orders from the council of elders. The council told us what we all knew. Questions had been raised about the wisdom taught by the Guild. Heresies were being debated. Some Mages had fallen completely into error, becoming ensnared by the slut of the Mechanics."

Alain heard Mari's muffled growl of anger. The elder must have heard as well, but ignored Mari, still speaking only to Alain. "The council said it was necessary to prove that their authority was undiminished, to provide an example of the discipline expected of Mages, to show the hard path that represents the only wisdom. All in this Hall would enter the next dream, showing that we would follow the path dictated us, that we did not fear to leave this illusion and that those who had fallen into error were weak by comparison."

"Why did the council not kill themselves, then?" Alain asked. "Would that not have proven their dedication most strongly?"

He thought a flicker of the barest hint of a smile appeared on the elder's face. "You ask questions that challenge the wisdom of the Guild."

"Yes," Alain said. "It has become a habit for me. The elders here accepted those orders? They did not question the wisdom behind them?"

"Some elders questioned," the elder said. "Some elders died before the rest. Those twelve who came were prepared. We were not. When something occurs so contrary to all experience and all wisdom, even elders such as this one will question what illusion we are seeing. The delay while trying to understand was fatal to many."

"Why did you not kill yourself like the others?"

"Because I asked the same question as you, young Mage. And because I was curious." He finally looked back at Mari. "This one wished to know why others sought new wisdom, what teachings led them off the path demanded by the Guild. I asked, since all is an illusion, since others are but shadows, the Guild itself an illusion as well, why is it wise to act as if the authority of the Guild is real when the Guild itself is not?"

The elder paused, a dark memory reflected in his eyes. "The elders who came here with the orders had the fire of belief in their eyes. They had been selected for that, this one believes. They killed the other Mages, quickly and silently, room by room, while the Mages still sought to grasp what was happening. A few managed to fight back, but all died. Then those elders who had come here killed all of the acolytes. They killed the acolytes. There is no wisdom that justifies such an act. There is no wisdom in those who would order it, and no wisdom in those who would obey such orders. Then the elders who had come turned their knives on themselves, so that none could question them and learn of their orders. I chose to live, Mage, so that I could tell what happened here and why."

The elder's eyes went to Mari again. "The orders from the council of elders commanded that the killings take place when we heard that the shadow claiming to be the daughter of Jules approached the city. We were to create the illusion that we had all been killed when that shadow arrived. Do you see? The council of elders wished to create the illusion that she had done this. They tried to create a spell to alter the illusion of the world by using not power but the blood of all in this

Hall. I am an elder. I have sought wisdom for many years. And while much still evades me, I know that spells wrought from blood have no place in the pursuit of wisdom."

"Will you tell others of this, elder?" Alain asked, badly shaken by what he heard.

The elder eyed Alain. "Your discipline has weakened, Mage, for I see feelings in you. But I also sense strength in you. I care not whether the wisdom you seek is a better path. The acolytes who have passed into the next dream will never have a chance to achieve wisdom. The acolytes in other Halls must be protected against those who would order their deaths for reasons that no Mage should accept. Yes, I will tell others. They will know I do not lie. The council of elders lacks wisdom and is given over to pursuit of power and other illusions. You may be wrong, but they are not right."

Alain nodded. "Do you wish to stay here, elder?"

"I will stay. It is certain that in a few days or less, Mages will be sent here on some errand, to find this Hall filled with dead. The council of elders would proclaim their shock, and announce that only Mages allied with the Mechanic could have successfully done such a thing. But I will be here, and I will tell them the shadow did not commit this act. I will tell them that those who claim wisdom did this."

"Can this one do any service for you?"

The elder touched his chest where the blood was still wet. "No. This one will live long enough to say what must be said. This one deserves to live no longer than that, for I stood and watched as the acolytes died. Their blood is on my hands as well, for I did not stop what I knew was wrong. You have seen them, the acolytes?"

"I have seen them," Alain said.

"Do any still have a trace of life in them? Has the Mechanic's wisdom shown you how to change a shadow, Mage, so that you might heal them?"

Alain shook his head. Even though commons had been led to believe that Mage spells could affect people directly, Mages could not actually do so. The elders claimed that was because no Mage had ever succeeded in being completely certain that others did not exist, that a tiny sliver of belief in the reality of those others kept spells from working on them. Alain had already decided that was wrong, but he did not yet know what was right. "I believe it is showing me the way to such wisdom, but this one is still far from there."

The elder looked at Mari again. "Your feelings are easy to read, shadow. You do not bear responsibility for what was done here," he said, surprising Alain by speaking to her. "The blame lies with those who did the acts, and with this one for not being strong enough to stop them. This one sees the daughter of the prophecy in you. Go and overthrow the Mage Guild. It has fallen into error and must cease."

The elder closed his eyes. Alain could see him withdrawing again, denying not only the shadows around him but also the world illusion that had betrayed him.

Alain stepped back. "We should go," he told Mari. "He will rouse again when other Mages come."

"But he's weak—"

"He will endure long enough to tell his story. Then he will cease, by his choice."

"There's nothing we can do?" Mari asked.

It was like her, Alain thought, that even when surrounded by death and facing someone who had once been ranked among her enemies, Mari still sought to give help where help was needed. "No. This elder has already set his mind on the journey to the next dream. He feels guilty, and would punish himself for his failure."

She nodded reluctantly, then backed from the room, clearly still not trusting the elder. Alain walked with her, leaving the elder with his bloodstained robes sitting in the corner, surrounded by the dead bodies of many others.

The silence as they walked back down the hallway felt oppressive. Alain felt the need to break it with speech. "The lives of the acolytes are supposed to be as nothing, but the council of elders know that a mass killing would arouse fear and anger in Mages who are not supposed to admit to either emotion. Fear and anger to be directed at you, along with the rejection of any suggestion that other paths of wisdom might be explored."

"I suppose if you don't care about individual life," Mari said in a low voice, "then it's a lot easier to give orders to end a lot of lives."

"It is a flaw in the wisdom of the Guild," Alain said.

"A *flaw?* Alain, flaws are things like a crack in metal or a design with too little attention to detail. Something that leads people to order mass murder is not just a flaw!"

"It is a bigger thing," Alain agreed. "I do not always use words well."

"I'm sorry. I know that. And I can see how upset you are inside by this. That elder cared, didn't he? He didn't show a trace of it that I could see, but it sounded like he cared about the acolytes."

"He does, though he will not admit it even to himself," Alain said. "He did not live for his sake, but to ensure that their deaths did not serve the purpose intended by those who ordered the killing."

They stepped back into the open air, Alain turning to close the door behind Mari. It was no longer locked, but he did not fear any commons sneaking inside a place that filled them with terror.

Major Danel and several of his soldiers stood not far away, clearly tense but determined to help if needed. "What was done here is done," Alain told them. He raised his voice, speaking to the officials and people of Danalee watching nervously from a distance. "All but one of the Mages and acolytes inside are dead, by their own hands or by the hands of elders sent by the Mage Guild. More Mages will come. Do not hinder them. You will not be blamed, for there is one left alive inside who will tell the Mages who come that this ill act is the work of the Mage Guild." He walked slowly to where his horse waited, grateful that the air outside the Guild Hall was not tainted by the stench of spilled blood.

Even though Mari was clearly very upset as well, she took the lead in further conversation with the officials of Danalee. "When other Mages come, they won't even think to blame the city for what happened," she explained. "They know you couldn't have done it. If they ask you what you know, tell them honestly that you had no knowledge of it beforehand and had nothing to do with it. They'll know you're not lying."

That did not seem to greatly reassure the leaders of Danalee. Being forced to host a Mage Guild Hall was a worry they were accustomed to. Having a Mage Guild Hall full of dead Mages was a new and frightening thing. A clamor went up. "They're not human! They'll destroy the city! What can we do? We need the daughter here!"

"You don't need me. Just do as we say, and you'll be fine," Mari told them again.

"But they're Mages—"

"They won't blame you."

"How can you be sure? You must stay, so you can deal with them."

"Who the blazes knows more about Mages?" Mari yelled, her nerves worn. "Me, or you? I am telling you, they will not blame you for this! You couldn't have done it! They know commons couldn't have done this!"

She pulled herself into the saddle to make herself taller. "Listen! The Mage Guild sought to blame *me* for what is in that Guild Hall! Me! Not anyone else here, not anyone in Danalee! The wrath of the Mage Guild is aimed at me and will follow me to Dorcastle! As for the Mages who come here to see this Guild Hall, their wrath will be centered on the elders who run their Guild and ordered the massacre here!"

Alain put on his most impassive Mage voice, the lack of feeling in it contrasting more strongly than usual with the emotion in Mari's words. "Do you not believe the words of the daughter? Do you wish to delay us further? We are needed in Dorcastle."

That shut off the debate, either because they recognized the truth of his words or because they were afraid to argue with a Mage.

When they reached the rest of the column again and the delayed procession resumed, the crowds began cheering louder. Major Sten leaned close to speak to Mari and Alain. "The word racing through the city is that the daughter has confronted the Mages inside their own Guild Hall and defeated them."

"What lies in that Guild Hall is not anything I want to take credit for!" Mari told him.

"Enough heard the truth that it will eventually catch up with the rumor running ahead of it. The Mages who did this act were fanatics, then, willing to murder and kill themselves on orders from their leaders?"

"Apparently."

Alain spoke again, even though he wanted to sink into silent isolation. "It has become more and more widely known that Mages such as myself are accepting others as real and yet retaining their powers. This strikes at the heart of the wisdom the Mage Guild has long insisted upon. The elders have become desperate in their efforts to discredit Mages such as me, and to discredit Mari, who is called 'elder' by the Mages who follow her."

"Desperate people can do awful things," Sten commented. "At least actions such as this prove the Mage Guild thinks you are winning."

Mari closed her eyes. "If what happened inside that Mage Guild Hall was a victory for me, I hope I never win another like it."

Sten nodded somberly and reined in his horse to fall back into the rank of riders behind Mari and Alain. Mari leaned close to speak into Alain's ear so no others could hear. "They were trying to get me to stay in Danalee! Did you hear that? A lot of them wanted to leave Dorcastle to its fate as long as I stayed here to defend this city against a nonexistent threat from the Mage Guild!"

Alain shook his head. "A city such as this could not be defended against an attack the size of the Imperial expedition. It would fall easily."

"I thought so, too! Don't they understand that if Dorcastle falls, Danalee won't stand a chance?"

"They look no further than their own fears," Alain said, "and seek to wrap us in their own illusion. They will try again before we leave. We cannot let them slow our progress, for with every delay they will seek to impede us again."

She gave him a worried look, then nodded.

The city leaders of Danalee led the column into another plaza, this one home to the city hall, and announced a grand celebration and dinner to be held for the daughter, while the representatives of the refugees from Dorcastle tried not to scowl. "Join us inside the hall!"

"We can't wait," Mari said, staying in the saddle, her voice pleasant but as hard as the steel that Mechanics used in their weapons. "We need to board the barges and head downriver to Dorcastle as fast as we can get there."

"But if you're here when the other Mages arrive, and you say your army is coming along behind, so you should wait—"

"Hold on!" a Confederation official objected.

An argument broke out among the representatives of Danalee and those of the Confederation and the refugees from Dorcastle. As words grew more heated, Major Sten, trying to look impassive but obviously unhappy to Alain's eyes, beckoned to Mari and began riding toward one of the streets leading off the plaza. Mari and Alain followed, the Tiae cavalry staying with them.

"Where are they going?" Alain heard one of the city officials demanding.

Mari heard as well. She rose in her stirrups and yelled a reply that filled the air. "I'm going to Dorcastle!"

The roar of approval from the crowd drowned out whatever answer any of the city leaders might have made.

A few more blocks took them to the docks on the Silver River, where barges were lined up, including large open craft with ramps leading aboard for the horses. The area erupted into a bustle of soldiers dismounting, collecting gear and saddlebags and weapons, being assigned to barges, and tramping aboard with relieved smiles because they would be able to make the last leg to Dorcastle on wooden decks, considerably more comfortable than staying in the saddle.

Major Sten, looking despondent, gestured toward the nicest of the waiting barges. "For you, Lady Master Mechanic, and you, Sir Mage."

"It is not your fault," Alain said.

Sten stared at Alain. "They tried to delay her here when every moment matters. My own people, and they—"

"Are afraid. For their homes and families." Alain nodded toward Major Danel, who stood speaking with a few of his cavalry before they boarded a barge. "I was once taught to forget what 'help' meant. It was forbidden even to speak the word. Mages are taught to care about none but themselves. Perhaps that is why I see help the more clearly now. To think of others when danger threatens you is not an easy thing. I am grateful for those like you and our escort from Tiae, who will risk all for those who need it. That is all that matters."

"Thank you, Sir Mage," Sten said, his face working with emotion. "It will be a great honor to fight alongside you and the daughter at Dorcastle. I hope we are not too late."

Alain followed Major Sten and Mari aboard the barge, standing by the large, shoulder-high deckhouse as the barge pushed off and the crew began poling out into the river where the current would help drive the boat downstream. Mari held onto Alain to keep herself steady as she waved back to the people seeing them off, holding the position until the crowds had dwindled and the tallest buildings in Danalee had disappeared behind them as the sun set.

Mari finally collapsed onto the blankets placed on the deck for bedding. "I don't want to move again until we reach Dorcastle," she told Alain.

"I will bring you food and water," he said.

"No! You shouldn't wait on me!" But before Mari could struggle to her feet again a soldier came by bearing trays of grilled meat, fruit, and jugs of watered wine for both her and Alain.

They sat on the barge's deck, their backs against the deckhouse, watching the river banks roll by and the stars appear overhead. "You have become suddenly more tense," Alain said. "Is it concern for what may come?"

Mari shook herself slightly to try to relax. "No. I'm sorry. It's memories of old fears. The last time we were on a river was our escape from Marandur. Everything reminds me of something scary or dangerous now, Alain. By the time this is over, will there be anything we can just enjoy?"

"Each other, I hope," Alain said, wanting to take her mind off of past and future dangers. "I have decided it is that star," he added pointing upward.

"What star?" she asked, squinting at the sky.

"The star the great ship came from, the star that warms Urth. You see the Great Roc?" he said, gesturing toward the arrangement of stars that formed a constellation resembling the outline of an immense bird. "Just beyond and above it, there, as if the Great Roc is flying to it. I have decided that is the star."

"I hope you're right!" Mari said, laughing. "Wouldn't it be wonderful if it was that star? Won't it be wonderful when the librarians can finally use that transmitter to try to speak with Urth? There is so much to learn. I hope I have time to learn everything."

"You would not be happy if you knew everything," Alain said.

"I guess not," she agreed, snuggling down next to him. "I like learning new things. I hope… Alain, have you had any visions of Dorcastle since that one of the battle? Anything that could tell us how it will go?"

He stared at the sky, wishing that she had not asked that question. "Do you want to know?"

He felt her body grow rigid again. "Is it about us losing?"

"No. What I have seen tells nothing of that."

"But you don't want to talk about it. I can tell." She sat up, looking at him. "You saw something about me, didn't you?"

"I did," Alain said, desperately wishing that she would not ask for more.

"Something about me that you don't want to talk about." Mari inhaled a long shuddering breath. "Dead?"

"No."

"That's…good."

"I do not know if it showed anything at Dorcastle. All I saw was you. You were…hurt."

"It could have been a warning about someplace else?" Mari rubbed her face with both hands.

"Something that could happen," Alain said. He believed that, he told himself. He would not allow himself to believe that what he had seen was certain to happen.

"That's not as bad as I feared. I mean, it sounds like what we've been worried about for years now. One of us getting hurt. And we already have been hurt, sometimes." Mari relaxed herself slightly against him again. "I'm too tired to worry about another possible thing that might happen. It's not like I haven't been dealing with my fears of just that. I wish you had seen something nice, though."

Despite his own weariness, Alain remained awake long after Mari had dropped into exhausted slumber. He could not stop thinking about the carnage inside the Mage Guild Hall. All Mages knew that the elders could be ruthless. But he had never heard of anything like the mass death in the Guild Hall.

Desperation. As Major Sten had said, that was the only explanation that fit. The elders, who were supposed to be above any such emotions, were so worried about the numbers of Mages joining Mari's forces in search of different paths to wisdom that they had become desperate enough to take extreme action. Just as the Great Guilds had become desperate enough to risk giving the Empire power over enough of the world to potentially make the Empire too powerful for the Great Guilds to control.

Complacent foes, certain of victory, would limit their moves. Desperate foes might do anything.

Alain remembered what Mari had said, that she wished he had seen something nice. He realized only then that he had seen nothing of the two of them after the war, no foresight visions of them together and at peace. Part of him knew that meant nothing, that foresight never showed everything and might not show anything. But another part of him worried, because that vision of Mari badly hurt was the last he had seen, and nothing beyond that.

He fell asleep at last and dreamed he was once again among the awful ruins of the dead city of Marandur. He was alone, searching for Mari, and he could not find her.

* * *

Despite her tiredness, aches from the long ride north woke Mari early. Even with the barge crews adding their efforts to the swift river current, the journey downriver to Dorcastle would require all this day and the following night. With luck, they would reach the city the next morning.

The chance to rest was both welcome and hard to accept. While she needed the time to recover, Mari chafed at inactivity when the Imperial expedition might arrive at Dorcastle at any moment. What if they made it too late, encountering the defeated remnants of the Confederation forces fleeing south?

"There isn't any other place to make a stand if Dorcastle falls," Major Sten said gloomily. He stood near Mari, looking north as if he might catch a view of events taking place far beyond their sight. "Jules warned about that when the Bakre Confederation was founded. Hold Dorcastle, she said, or you will lose the Confederation. From Dorcastle the Imperial legions would be able to march all the way to Danalee and take that city, then either turn west to seize Debran and the areas around Lake Annan, or continue south to assault Tiae. Your army would have to try to defend the line of the Glenca River, but that's a very long front to cover."

While riding the barge offered physical relief, it didn't offer much in the way of emotional respite. The barges carrying Mari, Alain, and the Tiae cavalry passed barges being towed upriver, each one loaded with anxious children and elderly commons leaving the Dorcastle area. The road alongside the river hosted a constant stream of refugee traffic, heading for the dubious refuge of Danalee.

Major Sten had ordered that Mari's banner be posted on the barge, which told all who saw it that the daughter was heading for the endangered city. Mari had to meet the pleading and frightened gazes of all they passed. She tried to project cheerful confidence despite the fears gnawing at her guts as the day passed and they drew ever closer to Dorcastle.

Sten cupped his hands around his mouth and shouted at a courier who had come into sight riding south at a fast clip. "What news?"

The courier slowed his horse long enough to yell a reply. "The Imperials had not yet arrived when I left! I have been sent to ask that any regular troops that can be spared be sent north!"

"Ride on, then!" Sten shouted. "Tell anyone you meet that the daughter is on her way to the city, and brings with her a valiant band of cavalry from the Kingdom of Tiae to help fight for the freedom of us all!"

"Then hope still lives! I will tell everyone, sir!" The courier urged his horse back to a quicker pace and soon vanished from view.

Mari tried her far-talker several times throughout the day, first attempting to contact any of her forces which were close enough, then shifting frequencies to try to overhear anything said by Mechanics still loyal to the Guild. But she heard nothing from her own people, and only a few faint words from Mechanics Guild loyalists before those were lost.

"It is broken?" Alain asked. He had learned enough about Mechanic devices to know that when Mari shook one in frustration that it probably wasn't working.

"No," Mari sighed, looking up into a sky dotted with clouds. "We're in a river valley, moving deeper into it as we get closer to Dorcastle. There's something about the air in places like this that stops far-talkers from being able to hear each other."

"Something stops the invisible waves?"

"I guess you could say that."

Alain looked upward as well. "Like invisible cliffs?"

"I don't know. It's something to do with pressure and temperature in the air. The Senior Mechanics never let us learn that kind of thing, but I've gotten that much from some of the banned technology texts we recovered from Marandur." Mari's attention had been focused to the north for a long time, but now she looked south and west. "Do you think the Syndaris have attacked Pacta yet?"

"It is possible. Sien will not let Pacta fall. And she has the help of Mechanic Alli. I am certain that Alli will give the Syndaris a welcome that will be long remembered."

"I hope you're right. I'll be surprised if we don't hear the sound of Alli's welcoming explosions even from this far off." It could be happening right now, Mari thought: people fighting for their lives as well as their freedom from the Great Guilds. Queen Sien could be leading a last desperate charge or commanding a rear guard or be dead in the rubble of the ancient buildings or the new workshops. Alli would retreat, wouldn't she? Or would she stand by her guns, firing at the approaching enemy until overrun?

Mari felt guilty for not being at Pacta to help, guilty for not being with her friends when they faced such a threat. It was absurd to feel that way, since she was heading for what was likely to be a far worse fight at Dorcastle, but Mari felt bad nonetheless. Those people being attacked were at Pacta because of her, they were being attacked because of her—

"You are blaming yourself," Alain said.

"How did you—? Never mind."

"Remember the Storm that threatens this world," Alain said. "A Storm created by the frustrations and anger of the commons who have been forced to follow the will of the Great Guilds for centuries. Yes, there is war because the commons see that the daughter has finally appeared, but if she were not here—if you were not here—already cities would be collapsing into chaos as the people rioted, just as we saw in Palandur."

"I'm the lesser evil?" Mari asked.

"You are not evil at all," Alain said, taking her absolutely seriously as he always did. "This war we face is by far the lesser evil compared to what would happen otherwise."

"I know." Mari looked at the refugees trudging toward Danalee, feeling a sick knot in her stomach at the sight. "I'm still glad that I feel badly about it. If the cost of this didn't bother me, I would have become the sort of person I never want to be."

That evening she forced herself to eat a full meal despite the nervous tightness in her stomach. The next morning they would reach the city.

* * *

Mari stood by Alain, not speaking but sharing the silence between them, as the barge drew closer to the boat landing on the outskirts of Dorcastle. Instead of bustling with activity, the landing and the nearby road were nearly deserted, only a scattering of soldiers loading supplies into a wagon. The barge slid alongside the landing, weary crew members hastening to tie it up securely.

Mari had barely stepped from the barge when a courier came riding fast from the direction of the city, reining her horse to a hard halt nearby and staring at the arriving barges. "Is the daughter here in truth?"

"Yes," Major Sten called back. "What message?"

"You made it just in time! Scouts have come in reporting that the Imperial expedition is just up the coast and will reach the city before nightfall!"

CHAPTER FOUR

ANY SENSE OF quiet and calm vanished as the soldiers of Tiae came ashore in a rush. Ramps came down and horses were led onto the landings to be quickly saddled and bridled. Restless after their time confined on the barges and picking up urgency from their riders, the horses shifted about, nipping at each other.

Mari hauled herself up into the saddle, any physical discomfort forgotten for the moment. Directly behind her and Alain, Major Sten and Major Danel were mounting their horses as well. Right behind them were two troopers, one carrying the banner of the New Day and the other the banner of Tiae. The road into the city was broad and nearly empty, so the rest of the soldiers formed a column riding four abreast.

They rode at a brisk clip, out-pacing the courier whose weary mount couldn't keep up with the rested cavalry horses. Passing through the outlying portions of the city, Mari was struck by how eerie Dorcastle felt with most of the population gone. Since almost all of the defenders were massed near the first wall down at the harbor, these portions of the city might almost have been deserted. All she saw were small patrols ensuring security in the empty streets.

Dorcastle occupied a river valley that represented the only significant break in the cliffs lining the southern Sea of Bakre from the desert waste in the east to Gullhaven in the west. The valley, with steep, unclimbable rock faces on either side, widened and dropped as it and the Silver River headed for the sea. Seven massive walls defended the city, the first and longest near the waterfront, the seventh and shortest just before the city gave way to the open land beyond. Anyone wanting to invade the Confederation or lands south of it had to besiege Dorcastle first. It offered the only route inland short of Gullhaven, and anyone who tried to bypass Dorcastle would be at the mercy of the fortress city, which couldstrike at them from behind and sever their lines of supply from the east.

"The Imperials have attacked Dorcastle several times over the centuries," Major Sten said as they rode. He seemed to feel the need to break the oppressive silence of the empty city. "One attack got as far as the fourth wall. No enemy has ever made it any farther."

Alain's impassive voice sounded odder than usual with the vacant buildings around them echoing back his words. "But there has never been an attack of such magnitude, nor one with the full backing of the Great Guilds."

"That is so," Sten said. "But we've never had the daughter of Jules fighting to defend the city."

Mari tried not to laugh at the idea that she, alone, counterbalanced so many Imperial legions and the force of the Great Guilds.

As they passed through a gate in the seventh wall, the farthest from the waterfront, Mari studied its thickness at ground level, trying to draw reassurance from its strength. Hopefully the might of this last wall would never be tested.

Their route passed through three more walls before reaching the central plaza surrounding the city hall. The plaza was choked with the instruments and means of war. Mobile ballistae waited in long ranks to be loaded with projectiles. Wagons held crates of food, much of it meat jerky and hard breads or crackers that would not spoil. Many other wagons bore the painted image of a red serpent curled around a staff, indicating they served the healers who would try to treat and save the wounded. The men and women in healer's garb who stood around those wagons were talking quietly among themselves.

"They know they're going to be very busy soon," Major Sten commented in a low voice.

"Soldiers and healers have that much in common," Major Danel said. "When we are busy at our trades, it means others are suffering."

The low rumble of conversation among the people in the plaza rose to a mild roar as they spotted the column of cavalry with Mari's banner alongside that of Tiae. She once more heard cries of "The daughter!" But alongside that were calls asking about the Tiae cavalry, and cheers when word was passed that they had come to help defend the city.

Mari glanced back to see the soldiers of Tiae riding proudly, some of the older ones nearly in tears from the fervor with which they were being greeted.

"Forward command is at the harbor administrator's building!" an officer called to Major Sten, who waved acknowledgement and led the column onward.

The streets were showing more and more signs of life as they drew near the water, but with rare exceptions everyone they saw and every activity related to the defense of the city. The city of Dorcastle that Mari remembered, filled with people living their lives and doing their work, had been emptied out. What had been a living city was now a citadel with only one purpose: to stop what seemed to be the unstoppable.

They went through two more walls, the armored gates standing open but with numerous sentries controlling all traffic, before reaching the business area near the docks, now given over totally to the business of war. Major Sten guided the column toward an imposing building in the shadow of the first wall facing the harbor.

Soldiers already lined the battlements at the top of the wall. Others waited in groups on the ground, ready to be rushed into the fight to reinforce threatened areas or counterattack any force breaching the wall or gates at ground level. The quiet resignation with which they awaited the arrival of the Imperials was broken as more and more caught sight of the column and Mari's banner, replaced by wild cheers.

Knowing how much her presence meant to these men and women, Mari stood in her stirrups to wave and pump her fist to the sky, feeling like a fraud because of the fear inside her.

Officials, some in uniform and others in civilian clothing, came spilling out of the harbor administrator building. Mari stopped her horse a few lances short of the waiting officials and managed to dismount fairly gracefully.

Alain stepped beside her. Mari beckoned to Major Danel and Major Sten, then walked the remaining distance to the waiting dignitaries. The soldiers saluted her while the civilians bowed slightly. Apparently word had reached them that the daughter of Jules didn't like having people kneel to her.

"You came," one of the men said, his fine suit betraying his high status, his face lit with joy. "I am Eric of Larharbor, Confederation Vice President for War. We have been *anxiously* awaiting you."

"But we never doubted that you would honor your word," added the well-dressed woman beside him. She indicated herself. "Jane of Danalee, Confederation Vice President of State. The people of the Bakre Confederation will never forget that you came to stand with them, daughter."

Mari did her best to smile in return despite her nerves. "I prefer Mari or Lady Mari, if that's all right with you. This is Sir Mage Alain of Ihris. I assume that you know Major Sten, who brought your message south and escorted us north, and this is Major Danel of the army of Tiae."

Everyone looked at Danel as he stepped forward and saluted. "By order of Queen Sien of Tiae, my unit has escorted the daughter to Dorcastle, and will now place itself at the disposal of the forces of the Confederation to assist in the defense of the city."

Surprise lit every face on the Confederation side. Vice President Jane looked over Danel's troops. "You should know that you are the only force that has come to our aid, Major. The Western Alliance, the Free Cities, and all others are husbanding their forces to defend their own lands and interests."

Vice President Eric nodded, smiling. "But Tiae, the kingdom so recently broken, sends us help. This selfless aid will never be forgotten."

Danel cleared his throat and brought out a paper, reading in a voice loud enough to carry. "Sien of Tiae, Queen by birth and the will of her people, sends this word to the people of the Confederation. Just as the daughter of Jules seeks a New Day for all, the reborn Kingdom of Tiae seeks a new day in its relations with you. We extend our hands in friendship, and offer our hands to aid you in your hour of need. Let this form a foundation for a future of peace and cooperation between us when the daughter's victory has been won."

Vice President Jan nodded solemnly to Major Danel. "We look forward to that future alongside the kingdom."

"A force small in size but large in purpose," said an older military officer wearing multiple bright stars on his shoulders. "I am Field Marshal Klaus, Lady, commander of the Confederation forces defending Dorcastle."

Mari nodded politely to Klaus. "This small force has a large sting. I've got a new rifle with me, and the Tiae cavalry have fifteen more, along with a good supply of ammunition."

"Fifteen? Those are the daughter's rifles?" Eric asked. "Not Mechanics Guild models?"

"Yes," Mari said. "I'm sorry we couldn't bring more. My army is coming, with a lot more rifles."

Everyone craned to look, as if expecting Mari's army to begin marching into sight at any moment. Embarrassed again, Mari shook her head. "I don't know how far behind me they are. Only a few days, I hope. They're coming. I promise."

"Fifteen rifles," Klaus commented. He was stoutly built, and carried with him the same sort of strong aura as the wall looming over them. "The Mechanics Guild has slowly robbed us of any working models of their rifles. We have only three of those to defend the city, and only twenty bullets total to share among them. What does 'a good supply of ammunition' mean, Lady?"

"About eighty rounds for each rifle," Mari said. Despite the tension of the moment, she had to smile at the looks of astonishment that greeted that news.

"Tiae has sent us a very great gift indeed," Vice President Jane finally managed to say.

Mari didn't correct Jane, deciding to let Sien take credit for the contribution of the rifles as well as the soldiers from Tiae. "I understand the Imperials will be here soon."

"They could come into sight at any moment, Lady," Eric said, sagging a bit with worry. "Your army *is* on the way, you say? The sooner they arrive the better."

Field Marshal Klaus, who seemed to be a man of few but well-considered words, looked south. "How many? Our last reports said you had five thousand under arms."

"I had to leave several hundred soldiers to protect Pacta Servanda, but the army coming numbers more like six thousand," Mari said. "With about five hundred rifles like mine."

"Five *hundred?*" Even Klaus's composure was tested by that news.

"We could hold a paper box against the legions with five hundred rifles," Vice President Eric exulted.

"They're not here yet," Vice President Jane said. "But when they do arrive… We've heard stories, we've received reports, telling us how many Mechanic weapons you had, daughter…excuse me, Lady Mari… and how many bullets you were making for them, but nobody believed any of it. Everyone thought that you had succeeded in Tiae because of a vacuum of power that you had been clever enough to exploit."

"If we are fortunate," Alain said, speaking for the first time, "the Great Guilds and the Imperials have also discounted such reports."

No one answered for a moment. Mari saw their discomfort at not knowing how to speak with a Mage. "Treat my Mage as you would me," she said. "Speak to him as you would me. He is not dangerous to anyone except our enemies. Alain can be trusted in all things."

"Then…Sir Mage…I can guarantee you that our enemies have not believed the reports," Field Marshal Klaus commented. "We should go inside and discuss the defenses in detail, Lady. Major Danel, is it?

Please report to General Sanj over there to the left, you see her command flag? She will see to you while we decide the best way to employ your forces."

Mari turned to the Tiae cavalry. "I'll be seeing you as we defend the city!" she called, waving and wondering whether any of them would survive the battle.

They walked into the building, where the large central meeting room had been turned into a headquarters with big tables covered by maps. Wooden blocks represented different units of defenders. "Lady Mari," Vice President Eric said, "since you are going to assume command of the defense—"

Mari held out both hands. "I'm not assuming command."

"But—"

"I'm a Mechanic. If you needed some equipment fixed, I'd be the expert. But this is another line of work." Mari nodded to Klaus. "One in which Field Marshal Klaus is the expert. The commander of my army, General Flyn, told me that Klaus is the finest there is."

Flyn had actually told Mari, while discussing Confederation commanders some months ago, that Klaus was the Confederation's best at fighting a defensive battle. "I could take Klaus easily if he was on the attack," Flyn had remarked, "but if Klaus was dug in and holding his position, I would have a very hard time of it." Since the fight for Dorcastle would be a defensive one, Mari didn't feel as though she had misstated Flyn's opinion.

And her words had clearly pleased the field marshal, who bowed toward her. "General Flyn's reputation is well known. I am honored by his appraisal of my skills."

"What then is your intended role?" Vice President Jane asked.

Mari gestured toward the outside. "They need to know the daughter is with them, is fighting for them, is fighting alongside them. If you want to declare that I'm leading the defense, that's fine, and I will accept a role overseeing the defense, but I want Field Marshal Klaus to be formulating the strategy and making the tactical decisions on a moment-by-moment basis."

Jane nodded, her eyes on Mari. "While you fight on the walls alongside our defenders?"

Mari nodded, wincing inside at the thought. "Yes. So they know I'm there."

"When you're seen by the Imperials, and the Mechanics, and the Mages," Eric said, "they'll bend every effort to killing you."

"I'm actually kind of getting used to that," Mari said, trying to make a joke of the danger to help hide the tightness in her gut.

"I will be with her," Alain said. "At all times."

Klaus bowed again, this time to Alain. "Sir Mage, I admit to great worry about the danger posed by the Mage Guild. There will be many Mages coming, I fear, and our ability to counter their spells is very weak."

"Many Mages are no more threat than a few" Alain said. "The power that Mages must draw on to create their spells is limited in each area. Once that power is exhausted by a handful of powerful spells, the only threat that Mages can pose is from their knives."

That news earned him looks of surprise and, Mari saw, some skepticism. They had difficulty believing anything told them by a Mage. "He's speaking the truth," she said, her voice harder than she had intended. "Mage Alain is telling you things that the Mage Guild has kept secret so that you wouldn't know about their limitations."

Field Marshal Klaus nodded, his expression intent. "So, this power the Mages employ, Sir Mage, it is like the bullets for the Mechanic rifles in a way? Only so much is available, and once used the weapon loses its potency?"

"That is exactly so," Alain said. "The larger the spell, the more power it uses. Once depleted, the power will slowly rebuild, but over a span of weeks and months."

"How much power is there around this part of the city?" Mari asked him.

"As is usual near water, there is some, but not a great amount," Alain said. "I sense more power in other parts of the city, but here at the first wall it will be quickly used up if many Mages seek to employ it, especially if major spells are cast. After a few such major spells, the Mages before this wall will be of no greater threat than any other man or woman."

Vice President Eric grinned with relief. "We feared being overwhelmed by a hundred Mages doing their worst all at once. Can this news of yours be shared, Sir Mage?"

"It is a secret of the Mage Guild," Alain said. "For which I care nothing. Tell anyone you wish. Tell it widely."

"It will be immensely reassuring to our defenders," Klaus said. "This is the second best news of today, after only your own arrival, Lady." He gestured to one of the aides standing by attentively and ordered that the word be passed around the defenders, then faced Mari again. "What do you think the Mechanics will bring to the fight?"

"Rifles," Mari said. "Just how many the Mechanics Guild has is a secret I haven't been able to learn, but some of what they had my forces have acquired, and some of what they have left will have been kept back to defend Mechanics Guild Halls. From what I know, I'm guessing about a hundred rifles will be employed here, but probably with not more than twenty or thirty bullets for each, and most of the Mechanics using them won't be well trained in that task."

"Except for the Assassins," Alain said.

"Yes," Mari agreed. "There's a special unit of the Mechanics Guild that consists of trained fighters. I don't know for certain how many of those are still around, but the best information I have says there are about forty left. Aside from the rifles, they will use explosives to try to blow open gates, and some light and medium caliber artillery. But there are only a few artillery pieces, and not much in the way of shells for them because the Senior Mechanics deliberately limited the number made. They didn't want commons capturing the artillery and using it against Mechanics Guild Halls."

"We've heard that you have much larger artillery than the Mechanics Guild," Vice President Eric said.

"I do. Some of it is with my army, and the rest is dug in to defend Pacta Servanda from an expected large attack by the Syndaris."

"There was a large explosion in Dorcastle a few years ago," Klaus noted. "It destroyed a warehouse. Rumor since then claims it marked your first appearance."

Mari wondered if they could see her embarrassment. "Yes. That was me. It wasn't explosives, though. It was a steam boiler that I deliberately caused to over-pressure and explode. It's not impossible that the Mechanics Guild might bring in some boilers on barges and try to explode them against the sea-gates, but deliberately making a boiler explode is completely against Guild practices, so I don't believe that even under these circumstances the Senior Mechanics would allow it, or even think of doing it. What about the rail yard in Dorcastle? Have you occupied that?"

"We have," Klaus said. "That is, we swept through it after the Mechanics withdrew to ensure none remained, and are maintaining a watch on the rail yard in case some of them try to sneak back in. The rail yard is inside the second wall, so we couldn't leave it as a potential threat. But we have no one who knows how to use the Mechanic devices left there."

"They have probably been disabled," Mari said. "If we get a chance, I'll check them out."

"Which leaves the legions," Klaus said. "You have both fought them, so I need not brief you on the danger they pose. We have received reliable reports that the Emperor has sent every active legion into this attack, leaving the defense of the Empire itself to reserves and auxiliaries."

"That is a large risk," Alain observed.

"That's a lot of legions," Mari said. "How did the Empire get enough shipping to carry them?"

"Apparently they and the Great Guilds took possession of everything they could seize," Vice President Jane said. "The Sea of Bakre has been almost stripped of ships. Any vessel that evaded them is hiding in port."

"Some Confederation warships have been ordered to harass the Imperial expedition," Vice President Eric said. "But it's too large to mount an attack on. The decision was made by those above me to hold back most of our fleet to defend the Strait of Gulls."

"Little good holding the coast will do us if the Imperials succeed in ripping out the Confederation's guts," Klaus commented. Another aide arrived, rushing up to the field marshal.

"Still no sign of the Imperials, sir."

Klaus nodded. "What about the Mechanic and Mage Guild Halls? Any activity?"

"No, sir. Nothing," the aide said. "You can't even tell anyone is alive inside."

Mari flinched before she could stop herself. "Alain?"

"The Mage Guild Hall is occupied," Alain said. "I can sense the acolytes and many of the Mages." He paused, seeming perplexed. "And an elder who is familiar to me. Why is her presence so clear?"

"She wants you to know that she's here?"

"Yes." Alain looked at Mari. "While time permits, we should go by the Mage Guild Hall. I will not go inside, but perhaps she will come out to speak with me. It is important to know what those Mages intend."

"We can take a look at the Mechanics Guild Hall as well," Mari said. "So I can size that up." She hesitated as a thought occurred to her. "Do you have city records of any groups of Mechanics arriving in the last few weeks?" she asked the officials.

"We do keep track of their comings and goings," one of the city officials admitted. "This is important?"

"If a group of ten or twenty showed up recently, the Senior Mechanics could have sent in part of the Assassins unit in advance," Mari said. "If they charge out at a critical point, twenty Mechanics with rifles—"

"Behind our lines," Klaus said, alarmed.

Another official hurried up, paging through a ledger. "Three weeks ago. Exactly twenty-one Mechanics arrived at the docks and went to their Guild Hall. No rifles were visible, but they had large packs with them that could have easily concealed something of that size."

"You called it," Eric said admiringly to Mari.

"We've got sentries watching that Guild Hall," Klaus said. "We're going to have to post some stronger forces there without tipping off the Mechanics that we suspect what they are planning."

"Let's get you to the Mage Guild Hall," Jane advised Alain. "We don't know how much time we have left, and we need to know if we have to defend against the Mages, too. Thank you, Sir Mage, for your help. I did not truly believe that any Mage could ever… I was wrong."

Alain nodded to her. "Before I met Mari, I had forgotten the words thank you, and no longer knew what the word help meant. Your thanks should go to her."

"People should stop crediting me for their own accomplishments," Mari said. "Let's go."

To Mari's relief, instead of mounting horses they were hustled into a coach that tore off through the streets of Dorcastle, wending its way through the defenders and their piled-up supplies. The many sheaves of spears, piles of spare swords, and boxes filled with crossbow bolts gave the appearance of a vast open market dedicated to the instruments of war.

She recognized more landmarks in this part of Dorcastle as the coach thundered through the streets, but seeing the city prepared for war felt strange to her as she recalled the bustling trading center she had first visited.

The coach shuddered to a halt on the edge of the plaza facing the Mage Guild Hall. Like its counterpart in Danalee, the Mage Guild Hall had been designed to reject the world outside, only a few small, narrow windows and forbidding-looking doors visible on the unadorned and harsh exterior.

Mari stopped Alain when he appeared ready to stride toward the front entrance. "How dangerous is this?"

"Compared to coming to Dorcastle?" Alain asked.

"Don't try to be funny. We're walking toward that building together, so if you have any concerns, now would be a good time to share them."

Alain looked toward the building. "I do not sense danger. There is…no feeling of tension inside. Only the normal lack of emotion."

"Most people don't consider that normal," Mari said, checking that her pistol was ready. "All right. Whenever you're ready."

As the Confederation officials watched nervously, Mari and Alain began walking slowly across the plaza. They had gone only partway when the main entrance opened to reveal a single woman in the robes of a Mage elder. The elder walked toward them with the measured gait of someone very old, using a cane to occasionally support her steps, so that they met well away from the Hall.

"This one is honored to speak with you again," Alain said to the elder.

The old Mage raised her eyebrows very slightly at Alain. "Honored? You speak of feelings, young Mage?"

"I speak of feelings, I admit to feelings," Alain said. "My powers remain."

"So rumor holds," the elder said, "though the council of elders insists that you have become powerless." She studied Mari dispassionately. "So, this young Mage saw clearly before he spoke to me years ago. I see the hope of the world in you, shadow. Why have you come back to Dorcastle, daughter of Jules?"

"To help the people here defend it," Mari said. "To help overthrow the Great Guilds."

"This young Mage has done much to trouble the Guild already," the elder said. "There have been many challenges of late to the wisdom of the elders."

"This one has questions," Alain said.

"Dispense with formality, young Mage, for I sense great urgency in you and this shadow."

"How is it with this Guild Hall?" Alain asked. "Will any there assist in the attack on the city?"

Mari was surprised to see a trace of a smile appear on the elder. It usually took a while for Mages who had left the Guild to reveal any feelings.

"This one, and others, have received instructions," the elder said. "But the instructions have been judged to be unclear. We are meditating on their meaning and will do nothing while thus engaged. You should know," she added, "that over time there have come to this Hall those who have doubts of the wisdom of the Guild. It has become a place where most have concerns, but have not yet been willing to discard the old wisdom."

"Thank you," Alain said, drawing another faintly surprised look from the elder. "I must tell you what was found in Danalee." He quickly described the deaths there and the living elder they had found, while open dismay appeared on the face of the elder.

"This is a great ill," she said when Alain had finished. "A failure of wisdom such has never been known. I will tell the others. You need fear nothing from those in this Hall, young Mage." The elder looked at Mari, her eyes taking on the same aspect as Alain's when he experienced foresight. "Do you know of this?" she asked Alain when the moment passed, still watching Mari intently.

Mari felt a chill run down her spine, remembering what Alain had told her of his vision of her hurt.

"Yes," Alain said. "It will not happen."

"So?" The elder studied Mari a little longer. "Perhaps not. No future is certain. But…know this also, young Mage. If you stay with her, hope remains. I see this. Do not forget, for if this one is real to you, as rumor claims, you must stay beside her. Let none separate you. Then…perhaps."

"This one will not forget your words," Alain said.

The elder turned without any farewell and began walking arduously back to the Mage Guild Hall.

Mari ran one hand through her hair, then looked at Alain. "Your vision of me was that bad?"

"The elder said that hope remains," Alain insisted.

"All right." She refrained from pointing out that "hope remains" wasn't exactly the strongest reassurance. Mari took a deep breath to calm herself, resolving to try to put from her mind the foresight of Mages. "Let's go over to the Mechanics Guild Hall. I don't intend actually exposing myself to the gun-sight of anyone in there, but I'll call with my far-talker."

That proved to be as frustrating as she had expected. Mari called on the standard Mechanics Guild frequency, asking to speak to anyone and repeating her usual promises about protecting Mechanics and their families once the Mechanics Guild no longer held power. But there wasn't even a brief hiss of static to hint at a reply. "If you have to," Mari told the Confederation officials, "you can cut the pipeline bringing water to the Guild Hall. There are cisterns inside, but they won't be able to hold out for more than a couple of weeks if you cut off their supply. I'd prefer you not do that if possible."

"It wouldn't help in time to make a difference now," Dorcastle's mayor sighed. "You're certain that the Mechanics in there will be of great importance to this city if— I mean, when we have won?"

"Have they been important in the past?" Mari asked, knowing the answer was yes. "In the future, the number and capabilities of Mechanic devices are going to grow hugely. The more Mechanics any city has, the more it will be able to make use of those devices and create new ones. They can serve the city, instead of the city serving them."

"They can, but will they, Lady?"

"I think many will. I really do."

"We must get back to the waterfront," Field Marshal Klaus urged. "I've given the orders to redeploy some of our reserve forces around the Mechanics Guild Hall. If those assassins sortie out during the fighting, they'll run into an unpleasant surprise in the form of massed crossbow fire from concealed soldiers."

Mari often felt depressed thinking of Mechanics dying in the war. But the Mechanic Assassins, ruthless and fanatical, were another matter. "Good."

The sound of pounding hooves warned of another courier racing their way. "The Imperial fleet has come into view!"

Mari looked toward the harbor. "I wish I'd had the chance to eat lunch before the war started." It wasn't until everyone except Alain gave her funny looks that she realized how odd that sounded.

"The lead ship is flying a parley flag," the courier added breathlessly.

"Parley," Field Marshal Klaus commented. "They don't want to discuss terms. They want us to surrender without a fight."

"Let's see how long we can stall them," Vice President Jane said. "It looks like you will get a chance at lunch, Lady Mari."

* * *

They waited at the harbor to receive the Imperial representatives. Three soldiers stood on the landing, each holding a flagstaff from which a banner flapped gently in the sea breeze. In the center was Mari's banner, blue with a many-pointed gold star. To the left was the flag of the Bakre Confederation, deep red with symbols of the various cities arrayed on it, including in the upper right the crossed swords of Jules herself to represent Julesport. And on the right was the green and gold flag of the Kingdom of Tiae, held by one of the cavalry who had escorted Mari and Alain to Dorcastle.

Mari stood with the flags at her back and Alain by her side. In contrast to the glittering armor and bright uniforms of the soldiers and the fine suits of the two vice presidents, she wore her dark Mechanics jacket and Alain wore his Mage robes. Even though Mari had wanted Field Marshal Klaus to stand beside her, Klaus and the other Confederation officers and political representatives had insisted on forming a rank behind her. With them stood Major Danel, his green uniform of Tiae standing out amid the red uniforms of the Confederation.

Well behind them all, separated from the water by rows of warehouses and other buildings, the first wall of Dorcastle stood. Along its top, the barely seen shapes of soldiers and their banners formed a solid display of defensive might.

Mari thought it all impressive. But she doubted it was enough to cause the Imperials to call off their attack.

It was late in the afternoon by the time a launch so large it was almost a small ship in its own right came toward them across the harbor, banks of oars rising and sweeping in unison to drive it over the water. Bright Imperial banners flew from the bow and stern, and legionary officers standing in the launch wore red capes that matched the high red plumes on their helmets. Where the uniforms of the Bakre Confederation were a bright scarlet, those of the Imperial soldiers were a darker wine red. Among the soldiers were a few high-ranking Imperial officials, their bright white ceremonial suits glistening in the rays of the lowering sun.

A small dark cluster on the launch's deck marked the presence of several Mechanics. A similar cluster of Mages stood in a position as far away from the Mechanics as the size of the launch permitted.

"The Mages are not elders," Alain said to Mari in a voice loud enough to be heard by the others waiting with them. "Even now, elders will not stoop to admit the existence of common people or Mechanics."

"Those look like Senior Mechanics on the launch," Mari commented. "They probably didn't trust regular Mechanics to do and say exactly what they were told when dealing with us."

Vice President Jane spoke up. "The Imperial officials are led by Crown Prince Maxim. The only one in the Empire who outranks him is the Emperor himself."

"Who is the woman next to him?" Field Marshal Klaus asked.

"Crown Princess Lyra. Equal in rank to Maxim."

"So which one is in charge?"

"From the way they're standing, Maxim has the lead," Jane said. "You know how the Imperial household works. Survival of the fittest. Maxim probably convinced the Emperor to give him command, but Lyra is along to take over if Maxim bumbles the task. She'll be watching for any hint of failure on his part that will allow her grounds to take over command of the expedition, but if she fumbled after that Maxim could resume being in charge."

"That ought to motivate everyone," Vice President Eric commented. "Is there any chance they will sabotage each other and benefit us?"

"Things like that have happened," Jane said. "Not officially, but we know of them. However, in this case I don't think we can count on that. The Imperials want to take this city too badly." The group fell silent as the launch approached the landing, its rowers checking their motion with precise skill that brought the craft to a gentle stop. Sailors leaped ashore and wrapped lines around the landing's bollards to hold the boat fast.

For a few moments no one moved, the only sound that of the banners of both sides flapping in the wind.

Crown Prince Maxim began walking, every Imperial official matching his steps. He set foot on the landing with the attitude of a conqueror treading on already-subdued territory, Crown Princess Lyra right beside him, the other Imperial officers and officials following.

Maxim strode toward Mari, but looking past her. She realized he was heading toward Field Marshal Klaus.

Coming to a halt, Maxim gazed around at Dorcastle as if unimpressed and already bored with this provincial backwater.

Another Imperial official addressed Klaus. "Crown Prince Maxim is prepared to accept your surrender."

Klaus shook his head. "If you're here to talk, you need to talk to our leader. She's right there. You can't miss her."

The Imperial kept his eyes on Klaus. "There is a dead person there. I do not speak to the dead."

Mari decided it was time for her to join in. "The Emperor's rule does not extend to the Confederation. He is not in charge here. Neither are you. The people of the Confederation, like those of the Kingdom of Tiae and the Western Alliance and the Free Cities, make their own rules."

The Imperial official paused, clearly uncertain how to handle the situation.

Crown Prince Maxim saved him, waving an indifferent hand and looking directly at Mari. "You have proven very difficult to kill. Do not make the mistake of assuming that means you *cannot* be killed."

Mari kept her own voice steady as she replied. "Do not make the mistake of assuming that I am not prepared to die in order to ensure that the Great Guilds are overthrown and that Dorcastle does not fall." Inspiration gave her more words. "The Empire has tried to kill me many times. And failed. I understand that you Imperials think you know the reason for that."

Tall, bright Princess Lyra laughed mockingly. "I see you in the light of day, rather plain in appearance and with the greasy hands of a Mechanic. There is little of the undying beauty of the Dark One about you."

That should have stung, and it did a bit even though Mari had never considered herself to be gorgeous, but Mari found herself smiling. "There is enough of the Dark One to take me in and out of Marandur twice, and through every obstacle the Empire could put in my path. Your legions have always failed against me."

"They will not fail this time," Maxim said in a way that made it clear he was reasserting who was in charge of this negotiation. "Since these others have foolishly placed you in charge, I call on you now to yield this city. Otherwise, every drop of blood spilled here will be your responsibility."

"We fight in defense of our freedom," Mari said. "Responsibility for loss of life lies with whoever attacks us."

"Apparently," Prince Maxim said, running his gaze over the various officers and officials, "none of you understand what will happen to this city when the legions take it. If you had even a hint of what would happen, you would yield immediately."

"I know exactly what will happen," Mari said. "I've seen Marandur, from the inside. Have you? How many of the bone fragments in the ruins of that city once belonged to Imperial legionaries? Is that what you want to be remembered for? As the one who shattered the Empire's legions against the walls of Dorcastle?"

"I have seen enough of Marandur," Maxim said. "I know that it shows the Empire's strength."

"Then why," Alain asked, "does the Empire forbid anyone to enter the remains of the city? Does it fear that others will see that all of the Empire's force could only produce a victory that cost more than the worst of defeats?"

No matter his other skills, Crown Prince Maxim clearly lacked

much experience with speaking to Mages. Not that there was any surprise in that, since in most of the world no one talked to Mages unless
they had to and Mages talked to no one unless they must. Maxim
glanced back toward the Mages standing with silent, hooded menace.

"That one is nothing," one of the Mages said in a toneless voice that
begrudged the act of speech.

"This one has been to Danalee," Alain said. "This one has seen what
the council of elders ordered in Danalee, orders told me by an elder
who defied those commands. All others in that Hall, from acolyte to
elder, died by murder or at their own hands. That is the wisdom the
Mage Guild offers you."

The Mages did not reply.

"An obvious lie," Maxim finally said, annoyed.

"They haven't called him a liar," Mari told Maxim, "because Mages
can tell when someone is lying, and when they're not. They know that
Mage Alain told them what did happen at Danalee."

"I weary of this," Maxim said, his voice taking on overtones of
anger. "Yield. Now. Or die in the ruins of this city."

"We will fight," Mari said, wondering if she sounded as breathless
as she thought she did. "All of us."

"All of you? You stand alone."

"Tiae stands with us," Vice President Jane called, indicating the
banner, and then pointing upward where every soldier sent by Queen
Sien had been placed along the battlements. "And the daughter of
Jules leads us. You know what the prophecy says. You cannot triumph
here."

One of the Mages finally spoke again, her voice also totally lacking
in feeling. "There is no prophecy. There has never been a prophecy."

Alain answered, putting a bit of feeling into his own voice. "The
word of a Mage," he said. "Worthless. The elders have taught you that
there is no truth, so you do not hesitate to lie. Have you never thought
that if truth does not exist, then what the elders tell you must also be
lies?"

"Fool," the female Mage replied, the lack of emotion behind the word somehow making it sound terrible. "You will cease here."

"I will fight for what is real here," Alain said. "The prophecy does exist. And you know when you look upon Master Mechanic Mari that she is the daughter whose coming was foretold. Over the centuries the Mage Guild has slain every woman who might have become the daughter, but you have not slain her. She, and those Mages who look to her for wisdom and call her elder, will show you a truth you will not admit to."

"Elder? That shadow?" another one of the Mages spat, startled enough to let some tones of disbelief enter his voice.

"Silence," the female Mage said before directing her attention back to Alain. "You are nothing. You have lost your powers in pursuit of a shadow."

"If you are right, then you need not fear me," Alain said.

The silence that followed that statement was finally broken by one of the Senior Mechanics who had come with Maxim, speaking with open scorn. "I told you this would be a waste of time. She's out of her mind with delusions. Just kill her and these others."

Mari felt the old anger at the contempt with which the Senior Mechanic regarded her and all others. "You, and all of your like, have dared to enslave a world, have kept from us the sort of Mechanic technology that could have bettered the lives of everyone, and now think you can control the Empire by giving it too much to swallow? Crown Prince Maxim, I have sent some of that banned technology to you, to the Emperor himself, to see what the Guild has denied him and every one of his subjects. To show the Emperor that the knowledge will be shared with all."

Maxim smiled. "But we don't want all to have it. Those texts you offer came from Marandur, from Imperial lands, and already belong solely to the Emperor. We are coming to get them back."

Mari saw the Senior Mechanics, behind Maxim and out of his sight, exchange smug glances. They doubtless had their own plans for those banned technology texts. "If you want that technology so badly that you'll attack Dorcastle, I'll guarantee you that you'll get it back, one bullet at a time, one artillery shell at a time, until every legionary who tries to take these walls is dead."

Vice President Jane spoke up again. "Surely we can negotiate, Crown Prince? Let us talk and find a means to avoid a battle which will only drain the Empire of the strength needed to deal with the arrogance of the Great Guilds."

"She's just trying to stall," another Senior Mechanic called to Maxim in the tones of a teacher to a dull student.

Mari saw Maxim's jaw tighten but his voice remained level as he replied. "Thank you, honored Senior Mechanic. You who call yourself the daughter are beyond reason. I call upon those who represent the Bakre Confederation. Know that if I leave this landing without your surrender, there will be no second chances and no further negotiations. I demand for the last time that you yield this city to the dominion of the Emperor."

Major Danel spat onto the stone before him. "We in Tiae have had enough of warlords, even those who style themselves as princes and emperors. By order of Queen Sien, and trusting in the daughter, we will fight as long as there is life in us."

"Tiae speaks for us as well," Vice President Eric said.

"Tell your legions that they will die in a battle they cannot win!" Mari said loudly enough to ensure that everyone in the Imperial delegation could hear. "We fight for the freedom of this world, and we will not fail!"

Maxim spun on his heel, the others in the delegation hastening to keep up as he strode back to the launch. "You will soon see the wrath of the Empire's legions," he called as a parting shot.

"We'll see your legions," Field Marshal Klaus replied. "We'll see them lying dead before our walls."

As the Imperial launch pulled away, Vice President Jane sighed. "I've had negotiations go better. But it's clear that Maxim never intended to strike a deal. He thinks victory is certain. A wiser or less ruthless man would have offered good terms to spare the legions the losses they'll take and spare himself the time needed to assault the city."

"The storm will strike soon," Klaus said. "Let us take up our weapons and prepare to face it."

Mari stood a moment as the others began moving back to the wall. She gazed out across the harbor to the forest of masts in the sea beyond that marked the immense Imperial expedition and its backers, the Great Guilds. Victory seemed impossible.

"I'm not going to let you win," she told the distant figures of the Senior Mechanics, the elders of the Mage Guild, and the Imperial multitude.

CHAPTER FIVE

"THEY PROBABLY WON'T hit us until just before dawn," Field Marshal Klaus said as the group stood on the battlements of the first wall, watching the rays of the setting sun gild the Imperial ships outside the harbor. "Too many things can go wrong when it's dark. The Imperials will come charging in at first light, planning on overrunning the waterfront area and hitting this wall as fast as possible."

"I take it we're planning on doing something about that?" Mari said.

"Oh, yes, Lady, we are indeed. The legions will find themselves facing some serious delays. We commons may not have access to Mechanic arms and explosives, but there are simpler weapons."

"Expensive, though," Vice President Eric commented. "You should have heard the merchants screaming about the trade goods still in those warehouses on the waterfront."

Klaus smiled slightly. "I did. I told them I could do nothing about it, being a simple soldier, and they should speak with the representatives of the government. Such as you."

"Well played." Eric leaned forward on the battlement. "You understand that even though I could try throwing my weight around I have no intention of doing so. You and Lady Mari have command of the defense. I will do what I can to assist you. It's an odd feeling, isn't it?"

"What's that?" Klaus asked.

"To see the sun set and wonder if you'll see it rise again. I did militia service, but nothing really hazardous." He glanced at Mari. "Is this the worst you've faced, Lady Mari?"

Mari shook her head. "It doesn't feel like it yet. The worst…I guess being chased through Altis by the assassins. The final voyage of the *Terror* was horrible, but I was so tired and numb that I didn't really feel it at the time. It's worse in memory." She turned a questioning look on Eric. "How did you and Vice President Jane end up here?"

Eric gave a brief, derisive laugh. "My boss, the Bakre Confederation President of War, said someone needed to be here. He proposed one of my assistants. Jane's boss, the Bakre Confederation President of State, replied by saying that she was sending Jane because the defenders deserved that much. So my boss said he was sending me. I guess you could say we ended up in Dorcastle as part of a game of one-up-manship by our superiors."

"You're not elected?"

"No. The Presidents are. Jane and I were appointed to our jobs." He smiled crookedly as the sun slipped beneath the western horizon. "I was really happy when I got the appointment. Celebrated and everything."

Mari laughed, too. "I didn't exactly volunteer for the daughter job, you know."

"You've done more with it than many thought possible," Eric said.

"I'm going to do my best. So will Jane."

"You will do fine," Field Marshal Klaus said. Mari wondered how many times in his military career Klaus had said the same thing to nervous soldiers before a battle.

Klaus looked up at the sky, where the stars were coming out as night fell. "The Imperials may make attempts to slip some units in during the night, so we'll have to stay on alert. Our scouts near the waterfront should spot any serious incursions. With your permission, Lady Mari, I will pass orders for double sentinels to be stationed tonight, but otherwise for everyone to get as much sleep as they can."

"That sounds like a good plan. Where do you think is the best place for me and Mage Alain?" Mari asked.

"Right here." Klaus patted the stone rampart before them. "This is almost atop the main gate. It is certain to be a target for the Imperial attack, because that's how Imperials think. It's the main gate, so it's the most important gate, and they will by all the stars above take the most important gate. Maxim will try to smash his way through here and keep going. They will probably also hit the two other secondary gates in this wall as well as the two sea gates, but those should be lesser efforts."

"Even if the Imperials weren't so inclined, seeing Lady Mari will guarantee they attack in great strength at this spot," Vice President Eric commented. "Is that wise?"

"I have to be on the walls with the defenders," Mari said, trying to sound matter-of-fact about it. Alain gave her a side glance, showing that he had detected the uneasiness in her voice, but he said nothing.

"You'll have your rifle?" Klaus asked. "I'll assign ten of the Tiae rifles here as well. Even the legions won't be happy to be facing that."

"We may see worse than legions," Alain said.

"That reminds me." Mari looked down off the inside of the wall. "Where is the wagon we came with? There are two DKs in it. I need them close by."

"DKs?" Eric asked.

"Dragon killers," Mari explained. "And, yes, they do exactly what their name says."

Klaus and Vice President Eric went off to check other parts of the city. As night fell the areas that Mari could see presented strange contrasts. Just behind her, inside the first wall, lanterns and torches illuminated frenzied activity as the defending forces made last-minute preparations. On the wall itself, the only light came from the stars overhead and a few shaded lanterns that could not be seen by anyone outside the wall. Nothing moved in the open stretch in front of the wall, left clear of buildings or other cover so that attackers would face the full force of the defenders' wrath. Beyond that open space the waterfront of Dorcastle lay dark and silent, the warehouses, offices, and taverns that would normally be full of life and light sitting empty as the city awaited the assault. The harbor, which Mari remembered always being crowded with shipping, was dark, its navigational buoys removed by the defenders and the lights on the breakwater extinguished.

Outside the harbor, the Imperial expedition glowed in the darkness, every ship apparently having lit every lantern and torch available to display the size and power of the attacking force. Mari could spot three Mechanics Guild ships out there, their electric lights gleaming with a steady white glow contrasting with the yellowish flickering of the torches and lanterns on other ships. One of the Guild ships also had a searchlight mounted, its beam occasionally sweeping across the wall to intimidate the defenders.

Mari remembered having toured that ship when it visited the harbor at Caer Lyn. How old had she been? Eleven or twelve. Part of a group of Apprentices taken to see the ship and learn about the devices on it.

She recalled being thrilled to see the steam boiler that provided propulsion and light for the ship. Her friends Alli and Calu, a few years older and adopting the jaded attitude of teenagers, smiling indulgently as Mari threw question after question at the Mechanics and Apprentices who worked the boiler. Alli had reserved her questions for the crew of the deck gun, of course.

Were any of those Mechanics still aboard that ship? Were any of the men and women she had known as Apprentices at Caer Lyn part of the crew?

Many of her former co-workers were here to destroy what Mari had tried to build, and to kill her as part of that destruction. Mari had gone from being a loyal member of the Mechanics Guild to someone sworn to destroy it, from being an operator of steam locomotives and writer of thinking ciphers for calculating and analysis devices to being the symbol of the New Day and the overall commander of the forces defending Dorcastle.

She could retrace every step that had brought her from there to here, from then to now, but it still felt unreal at times.

Other than the electric lights, steam funnels, and a field gun mounted on each, the Mechanics Guild ships were otherwise like the ships around them, built of wood, with soaring masts and spars to hold sails. Professor S'san had told Mari that old records showed the Mechanics Guild had centuries before possessed four ships built entirely of metal. By the time that Mari became a Mechanic, only one of those ships remained. The others had deteriorated over time and were cannibalized for parts and metal to keep the last ship working.

A few months ago Mari had seen one of her ships, the *Pride*, sink that last metal ship. The Guild's technology was slowly falling apart, but rather than make any changes that might imperil their hold on the world, the Senior Mechanics would rather cling to old policies and ideas. If the Guild was going to fail, the Senior Mechanics were determined that the rest of the world would go down with it.

Mari lowered herself to sit down, resting her back against the battlement. The coolness of the stone spread through her clothing to give her a slight shiver. Above, the stars gleamed in uncountable numbers.

The dragon killers lay beside her, her rifle next to them, constant reminders of what the morning would bring.

She was glad that Alain sat beside her, offering human warmth and comfort.

Some soldiers came walking along the wall, stopping when they reached her. "Lady Mari? I'm Colonel Teodor, commander of the Third Regiment."

Mari struggled to her feet. "This is Sir Mage Alain. What can we do for you?"

"Ah…" The colonel seemed at a loss for words.

It took Mari a moment to realize why. Like all other commons, the colonel had spent his life being taught never to question or challenge Mechanics, only to do as they ordered. He had no idea what to do when a Mechanic asked him what he wanted.

The colonel recovered quickly, though. "Lady, my regiment is responsible for defending this portion of the wall. This is Sergeant

Kira. Her platoon is stationed at this spot. We are at your service and command."

"Thank you," Mari said. "You have orders from Field Marshal Klaus?"

"Yes, Lady."

"Follow them. If I need anything else, I'll let you know. Mage Alain and I will help deal with any threats here." Mari pointed down at her weapons. "I've got two dragon killers, and my rifle, and a pistol. I understand that the field marshal intends stationing some of the cavalry from Tiae along here with their rifles."

"Yes, Lady," Sergeant Kira said. She was several years older than Mari and wore her light armor with the casual ease of a veteran. Kira gestured to the side. "They're right over there, just above the gate."

"Sergeant Kira," Colonel Teodor added, "is one of the Confederation's best shots with a Mechanic rifle."

"You're not carrying a rifle," Mari said, seeing only her sword and a crossbow.

"It broke," Kira explained. "The Mechanics took it to repair, said they'd return it, but that was months ago and it never came back."

"And they made us pay in advance," the Colonel grumbled, then looked apologetic. "I'm sorry, Lady, for my harsh words."

"Don't worry about it," Mari said. "You're talking about the actions of the Mechanics Guild, which we are all fighting. I'm going to be busy, probably using the dragon killers, when the Imperials hit. If you're a good shot, would you like to use my rifle for a while, Sergeant?"

Even in the darkness it was possible to see Kira's eyes widen. "That—? It's— Thank you, Lady!"

Mari bent down, picked up the rifle and handed it to Kira. "It's called an A-1. Accurate out to half again the range of the old Mechanics Guild repeaters at their best. There's no lever to work. It's clip fed. Every time you pull the trigger it automatically loads a new bullet until the clip is empty. There are twenty rounds in this clip, and uh…" Mari dug into the pockets of her jacket. "Here are three more clips.

Oh, I may call these magazines sometimes because that's what the banned technology texts call them, but I'm used to thinking of them as clips because that's the term the Mechanics Guild has always used. Don't ask me why."

"Eighty…bullets?" Colonel Teodor asked in disbelief. At the prices the Mechanics Guild had charged for bullets, the number represented a not-so-small fortune. Entire armies had gone into battle with less than half as many rounds as that.

"I know you won't waste any," Mari said. Which was true. With bullets so rare and expensive, anyone taught in the traditional ways of using the old Mechanic repeating rifles would fire only at high-value targets that offered a high chance of a hit. "You're going to be near me when the Imperials attack. There are some important targets I'll point out to you if I see them."

"Yes, Lady!" Sergeant Kira ran her hands over the rifle. "I will use it well."

"Thank you." Mari realized that she had just described some other people, Mechanics and Mages, simply as "targets." But she knew from experience that in the heat of battle that's all they would be. It was only afterwards, when she had time to think and remember, that the faces haunted her.

Colonel Teodor and Sergeant Kira walked off a short distance, speaking to each other. Mari lowered herself back to a seat on the cold stone. Alain sat with her. To either side she could hear soft conversations among the defenders occupying this part of the wall. From inside the city came the occasional sounds of a unit marching by or the clatter of hooves as cavalry or wagons went past. It all felt strangely peaceful and calm.

"What bothers you?" Alain asked in a low voice.

She wasn't surprised that he had picked up on her unease. "Shooting at people wearing Mechanics jackets. I've had to do that before, but this time it's much more likely to be people I might know. I'll do it because I have to, but every time I have to think about doing it, it still feels so wrong."

"Would you be happy if you accepted it without any misgivings?" Alain asked.

"You know I wouldn't."

"The Senior Mechanics who give the orders to those we fight have no misgivings about telling other Mechanics to kill you, or anyone else."

Mari shook her head. "Alain, I know we're not morally the same as them. That doesn't make me feel much better. We have to win, but I don't have to enjoy what that requires of us."

When Alain did not immediately reply, she knew he was thinking.

"Soon after I was taken to the Mage Guild Hall as an acolyte," Alain finally said, "one of the other new acolytes rebelled, shouting that what the Mages did was wrong. It was not fair to treat others so. The acolyte was harshly disciplined, to show the rest of us that anyone who believed in ideas like fairness was foolish. The illusion which is this world contains no fairness, we were told. It simply is. The illusion does not care."

Mari stared at him. "Are you trying to cheer me up, darling? Because if you are, it's not going so well."

"What I am attempting to say," Alain explained, "is that I came to realize the fallacy in what the elders claimed. They argued that the world illusion was responsible for their actions against the acolyte. Yet if the world we see is an illusion which Mages must deny in order to make changes to the illusion, how can we blame the illusion for our actions? The illusion did not harm that acolyte. The elders did. Perhaps the world does not care what choices we make. But they are our choices."

Mari gazed at Alain. "I still don't quite get it."

"The world illusion has forced us into this." He waved about to indicate the wall they occupied and the attacking force beyond the harbor. "Those who give the orders to attack Dorcastle do not care that others will die. You care that your actions, no matter how well intentioned, will cause harm to others. They feel no remorse, no responsibility. You do. That is an important difference."

"So," Mari said slowly, "I should feel good about feeling bad about it?"

"Yes. You understand."

"Um…yeah. You know, engineering isn't nearly this complicated."

"There is something else," Alain said.

"Why did I let you get to know me so well?" Mari squeezed her eyes shut, breathing deeply. "I keep remembering that Mage elder saying *hope remains*. That's a lot better than *no hope remains*, but still…"

Alain's voice took on enough somberness for Mari to hear it. "My thoughts also dwell on that. But then, I have been worried about you for so long."

"Two years now?" Mari said, opening her eyes to look at him. "About two years. We started out together being chased by people who wanted to kill us."

"They wanted to kill me," Alain said. "They just wanted to kidnap you."

"Oh, yeah, so much better. Then we almost died of thirst in the waste… And the train almost went off that broken trestle on the way to Dorcastle…on the way to here." She leaned closer to him. "That's when I knew I was doomed. I was watching the gap get closer and closer while we tried to stop the train, and all I could think about was you getting hurt or dying." Mari had to pause before she could say more, as she finally realized what had lain beneath her other worries. "Just like now. I'm scared for both of us. You keep saying that you'll die to protect me. Don't do that, Alain. Don't."

This time he stayed silent.

"Alain, will you promise me—"

"No." He touched the promise rings on his hand and on hers. "I have made my promise to you. And you have made yours to me. Let those be the promises that guide us."

She exhaled loudly, exasperated. "I don't want to live in this world without you."

"Then we both must survive the battle," Alain pointed out.

"Serves me right, for trying to argue with a Mage." Mari turned her head and smiled in welcome as Sergeant Kira returned, grateful for the distraction.

"Lady Mari?" Kira held the rifle as if afraid that someone would take it from her. "Where do wish me to stand, Lady? When the Imperials come?"

"Is over there all right?"

"Yes, Lady." Kira paused, then spoke in a rush. "I didn't believe it when I first heard people saying that the daughter had finally come. And then I didn't believe it when I heard she was a Mechanic. I'm sorry."

"I'm sure you've had your share of unpleasant encounters with Mechanics," Mari said. "But all Mechanics aren't like that. Please sit down. Talk."

Kira sat down nearby, crossing her legs, the rifle in her lap. "They say you're from the Sharr Isles."

"That's right. Caer Lyn. Are you from Dorcastle?"

"Me? Yes, Lady."

"So you're defending your home."

Kira looked into the city. "Home and family. I've no man of my own nor children yet, but my parents are from Dorcastle, as were their parents. It's a nice place. My brother lives here, as well, with his promised wife and children."

Mari nodded slowly. "Is your brother on the wall, too?"

"No, Lady. He's at sea. His ship is somewhere in the Umbari, still safe, we hope. His family left several days ago, going south to Danalee."

The Umbari Ocean was where the Syndaris were preparing to hit Tiae. They might have already attacked in the south. "What will his ship do if they see any Syndari ships?"

"Do their best to stay clear and lose them," Kira said. "No one smart lets a Syndari get within reach of their back. We hear the Syndaris have gotten a taste of their own medicine lately, though, from pirates." She gave Mari a grin.

Mari returned the smile. "The pirates haven't sought out the

Syndaris, but they have given Syndari ships some bloody noses when pushed," she said.

"I see your knife," Kira said. "A gift?"

"Yes." Mari touched the sailor's knife at her belt, given her after she had helped capture her first ship. "I suppose Jules would approve." She still wasn't used to being thought of as a descendant of the old pirate. It felt odd to have sailors want her touch to bring them luck at sea.

Kira chuckled. "I'm certain that she would, Lady. My brother said his ship never fears a ship flying your banner. I'll have to tell him I met you. He'll be jealous." Kira paused. "They say you've never lost a battle, never been defeated. Is that true?"

Mari thought about that. "I guess, in a way. Mage Alain and I have had to run more than once, but in the end we've always managed to achieve whatever we set out to do. Sometimes that was just staying alive, though."

Sergeant Kira hesitated again. "You, and a Mage— How did you and— I mean, how could— No. Forgive me."

Alain, who had been sitting silently beside Mari, suddenly spoke, his voice carrying more feeling than usual so that it sounded almost natural. "Master Mechanic Mari has bound me to her with a spell that is impossible to break."

Kira stared at him.

"Alain!" Mari punched his shoulder. "She'll think you're serious!"

"I am," Alain insisted. "I am bound to you by love, the most magical spell of all, which instead of quickly fading can grow more powerful over time."

She couldn't help smiling at him. "You're trying to distract me, aren't you?"

Alain nodded. "Unsuccessfully, it appears."

"I appreciate the effort. Sergeant Kira, the truth is—" Mari felt Alain's body suddenly grow rigid with tension. "What is it?"

Alain scrambled to his feet. "Mages are on the waterfront or near it. They use spells to hide themselves from sight." He pointed. "There. And there. And there. Six Mages at least."

"Colonel Teodor!" Mari called, her voice piercing the night. The colonel came running up, but before he could say anything Mari gestured to Alain. "Mage Alain senses Mages coming onto the waterfront. They're using spells to make themselves invisible."

"They're scouting us?" Teodor asked.

"No," Alain said. "Mages would not be employed just to scout. Their goal is to find and kill your scouts before they can sound an alarm. In this case, I would expect the Mages to then come close to the gates in this wall so they can allow entrance for Imperial forces, who will strike without warning."

Mari wondered why Teodor and the others were hesitating. "What's the matter? Didn't you understand?"

"Yes, Lady," Colonel Teodor said, "it is just that…"

She heard the worry in his voice and realized that it was not aimed at the enemy. "My Mage," Mari said, trying not to get upset. "My Mage just told you something and you don't believe him? Is that what's happening here?"

From the reactions of the soldiers, she apparently hadn't done too well a job of keeping anger from her voice.

"Forgive us, Lady, it's just that…a Mage…"

"I'm a Mechanic!" Mari said. "Do you trust me?" Without waiting for a reply, she pointed to Alain. "Yes, he's a Mage. Any Mage who follows me will tell you the truth, but Mage Alain in particular is absolutely trustworthy. You must have heard what he did in the Northern Ramparts! And you hesitate to believe him?"

"I'll go to the Field Marshal and tell him of the warning," Sergeant Kira volunteered.

"Yes," Colonel Teodor agreed. "As quickly as possible. Let him know the scouts and our sally gates may both be in danger. Sir Mage, my apologies," he added as Kira ran off.

Mari was pleased to hear Alain's voice stay even but not emotionless. "It is nothing," Alain said. "In an emergency, it is important to know who can be trusted."

"It is," Teodor agreed.

Mari peered into the night. "Can you spot any of them?" she asked Alain.

"Not directly," he said. "From this distance I can only sense the spells and the general direction."

Soldiers all along the wall were stirring as the alert spread. Her attention on the waterfront, Mari was startled when Field Marshal Klaus, breathing heavily from his run to the battlement, arrived beside her. "Where and how many, Lady?"

Alain pointed again several times.

"They want to take out our scouts?" Klaus asked Alain.

He nodded. "To clear the way for legionaries."

"Or Mechanics," Mari said.

Klaus nodded, one hand cupping his chin, his eyes narrowed in thought. "I have seen this done, though not in conjunction with Mechanics. Mages take out the scouts without us knowing, then the Imperials post special attack forces near the sally ports to try to force them by surprise."

"The Mages can also create temporary openings in the gates to allow sudden entry at the desired moment," Alain said.

"I have seen that, too. With our focus on that Imperial fleet lit up to draw our attention, it might have worked." Klaus paused. "We must bring the scouts in, but the risk to them will be high if they retreat now."

"They will all die if they remain where they are," Alain said. "If they come in quickly, I may be able to save some of them."

"Good enough and more than I had hope for, Sir Mage. Vern! Sound the alert, followed by the recall."

One of the field marshal's aides stepped to the edge of the battlement, raising a trumpet to his lips. Two tones rang out, carrying easily through the silence of the night. After a pause, he played the tones a second time, then a third. The aide waited for a longer pause, then played three sharp notes, followed by the same three again.

"Kaede, Bruno," the field marshal ordered two lieutenants, "get to the sally gates and let them know that there may be Mages and

legionaries pursuing our scouts. Be ready to hold those gates shut."
Klaus sighed. "In the face of the scouts, if necessary."

"But Field Marshal—" Bruno began.

"They knew the odds. Get going."

As the two aides dashed off, Alain spoke. "I have to go to one of
these sally gates."

"Then I'm going, too," Mari said.

"Lady, the risk—" Klaus began.

"My Mage is going! So am I."

Klaus nodded, wisely deciding not to argue further. "Follow Lieutenant Kaede. The sally gate she goes to will have the most scouts
heading to it for safety. My thanks to you, Lady, and to you, Sir Mage."

Alain began running, Mari following as closely as she dared with the
stairs down only dimly visible. They rushed past others who stood aside
to let them past, before finally reaching the pavement and running along
the inside of the wall, which was bolstered by buildings built up against it.

Lieutenant Kaede darted to the side, Alain following her and Mari
right after him. They went through a small, open, heavily armored
gate, down a tunnel formed by the wall, and came to a stop at another
small, armored and sealed gate.

"Stand by...for the scouts to...return," Kaede gasped to the sentries at the gate as she tried to catch her breath. "There may be...
Mages behind...them, and...legionaries."

"I will know if there are Mages close to them," Alain said. He faced
the sally gate, his brow furrowing slightly with concentration.

Mari drew out her pistol and waited, controlling her own breathing. *Stay calm, stay ready*, she repeated to herself.

Minutes crawled by. "How will we know when the scouts get to the
gate?" Mari whispered to Lieutenant Kaede.

"Voice relay. They flash a signal to the soldiers on the battlements,
and the soldiers call down to us," Kaede replied.

"Mages come this way," Alain said. "Three...four of them."

"There should be six scouts heading for this sally gate," Kaede said.
"They're all very good at remaining concealed even when moving."

"Even very good scouts are easy prey for Mages who use their spells to hide from sight," Alain said. "The Mages have begun moving faster."

"How close?" Mari asked, holding her pistol in a two-handed grip, ready to use.

"Not close yet. Coming fast."

"Get that gate open," Mari ordered before she realized that this wasn't her army and the soldiers might not jump to obey.

But she was the daughter of Jules, and they had been told that Lady Mari was in overall command of the defense, so the soldiers didn't hesitate. Many of the bars holding the gate shut had already been loosened, and now the soldiers fell to with a will to release the rest. As the last bar dropped, several soldiers tugged on the gate, forcing its ponderous weight into slow, reluctant motion.

As soon as the gate was open far enough, Alain darted through it. Mari, muttering a curse at his recklessness, followed into the night beyond. They stood next to the wall, in the cleared area between it and the nearest buildings. Mari, the wall at her back, felt suddenly very vulnerable.

There were several figures coming toward them, difficult to see in the dark, crouched as they moved cautiously, trying not to be spotted. "Run!" Mari yelled. "As fast as you can! We'll cover you!"

The scouts leaped to their feet and raced toward the gate, but Mari could see that Alain's attention was focused beyond them. She knew he could spot the location of Mages using their invisibility spells, and so waited, her weapon now pointed forward and held steady in both hands, as the first scouts reached the wall by her. "Get inside!" she snapped to them.

Alain's hand came out, palm up, as he prepared his heat spell.

The wall of a warehouse just on the other side of the open area suddenly exploded as intense heat struck the bricks. Mari saw two figures in Mage robes abruptly appear, staggering away from the fragments of brickwork that had pelted them. She aimed and fired twice at the first figure, then switched aim to the second and fired twice more.

Alain had already turned and focused on another target. This time a window exploded, shards of glass striking another Mage who suddenly appeared there. Mari fired again, seeing that Mage jerk from the impact of the shot.

That left one Mage unaccounted for, but the last of the scouts had reached them. Mari spun inside around the edge of the gate as Alain backed toward it. She saw his long knife come out, then twist up to block a blow from another long knife that had seemingly appeared out of nowhere.

She put a bullet into where the attacker should be, seeing the fourth Mage appear and reel to one side as the bullet hit and Alain's knife cut across the Mage's throat.

"Get inside!" Mari yelled at Alain.

Still Mage-calm, Alain dropped back to join her. "There are no more Mages near."

A crossbow bolt struck the frame of the gate.

"Imperials! Get it shut!" Lieutenant Kaede yelled.

The soldiers put their backs to the task, shoving the gate closed as several more crossbow bolts slammed into it, then hastily shoving the locking bars back into place.

"What happened at the other gate?" demanded one of the scouts who had made it to safety. "We had four people heading that way."

Alain shook his head. "That gate is to the left of us? The Mages there have dropped their spells, but remain outside the wall." He looked toward the outside. "They retreat toward the water. The other scouts must have been caught or killed."

"Monster! Why couldn't you—!" the scout yelled at Alain, his fist tightening on his dagger.

Lieutenant Kaede shoved the scout against the wall. "Shut up, you fool! He's the daughter's! The only reason you and these others are alive is because that Mage warned us and then came down here to face four times his number of enemies to save your butt! He couldn't be in two places at once!"

The scout stared at Alain, then at Mari. "The daughter's. I'm…I'm sorry. Sir Mage." The scout bowed his head toward Alain, his voice shaking with reaction. "Thank you for the lives that you saved. I will accept your punishment for my words and actions."

Alain shook his head again. "It is hard to lose friends. I heard and saw nothing worthy of punishment."

Everyone but Mari stared at him.

"Mages can be human, too," she told them, feeling depressed about the four scouts they couldn't save and at the survivors' immediate reaction to focus their anger on Alain. "The Mages who follow me are different. Give them a chance to show you that. Let's get back up on the wall, Alain."

The walk back was at a much slower pace, and going up the two flights of stairs next to the wall took a lot more effort than coming down them had required. Field Marshal Klaus was waiting for them. "A valiant action, Lady Mari. Rumor has not done justice to you or to Sir Mage Alain. We could see much of it from here."

"What happened at the other gate?" Mari asked.

Klaus looked directly at her. "The gate was not opened when the scouts sent the signal. I ordered that, because there was no way to know if Mages were among them unseen. The scouts there were told to make their way back into the dock areas and try to remain concealed. They did not succeed."

She felt anger, not at Klaus, but at fate. "If we'd only had another Mage with us. Mage Asha, or Mage Dav, or—" Mari rubbed her eyes. "I'm sorry."

"Try to get some sleep now, Lady. Tomorrow will likely be a long and hard day." Klaus saluted her, then walked off along the battlement.

Sergeant Kira was back, a short ways away. She gave Mari a brief wave and hoisted the rifle in both hands to show she and it were ready.

Mari waved in reply. Alain was leaning on the battlement, looking toward the waterfront, but saying nothing. Mari sat down again, pulled out her pistol, ejected the clip and reloaded it. "Alli always told me to reload at the first opportunity," she murmured to Alain.

"I would never argue with Mechanic Alli," Alain said.

"You did your best. You saved six of them."

"So did you," Alain replied. "But four died. It will be worse tomorrow."

"I know. A lot worse." Mari returned her pistol to its holster under her arm, looked over to reassure herself that the two dragon killers were still close by and ready for use, then leaned back, certain that she would not be able to sleep at all.

* * *

She woke to a touch on her shoulder and stared up at Alain, not remembering when she had fallen asleep after being sure she wouldn't be able to. "The Imperial fleet is moving into the harbor," Alain said.

Mari got to her feet and leaned forward against the battlement, holding her Mechanics jacket about her and gazing into the predawn light. Stars still glowed overhead, but they were nothing compared to the blaze of lights on the water as the Imperials brought their ships into Dorcastle's harbor.

The ballista towers alongside the harbor stayed silent.

"Why are we not firing, Lady?" Sergeant Kira asked in a hushed voice.

"Field Marshal Klaus said that a force of this size would simply annihilate the towers before they had a chance to do any damage," Mari said. "There didn't seem to be any sense in sacrificing people to no purpose."

As if to underline her words, one of the ballista towers suddenly shook, collapsing into a pile of rubble.

"Mages," Alain said. "They caused part of the foundation to vanish."

"Can they do that to our wall, Sir Mage?" Kira asked.

"Not easily. The wall is much thicker, requiring much more power, and any Mage concentrating on such a spell cannot also stay unseen."

"I understand," Kira said, fingering her rifle.

Field Marshal Klaus joined them, trailed by aides, looking unexcited as he surveyed the invasion force.

Mari brought out her far-seers and offered them to him.

But Klaus shook his head politely. "No need for those. We know all the landmarks here, and I can see everything I must well enough."

As the first ships of the Imperial fleet began reaching the waterfront, Klaus looked at Mari. "I think it is time."

"Go ahead," Mari said.

The field marshal gestured to an aide, who turned and shouted. "Shoot!" Mari heard the order being repeated along and behind the wall. A rapid series of thuds from behind the wall marked numerous ballistae hurling their deadly burdens into the sky.

Overhead, streaks of fire appeared, forming scores of beautiful arcs against the still-dark sky. The flaming projectiles fell down toward the harbor, plummeting onto the Imperial fleet. Many of the lead ships had covers of hides raised over their decks to deflect the fiery bombardment, but bright flames grew on other ships, racing up rigging and along spars.

"We have practiced for this," Sergeant Kira said, her voice low as she watched the ballista bombardment. "Every year for centuries. There are places marked to position our ballistae, and from each place we can tell exactly how to launch to land our projectiles at predetermined sites in the harbor and the city."

Legionaries were leaping from the lead ships, forming up and beginning to move rapidly in among the buildings and warehouses. Cohorts charged down the streets, heading for the wall.

But more and more of the blazing projectiles fired by the defenders were falling among the waterfront structures, where fires were springing up. "The rest of the Imperials will either have to march through that," Klaus said, "or wait until the fires burn out."

"It can't be easy to set fire to part of your city on purpose," Mari said.

"It's not," Klaus said. "But it's about saving the city by sacrificing some of it to save the rest. Crown Prince Maxim wanted to charge straight to the wall, but he's going to have wait a while, because even the legions aren't fireproof."

Alain was also watching the fires spread, and the first legionaries to land and charge through to the open area before the wall. "They will be trapped," he said. "Between the fires behind and our forces in front."

"They won't be trapped for long, Sir Mage," Field Marshal Klaus said. "But we'll wait until the fires get worse before we hit them."

The fires in the waterfront area grew and merged. Mari lost sight of the legionaries who had been among the waterfront structures and wondered if they had made it out again as the conflagration raged ever larger and hotter. Several cohorts that had made it through before the fires grew too intense were standing with shields raised against the defenders in front of them and the heat of the growing fires behind.

Mari felt a breeze blowing from her back toward the fires, and realized that they were burning so strongly that they were pulling oxygen into themselves to feed the destruction. "Alain, remember when we were first in Dorcastle? I'd noticed that the buildings on the waterfront looked newer than in the rest of the city, but I never learned why until now." She tried using her far-seers to figure out what the Imperials were doing along the waterfront.

"Can you see anything, Lady?" Klaus asked. "We had oil trails laid along the piers to carry the fires into the Imperial ships, but that's more of a hopeful strategy than a reliable weapon."

"I can't tell," Mari said, lowering her far-seers and rubbing her flame-dazzled eyes. "Between the smoke and the heat of the fires that is distorting the air so badly, I can hardly make out that there are ships in the harbor, let alone what's happening to them."

Klaus gestured to Lieutenant Kaede. "Call to those cohorts on our side of the fires and ask them if they want to surrender or to die."

Kaede soon reported back. "They refuse to surrender."

"As expected. General Sanj!" Klaus called down the street. "Hit them!"

Mari saw gates opening in the wall, foot soldiers armed with crossbows and pikes marching out to spread and form a solid line facing the defiant, trapped cohorts. Crossbow bolts were released into the Imperial formations, weakening them, before the lines of pikes charged forward.

The trapped cohorts couldn't hold against the weight of the defenders' charge. Some of the legionaries died on the point of a pike, a few tried leaping through the pikes to attack with their swords and also died, while the rest were forced back into the ravenous flames.

Even Imperial legionaries couldn't stand against that. The formations broke. Most surrendered, but a few rushed into the fires, shields held over their heads, in a futile attempt to escape.

"We'll put them under the care of militia guards and marching to Danalee before the sun sets," Klaus told Mari. "Get them out of the city, where we won't have to worry about them. It's a small blow against the Imperials, but it gives us the first win of the fight. That's good for the troops to see."

The firestorm raged all through the morning, putting off so much heat despite the protective distance offered by the open area before the wall that Mari began standing behind the shielding stones of the battlement. The flame-born wind grew stronger as the greedy fires fed, until it felt like a gale blowing toward the burning waterfront.

Noon passed, the blazes finally beginning to subside in places, but the waterfront remained an impassible barrier of flames.

By late afternoon the fires were still burning, but were now mostly confined to the ruins of the structures themselves. Mari, gazing through her far-seers, could see formations of legionaries locking shields around themselves to protect them from the heat as they began advancing again down the center of the roads leading from the waterfront.

Field Marshal Klaus had been waiting for that.

Ballistae fired again, this time hurling clouds of fist-sized and larger rocks aimed to land in the center of the streets. As Sergeant Kira had said, the defenders had spent generations carefully working out exactly how to fire ballistae placed in certain spots to ensure their loads were delivered exactly where needed.

Mari watched, willing herself to accept what had to be done, as she saw the deadly hail fall on the advancing legions, smashing shields, arms, legs, and heads.

They kept coming, a seemingly endless stream of attackers, now racing the sun to try to take the first wall before darkness fell.

The word came down the battlements. "Stand to the ready."

Looking up and back, Mari saw that her banner had been placed right behind her, fluttering in the breeze. It told all of the defenders that the daughter of Jules was here. It would also tell all of the attackers where the daughter was.

Mari had been in battles before, but this fight was much bigger than any she had experienced, and the stakes of winning or losing much higher. As she watched the legionaries advancing through the flame-bordered streets toward the wall, her heart was beating so loudly she thought that everyone near her must be able to hear it. Her throat suddenly dry, she took a quick drink from her water flask.

Alain touched her arm. "I am beside you."

"Thanks," Mari replied. She tore her eyes from the spectacle as another volley of ballista-launched rocks landed on the oncoming legions. "Alain, if I die here—"

"Mari—"

"*If* I die here, I want you to know that it was worth it. If living for a hundred years more meant I never would have known you, and the Storm would have triumphed and destroyed so much and so many lives, I'd still want to die in Dorcastle beside you, both of us trying our best."

"You will not die," Alain said in a way that caused her to look long and hard at him.

"Do not do anything stupid," she whispered, fearing for him now more than herself. She kissed him, trying not to think about the possibility that it might be their last.

The crash of artillery fire brought her attention back to the fight. With the fires subsiding, the Mechanics Guild ships had come close enough to begin firing their deck guns over the still-burning ruins of the waterfront. Unlike the high arcs of the ballista projectiles, the Mechanic artillery shells flew in low, flat curves to strike the wall.

Mari could feel tremors in the wall as the Mechanic shells exploded. But the massive stone blocks that made up the outer wall were too tough for the light and medium guns that the Mechanics Guild had limited itself to. For centuries, guns that size had been enough to turn the tide against foes whose best weapons were ballistae and crossbows. Mari leaned out enough to check where the shells had struck, seeing that only shallow spalls had been knocked from the rock.

"They're going to shift their fire to hitting the battlements when they realize how useless those guns are against the wall," she told Alain. "Do you see the biggest gun there? The one on the ship to our right?"

He squinted. "Yes."

"Can you put heat on the ammunition stacked next to it?" There were men and women in dark Mechanics jackets working that gun, but she couldn't afford to think about that.

Alain shaded his eyes with one hand. "The pile of objects near the weapon? I can barely see it, but it shines like the shells of Mechanic Alli's guns."

"Yes. That's the brass of the shell casings."

"I can see it well enough to put heat there. It will be good to use some of the power available before the attacking Mages drain it." He held his right hand out before him.

Mari felt the growing heat radiating from the spot above his palm where Alain was, in his own words, creating the illusion of great heat to place on part of the immense illusion that was the world he saw. She noticed Sergeant Kira and the other nearby soldiers watching with awe. Odds were, none of them had seen a Mage working a spell from so close before.

Alain relaxed.

The sharp reports of the Mechanic artillery were interrupted by a much bigger explosion as the ammunition for the medium deck gun exploded. The front of the ship blew apart in a flurry of wood splinters, a cloud of smoke rising into the sky.

Cheers rolled across the wall as the defenders applauded the setback for the Imperials and the Great Guilds. The other two Mechanics

Guild ships began backing away frantically, rendering their deck guns useless. "They're not used to this kind of setback," Mari said to Alain. "They're spent their lives being able to pound on commons from a distance with impunity."

But even though the Mechanics Guild artillery was temporarily out of the fight, the Imperials and their ships kept coming to the docks, avoiding wreckage to offload what seemed to be a never-ending stream of legionaries and siege weapons.

"Mages are preparing spells," Alain said. "They are in front of us." He pointed straight ahead, where the roads from the waterfront opened out.

Mari used her far-seers again, spotting some Mage robes among the advancing legions but searching in vain for the dark jackets of Mechanics. "They're not going to coordinate their attacks with the Mechanics like my army does, are they?"

"The elders of the Mage Guild would not deign to do so," Alain said. "Our former guilds are surely competing with each other. One will strike, then the other."

"I didn't think they'd be that dumb. They must have heard reports of how my army fights. If Mechanics were getting in position to fire on us with rifles we'd have a much harder time coping with the Mages. Hopefully we can hit them before—"

"Let the largest spells be cast," Alain said.

Mari gave him a frown. "Why?"

"First, because they will use up almost all of the power available in this area. That will leave little for all of the other Mages to use." Alain nodded down the battlement toward some of the soldiers waiting for the attack. "But also because our troops are worried by the size of this assault and how it has the full backing of the Great Guilds. If the Mage Guild throws its worst at you, and you destroy their worst with the dragon killers of Alli, it will greatly bolster the confidence of our comrades."

Her frown vanished as Mari nodded. "You are one smart Mage. I'm glad I married you. All right. Hold off using any more spells, keep your strength, until the Mechanics make their play. I'll see if I can handle the Mage Guild threat."

"Your chance will come quickly." Alain pointed again. "Much of the power available has just been used. A mighty spell was cast there."

Mari bent down and grabbed a dragon killer.

Cries of alarm burst out among the defenders as a huge shape appeared on the edge of the open area facing the wall. The dragon was tall enough to overtop the battlement, charging straight for the wall near the main gate with its claws extended.

Mari ran along the battlement, trying to get directly in the path of the oncoming monster.

CHAPTER SIX

MARI DODGED PAST defenders who were, perversely, blocking her by standing their ground. Even worse, an officer who got a glimpse of her running past flung out an arm to stop her. "Get back to your post!"

"I'm not running away!" Mari yelled at the startled officer. "I'm trying to stop that thing!"

The open area between the nearest buildings and the wall had seemed pretty wide when she had walked across it yesterday after their failed negotiations with the Imperials. But at the moment, with the dragon making long strides, it seemed far too narrow.

Fortunately, she gained some time when the dragon paused, its eyes scanning the battlement.

Those eyes fell on her.

The dragon's roar seemed to shake the wall. It leaped forward toward her as Mari shoved aside some soldiers and rested the dragon killer tube on the battlement. "Make sure no one is behind me!" She aimed at the upper chest of the spell creature, breathing slowly, her finger slowly squeezing the trigger.

In the back of her mind Mari remembered a time years ago, when Alli had been teaching her to shoot, explaining how the easiest shots were against something coming straight at you. *There's no way you can miss that kind of shot, Mari.*

Yeah, yeah, Mari had said. And then had missed the practice target right in front of her.

❖ The dragon was less than ten lances from the wall when the rocket fired, trailing a stream of smoke until it struck the beast hard enough to knock it into a sideways stagger, the sound of the warhead's explosion echoing off the wall. The creature's stagger continued for two more steps to Mari's left, the smoke of the explosion clearing to reveal the size of the hole in its chest, then the clumsy sideways movement turned into a fall.

Mari had just inhaled deeply when Alain called urgently. "Another dragon is being created! There!"

"I thought you said the first one used up a lot of the available power!" Mari ran back to where the second dragon killer lay, soldiers shocked by the destruction of the first dragon once again milling about in her path. She reached the weapon and picked it up just as the second dragon appeared. It wasn't quite as large as the first, but still terrifying as it charged straight for where Mari's banner waved on the wall.

That made aiming easy again, which was fortunate given how close the monster was. Mari barely had time to ready the weapon, settle the tube on her shoulder, aim, and fire.

In her haste, she had aimed too high, and almost missed.

The rocket struck the dragon on the muzzle, sending its deadly spray of explosive through the spell creature's head and out the back. The beast reeled, then fell to lie in a heap at the base of the wall, still twitching.

Sergeant Kira's rifle barked, then a moment later fired again. Mari looked over to see Alain pointing out to her the Mages who had created the dragons, standing on the far side of the open area as if trying to understand how their creatures had been so quickly dealt with. One of the Mages fell to lie still. The other dropped from the impact of Kira's second shot but then began crawling away, hidden by the legionary formations that were steadily growing as more and more Imperials got through the dwindling flames of the waterfront.

Mari stood up, still holding the last, empty dragon killer weapon. The single-shot devices were useless now.

It felt unnaturally quiet. Everyone on the battlements within eyesight was staring at her, as were the masses of legionaries looking up at the wall.

She turned to say something to Alain, then lurched as the defenders erupted into cheers that nearly deafened her as they finally absorbed that she had killed two dragons nearly as fast as they could be created.

"I guess you were right about the morale thing," she shouted at Alain over the noise. Even though she felt ridiculous to be doing it, Mari raised up the empty dragon killer tube and waved it triumphantly, setting off more cheers.

She wondered what the cheering defenders would say if they knew that she had used up all of her dragon killers.

"More spells," Alain shouted back to her over the tumult. "Not dragons. Not enough power remains here for more of them. Five of one spell and something else. A roc."

A roc. To carry word somewhere else, or to attack the battlement? "Sergeant Kira," Mari said. "Give me back that rifle."

She had barely taken the weapon when Mari saw the roc appear, the huge bird gliding out of the smoke rising from the waterfront fires, its claws extended to rake the soldiers on the battlement.

It was moving very fast, but Mari had been practicing since almost being killed by a roc at Minut. She had learned how to aim at a fast-moving object by firing at targets pulled behind rocs created by her own Mages. As the roc approached, wings extended, to Mari's right, she aimed at the Mage on the back of the bird, her rifle muzzle moving smoothly to give her a slight lead on her target. A target who was a Mage perhaps like Mage Alera or Mage Saburo.

A Mage who had to die. Mari squeezed off the shot, and a moment later the Mage on the roc jerked backwards and then forwards before falling limply from the bird to plummet down to the stone below. Unguided, the roc swerved upward, flying about aimlessly in futile search of the Mage who had created it and now lay on the ground unmoving.

"The others are trolls," Alain said. "There is almost no power left on that side of the wall for the use of Mages. They can do nothing more to concern us."

"That's good news." Mari spotted Colonel Teodor. "We've got trolls coming!"

"Trolls?"

"Five of them!" She looked to where Alain was pointing. "There! All coming toward this gate!"

"We can handle trolls!" Colonel Teodor called back.

The large, misshapen spell creatures came lumbering toward the gate. Five trolls, just as Alain had said. Slow, but very strong.

Mari tossed the rifle back to Sergeant Kira. "See how many more Mages you can take out."

Sergeant Kira aimed and fired, taking time between each shot. Mari saw more Mages fall. They weren't seeking cover, apparently oblivious to the danger as Kira's rifle killed one after another.

"The Mage Guild elders have told them that Mechanic rifles are toys, incapable of threatening them," Alain said. "Just as they told me, even after the caravan I was supposed to protect was destroyed in the Waste."

Colonel Teodor ran up, saluting Mari. "If those dragons and the roc had cleared these battlements, we couldn't have stopped the trolls. Thank you, Lady."

"Why aren't the legionaries firing?" Mari demanded. "If they were hitting us with crossbow volleys—"

Alain answered, his voice toneless. "Mages have no need of aid from shadows. The Mage elders would have demanded that the Imperials stay out of their way."

Wondering just how many people had died over the centuries because of the arrogance and ignorance of their superiors, Mari watched the defenders nearest the gate wrestling barrels close to stone spouts angling down from the battlement.

As the trolls neared the gate, the barrels were tipped, thick liquid gushing into the spouts and arcing out from the top of the wall.

Flaming torches were hurled from the battlement, and the oil on and around the trolls caught with a whoosh and gouts of dark, greasy smoke.

Mari looked away, flinching, as the trolls burned.

They kept coming, because that was all they knew to do. Two trolls fell, still burning. Three of the trolls made it all the way to the gate before crumpling into smoldering heaps.

Temporarily out of valuable targets, Sergeant Kira pointed to the masses of legionaries. "Look at them! They thought with the Mage Guild giving them support they could just walk right over us! And instead they've seen the Mages' weapons rendered useless!"

"Will there be more?" Colonel Teodor asked anxiously.

Alain shook his head. "I can still draw on power behind this wall. But those Mages have used all but a tiny amount of what power was there. You will face no more spell creatures attacking this wall."

"Get that word to the field marshal," Teodor ordered a nearby soldier, who dashed off.

Mari turned to say something to Alain and saw the nearby soldiers staring at her, some smiling, others displaying awe that made Mari feel uncomfortable. "What?" she asked Sergeant Kira.

"You're asking what?" Sergeant Kira shook her head in disbelief. "Lady, they're looking at you because you killed two dragons and the Mage on a roc as quickly as if they had been two chickens and a pigeon."

"Thanks, but I didn't kill them all on my own," Mari said. "Mechanic Alli built those dragon killers. Mechanic Calu helped me figure out how to hit something moving as fast as a roc. Mage Alain told me what to expect and where they would come from." She raised her voice, so her words carried down the battlement in both directions. "It's a team effort, don't you see? We're all going to hold Dorcastle from being taken by the Imperials. We are all going to overthrow the Great Guilds. All of us, fighting together."

"I hear you," Sergeant Kira said. "Teamwork is very important. But so are leaders."

Klaus himself appeared a few minutes later, eyeing the situation outside the wall. "The legions still aren't moving," he commented to Mari and Alain. "The Mage Guild has made its try. Am I right that the Mechanics will now insist on their chance?"

"Could anything other than a demand by one of the Great Guilds have restrained Prince Maxim from throwing the legions against this wall already?" Alain asked in turn.

"I cannot think of anything, Sir Mage." Klaus gave Mari a keen look. "I have been told that your army has been very successful using Mages and Mechanics. Is this how you fight, sending in one kind and then the next?"

"No," Mari said, watching the numbers of legionaries continuing to swell. "In my army, everyone works together, the Mechanics and the Mages supporting each other as well as the commons."

"How would that have worked here?"

Mari pointed to where the legions were gathering. "Commons with rifles and crossbows would have kept our heads down while Mage creatures cleared a path to the gates and Mechanics came close behind to plant explosives. Other Mages on rocs would fly above, Mechanics on them with far-talkers telling us everything that was happening and what the enemy was doing. And my artillery would be dropping shells where they were needed to break the defenders."

Klaus pondered her words as he gazed at the waiting, silent legions. "I am feeling fortunate to be among your allies and not your enemies, Lady. Lacking preconceptions of how battles should be fought, you created a new system to maximize the advantages of your forces. I hope I get the chance to discuss tactics with your General Flyn."

"I'll make sure that happens," Mari said. Field Marshal Klaus headed off the check other parts of the wall, leaving Mari gazing at the apparently endless stream of legionaries still gathering for the assault. She had seen many legionaries fall under the blows of ballista projectiles, but for each that fell many more appeared. It was like fighting a beast which added more claws for each one severed.

Colonel Teodor came quickly along the battlement. "Do you know what will come next, Lady?"

Mari closed her eyes, thinking. "There's a weapon the Mechanics Guild has. I'm sure they'll use it. I can't stop it." Mari saw immediate looks of dismay "But Mage Alain can. When it shows up, I'll show you how to deal with it."

Most of the bombardment so far had been from the defending side, its projectiles falling on the legions and the Imperial ships. But as the waterfront fires subsided, the Imperials were getting ballistae ashore, and some of the ships in the harbor had gotten the range. Enemy projectiles had begun plummeting down. Only a few hit the battlement, most either thudding against the thick stone of the wall or passing completely over to crash among the buildings behind the wall. Some of the Imperial projectiles were aflame, starting fires behind the first wall that threatened to trap the defenders just as the legionaries had earlier been penned in. One of the flaming shots struck the battlement directly not far to Mari's left, sending sparks and burning fragments in all directions.

The reserves on ground level were rushing to put out the fires started by the Imperial bombardment. With the Imperial legions still standing in place, there was more activity behind the wall than before it.

The defenders' ballistae shifted their aim from the streets leading from the waterfront and began dropping their deadly rain on the ranks of legionaries drawn up on the far side of the open area. The legions locked shields above them, offering some protection from the bombardment but not nearly enough.

Mari raised her far-seers and spotted a cluster of Imperial officials behind the legions who appeared to be arguing with a group of Mechanics. "The Imperials aren't happy with their allies. I'm guessing that the Imperials don't want to stand there getting bombarded and the Senior Mechanics are telling them they have to while the Mechanics get their act together." Another Imperial projectile came down just behind the battlement. "I have to stand here and look calm," Mari told Alain. "How am I doing?"

"You could get behind the battlement and be safer," Alain told her.

"No, I can't hide or look afraid." She pointed up to the banner of the New Day flapping in the breeze. "Everyone knows who's standing here."

"The legions will not turn aside just because you do not appear afraid," Alain said.

"The legions will lose because they'll decide they're beaten before we do. I know you're scared for me, but I have to do this," Mari said. She nodded to him, letting her fear show for just a moment, then controlled her expression again. "I'm putting my Mage face on," she added. For some odd reason, that struck her as funny. She grinned, and noticed the soldiers within view smiling at her apparent display of confidence.

For his part, Alain appeared resigned to accepting that Mari would do what Mari thought she had to do. "Tell me what device the Mechanics will send against us," he said.

She stood a little back from the front of the battlement and waved to both sides at the defenders in view before answering. "You said the Mage Guild's creatures drained almost all of the power on that side of this wall. How much can you do?"

"Several intense heat spells without growing too exhausted"

"Good." Mari leaned forward on the battlement again, tense as she surveyed the Imperial forces still coming ashore. "The Mechanics Guild has a weapon that's actually very crude. It's an armored wagon loaded with a lot of explosives. They roll it up next to something like the gate here, detonate it, and blow a really big hole in the wall."

"How do they roll it?" Alain asked, already looking for such an object in the fires and smoke of the waterfront. "Does it use one of the Mechanic boiler creatures?"

"No," Mari said, letting old anger enter her voice. "They once could do that, using an armored steam-powered tractor that could push the bomb wagon into position. But the last of those tractors broke a long time back, and the Senior Mechanics wouldn't allow any fixes that changed anything important about the tractors, so they've stayed broken. The wagon will have to be pulled and shoved into place by a lot of people, probably legionaries ordered to do the job."

"What must I do?" Alain asked.

"When I point it out to you, and show you where to hit it, you have to use your heat spell to detonate the explosive before the wagon gets too close to the wall." Mari sighed, her thoughts bleak. "All those legionaries pulling it will be blown to pieces."

Alain nodded to her. "Such a loss will cause the Imperials to be more mistrustful of their Mechanic allies."

"It should show up any moment now. Judging from that argument I saw, the Imperials are already as mad as blazes that the Mechanics are taking so long to get it ready. Alain, I've become entirely too used to shooting at people, but I still cringe at the idea of blowing up a lot of them."

"If you think of the illusion—" Alain began.

"I cannot see other people as illusions or shadows, Alain," Mari broke in.

"That is not what I meant. All see the illusion which is the world in their own way. Some want to force all to see the illusion in that one way, their way. The men and women of the legions believe that the Emperor keeps them safe, but because of that they also believe it is right to require others to do as the Emperor commands. The Great Guilds want to force all to continue to live in an illusion that they control. You, Mari, and those with you, want to let everyone decide which form of the illusion to accept and to follow."

"And that's why I have to blow up people," Mari said, wondering why Alain thought his explanation would help her feel better about doing it. She spotted movement on one of the streets leading toward the main gate. "I think they're coming."

From the outside, the formation resembled some sort of turtle, locked shields forming a solid barrier against attack as about forty legionaries dragged the heavy Mechanic bomb wagon toward the gate. In the center of them, Mari could catch glimpses of the wagon itself. "Can you see enough of it to place a spell?"

"No," Alain said.

"Sergeant Kira," Mari called. "Go down to the Tiae cavalry. I want all of you with rifles to clear enough legionaries from around that cart they're hauling to give my Mage a good shot at it."

"Clear the legionaries from around the cart so the Mage can see to strike at it," Sergeant Kira repeated. "Yes, Lady. It will be done."

"And when I yell *duck*," Mari called as Kira ran to the right, "make sure you get behind the battlement!"

She waited, tense, as the legionary tortoise crawled toward the gate. The formations on the far side of the open area had also locked shields to protect themselves from the effects of the coming explosion, but behind them Mari could see crossbows being raised into position. It looked like the Imperials were finally going to act in support of one of the Great Guilds' attacks.

Distant orders were called among the legionaries, and with the *whack* of hundreds of crossbows firing at once, a storm of bolts flew toward the battlements near the gate. "As you warned, they will try to force us to keep our heads down," Alain said, standing beside her.

"I didn't want to be right about that. Get down, Alain!" Mari, thinking that any rational person would be hiding behind the battlement right now, crouched a little lower but stayed exposed as bolts slammed into the wall beneath her, into the sturdy stone of the battlement, or passed overhead to menace those behind the wall. Some of the defenders were hit and fell, but Mari held her ground, knowing that she had to spot the instant Alain had an opportunity to strike at the bomb wagon.

A ragged volley of rifle fire sounded to Mari's right. Several legionaries whose shields protected the bomb wagon fell, leaving a clear view. "Alain, see that rounded object? As much heat as you can, right on it!"

Alain inhaled deeply, concentrating. Mari saw legionaries trying to cover the sudden gap in the wagon's protective shell, then part of the metal casement suddenly glow white as Alain sent his heat onto it.

"Everybody down!" she shouted, ducking to set a good example.

She hadn't quite made it all the way when a titanic roar sounded and even the massive stones of the wall shook from the force of the explosion. As she lay against the battlement, Mari's eyes fell on her banner, seeing it ripped by the shockwave passing above her.

The echoes from the blast were still resounding when Mari hauled herself up to look. An impressive crater marred the spot where the bomb wagon had been.

There was no trace of the legionaries who had been clustered around it.

The formations behind them had been battered and thrown into disorder by the explosion. Despite their locked shields, some of the legionaries were not able to rise again.

Scattered, derisive cheers began along the battlement, merging into a loud celebration by the defenders mocking the attackers.

But as the cheers rolled over the still-burning buildings of the waterfront, Mari saw the legionaries reforming, their numbers still growing as more and more marched in from the waterfront.

Colonel Teodor approached her. "Lady, do you think the Mechanics will try again?"

"No," Mari said. "Right now the Senior Mechanics are trying to figure out what made that bomb wagon explode before it reached the gate. Until they reach some conclusions, they won't send another. That's procedure, and I know from painful experience that the Senior Mechanics will stick to procedure no matter what."

Teodor looked at the massing legions. More Imperials were coming into view bearing scaling ladders, and near the waterfront siege towers could be seen rolling off of large barges that had been towed to Dorcastle. "I will inform Field Marshal Klaus that the Imperials will strike us soon."

As Teodor rushed off, Mari looked to the west, where the sun was sinking toward the horizon. The fiery sacrifice of the waterfront buildings had bought the defenders the majority of the day, and the repulse of the Mage attacks and then the Mechanic effort had used up still more daylight.

But there was still enough time for the Imperials to try brute force where Mage spells and Mechanic devices had failed.

Sergeant Kira came back to stand near Mari, smiling proudly. "What has you so happy?" Mari asked.

Kira gave Mari a surprised look. "I'm fighting alongside you, Lady. I helped you destroy that Mechanic wagon. It is something to be happy about, to be proud of."

Mari looked back at her banner, its edges tattered by the force of the explosion of the bomb wagon. "We'll be prouder when we've thrown the legions back into the sea."

Sergeant Kira grinned.

Before anything else could be said, a low, rhythmic chant arose from the massed Imperials. Mari leaned on the battlement as the chant swelled in volume. The legionaries sang, their voices filling the air with vows to destroy the enemies of the Emperor, to honor their families, and to continue the fight to the end. There was something majestic about the huge chorus of legionaries, facing the might of the first wall of Dorcastle, singing their paean to death and glory. Something majestic—and frightening.

As the last choruses were sung, the legionaries began clashing swords and spears against their shields, the dull thud of metal on metal magnified by the thousands upon thousands of weapons and shields so that the sound echoed just as the earlier explosions had.

"Stand by. Stand by." The word came racing down the battlement, where the defenders stood ready, no longer cheering but grim as they awaited the Imperial onslaught.

The last word and the last clash of metal on metal came together, as several siege towers were rolled into the open area and hundreds of scaling ladders were hoisted.

The brass horns of the Imperials blared their harsh notes across the waterfront, two rising notes repeated, ordering the legions to battle.

The legions let out a deep, sustained yell. Imperial crossbows fired a massive cloud of bolts at the battlements. Imperial ballistae unleashed their projectiles.

The legionaries charged the wall.

Mari, like the other defenders, crouched behind the battlement as the swarm of crossbow bolts slammed into the wall or flew past overhead.

"Up! Up! For Dorcastle! For the daughter!" The cries rang along the wall and the defenders rose again to hurl their own wave of crossbow fire at the charging legions.

Mari stared at the thousands of legionaries shouting their battle cries. Their numbers seemed endless. For every one that fell to defensive fire another hundred moved forward.

Sergeant Kira fired.

Mari watched an Imperial officer fall as her shot went home.

She drew her pistol, thinking the weapon felt very small against such foes.

Imperial crossbow bolts were flying in a continuous, deadly barrage, most missing but some hitting defenders.

Alain let out a gasp of effort, and Mari saw one of the Imperial siege towers erupt into flame despite the layer of thick hides protecting it.

Another siege tower caught fire, then a third.

Alain sagged down next to Mari. "Must rest," he muttered.

"I've got it," Mari told him.

The wave of Imperials reached the wall, the scaling ladders rising, other legionaries throwing up ropes with grappling hooks on the end to gain firm purchase on the battlement.

The soldiers near Mari were grabbing spears from the baskets set along the battlement, hurling them into the mass of legionaries below. Baskets of stones and piles of bricks provided other projectiles, and near the gate itself more oil poured down to be set afire and block attempts to bring battering rams into play.

Mari could no longer hear any clear orders or cries, just a loud, continuous roar of thousands upon thousands of voices and the constant clash of metal on metal and metal on stone.

The soldier on Mari's left cast another spear, then staggered back, a crossbow bolt buried in his chest.

Men and women with armbands showing the red serpent and staff were running along the battlement, crouched over as they ran to avoid being hit by Imperial projectiles, tending to the wounded where they could and moving aside the dead who were beyond any human help.

Alain sat, his back to the battlement, regaining his strength. Mari rested her free hand on Alain's shoulder, comforting both him and herself, as Sergeant Kira fired again and again. She could hear the Tiae rifles barking nearer the main gate, mowing down Imperials with a barrage that combined with the burning oil to keep the gate safe.

The top of a scaling ladder thudded into place next to Mari.

A soldier ran up with a spear, lodged it in the ladder and began trying to push it off. Mari added her strength to the effort and the ladder tilted back and fell.

There were so many ladders.

Imperials were reaching the battlement to clash swords with the defenders. Mari aimed and fired, dropping a legionary who had just reached the top. She walked rapidly down the battlement, her heart pounding but her head oddly calm as she fired again and again, putting shots into every legionary who tried to get onto the battlement.

Alain had gotten back to his feet.

A fourth siege tower, nearly to the wall, suddenly began burning.

Mari, reloading her pistol, saw among the mass of Imperials a group in the dark jackets of Mechanics running toward the main gate, carrying something heavy. "Sergeant! Get those Mechanics!"

Later, she would wonder if she had ever known any the Mechanics who died one by one as Sergeant Kira fired with deadly accuracy. Right now, the battle raging around her, she thought only of the need to stop them. When half their number had fallen, the survivors dropped their burden and fled, two more of them falling to Kira's bullets before they got out of range. The object they had been carrying was left behind on the pavement, the attacking legionaries obviously unaware of what lay among them. "Alain! Can you manage another heat spell strong enough to set off that smaller bomb?"

"I will," Alain said.

She grabbed him as he fell, exhausted by the effort, hearing the boom of the explosion and knowing that another Mechanics Guild bomb had killed its share of legionaries. She lowered Alain to a sitting position again, feeling no pity for the attackers, thinking only the cold, hard truth that the Empire's ill-chosen Great Guild allies had to this point killed far more legionaries than they had defenders of the city.

"Are you hurt, Lady?" someone cried.

Mari looked over to see a worried lieutenant gazing anxiously at her and realized again how many eyes were watching the daughter.

She stood up, facing the storm of the Imperial assault, and raised her hand holding her pistol high. "Freedom!" she called, certain that her voice was lost in the cacophony of yells and clash of weapons, punctuated by the crash of rifles near the gate. But her call was picked up by the nearest soldiers and repeated down the battlement, shouts of "freedom" and "the daughter" rising over the bedlam.

As Mari lowered her pistol she noticed the low rays of the sun lighting it. Looking to the west, she saw the sun was near setting.

But the legions kept coming, like the waves on the Sea of Bakre, endlessly crashing against the wall, wearing at the defenders despite mounting piles of their own dead on the streets of Dorcastle.

Fresh Imperial forces were appearing, unleashing a new rain of crossbow bolts. Here and there, Mechanic rifles boomed amid the Imperial ranks as well. Mari saw one of those Mechanics fall as Sergeant Kira fired again. She had to fight down fear that every rifle shot from the attackers was aimed directly at her, then realized that many likely were, since she was the only figure on the battlement wearing a Mechanics jacket and she was standing by the banner of the New Day that still waved behind her. "If I was smart I'd take off this jacket," she told Alain. "But then, if I was smart I'd be a long way away from here."

Alain, rising to his feet again, gave Mari a look in which she could read his fear for her. He rarely showed his feelings so clearly. "It would be wise to remove it. If you do, you would be safer."

Mari looked down at her jacket, remembering all that it had once meant to her, all that it still did mean to her, and all that the daughter meant to the men and women dying around her. "No. This is part of what people expect to see, and even now I want people to know I am a Mechanic. I worked for this jacket. If I'm going to die, I'm going to be wearing this jacket when I do."

"Do not say that."

"Don't worry, darling. I'm not dead yet. Hang on. I've got to help take care of something."

Mari ran down the battlement to where a new siege tower was lumbering into contact. As the ramp on the tower fell onto the battlement and legionaries began pouring out, Mari emptied her pistol into them, halting the attackers' charge in a welter of falling bodies. The soldiers around her cheered and hurled torches into the opening in the tower left by the dropped ramp, turning it into a tower of flame from which legionaries fled or fell.

She raced back to Alain, reloading again, trying to remember how many clips of ammunition she had brought.

Sergeant Kira was standing by Alain, her rifle searching for targets worth a bullet. "Your Mage is all right, Lady! We will see to him!"

"Thank you." Mari searched her pockets, counting the bullets she still carried. "If this keeps up, I may have to learn how to use a sword."

Kira fired, and a moment later another Imperial officer fell. "You don't know how to use a sword, Lady? I must teach you! Every woman should have that skill."

"Maybe later," Mari said, gasping for breath. There was a lull in the Imperial assault as the legionaries regrouped under the hail of stones, bricks, and spears still being thrown from the battlement. But the supplies of those projectiles on this wall were nearly exhausted. "It's almost dark."

"A bad time!" Sergeant Kira warned. "Still light enough for the Imperials to see, but getting dark enough that we can't spot what they're doing!"

As if her words had triggered the event, Mari heard a large explosion far to the left of her. "A bomb wagon," she told Alain and Kira.

"The Mechanics used another, and unfortunately were smart enough not to send it against this part of the wall."

Trumpet calls were sounding along the wall, accompanied by messengers running to pass the word. "Lady," Colonel Teodor reported, blood from a cut on his face painting half of it black in the growing dark, "the Imperials destroyed the secondary gate down that way and breached the wall. We have orders to fall back in stages to the second wall."

"Do that," Mari said, looking at Alain. "Can you walk?"

He pushed away from the wall, nodding.

Lieutenant Kaede appeared. "Lady, Field Marshal Klaus has ordered a fall back. The reserve forces on the ground have contained the Imperial break-through, but we won't be able to hold them all night." She pulled Mari's banner from its holder. "I will accompany you to the second wall."

Mari looked at Sergeant Kira. "You're not coming yet?"

"In stages, Lady, so the Imperials don't realize we're falling back and come up along the entire wall," Kira said. "I will meet you on the second wall."

"All right. Make sure you do. You've promised to teach me how to use a sword."

As Mari turned to go, a Confederation captain walking along the battlement to pass on orders reeled from the punch of a crossbow bolt and fell. Mari ran to his side as healers followed, but the captain was already dead.

Throughout the assault, Imperial ballistae had continued to hurl flaming projectiles behind the wall. Only now, looking back, did Mari realize that fires were blazing all over the area the defenders would have to retreat through between the first and the second walls.

And with hoarse shouts the Imperials were coming at the wall again.

CHAPTER SEVEN

ALAIN WENT TO the edge of the battlement, looking out to see a newly arrived siege tower rumbling toward the wall above the main gate. He could feel that some power still remained in the area behind him, so he called on all of that power that he could, imagining intense heat above his palm, then imagined that illusion into the illusion of a siege tower filled with Imperial legionaries.

It was much easier to think of them as shadows as the tower became a torch and legionaries fell, blazing, from the ruin. This was one of those times when Alain wished that he could still believe that others were not real. Feeling tired from the spell, but glad that he had used up power that now could not be employed by the Mages still loyal to the Guild, he turned to see Mari crouched by the dead captain who had just been slain by Imperial weapons, and put from his mind any concern for those attacking this city. He touched Mari's shoulder. "They will not leave until we do," he told her, nodding toward the soldiers defending the wall.

"All right." Mari straightened up, Lieutenant Kaede standing right behind her with her banner, and waved to the defenders still in sight as the last light of day faded. "I'll see you all on the second wall!"

They headed down the stairs to street level. Alain stayed at the rear so that Mari would not notice how tired he was. She would slow down if she saw that, refusing to leave him, not realizing that he would find the strength to move fast enough to keep up with her as long as she stayed ahead.

The sky above would normally be given over to the stars and the moon sitting low to the northwest, the light of the twins faintly visible as they continued their eternal pursuit of the moon. But the light of the fires ahead dimmed what little radiance pierced the clouds of smoke from burning buildings everywhere, further veiling the heavens. "It is as if the stars themselves do not wish to view this," Alain murmured to himself.

Mari heard. "I don't blame them." She sounded worn out but her steps stayed steady. "We need to go by the wagon."

She led the way to the wagon which had come from Pacta Servanda, reaching in to pull out several packs. "This is the remaining ammunition," she told Lieutenant Kaede, handing two of the packs to Alain and shouldering three herself. Kaede grabbed two passing soldiers to carry the remaining four between them. Mari paused to frown at the packs. "This is too much. Alli sent a lot more ammo than she told us she had."

"She would not have sent it if she could not spare it," Alain said.

"If she didn't *think* she could spare it," Mari grumbled in a voice only he could hear. "I hope she was right."

Leaving the wagon, the group joined a stream of retreating defenders moving through the neighborhoods behind the first wall, soldiers on foot mingled with a few mounted cavalry and many wagons. The horses danced with fear as the broad road ran between buildings burning and crumbling with fire on every hand, sparks and glowing wisps falling in strangely gentle showers on the men and women, horses and mules, heading south to the second wall as another part of Dorcastle burned around them. Coughing in the smoke that blew across the road, Alain looked behind, seeing the rear guard falling back as well, their movements highlighted by burning embers drifting down around them.

Alain, judging the feelings of those around him, was surprised to see that they were tired from the recent fight but still in good spirits.

Some joked among themselves, others sang, and the sight of Lady Mari and her banner roused new cheers.

"Everyone knew we'd only hold the first wall for a short time," Lieutenant Kaede said, sounding breathless. "It's too close to the water, too easy for the attackers to hit with all their strength. The second wall is another matter. They won't get through that so quickly."

"How many times has this happened?" Mari asked in a low voice. "How many times have invaders taken the first wall while the defenders fell back to the second?"

"I don't know, Lady. Five times, ten times, something like that. The legions come and hit us, the city suffers, but in the end the legions always retreat and the city remains."

But always before, Alain thought but did not say, the Great Guilds had intervened to ensure that Dorcastle did not fall. Always before, the Great Guilds had wanted above all to keep things unchanging, to prevent the world from altering in any way that might weaken their control. An Empire that controlled too much of the world, that sought to control all of the world, could have challenged the Great Guilds. This time, faced with a threat they could not defeat with those old tactics, the Great Guilds had thrown their power behind that Empire.

Mari glanced back at him, her face lit by shifting patterns cast by the fires burning on either side, and he read in her eyes that she shared the same thoughts.

They finally reached the open area before the second wall, Lieutenant Kaede holding Mari's banner high so that the fires could illuminate the blue and gold for all to see.

"Where are you from?" Alain asked the lieutenant.

She cast a startled glance at him, and he finally noticed a cut on her forehead. "Julesport, Sir Mage. Lieutenant Kaede of Julesport."

"The city of the pirate Jules," Alain observed.

"Yes." Kaede cast a glance at Mari. "I grew up learning of Jules, and hearing of the daughter. We'd stopped believing she would ever come. But she did."

Mari looked back at the burning buildings now behind them. "Maybe she shouldn't have."

"No, Lady. Don't say that. We had nothing left. Nothing to live for, nothing to expect but a lifetime of serving masters who cared nothing for us. We follow you not because we must, but because you will bring us the new day in which the Great Guilds no longer rule everything." Kaede followed Mari's gaze. "Even if I don't live to see that day, others will. These buildings burn, but we can replace them. We've replaced them before. The cost will be small when we finally gain our freedom."

They went past ranks of defenders standing ready at the main gate, through the tunnel inside the wall, and out into the area behind it, already filled with the implements and the human cogs of the machine of war. Alain followed Mari up the stairs inside the wall, reaching a place above the gate where Lieutenant Kaede planted Mari's banner once more. "I will return to headquarters now. The field marshal wanted me to tell you that he will stop by to discuss the defense of the city."

"Thank you," Mari said.

Alain leaned on the battlement of the second wall, gazing at the fires blazing in the buildings before them and the streams of defenders retreating to their next defensive position. "I see your Sergeant Kira," he told Mari.

"You do?" Mari leaned on the stone next to him. "Yeah. Good. And there are the Tiae rifles that were at the gate. There are only eight of them, though." She sighed sadly. "Blast. I wonder how many people we lost on the first wall?"

"The field marshal may be able to tell you," Alain said.

"I'm not sure I want to know. When did Sergeant Kira become mine, by the way?"

Alain gestured toward Kira, hurrying along with the other members of the rear guard. "You are obviously fond of her, and she of you."

"I like who she is," Mari agreed. "I don't know who she is seeing in me, though. Master Mechanic Mari of Caer Lyn? Or the daughter?"

"Perhaps both."

"I know it's the same for you, in a way. Do people look at you and see Alain, or do they see a Mage?"

"I am both. Thank you for showing me how to be a Mage that sees others as real." Alain studied the ground before the second wall. "We will have to worry about Mage spells once more."

"How much power is left out there?"

"One dragon. Some lesser spells."

"Why would they try a dragon again?" Mari asked. "They don't know that I'm out of dragon killers."

"They will try a dragon again because the last two dragons failed," Alain explained, seeing Mari's instant skepticism. "You must think as someone who has never experienced such failure. When you hear of it, when you see it, do you believe it? Or do you discount it as a flaw in the illusion? The elders have been told that two dragons failed. They will not accept that. They will blame the Mages who created the dragons, say that those Mages produced flawed illusions of Mage creatures which failed because of those flaws, not because of what you or any other shadow did."

"Didn't Sergeant Kira kill at least one of those Mages?"

"There will be more Mages who can create dragons," Alain said. "The elders will tell one of those to try next, to prove that the failure of the first two was the fault of the Mages who created them," he repeated, "and does not reflect any flaw in the wisdom of the Guild."

"Do you think word is getting around among those Mages about what happened in Danalee?" Mari asked.

"I will know if it is," Alain said, sweeping his hand in a gesture across the burning city before them. "I can dimly sense many Mages beyond. If that number begins to fall enough that I can sense it, I will know that Mages are deserting the cause of the Guild."

"Can you really spot Mages from this distance?" Mari asked, waving to Sergeant Kira as the rear guard entered the gate. The ranks of defenders outside the gate stayed firm, though, waiting on stragglers.

"Not individual Mages," Alain said. "Not unless they cast a spell. But the others I can sense like…" He pointed to the nearest burning building. "A fire. A large blaze tells me many Mages are present. A smaller one would say their numbers have dwindled."

"Like my bonfire?" Mari commented dryly. "I wonder what Mage Asha is sensing of me now."

Alain looked south. "I wish we knew what has happened at Pacta Servanda. If the battle has yet been joined there, and what has occurred."

Mari smiled, but Alain could see how forced it was. "I for one would not want to face Queen Sien in battle. Nor would I want to face whatever Alli came up with in the way of defenses."

Sergeant Kira and the rest of the Third Regiment came up onto the battlement, looking tired but ready. Alain judged their numbers with his eyes, estimating the losses on the first wall.

He gazed down at the stones beneath his and Mari's feet, seeing a chilling similarity to those in his vision of her lying badly injured. But as on the first wall, these definitely were not the same stones as in the vision. He wished that meant she was safe here, but it only meant that on this spot she would not suffer the injury he had foreseen. Mari might still be badly hurt here, in a place not foreseen. As Mari had often complained to him, foresight rarely brought comfort.

Before he could say anything else, the staccato sound of rifle fire erupted behind them.

Mari stiffened. "The Mechanics Guild Hall. That's where the shots are coming from. I should—"

"You should not," Alain said. "The defenders will already be concerned by the sound of fighting behind them. If they see the daughter running from the wall, they will think the worst."

"Blast! You're right. I hope Field Marshal Klaus had enough reserves watching to handle the assassins."

As the sound of rifles continued to echo through the night, Colonel Teodor came by. "Lady, this is something you expected?"

Alain heard the worry under the calm words and answered. "Lady Mari knew that the Mechanics in the Guild Hall would try to sortie out and disrupt the defense. She and Field Marshal Klaus prepared for such a thing. The sounds you hear are those of the Mechanics being defeated and driven back into their Guild Hall."

Teodor smiled with relief. "I will pass that word along the wall, Sir Mage."

Mari leaned close to him as she continued looking toward the sound of rifle fire. "Have you had some sort of vision that showed what you just told him about the Mechanics being defeated?" she murmured.

"No," Alain said. "But I have…belief? In the field marshal."

"Confidence in him, you mean." Mari nodded, smiling without revealing any hint of worry as she listened to the fighting, even though Alain could hear the concern in her voice. "One thing is for sure, the battle isn't moving toward the wall. It's staying around the Mechanics Guild Hall."

The sound of rifle shots dwindled into a few scattered bangs, then ceased.

"I hope they were all assassins," Mari told Alain. "I hope they didn't force any of the other Mechanics in that Hall to attack with them."

Cheers came down the wall toward them. "We beat the Mechanics!" Alain heard.

The phrase was repeated until it reached them, then faltered as the soldiers looked at Mari. "It's all right," she said. "Those Mechanics sought to hurt and dominate you. Celebrate defeating them, but don't forget there are other kinds of Mechanics. Like me."

As the news passed them on down the wall, Mari looked at Alain. "How about the Mage Guild Hall?"

"All is quiet," Alain said. "I sense only meditation. Those inside do not aid us, but neither do they attack. That elder spoke the truth to us."

"It's funny, but I never doubted her." Mari gave Alain a sharp look. "Speaking of that elder, why did you want me to take off my jacket so badly? It has something to do with that vision, doesn't it?"

Alain knew that he could not lie to her. "Yes. In the vision, you are wearing that jacket."

Mari shook her head. "So if I take it off that will instantly cancel the possibility of the vision coming true?"

"I do not know," Alain said.

"And if it did cancel it, might it be at the cost of us losing when we might have won, because the people defending Dorcastle could no longer easily tell the daughter was still in the fight?"

"That is possible," Alain admitted.

"I said it before, Alain, and I still feel that way. If I'm going to die, I'm going to die wearing this jacket, not hiding and hoping no one notices me." She stared out at the fires. "When I walk into what you call the next dream, no matter when that happens, I'm going to walk in wearing this jacket. I earned it. And despite everything I have learned about the Mechanics Guild I am still proud of it."

A column of cavalry appeared out of the fires, riding hard. On their heels, legionaries streamed into the area before the second wall.

The cavalry raced through the gate, the defenders falling back inside after unleashing a volley of crossbow fire that staggered the legionary charge.

Alain heard the low boom of the heavy gate as it sealed and felt through the stone of the wall the impact of the main gate closing.

Field Marshal Klaus appeared soon afterwards, striding along with a ponderously confident gait. "Everyone is talking about the daughter," he advised Mari with a smile. "How she held the main gate and cast down dragons with one blow."

"They should be talking about everybody else who held that gate," Mari insisted. "The defenders of Dorcastle are amazing."

Vice President of War Eric was with Klaus once more, and smiled at her words. He wore a sword belt over his suit and looked haggard. "Your warning about the Mechanics Guild Hall served us well. Twenty-some Mechanics charged out, but halfway across the plaza were met with fire from crossbows positioned in the buildings and alleys around them."

"About ten made it back inside the hall," Klaus noted with a thin smile. "If they had made it to the gate they were headed for, they could have caused enough disruption for the Imperials to have broken through." The smile vanished. "The Imperials got through the secondary gate on the first wall using another one of those big Mechanic bomb wagons. How many more do they have, Lady?"

"I don't know," Mari said. "Probably not too many. The Senior Mechanics hated wasting money on things like excess ammunition that they couldn't sell. There will be more of the smaller bombs, too."

"Can you tell us anything of what the Mage Guild is up to, Sir Mage?" Klaus asked Alain.

Alain looked to the north before answering, straining his senses for any indications. "As I told Lady Mari, I expect another dragon tomorrow. That will leave little power for any other Mage spells. Tonight there may be attempts to force sally gates, but only a few because the Mage elders will want to preserve the power for the much larger dragon spell. I will warn if I detect such attempts. Ensure that those guarding such small places keep some always on alert. Any Mage who creates an opening in a gate will be standing before it. Crossbows will eliminate both Mage and opening if fired quickly and accurately enough."

"Make sure that gets passed around," Klaus told Lieutenant Bruno and Lieutenant Kaede. "Get word to every sally port and gate guard. Sir Mage, surely the Imperials would prefer forcing some gates in the night to the creation of another large and showy dragon, dangerous as dragons are."

"It is not a matter of what the Imperials want," Alain said. "It is a matter of the elders of the Mage Guild wanting to prove that they are right. They will not bend before Prince Maxim or any other."

"Even when their control of the world is on the line," Mari remarked, "the Great Guilds are still the Great Guilds, arrogant and set in their ways. General, has anything happened at the Mechanic rail yard? Have any Mechanics tried to enter it today?"

"No, Lady. I've received no such reports."

"I may be able to set a trap there," Mari said. "Just in case we can't hold this wall."

Klaus leaned close to her, his voice low so that only Alain and Mari could hear it. "Given the size of the Imperial force, it is a certainty that we will be forced to retreat to the third wall, Lady. But we can make the Imperials pay a mighty price for this wall."

"Why do you not wish others to hear this?" Alain asked in the same low tones.

"Because, Sir Mage, they must fight for this wall as if they never intend to retreat. Tell people they are expected to retreat and they will do it, most likely much faster and much more easily than if they believe they are expected to hold."

Alain nodded, thinking that even soldiers worked with illusions. Field Marshal Klaus felt that giving his soldiers the illusion that they could hold this wall in the face of the Imperial onslaught was vital to winning the battle. Whereas giving them the illusion that the wall was certain to fall would guarantee that to happen. "I see," Alain said out loud, pitching his voice to a louder volume. "So we will hold this wall."

"Yes, Sir Mage," Klaus agreed.

Mari gave them both a look that said she wasn't happy with misleading people, but she only nodded as well.

Alain looked north. The fires burning in the buildings there shone off the armor and weapons of countless Imperial legionaries flooding into the area between the first and second walls.

"They're moving fast down there, but you can see the lack of scaling ladders. They left the burden of those behind in the hope of catching up with us before we got the gates closed. I think it very likely that they won't hit us again until dawn," Klaus remarked. "This time Maxim may insist on using his legions first and not waiting for the Great Guilds to fail. It will be a hot day and a long day."

After the field marshal and his aides had walked down the wall to inspect other areas, Mari went to the surviving rifles from Tiae, handing out some of the remaining ammunition. "We might see another dragon tomorrow," she cautioned. "If we do, aim for its eyes and inside its mouth. That'll be your best chance to hurt it."

"Gast'n's weapon was broken when he was killed," one of the cavalry told her. "But we saved Lind's."

"I'll take it," Mari said. "Keep on fighting well. I know your Queen is very proud of you, Tiae is very proud of you, and so am I."

"Lady?" one asked. "Will you tell her we died well?"

Alain saw Mari stare at the soldier, then inhale slowly before replying. "Yes. If it comes to that. Let's all focus on making the Imperials and their Great Guilds masters die in enough numbers to discourage any more attacks on us."

When they had returned to the spot on the battlement where they had started, Mari set the rifle with the packs of ammunition. "Could you watch these for a while?" she asked Sergeant Kira. "Field Marshal Klaus says the Imperials won't try anything else tonight."

"Probably not," Kira agreed. "They're worn out, too, and you see those clouds coming in? On top of the smoke that's already out there, those clouds will cover the moon and stars so it's too dark to organize another attack once the fires across the way burn down enough."

Mari nodded, grimacing. "Alain, would you like to take a walk? There's something I need to check on. I'll be back," she told Sergeant Kira.

"I'll come along, Lady," Sergeant Kira said.

"No need. Stay with your unit. Get some rest."

"But, Lady—"

"We'll be fine."

Alain followed Mari back down the stairs to street level. "What is this thing you must check on that you do not wish to do?" he asked her.

"I'll explain when we get there," Mari said, walking down the wide street from the gate toward the third wall. "Are you from Dorcastle?" she called to a woman controlling military traffic at an intersection. "Where is the Mechanic rail yard? Where the trains come in?"

The woman pointed to one side. "Just a little way in that direction. You're almost there." She stared, hauling out her sword, clearly ready to shout a warning. "A Mechanic?"

"Yes," Mari called, holding her arms out as she walked closer. "It's all right. I'm Lady Mari."

Soldiers rapidly converged, surrounding them with open hostility that led Alain to place one hand on the knife beneath his robes, wondering if he would have to use it to protect Mari from "friendly" forces.

But the emotions Alain sensed changed quickly when an officer bulled her way through the sudden crowd. "It's the daughter, you fools! I saw her ride by two days ago with the field marshal! How many Mechanics have you ever seen walk around with a Mage by their side?"

Anger and fear changed to joy and reassurance as the soldiers relaxed and stammered out apologies.

"Lady," the officer said, "you should have an escort. In the dark, when fighting has left nerves raw, mistakes are too easily made." She stepped to one side, stopping a small unit marching by. "Where are you headed?"

"The wall," the commander said, saluting.

"Not yet, you're not. You are to escort the daughter, Lady Mari, where she wishes to go, and then escort her back to the wall. After that, return to your other orders."

The commander, obviously worn out and apparently disposed to argue the orders, shut his mouth at the officer's words. "The daughter? It will be our honor to escort her to the ends of the world if need be."

"It's not that far," Mari said. "Thank you," she told the officer.

"It was my honor to assist, Lady," the officer said, turning to the other soldiers present and ordering them to spread the word about how the daughter looked and that she always traveled with a Mage by her.

Mari nodded to her new escort, then set off in the direction of the Mechanic train yard. Alain, surprised that Mari was able to maintain such a brisk pace after the labors of this day, walked beside her. After only a short time they encountered a pair of guards.

"Halt!"

"It's the daughter," the commander of their escort called. "All's well."

Mari smiled reassuringly at the guards and kept going. A short distance farther, Alain found himself gazing on a familiar place. "This was where the Mechanic train brought us when we came to Dorcastle from Ringhmon."

Mari nodded, bringing out a Mechanic hand light and pointing toward two hulking shapes. "I figured the Mechanics Guild would leave these here."

"Locomotive creatures?" Alain asked. "Why would your former Guild have left their locomotive creatures instead of taking them, or causing them to cease?"

"Dearest husband, some day I am going to get you to understand that locomotives are machines, not creatures like dragons or trolls." Mari looked toward her escorting unit, who appeared nervous at the idea of entering the Mechanic facility. "You can wait here. I shouldn't be too long."

She walked toward the locomotives as Alain, reluctant to approach the creatures, followed her. "They can't leave their tracks, and they don't just cease like a Mage creature," Mari explained to Alain. "How many times have we talked about this?" She paused, standing near the closest one, running her light across its surface and looking at it with a sad face. "As far as I know, only one new locomotive has been hand-built by the Mechanics Guild in the last few decades. These very likely are several decades old, if not older."

"Why have we come here?" Alain asked.

"Because I'm going to make them cease, Alain. Do you remember how we killed the dragon on our first visit to Dorcastle?"

He stared at her. "You wish to do that again? Using these?"

"I don't wish to," Mari said, sounding sick at heart. "But if we have to fall back to the third wall, these can ensure that the legions get a very warm reception when they chase us. You can wait here or come with me."

"I will come with you." Alain stayed close to Mari until she climbed into the back of the nearest of the creatures, the light she held shining from the windows on the back. He touched the side of the creature tentatively, surprised to feel the hard surface cold to the touch. Always before when he saw a locomotive creature it had been hot, rumbling inside as it breathed out clouds of warm mist. "Is it dead?"

She stuck her head out of the back. "It was never alive," she said with a pointed look before disappearing inside again.

"Like a troll," Alain said.

"*Not* like a troll!" Mari came out, dusting off her hands. "They safed them as well as they could. Fuel tanks drained, throttles removed, brakes locked. Unfortunately for them, that won't be enough to stop what I have to do." Alain watched her clamber along the outside of the creature, stopping to examine one of the things sticking up from the rounded top. "Alain? Can you get me some ballast?"

"What is ballast?"

"Those rocks over there. The ones that get laid along the rails in open country."

"Why do you not just call them rocks? Are these like the rocks that burn?"

"We call them ballast because they're special rocks," Mari said. "And no, they are not coal. Coal is black and sort of shiny, remember?"

"It is very dark," Alain pointed out.

"Oh, yeah. Sorry. I guess the ballast does look black from here. Everything looks black from here." She waved the light around, pausing it on a few places. "I've never seen a train yard deserted, Alain. It's sort of unnerving. I have to keep telling myself that when we win there will be a lot more train yards, and more trains and tracks, and places like this will be alive like never before."

He went to the pile and collected an armload of the rocks. They were a mix of sizes but none larger than his fist. Mari took them one by one, examining them, tossing some away and carefully pushing others into the thing sticking up from the top of the creature. "This is the safety valve, Alain. Do you remember what we tied down on that barge? This is like that, only the way it's designed on this locomotive it can't be tied down. But I can jam rocks in here that will prevent the valve from lifting. Are you understanding any of this?"

"No."

"All right. Bring me some more rocks." Mari went to do the same thing to the other locomotive creature, but stopped moving when she got into the back. "Oh, no."

She sounded so upset that Alain forgot about getting more rocks, overcame his worries about the creature, and jumped up into the back as well.

Mari sat staring at the controls before her. "Alain, this is Betsy."

"Betsy?"

"This locomotive. It's Betsy. I trained on her." Mari hit the inside of the cab. "Why did Betsy have to be here?"

Alain bent to look, surprised to see tears in Mari's eyes. "I do not understand. You keep telling me they are not alive."

"They're not! But Betsy...she's over a hundred years old, Alain. Betsy's a legend! She's trained countless Apprentices how to be Mechanics. I helped fix her once. And I'm going to have to..." She hit the side of the creature again.

Alain rubbed the back of his neck. "I do not understand. Always you tell me that the creations of Mechanics are not like Mage creatures. But I see you here, I see how you feel, and all I can think of is Mage Alera bidding farewell to her roc Swift."

Mari sat wordlessly for a little while. "I guess you're right after all. We Mechanics tell ourselves that these are just machines formed of metal and fired with oil, soulless creations who owe their existence only to us and that have no feelings and no sense of their own. But we give them names and we feel their moods and we talk to them...and when they reach their final end we feel very sad to lose them."

She got up. "I can't do it. I'll rig the other one, but not Betsy. I will not be the one who kills her."

Mari jumped down, enlisting Alain's help in pushing a cart with a barrel on it to the first of the creatures. "This locomotive runs on fuel oil. I couldn't do this if we were up north or in the east where the locomotives burn coal, because someone would have to stay here and keep feeding the fires. But here they burn oil. I need to load enough into this tender to keep the fires in this locomotive burning hot enough and long enough to overpressure the locomotive's boiler."

"I remember those words," Alain said. "Master Mechanic Lukas said that must never be done."

"Yes," Mari sighed as she worked a hand pump. "And he was very unhappy to hear I had already done it once. He's not going to be thrilled that I'm doing it again. If we can hold the second wall, I won't have to."

After she had finished that task, Mari went into the back of the creature. "I'm presetting most of the controls and locking them," she told Alain. "If we're falling back through here, I might need your help starting the fires, so save one of your heat spells for that."

"Will we have to wait by it again?" Alain asked.

She paused to stare at him. "I can hear that you're worried. You must be really scared of doing that, and given how much damage an exploding boiler can do you're right to feel that way. No, we won't have to stay by it this time. I'll get the fires going, make sure there's enough water flowing into the boiler, and then we run. With the safety valves blocked and the fires going hot, this locomotive will explode when the pressure gets high enough, and when it blows hopefully the only people nearby will be Imperials and Senior Mechanics and Mage Guild elders." She looked over at the other Mechanic creation. "And hopefully Betsy won't be too badly damaged."

When they had finally finished, Mari paused, shining her light around the rail yard. "Destroying this place really feels like a crime to me. I hope we don't have to blow it up."

"I hope this as well," Alain told her.

"We're not going to be anywhere near it this time!"

"It is not that," Alain said. "It is because the idea of doing it makes you sad, and you do not wish the locomotive creature Betsy to be harmed."

"I've done worse things," Mari said, "when I had no other choice. But thanks. Let's back to the wall and try to get some rest."

The unit escorting them seemed as relieved as Alain to leave the

Mechanic rail yard and head toward the wall. Alain noticed Mari looking back and off to the side a few times, and guessed she was gazing toward the place where the Mechanic Guild Hall lay. But she said nothing, and since the soldiers escorting them were close enough to hear any conversation, Alain also stayed quiet.

At the stairs leading up, Mari bade farewell to her escort, ordering them to tell their superior that they had done an important service for her. She watched them go, holding herself with her arms. "I got scared back there, Alain, when all those soldiers crowded around and yelled *Mechanic* at me. I've gotten used to having commons be happy to see me, and forgotten what can happen to a Mechanic who isn't the daughter. What if that had been Alli or Calu? They could have been badly hurt, or killed, because they looked like the enemy."

"I was worried as well," Alain said. "It did not occur to me to worry, either, until we were surrounded. Our perception of the world illusion has changed in ways that do not fit the illusion others still see."

"Like when everybody here looked at you and saw only a dangerous, inhuman Mage?" Mari asked. "That's just one more thing we have to change, right?"

"Yes. We will change it." When Mari said such things, Alain found himself believing they could happen.

Once more on the battlement, Alain looked upwards, thinking the darkness had grown. As Sergeant Kira had said, clouds were moving in, further obscuring the starlight. Mari lay down, her head on one of the packs holding ammunition for her weapon. Alain sat right next to her, his back to the battlement.

Sergeant Kira saluted Mari. "Welcome back, Lady. I've been looking for targets lit up by the fires, but all the high-ranking Imperials seem to have figured out that showing themselves within range of your new rifles is a bad idea."

"I hope they learn quickly enough to give up trying to beat us. I'm pretty tired, Kira. We'll have to do that sword training tomorrow," Mari told her. "Tell whoever stands sentry to wake me just before dawn."

"Yes, Lady."

"And get some sleep yourself. I don't want you staying up all night standing guard over me."

"Yes, Lady."

"And stop calling me Lady all the time."

"Yes, Lady."

Alain, huddled into his robes, reached out to touch Mari's shoulder. "You may have met your match in Sergeant Kira."

"You may be right." Mari looked at him. "Don't you dare die."

"Don't you."

"All right. I guess we'll both have to live through this."

Alain closed his eyes, wondering how long the illusion of the world would have both him and Mari in it.

* * *

"Alain?"

He blinked, trying to come out of the fog of a deep sleep. Alain usually woke up quickly and cleanly, but he usually wasn't as physically exhausted as he had been last night. The air held a chill, and the stars had not yet begun to dim in the east. "Are the Imperials coming?"

"Not yet." Mari looked toward the east as well. "It's about an hour before dawn. Field Marshal Klaus thinks the Imperials might jump off early to try to catch us unready."

Alain got to his feet, trying to stretch his muscles as he stayed behind the protection of the battlement. "I am hungry. If it is going to be a long and hard day, I would like something to eat beforehand."

"That's the other reason I got you up. They're bringing around food and water."

Alain accepted a small loaf of bread and some hard cheese from a young auxiliary who appeared to be terrified of being touched by a Mage. Mari must have noticed, because she made a point of reaching to hug Alain while the young man was still nearby. Alain ate quickly, reverting to Mage ways and not tasting what he was chewing, then washed it down with some of the watered wine from buckets being carried along the battlement.

"They didn't give us any chocolate," Sergeant Kira remarked as she finished her breakfast. "That's good."

"Why is that good?" Mari asked.

"According to rumor, they give you a ration of chocolate if they think you're likely to die carrying out your orders," Kira explained. "It means they think we're going to survive today."

"Or it means they did not have enough chocolate," Alain said.

Kira grinned. "Thank you for pointing that out, Sir Mage. You must be a veteran yourself."

He managed a small smile to her, receiving a look of surprise in return. It was still too dark to see much beyond the wall but the glowing embers of the fires that had raged the day before. Alain looked along the battlement, where new weapons were stacked ready for use: crates of crossbow bolts, baskets of spears, piles of rocks and bricks. Alain had watched soldiers pulling apart buildings last night and wondered at the reason. Now he saw that it was so those bricks could be used as weapons, as if the city itself was helping in its defense.

Mari stared toward the Imperial position, where preparations were still shrouded by darkness. "We'll be needed soon. Are you all right?"

"Yes. Are you?"

"Curiously calm, my Mage. Maybe I'm too scared to realize that I'm scared."

"Sometimes it's like that," Sergeant Kira offered. "Like our minds can't handle it, so they just say all right, get on with it."

"I guess I was like that before the *Terror* went down," Mari said. She rubbed her arm in the place where an Imperial crossbow bolt had left a scar.

"May I say something, Lady?" Kira asked.

"As long as you don't call me lady."

"Yes, Lady," Sergeant Kira said, leaning on the battlement next to Mari. "I'd only spoken to a Mechanic once before in my life, before meeting you I mean. It was just a job, me escorting a pair of Mechanics to work on the lights at the city hall. One of them ignored me, and the other was brusque but not unkind. Still, after that I didn't want to search out Mechanics for conversation. And Mages…Sir Mage, I once saw a Mage looking at me, a man a fair bit older than you, and it was the most frightening thing I ever saw. I ran, I admit it. I thought he might want me for something."

"You were wise," Alain said. "Too many Mages have taken to heart what the elders teach, that others matter not at all. He might have killed you on a whim, or used you badly in other ways."

"We're trying to change that," Mari told Kira. "Changing how Mechanics view commons, and how Mages view everyone. We're making progress. It'll probably be generations before we're all comfortable together, but down in Tiae we can all talk to each other."

"I'm not just talking to a Mechanic," Sergeant Kira said. "I'm talking to the daughter herself. I'll tell my children about it someday. Me on the walls of Dorcastle with Lady Mari."

Mari smiled. "That will be something, won't it? And I'll tell mine about being on the walls with Sergeant Kira."

"You want to have children, Lady? You and your Mage?"

"Yeah. Someday. I know that sounds weird, a Mechanic and a Mage having children, but not so long ago I never would've believed a Mechanic and a Mage could be married." Mari shrugged and smiled again. "Yet here I am."

Kira looked back toward the Imperial lines, her smile vanishing. "It's odd to speak of children and the future, isn't it, Lady? When the legions wait just over there?"

Mari sighed, following Sergeant Kira's gaze. "We're fighting for the future, Kira. Our children's future."

Kira nodded. "Lady Mari? You've fought the legions before this. They say you've gone to Marandur."

"Yeah. Twice."

"I'm serious, Lady."

"So am I, Sergeant Kira. Tell her, Alain."

"Marandur is not a place anyone would want to go even once," he said, remembering the awful ruins of the ancient siege. "But we have been there twice. I do not understand why the Imperials go into battle when they have such a monument to the cost of war on their own land."

"Maybe that's why the Imperial government doesn't want their people seeing it," Mari commented.

Alain sensed something off in the darkness. "Mages move. They prepare."

Sergeant Kira stared at him, then ran to tell Colonel Teodor. Within moments word was being passed rapidly down the battlement and to the reserves waiting below. Lieutenant Bruno ran up, saluting Mari. "Lady, Field Marshal Klaus reports that all is in readiness."

"Have him let me know if he needs anything from me," Mari said. "I'll be right here."

Almost as if her words had been a cue, a moment of silence fell. To Alain the world seemed to be holding its breath.

Imperial horns blared all across the front, echoing and reechoing so that it sounded like every legionary facing them had joined in that fanfare. Then from the darkness ahead burning ballista projectiles rose in a barrage that lighted the dimness of the pre-dawn twilight like a hundred tiny suns. Alain watched the smooth trajectories of the flaming weapons as they rose to their peaks, then arced downward toward the second wall and the buildings behind it.

CHAPTER EIGHT

DIMLY ILLUMINATED BY the fiery projectiles overhead, dense masses of legionaries charged toward the wall, siege towers moving slowly in their wake. Alain crouched behind the battlement as a brutal cloud of crossbow bolts slammed into the stones.

Behind him, Confederation ballistae launched their own deadly projectiles, mostly bundles of fist-sized and larger rocks that fell on the advancing legions, but mixed in with them flaming balls of oil-soaked rags that burst among the enemy to hurl fire in all directions.

Dozens of fires had sprung up behind the defenders as the Imperial bombardment struck. A few of the blazing Imperial projectiles hit the battlements, shattering into sprays of burning fragments.

Alain sensed Mages nearby, preparing spells. The closest ones were among the charging legions, just in front of the main gate. "The gates!" he yelled. "Mages prepare to create openings in the gates!"

That word, too, was repeated rapidly along the wall and behind it. Alain heard a sudden roar of triumph from the Imperials near the gate, but a moment later felt two of the Mages die.

Mari leaned out despite the rain of crossbow bolts and fired her rifle twice.

Alain felt the death of the third Mage.

There was a slight sense of familiarity in that one. Sometime, somewhere, he had met the Mage who had just died. Alain felt other Mages dying farther down the wall as they also fell to crossbows before they could allow the Imperials entry. Fell because Alain had told these commons exactly what to do to kill them and prevent their spells from aiding the Imperials. He searched his feelings for the sort of remorse that Mari felt when Mechanics died at her orders, and felt little. There were times when it was a comfort to have belonged to the Mage Guild, where personal relationships were regarded as both wrong and meaningless. Aside from Mage Asha, the friendships he had developed with other Mages had all come after he and the others had left the Mage Guild.

Shouts could be heard below and a brief clash of steel, as the few legionaries unfortunate enough to have used the Mage-created openings to enter the main gate found themselves trapped on the inside, massively outnumbered and unable to retreat.

Mari was exposing herself only enough to aim and fire her weapon, but Alain, looking out at the attackers immediately before the main gate, saw no target worth his own powers.

He got up, leaning out slightly over the battlement to look both ways down the wall.

Visible in the light provided by the battle and the dawning day, Alain could see siege towers far to his left and right. Apparently the Imperials had figured out that sending siege towers against the wall where the daughter's banner stood was a bad idea. What they had not realized was that Alain could place his spell on anything he could see.

He concentrated again, despite the crossbow bolts plucking at his robes, trying to draw power as much as possible from the area in front of the wall rather than behind it as he created great heat above his palm and sent it to the siege tower on his left, and then did the same to the tower on his right.

Both Imperial siege machines erupted into flame that turned them into towering torches, making it easier for the defenders to see the other Imperial attackers around them.

Alain dropped down behind the battlement, breathing heavily after the exertion.

"Dear," Mari told him, glaring, "are you trying to make it easy for the Imperials to kill you?" She aimed carefully, fired, then looked back at Alain. "I'm supposed to be the impulsive one, remember? —What?"

"A dragon," Alain said, sensing the spell draining almost all of the power remaining before the wall. "There." He got up far enough to point.

Mari's expression changed to surprise, then shock. "It's charging through the legionaries. I mean that. It's coming *through* them, plowing a path. Stars above, it's already wiped out at least a cohort."

"The elders would care nothing for that," Alain said. "They know where I am because I used the heat spells, they suspect I am responsible for the way the defenders so easily slew the Mages who tried to open passage through the gates, and they want me dead. The cost of that to their Imperial allies is of no concern to them."

Mari shouted down toward the Tiae rifles. "Remember! Aim for the eyes and inside the mouth!"

Alain stood up and the dragon burst into his view, charging straight for the place where he still stood at the battlement, legionaries frantically trying to escape the path of the monster, many being hurled aside or crushed.

Mari's rifle crashed, followed by that of Sergeant Kira, and then a rattle of several shots from the Tiae rifles. Sparks appeared on the dragon's head as bullets hit and were deflected. "What are you doing?" Mari yelled at him.

"You have told me it is easier to hit your target if it comes along a straight path," Alain said. "I stay here so the dragon will charge at me." The creature was getting very close, eyes gleaming with hate, teeth the length of swords displayed as the dragon prepared to snap at Alain. "But I will have to move soon," Alain said quickly.

Sergeant Kira's rifle barked, and the dragon's eye facing her suddenly went dark.

The dragon veered off, pawing at its injured eye, screaming with pain. Its powerful tail whipped about, cutting a swath through those legionaries who hadn't managed to get far enough away.

Mari fired and the dragon's head jerked back, blood coming from its mouth.

As it twisted in pain, Sergeant Kira, standing for a clean shot, put a bullet into its other eye.

The dragon screamed again and fell, twitching and jerking, taking out some more unfortunate legionaries with its death throes.

In the lull in the Imperial attack that followed as the legions waited for the dragon to finish dying, Colonel Teodor ran up, smiling. "Lady, once again you are a dragon slayer!" he told Mari.

Mari shook her head. "Not me. Sergeant Kira deserves the credit for this one."

"She struck the deadly blows," Alain agreed.

"Well done, Sergeant! You're a hero of the Confederation! I'll put you in for promotion to lieutenant."

Sergeant Kira waved away the praise, ducking as an Imperial ballista projectile smashed into the wall just beneath the battlement. "I know no good deed goes unpunished, sir, but I'm happy being a sergeant. Becoming a lieutenant would be a demotion of sorts, wouldn't it?"

"I suppose it would." The Imperials had recovered enough to begin launching flights of crossbow bolts again, so Teodor ducked behind the battlement along with the others. "But the field marshal will hear of this. Well done." He hurried back toward the gate, staying low.

"Now every time a dragon shows up, they'll call on me, won't they?" Sergeant Kira said, aiming and firing. Alain saw a Mage fall in the distance and felt him cease.

"Yes," Mari said. "Welcome to the club." She looked at Alain. "I guess you're right. The Mage Guild elders have decided that you are still a danger despite your love for a shadow."

Alain tried to feel for more Mage activity and felt none. "Mari, something has changed. Many Mages have died here and accomplished little. Prince Maxim has seen these things, as have his legionaries. They know that Mages can be killed more easily than they guessed. And they know that you and I still live despite the anger of the Mage elders."

"Do you think Maxim will move against his own Mage allies?" Mari asked.

"I think that if the elders at Dorcastle have any real wisdom they will not linger here."

"Doesn't that give us better odds. Sir Mage?" Sergeant Kira asked.

"We still face the legions and the Mechanics Guild," Alain said.

The harsh brass horns of the Imperials sounded again, this time followed by a deep roar from thousands of throats. A solid wall of Imperial soldiers moved forward against the main gate, shields forming an interlocked barrier to the fire of the defenders. Among them, another siege tower lurched forward, pushed and pulled by hundreds of legionaries protected by their comrades' shields. A storm of crossbow bolts augmented by the fire of perhaps a dozen Mechanics Guild rifles fell in a deadly rain upon the defenders of the main gate.

"Looks bad," Mari said to Alain. "There's something odd about that siege tower."

Alain nodded, having gotten the same feeling from watching it move. He rose enough to see the tower, and using the power still available behind the wall sent heat into it.

The hides protecting one side blackened and charred, but the tower did not burst into flame.

"It's lighter!" Mari yelled as she aimed and shot a Mechanic with a rifle. "They stripped off as much of the wood from the structure as they could, Alain. Put your heat on one of the corners, where there are still beams in place. Kira! Get all the Mechanics with rifles!"

As Mechanic after Mechanic fell from the combined efforts of Mari and Kira, Alain focused again, angry that his first attempt had failed.

He sent heat onto the nearest corner of the approaching siege tower.

Flames burst to life, running up the edge of the tower and along places where other wood beams must still be in place. But the tower kept coming.

It reached the battlement, the ramp falling in the front to offer a path for the legionaries packed inside to race onto the wall.

Alain, upset that his spells had failed twice, placed heat in the center of the ramp even though the effort right after the other two spells left him weak and dizzy.

Flames raced over the surface of the ramp, but legionaries charged across it into a wall of shields and spears held by defenders. The two sides pushed and strained, each trying to force the other back. Crossbows on the top of the tower fired into the defenders, creating gaps as soldiers fell, while Confederation crossbows fired back into the Imperial attackers.

The struggle ended abruptly as the burning ramp came apart. The legionaries on it fell, dropping with despairing cries.

A moment later the fires spreading along the remaining structure succeeded in weakening the siege tower enough that it bent and collapsed into a pile of wreckage against the wall.

Ballistae on both sides continued firing, the Imperial projectiles all falling behind the wall now, aiming to strike the defender's ballistae as well as supplies and the reserve forces waiting at street level. The bombardment from the defenders still fell among the massed legions, tearing holes in their tight ranks. Beneath the arcing fire of the siege machines, the legions and the defenders fought for the wall itself.

Scaling ladders were coming up all along the wall, the defenders trying to shove them off before legionaries could climb them and legionaries below striving to hold the ladders in place. "Alain!" Mari called. "Can you get that ram?"

"I am weary," Alain told her, but he focused on the wooden structure being rolled toward the main gate. He put the best effort he could into it, and flames began flickering along the largest wooden beams suspending the massive ram.

"Sergeant!" Mari called. "Those Mechanics! Don't let them reach the gate!"

Alain saw a group of several Mechanics running forward, carrying another one of the bombs. Legionaries surrounded them, their shields raised to protect the Mechanics.

Mari fired and a legionary fell, exposing a Mechanic. Kira fired, and the Mechanic fell. Mari fired again. Another legionary. Kira fired. Another Mechanic.

Mari's third shot produced a far different result.

A large explosion erupted from the center of the formation, annihilating the surviving Mechanics and blowing legionaries in all directions. The sound of the blast filled the area as the force of the detonation sent debris raining down. The Imperial assault faltered again as Mari stared, appalled. "How could a single hit have set off the bomb?" she asked. "One bullet hitting the casing shouldn't have been able to detonate it…unless the explosive was old and unstable! The Senior Mechanics always wanted to keep junk like that in inventory rather than replace it because that was cheaper in the short run. Didn't they care about sending Mechanics into battle with unstable explosives?" Mari paused, looking enraged. "Of course they didn't care," she answered herself out loud. "They weren't the ones carrying it."

As the Imperial assault paused in the wake of the explosion, Mari rested her rifle on the battlement, aiming at the distant figure of a Mechanic standing near some Imperial officers. "That has to be a Senior Mechanic," Alain heard her whisper. She fired. The Mechanic fell.

With another burst of battle cries the legions rushed forward again, closing their ranks, cohort after cohort charging toward the wall. Alain thought there seemed to be an endless supply of scaling ladders as well as soldiers on the Imperial side. Crossbow bolts kept flying in clouds and Imperial ballistae launched their burdens without pause.

A soldier near Alain hurled some bricks down on the attackers, then fell back, a crossbow bolt in his throat. All up and down the battlement, the ranks of the defenders were thinning under the unrelenting barrage.

A fresh unit of defenders came up the stairs, spreading out to cover part of the battlement and joining the fight with enough enthusiasm to hurl back the legions again.

"Lady? Do we have more bullets?" Kira asked.

"Here." Mari passed two of the clips to Alain, who passed them on to Kira. "How are you, my Mage?"

"Recovering," Alain said.

"Our ammunition won't last if we keep firing it at this rate." Mari set down her rifle and started picking up rocks and bricks from the nearest pile, throwing them down at the attackers.

Alain got back to his feet and joined in, finding some satisfaction in using such a simple weapon. Despite their upraised shields, the legionary ranks shivered under the downpour of heavy objects. The wave of attackers briefly receded, then came on again to meet another deadly hail of bricks and stones. As the shield walls broke, some of the defenders began grabbing spears from the nearby baskets and hurling them downward as well. Even if the spears only lodged in shields, their weight dragged down those shields, leaving legionaries exposed to other weapons.

But the Imperial barrage and assaults on the wall kept claiming defenders, who had to expose themselves to the hail of crossbow bolts and the occasional Mechanic bullet. More and more fell, while healers raced from place to place on the parapet, trying to save defenders who had not yet died from their injuries.

Alain saw a Confederation soldier fall with a crossbow bolt in one arm, then stagger up and continued hurling bricks using his remaining good arm until a second bolt lodged in his chest.

The ladders began rising against the wall again.

Alain stood beside Mari as she picked up her rifle once more. He saw a spot not far down the battlement where the ranks of defenders were much diminished, and put enough power and his own strength into another heat spell that caused the scaling ladder at that point to catch fire.

More reinforcements came up the stairs to join the fight.

Mari fired as more ladders thudded onto the top of the parapet. Defenders with pikes and spears once again shoved them off, some of them falling to legionary bolts, spears, and swords.

More ladders, legionaries swarming up them. Alain heard the dull boom of battering rams at the main gate. He saw that the defenders had poured more oil down on the attackers but that a hail of crossbow bolts was killing every soldier who tried to toss a torch down into it.

He placed heat upon the oil, seeing flames leap high and spread rapidly, the legionaries falling back from the inferno as Alain leaned on the battlement, exhausted for the moment.

Mari drew her pistol and aimed as a ladder came up nearby. Too weak to help, Alain could only watch as, aiming and firing carefully, she put a bullet into each legionary as they came up the ladder, replacing the clip in a few quick motions when the pistol emptied, then sighting in again and repeating the process.

Two defenders with pikes shoved the ladder back so that it fell among the attackers.

Mari knelt behind the battlement as she reloaded again. "How are you?" she asked Alain.

"Very tired. I have cast many spells."

"Don't exhaust yourself," Mari ordered. "Do you hear me? You have to be able to walk."

The attack paused as the legions reformed and brought up more ladders. Young auxiliaries scurried the length of the battlement, carrying water and food for the defenders.

Alain looked upward as he chewed some soft jerky without tasting it. The sun had risen high enough to be mostly obscured by the clouds, and smoke from the new fires set behind this wall was drifting high overhead, further darkening the sky. "It is nearly noon," he said.

"It feels like we've been fighting for a full day already," Mari said, her voice raw and weak. "I've got to stop yelling so much." She pointed out across the area behind the second wall. "Can you see? The Imperials are setting fires all over the place, except around the rail yard. They're trying to keep from damaging it with their bombardment."

"If you do the thing you planned for, blowing up the locomotive creature, that will damage the Mechanic rail yard."

"Yes, it will." Mari ran one finger across a slash in the arm of her jacket. "That one was close."

Alain held up the sleeve of his robe, showing off a hole and two rips. "We have been lucky."

"A lot of others haven't," Mari said, watching a badly wounded soldier being carried by on a stretcher. "If we've lost this many, how badly must the Imperials have been hurt already?"

Field Marshal Klaus came up the stairs, speaking with some of the defenders. He paused by Mari. "It has been going well, Lady," he told her.

"This is well? Really?"

"Yes." Klaus gazed along the battlement. "Some battles are quick, and go to the cleverest. Other battles are long, and go to whoever has the most endurance."

"My Mage says he thinks Prince Maxim may be fed up with the Mage Guild."

"The Mage Guild has done more damage to their supposed allies than they have to us," Klaus agreed. "Do you mean the Imperials might break their alliance with the Mage Guild?"

"I mean they may attempt to break the Mage Guild," Alain said. He stopped speaking, sensing something that he had trouble understanding. "The elders are angry. I have never felt elders reveal such emotions so clearly." He rose up, looking to the north. "The Mages move, that way, and my sense of them grows fainter."

Klaus peered toward the Imperial lines. "West and north? They're heading back toward the waterfront. Will they leave?"

Alain thought about the question before replying. "I do not believe so. While their anger must be directed at the Imperials, the Mage elders also do not want the Mechanics to be able to claim sole credit for an Imperial victory if such a victory occurred. They will remain." He tried to remember everything he had ever seen or learned about the elders who controlled the Mage Guild. "They would never admit to pride, but I believe that the elders suffer from it and let it guide their actions. So they withhold assistance, thinking that the Imperials will come crawling to them begging their aid once more."

"Pass that word around," Klaus ordered Lieutenant Bruno. "The Mage Guild should be out of the fight for a while. Where is Kaede?"

"Down on the left."

"Make sure she helps in letting everyone know that we've caused the Mages to withdraw. No other commons can claim that sort of achievement against Mages."

"How are we looking for reserves?" Mari asked.

"Still doing well," the field marshal replied. "We've had a harder time repelling the siege towers at other parts of the wall, but the Imperials have yet to gain a lodgment. The bombardment of the areas behind the wall has been intensive enough that I've started pulling back a lot of supplies and other assets behind the third wall, where the Imperial ballistae can't keep hammering them."

"Good," Mari said. "Anything else?"

Klaus knelt down next to her, speaking in a voice so low that only Alain and Mari could hear. "I'm concerned about pressure on the left. I'll be going there next myself to see things personally."

"Should Alain and I shift positions to there?"

"We can't afford to do that, Lady. The Imperials are still throwing their strongest efforts against the main gate. I'm going to shift some of the surviving Tiae rifles down to the left. That will not only give the troops there a morale boost but also offer a means to pick off Imperial leaders in that area." Klaus paused, betraying worry to Alain's eyes. "They're pushing harder than I expected, Lady. We must be facing every legion the empire has, just as that one report claimed, and they keep coming regardless of losses."

"We need to hold until my army gets here," Mari said.

"I wish I knew how long that would be," Klaus said. "Do you desire that I receive approval from you before ordering any more withdrawals?"

"No. I'm not in a position to see the big picture. I have confidence in you, Field Marshal, and have no doubt of your resolve. When you think we need to pull back," Mari said, "give the order to withdraw."

"Thank you, Lady." Klaus stood, but remained crouched to avoid the occasional flights of crossbow bolts coming from the Imperials even during this lull in the assault. "I'll check on the left."

"He is more worried than he showed," Alain murmured to Mari once the field marshal had departed.

"Act confident," she told him. "Everyone is looking to us."

"They look to you."

"No. They watch you, too. You've impressed them." Mari's head jerked about as a boom sounded from the direction of the Imperials. "That wasn't a rifle."

Alain stood alongside her, feeling the wall shudder from the shock of an impact. Mari had her far-seers to her eyes, trying to see through the drifting clouds of smoke cloaking the battlefield as a result of the fires burning behind the second wall. "It's an artillery piece, Alain. Mechanics Guild equipment. They must have off-loaded it from one of the ships."

"A weapon like Alli's big guns?"

"Not nearly as good as Alli's, but good enough to be dangerous if we don't do something about it."

Alain heard another boom, this time seeing a flash of light that marked the gun's position. But he could see little else. "Where are the...shells?"

Mari shook her head. "I can't see them. They might be behind that wall next to the gun. Maybe the Mechanics Guild has figured out you can hit whatever you can see. Or maybe that's just a coincidence. Sergeant Kira?"

"Lady?"

"Can you see the Mechanics around that gun?" Mari asked as the weapon fired a third time.

Kira squinted. "Yes."

"What do you think? That's a long shot."

"I can try." Kira rested her rifle on the battlement, aiming.

Alain watched for other dangers. The legionaries were busy regrouping and resupplying, leaving this fight to the Mechanics, but crossbows still fired at targets visible on the battlement. Little of Sergeant Kira showed, but Alain saw a group of Imperial crossbows clearly aiming her way.

He was rested enough to risk a heat spell. Alain imagined the heat above his palm, then thought it onto a crossbow near the center of the group.

The crossbow burst into flame and shattered, throwing burning fragments and splinters in all directions. The group of crossbows scattered.

Alain had barely turned his attention back to Sergeant Kira when the crash of her rifle sounded.

A long pause, while Mari looked through her far-seers.

"You got one!" she told Kira. "What a shot!"

"What are the others doing?" Alain asked.

"Loading again."

Kira didn't reply, aiming once more.

Another crash of a shot, another pause.

"Must have missed," Mari said.

"I won't waste the next one," Sergeant Kira vowed.

The Mechanic gun fired at almost the same moment as Kira's third shot.

"You got another!" Mari called as the wall shuddered from another hit from the Mechanic gun. Alain saw her squint again. "What's that?" she wondered.

"Ballista projectiles," Kira said. "Our own ballistae are targeting the Mechanic gun."

"Looks like the gun crew has decided that survival is more important than following orders from the Senior Mechanics," Mari said. "They're running. Oh, blazes. Here come the Imperials again."

The harsh notes of the Imperial brass horns signaled the charge, and another wave of attackers came against the wall.

Alain tried only to strike at targets worth a spell. There seemed to be far too few of those and far too many individual legionaries and scaling ladders. He brought out his long knife and used it as legionaries came up one ladder, fighting and killing with the emotionless skill taught to Mage acolytes. He kept his expression Mage-dead as he fought, seeing how that sight unnerved the legionaries he confronted.

Another lull, the sun far down in the west. Alain saw Mari counting the remaining ammunition and shaking her head. "Once I resupply the Tiae rifles," she said, "we're going to be—"

"Lady!" Lieutenant Kaede, a large bandage on one wrist, ran up and crouched nearby, breathing heavily. "All of the Tiae rifles on the left are dead. I've been sent to get the rest and bring them there."

"How did—?" Mari began, looking stricken.

"Crossbows, swords, and two died when an unlucky Imperial ballista projectile struck the battlement where they fought."

"Yes, go ahead and—"

Trumpets sounded on the left. Lieutenant Kaede grimaced. "Too late. The Imperials have a foothold on the wall." She paused as more trumpets called their message. "We've lost the secondary gate. The field marshal has ordered a withdrawal to the third wall."

Alain got to his feet, feeling weak from the effort he had expended all day, as the Imperials facing the main gate cheered and launched another assault. "They seek to pin us here," he told Mari. "Until our retreat is impossible."

"Discourage them," Mari told Alain. "Give it everything you've got."

He sent a rapid series of heat spells out, setting fire to several scaling ladders and throwing the assault into confusion. But the effort left him unable to stand, shaking as he clung to the battlement.

Sergeant Kira rejoined them. "We must go, Lady."

"I need your help," Mari told her. "Mage Alain can't walk on his own. Help me with him."

Kira stared. She turned long enough to fire a shot that dropped a centurion trying to get the assault going again, then turned back to Mari. "Lady? I've never touched a— He's a soldier, isn't he? Like me."

"Yes, he's a soldier, Sergeant," Mari said. "Help him like you would any other."

Kira got under one of Alain's shoulders while Mari supported the other, the two nearly carrying him down the stairs among the other retreating soldiers.

"This must be the first time your Mage has been carried by two women," Kira gasped as they ran.

"No. It's the second," Mari told her. "I think he does this on purpose sometimes so women will carry him."

"Not really," Alain corrected, still trying to get his strength back, "but that is a good idea."

"Quiet, Alain. Save your strength."

They had reached street level when Imperials began flooding onto the battlement of the second wall, bellowing cries of triumph as the last of the Confederation rear guard either fled or fell. One legionary with more speed than sense raced down the stairs toward them. Alain saw Mari use her free hand to draw her pistol and fire, knocking down the foremost enemy and slowing the charge of the others.

"I can walk," Alain gasped. Sergeant Kira stepped back as Alain found his feet. "Thank you, Sergeant."

"Anytime, for a comrade in arms," Kira said, turning to fire and drop the nearest Imperial officer.

"We need to go by the Mechanic train yard," Mari yelled at Sergeant Kira. "Tell Colonel Teodor."

"Yes, Lady!"

They ran past a solid formation of reserves ready to slow the Imperial advance, onto a street crowded with other defenders falling back. Alain, remembering that Field Marshal Klaus had sent most of the ballistae and wagons behind the third wall already, saw only foot soldiers and cavalry on this street, the horses shying from the burning structures on either hand.

Alain, still very tired, barely kept up with Mari as she ran back to the Mechanic rail yard and the locomotive creature she had worked on the night before. Sergeant Kira and a number of other soldiers from the Third Regiment stayed with them until they reached the rail yard. The guards that had been set around the rail yard were already gone, doubtless having joined the retreat.

"Wait here," Mari ordered Sergeant Kira and the other soldiers from the Third Regiment. Alain stayed with her as Mari ran to the locomotive creature she had prepared the night before and leaped into the back. "I need heat, Alain! Inside here!"

He looked, seeing a metal door standing open, darkness beyond. An oily smell came from it. Despite his weariness, Alain created the illusion of enough heat to set fire to oil, grateful that unused power remained here away from the wall. Once he thought the heat was strong enough, he imagined it inside the door, and saw flames suddenly erupt.

Mari slammed shut the door, making small adjustments to the controls, then paused to rest one hand on the creature. "I'm sorry."

She jumped down, Alain steadying her. Mari hesitated again, looking toward the second locomotive creature. "Keep your head down, Betsy!"

He urged Mari into motion again, out of the rail yard to where Sergeant Kira and other soldiers waited. For the first time, Alain noticed that one of the soldiers carried Mari's banner from the second wall. The entire group headed back to rejoin the retreating columns, while Alain worried about whether this side-trip had delayed them too much.

"Heating up the boiler that fast will crack the boiler lining," Mari said breathlessly to Alain. "But since I'm going to blow up the boiler, that doesn't really matter."

"How long do we have?" Alain asked.

"Long enough," Mari said.

When they reentered the main street they found one of the rear guard formations falling back quickly and joined in their retreat.

Confederation cavalry came out of a side street and charged at the Imperials rushing forward, scattering the legionaries. The cavalry rode back to the foot soldiers and the entire group moved back together.

Alain saw the buildings on either hand give way to the open area before the third wall. He could see defenders already on the battlement of the third wall, and ranks of pikes and crossbows protecting the gates as the last of the retreating forces streamed across the open ground and through the gates.

He staggered through the main gate alongside Mari, feeling incapable of any further effort and hoping he would not be needed again soon.

Mari stopped just beyond the gate, the soldiers around her stopping as well, watching as the formation outside the gate threw back a few assaults from tired, disorganized Imperial pursuers.

The formation fell back in perfect order, the two sides of the gate swinging closed the moment they cleared it.

"Lady?" Sergeant Kira asked, gesturing upward.

"Yeah. Let's go."

Alain went up the stairs with them, willing his legs to move up each step in turn. Cheers sounded as the banner of the daughter was planted on the battlement and Mari stood tall to wave in both directions.

Worn out, Alain leaned on the stone parapet. The sun had dipped below the overcast, sending slanting rays across the battlefield that illuminated strangely beautiful patterns in the smoke billowing from burning buildings below the third wall. He glanced at the stone beneath his feet, having almost forgotten in his exhaustion to see if it matched that of the vision, but once again it did not.

Looking outward once more, Alain could see Imperials flooding into the newly captured part of the city, columns of dark red uniforms and gleaming armor filling the streets towing siege machines with them. The sound of Imperial horns crowing triumph on the second wall carried easily to those on the third.

Mari put her arm around Alain, looking outward. "It ought to happen pretty quickly now, unless some Mechanics with the Imperials notice what I did and manage to shut off the locomotive's boiler fast enough."

The sound of the explosion rocked the city, large and small pieces of wreckage erupting from the Mechanic rail yard and tearing through nearby streets and buildings. Alain saw the Imperial columns on nearby streets break apart and scatter. Pieces of debris fell as close as the open area before the third wall.

The sound of the blast was still echoing, the soldiers around her cheering, as Mari stared at the devastation. "How many people do you suppose I just killed?" she asked Alain in a dull voice.

"Not nearly as many as will die if we fail," he tried to reassure her.

"That type of math doesn't make me like this any better." She looked to the right. "The Mage and Mechanics Guild Halls are both outside our lines now."

Mari pulled her far-talker from her jacket pocket, adjusting it and listening, calling several times, holding it up and getting no different result. "Nothing. Alain, why do you think none of our rocs have shown up here? Why wouldn't they have flown on ahead of the army with more rifles and Mages and other critical things?"

"I do not know," Alain said. "There must be a good reason. I was wondering why we have not experienced certain attacks from the Mage Guild. Perhaps the things we are both not seeing are related."

"What do you mean?"

"I have been wondering why we have not faced any Mages who can create the illusion of lightning," Alain explained. "Why have they not cast their lightning against the battlements? There are not many Mages with such skill, but it is odd that none of them are here."

Mari looked south. "You think maybe those lightning Mages are trying to hold up my army? They couldn't stop the army, but I don't imagine rocs could survive hits by lightning. That would be enough to keep them from flying ahead. Did our enemies out-think us this time, Alain? Did they set traps that aren't perfect but might have enough force to achieve their goals?"

"I do not believe that," Alain said. "The flaws in the methods of the past, dividing common and Mechanic and Mage, we have seen clearly here. We will triumph."

Mari smiled at him through the smudges of smoke on her face. "I made a Mage believe in something?"

"I have long believed in you. I also believe in what you do."

Field Marshal Klaus came walking along the wall, trailed by Lieutenant Kaede and Lieutenant Bruno. "Greetings, Lady. That went better than I expected."

"It did?" Mari asked.

"Yes. We had to yield the wall, but it cost the Imperials dearly." He waved out across the part of Dorcastle that had been taken by the enemy. "They'll have to bring up fresh legions during the night and withdraw the ones that have been in the thick of the fight. And with *their* Mages sitting out the fight for a while, we can hope for a quiet night."

"The Mechanics might try to sneak some bombs close to the wall during the night," Mari cautioned. "Some timers run long enough that they could plant a bomb in the night and it wouldn't go off until morning."

"We'll keep a close eye out for that, Lady. Are any of those bombs large enough to endanger the wall, or just the gates?"

"Just the gates. To blow a hole in the wall they'd need several of those bomb wagons, and even if they had them those wagons can't be brought up next to the wall without a lot of people noticing."

"Excellent." Klaus turned. "Are you the Sergeant Kira I've been hearing about?"

"Yes, sir," Kira replied, saluting.

"A dragon slayer, eh? Inspired by being so near the daughter?"

"Yes, sir," Kira said again, smiling. "I have been fortunate to fight near her."

"I understand she's under your personal charge? Good. I can't imagine a better soldier or a better unit than the Third Regiment for the task. I need to borrow the daughter for a short time, though. Lady, can you come for a briefing at my headquarters?"

"Yes," Mari said, beckoning to Alain.

The field marshal's latest headquarters was in an average-looking building that proved to be a small concealed fortress. The walls of the building were thick, the roof both reinforced and slanted to deflect anything striking it, and beneath ground level lay a very impressive basement with several escape stairways leading in and out to prevent those inside from being trapped. Alain looked at the soldiers rushing around to organize the room and update the maps, seeing order under the apparent chaos of activity.

Field Marshal Klaus brought them over to a large table, where once again a variety of wooden blocks portrayed different units and their positions. "We've taken our share of losses, but we're still in good shape, Lady. How many of the Tiae rifles are left?" he asked Lieutenant Kaede.

"Most of the soldiers carrying the rifles have been killed, their weapons either destroyed or broken, and one possibly lost, though we believe no ammunition remained for that rifle. Only four Tiae soldiers bearing rifles remain, sir."

Alain saw Mari close her eyes briefly before concentrating again on the field marshal's words.

"We'll deploy them on the right tomorrow, if that is acceptable to you, Lady. The Imperials normally alternate their primary blows, so I expect strong forces to assail the right of the wall as well as the main gate." Klaus paused. "Of course, the forces hitting the left will be strong as well. Just not as strong."

"We really did better than you expected today?" Mari asked.

"Yes."

"What do you expect for tomorrow?"

"The same as today, Lady," Klaus said, his eyes somber. "With one difference. Tomorrow we will not yield a wall. We will hold."

Alain nodded to Mari to show that Klaus meant what he said.

"We will hold," Mari echoed.

To Alain's surprise, she meant it, too.

He thought of the masses of Imperials, of the fresh legions being brought up in the night, and decided he might as well believe along with them.

They went back to the battlement to await the dawn.

CHAPTER NINE

MARI AWOKE WITH a jolt of alarm as a rock cast by an Imperial ballista crashed into the street not far behind the wall. She stared around in the darkness, her heartbeat rapid, for signs that the Imperials were staging a night attack.

"It's just a harassing bombardment," Sergeant Kira said. She was sitting, back to the battlement, not far away. "We've got a little while yet until dawn."

Mari sat up, seeing that Alain was still asleep. She moved over to sit next to Kira. "Thanks for helping me with Alain yesterday. I know that touching a Mage must have felt strange to you."

"Like you said, Lady. He's just one more soldier." Kira turned a curious look on Mari. "How did you two meet? The rumors say he sought you out to serve you."

"Not exactly," Mari said, looking upwards. Only a few stars were visible through rents in the clouds. A hush lay over the city, broken only by occasional soft noises from behind the wall and, once, the bray of a mule. "He did come looking for me when the caravan we were in was being wiped out, even though he didn't know who I was. We sort of saved each other, then we saved each other again, and then…saving each other became a habit, I guess. And then I fell in love with him, and he fell in love with me, and then everybody was trying to kill us. Just a typical meet cute guy in a deadly ambush followed by romantic adventure involving assassins and dragons, I guess."

"I never had that much fun on a date," Sergeant Kira commented. "Maybe I should have traveled with more caravans."

"It's possible to have too much of that kind of fun. Do you think a storm is coming?" Mari asked, looking at the overcast.

"Very likely. This time of year we usually have storms that we say come in easy and slow, then hit hard and fast. This looks like one of those. It might build for a couple of more days before breaking."

"If the storm hits, will it prevent the Imperials from attacking for a while?"

"Maybe. Maybe not. Storms make it a lot harder to pass orders and see what's going on, but they also provide cover and make it more difficult for the defenders to size up what's happening." Kira nodded toward the south. "I hope your army gets here soon."

"Me, too." Mari pulled out her far-talker, but heard even less than the day before. "Those clouds must be blocking the signal." She noticed Sergeant Kira trying not to stare at the device. "Here. Someday lots of people will have these. Even better ones than this. This is the on/off switch, and this dial sets the frequency, and this dial controls how loud it is."

Kira shook her head, holding the far-talker as if it were something fragile. "I'd heard rumors of Mechanic devices like this. I never thought I'd see one or hold one."

"Why don't you try it? Let me set the frequency. Go ahead. Push that and talk into that."

"What do I say?"

"Say this is Sergeant Kira of Dorcastle, and you're a common, and you're using a far-talker for the first time."

Kira smiled, then spoke the message into the far-talker.

"I'm sorry no one answered," Mari said, taking back the device and putting it in her jacket again. "The atmospherics are messing with its range, which means my far-talker can't talk very far at the moment. Maybe next time."

A growing murmur of noise along the battlement marked the arrival of another field breakfast. Alain woke and joined them, his expression impassive. "Any visions?" Mari asked him.

"No," Alain said. "I do not even recall dreams from this night."

"Me, neither." Mari realized that even though such battles fed her nightmares, while she was actually fighting them she had neither the energy nor the time to be tormented by memories of things seen and done. The idea of a battle bringing her internal peace was either ironic or awful, she wasn't sure which. Maybe both.

Alain looked to the north. "The Mages remain distant from this wall."

"Good. Too bad I can't discourage the Mechanics enough for them to do the same."

Kira rose up a bit to gaze over the battlement. "I hear something going on out there. We might have an early morning of it. Earlier than yesterday, that is."

She had barely finished speaking when Mari heard the *thunk* of a hundred ballistae firing and saw fiery projectiles rising from the north, like a false sunrise aimed at the defenders of Dorcastle.

"Here we go," Kira said, picking up her rifle.

The early Imperial attack proved to be a mistake. The darkness was still so thick that the Imperial units got intermingled, slowing the assault and resulting in large numbers of legionaries milling about at the foot of the wall as the defenders cast down rocks, spears, and bricks that could scarcely miss.

Mari and Kira added to the confusion by shooting every officer they could spot. Far down the wall to her right Mari heard the surviving Tiae rifles firing as well. She wondered how Major Danel and the other Tiae cavalry were doing, imagining they were doubtless frustrated to be waiting in reserve while others fought.

She also wondered what had happened to her, that she no longer flinched every time she fired, thinking of the person her bullet would strike. There were too many, there had been too many, and they would all kill her if given the chance, they were all trying to kill her right now. Like a Mage, she had walled off her feelings, not having the luxury to indulge in them when life and freedom were on the line.

The legions fell back, reorganizing as a red sun rose through the haze of smoke that now seemed to permanently engulf Dorcastle.

They came again, few siege towers visible today. Alain set on fire the two that were visible to him and a large battering ram being hauled toward the gate.

A group of Mechanics tried to deliver another hand-carried bomb to the gate, falling to Mari's and Kira's fire until the two survivors fled. Alain put heat on the abandoned bomb, the explosion hurling nearby legionaries in all directions.

Ladders thudded against the parapet. Defenders set pikes against the tops and shoved, trying to overbalance them and throw the ladders down. On the ground, legionaries pushed back or fired crossbows at the pike-carrying defenders.

Mari spotted a Mechanic with a rifle, but before she could fire Sergeant Kira's shot dropped him.

The legionaries fell back again, attacked again.

The ballistae continued to hurl their deadly projectiles, some solid and others afire, so that the buildings behind the third wall caught and sent clouds of smoke billowing up to join with the low clouds. Brief gaps in the overcast gave a glimpse of the sun and cast a few rays across the battlefield. Staring in astonishment, Mari realized it was almost noon.

The fallen on the battlement were carried off, some moaning in pain, others silent in death. The front defended by the Third Regiment grew shorter and shorter as the surviving soldiers drew together and fresh reinforcements came up onto the battlement to cover the resulting gaps.

How many attacks had been thrown back? Mari couldn't remember, the Imperial assaults running together in her mind.

Her rifle empty as another scaling ladder hit the wall nearby, Mari drew her pistol and leaned out a bit, ignoring the crossbow bolts being fired at the battlement. Aiming carefully, she fired several shots into the cluster of soldiers holding the base of the ladder. Some fell, others lost their grips. The top of the ladder swung out under the push of pikes wielded by other defenders, the legionaries trying to climb up the ladder gripping desperately or jumping off into the crowd below before the ladder overbalanced and fell among the attackers.

Another ladder thudded into the battlement nearby. Mari extended her arm and fired as a legionary who had ridden the ladder up tried to jump onto the battlement. Her shot hit the Imperial soldier and knocked him back.

More legionaries swarmed up the ladder as Mari reloaded. Defenders rushed to meet them with pikes and swords. Another ladder thumped up nearby.

Alain met the legionaries coming up, his long knife killing and wounding until the fire he had set in the ladder weakened it enough for it to collapse, spilling attackers back to the ground.

A soldier standing next to Mari took two steps backwards and fell, a bullet hole from a Mechanics Guild rifle in the center of her chest armor.

Mari wasn't sure how far past noon it was when the attacks ebbed. She sat behind the parapet, breathing deeply, staring at nothing.

"Eat," Sergeant Kira advised. She looked as haggard as Mari felt.

Lieutenant Bruno came by, saluting her. "Lady, the Imperials got onto the wall to the right for a short time, but we threw them back. The secondary gate on the right was badly damaged by a Mechanic device, but it's been braced and is holding."

"Good," Mari said, not sure what else to say. "We're holding?"

"Yes, Lady. We're holding."

A short time later, Mari heard shouts being passed along the wall. "Parley! There's a parley flag!"

She got up enough to look, seeing the traditional white flag with a wide blue band around the edge. Near it were a number of high-ranking Imperials.

"Those targets are tempting," Sergeant Kira murmured.

"They are," Mari said. "But behave yourself, Sergeant. Only shoot if they give cause."

"Lady Mari," Vice President of State Jane said as she came along the battlement. "At least you're easy to find," she added, gesturing toward Mari's increasingly tattered banner. "We're going to see what they have to say."

"Can we trust them?" Alain asked.

"No, Sir Mage. But we've got enough crossbows covering them that if they try to pull something we should be all right."

Mari and Alain followed Jane down the wall and to a small sally gate near the main gate. Field Marshal Klaus was waiting along with Lieutenant Kaede and Lieutenant Bruno. "Where's Vice President Eric?" Mari asked.

"He hasn't been seen since we pulled back from the second wall," Jane said. "I've trying to find out if he's in one of the field hospitals."

The gate opened and they walked out into a scene from a nightmare. The bodies of dead legionaries lay so thick at the base of the wall that it was difficult to walk without treading on them, and where bodies did not lie, blood pooled. Mari did her best not to look at any of the faces of the fallen, already having too many seared into her memory.

The Imperial parley group was not led by Prince Maxim or Princess Lyra, but the four eagles on the collar of the senior legionary officer identified her as a legion group commander, the highest Imperial military rank. "Are you prepared to end this useless struggle?" she asked.

Vice President Jane answered. "Certainly. Does that mean you're withdrawing?"

"I am here to accept your surrender and prevent more useless loss of life," the group commander snapped.

Mari shook her head, feeling stubborn and angry. "The only ones who can prevent more useless loss of life are you and the other Imperial commanders. You will not take Dorcastle. Stop trying. Stop wasting the lives of your legionaries."

"Your numbers dwindle," the group commander insisted.

"My army is on the way," Mari said.

"It will not arrive in time."

Alain replied, using his intimidating Mage voice. "Do you have foresight that grants such knowledge? The army comes. It will sweep away the legions."

"The word of a Mage," the group commander said. "Our awe of Mages has lessened considerably in recent days."

"This Mage," Mari said, "has cost you dearly in recent days. Don't forget that."

"Do you surrender? We are willing to offer terms for your soldiers. If we are forced to make them prisoner, they will not be released any time soon but will work at forced labor. If you surrender, we will grant them release once they relinquish their weapons."

Field Marshal Klaus's smile was grim. "You'll get their weapons on the same terms as for the last three days, point first and in the guts of your legions."

"How can you put your faith in a Mechanic?" the group commander asked. "Look at her! Arrogant in her jacket, already demanding the service of all of you! She is no different from any other Mechanic. All your sacrifices will achieve is a change in the name of your master."

"There you are wrong," Klaus said. "I have served Mechanics in the past because I must. I serve this one by choice. And count myself fortunate to do so, because she does not make me feel as though I serve, but rather that we are working together for a great and noble cause."

"It is you who serves the purposes of the Great Guilds," Vice President Jane added, "not the best interests of your Emperor."

"End this," Mari urged the group commander. "You cannot win."

"We will end it," the group commander said, "when the last wall has fallen, and you, Mechanic, are brought to the Emperor in chains to answer for your crimes."

"That's Master Mechanic," Mari corrected her.

The Imperials turned and walked away.

Mari and the others went back toward the sally gate, Mari feeling an itching between her shoulder blades as she worried about a bullet or a crossbow bolt striking there in defiance of the rules of parley.

Alain shoved her.

Mari stumbled to one side, cursing as she fell across some of the dead legionaries before the wall, but her words broke off as the sound of a rifle shot pierced the air and the snap of a bullet followed.

Another shot rang out from the battlement.

Lieutenant Bruno and Lieutenant Kaede put themselves between Mari and danger as she got up and hastened with Alain inside the sally gate along with Vice President Jane. Field Marshal Klaus followed, his expression dark, and then the two lieutenants. Mari didn't relax until the gate was shut and the locking bars across it once more.

A messenger ran up. "It was a Mechanic who shot, lying amid the Imperial dead farther from the wall. A soldier from the Third Regiment killed the Mechanic before she could fire again."

"An assassin," Mari said. She looked at Alain. "Thank the stars for your foresight."

"It gave no warning," Alain said. "I saw nothing. I just felt a need to shove you aside at that moment."

"I'll take whatever foresight offers in a case like this," Mari said.

"The Mechanics Guild broke the parley truce," Klaus grumbled. "The Imperials probably knew of it, but excused their dishonor by knowing the blame would lie with the Mechanics."

"I doubt there will be any more attempts at parley," Vice President Jane said. "I'll get a report off to the government about what happened here so they can be wary of similar treachery."

"It should be quiet for a little while," the field marshal added. "They wouldn't have tried a parley if they'd been able to mount another attack on the wall right away."

Mari and Alain made their way back to the spot where her banner flew. "Thanks, soldier of the Third Regiment," she greeted Sergeant Kira.

Kira nodded in reply, looking unhappy. "I didn't spot her before she fired. When she reloaded, she had to move to work the lever on the Mechanics Guild rifle, so I got her then, but that was too late to stop the first shot."

"I'm not complaining," Mari said.

"I thank you for that," Sergeant Kira said.

Colonel Teodor walked up. "I'm assuming they haven't given up?"

"No," Mari said. "The Imperials offered one small concession, but otherwise still just wanted us to surrender."

"It looks quiet out there," the colonel said, gazing out toward the buildings occupied by the Imperials.

"Field Marshal Klaus believes the Imperials will take a while to launch another attack," Mari told him.

"Good! I'll try to get some lunch…" Teodor looked at the position of the sun. "Or maybe dinner is the right word. We'll get some food and drink up here."

Mari slumped down against the battlement again. "The Third Regiment has been on the wall since the start of the fight. I'll talk to Field Marshal Klaus about rotating you off the wall for a break."

Sergeant Kira gave her an alarmed look, shaking her head. "I wish you wouldn't, Lady. I mean, you can. You're in charge. But you shouldn't."

"Why not?" Mari asked, baffled.

"We're an Old Line regiment, Lady. Us, the First and the Second as well. We don't back off from a fight. It isn't done. We stay in there until the battle is won. That's the way it is, because that's who we are. Everyone in an Old Line regiment knows the responsibility that comes with that."

Mari gazed at Sergeant Kira, not needing the skills of a Mage to see how much Kira meant what she said. "I won't do that, then, Sergeant. The Third Regiment will stay in the fight until it's won."

"Thank you, Lady," Kira said, grinning with relief.

Mari felt herself nodding off from fatigue as the last portion of the day ran out, the sun appearing only briefly as it sank in the west. From the north came the sounds of the movement of large numbers of people and siege machines as the Imperials prepared for the next assault.

But aside from Imperial ballistae continuing to fling projectiles at the defenders at irregular intervals, no other attacks took place.

Mari looked up as one of the Imperial missiles went past overhead, flaming brightly against the darkening overcast. A few days ago, she realized, she would felt the urge to duck. Now she just watched as the burning projectile fell among the buildings behind the third wall, spraying fiery fragments that the reserves raced to try to extinguish.

Alain, sitting beside her, placed his hand on hers.

"What are you thinking of?" Mari asked.

"I am thinking of you burning down the city hall in Ringhmon. Here we are, once again dealing with fire."

"I wasn't actually *trying* to burn down the city hall," Mari reminded him. "That just happened."

He ran his finger along the shoulder of her jacket, where a fresh score stood out. "This just happened as well."

"Thanks for shoving me out of the way in time."

"I hope I have a husband like you someday, Sir Mage," Sergeant Kira said.

"There's only one like him," Mari said. "And he's mine. —What's the matter?"

"Oh…just…we took a muster." Kira leaned back, her eyes closed. "It's easy in the heat of the fight not to notice too much who's fallen. But then you do the muster and you realize who's not there anymore."

Mari, feeling that words were useless, reached out to grip Sergeant Kira's shoulder.

Dinner came late, but for a wonder included hot soup and fresh bread. "They're using up supplies in case we have to fall back again," Kira advised. "And they know we need this. That's one thing about Field Marshal Klaus, he looks after his people."

The fires in front of the wall were burning down, but as the sun set the Imperials fired a volley from what must have been every ballista they had, the flaming projectiles racing across the sky to set off dozens of fires behind the third wall.

Field Marshal Klaus came by, saluting. "Lady, would you care to accompany me on a tour of the battlement?"

"Sure." Mari got to her feet, Alain beside her.

They walked to the left. The battlement seemed to go on forever, broken occasionally by defensive towers bristling with weaponry. Soldiers came to attention as Mari passed, saluting, smiling, looking at her with the hope of drowning sailors who had just spotted a rescue ship. After a while, Mari realized her face was hurting. Holding a false, confident smile wasn't easy on jaw and cheek muscles.

She saw the wariness with which many of the defenders regarded Alain, and so made a point of linking her arm in his and turning her smile on him frequently. Alain returned a look which told her that he appreciated her efforts.

And so they walked along the darkened battlement, their path illuminated by shielded lanterns, Mari greeting individuals, everyone expressing confidence, while to the north the brooding menace of the Imperial legions waited for the dawn.

After reaching the eastern end of the battlement, where the fitted stone met the living rock of the valley wall towering into the sky, they began retracing their steps along street level to speak with those in reserve and the support people like the cooks and the healers. Those reserve units not committed to fighting fires were trying to rest, but Mari greeted those who were awake. She spoke with Major Danel and his remaining cavalry from Tiae, feeling an odd sense of anxiety as she left them. That done, Field Marshal Klaus led the small group back on the wall where they walked down the right-hand side of the battlement.

Mari paused when she saw a single man in the uniform of Tiae saluting her. "Where are the others?"

"I'm all that's left, Lady. Of the rifles, that is. The Imperials have been concentrating their fire on us." He sounded proud of that.

"How are you doing for ammunition?" Mari tried not to let her distress show.

"Got plenty, Lady. Bullets the others didn't have a chance to fire."

He hefted his rifle. "Thanks for letting us make a big mark on the battle."

How did one respond to someone expressing thanks for the deaths of his comrades and his own likely soon to follow? "Thank you for being here."

When they reached her banner again, Mari was both physically and emotionally exhausted. After bidding farewell to Field Marshal Klaus, she huddled next to Alain, hoping she would have another night without dreams.

Unable to rest, she went through the remaining packs of ammunition, counting the clips and loading loose rounds into emptied clips.

That done, Mari gazed south, wondering how things were at Pacta.

"You should sleep, Lady," Sergeant Kira said, her voice soft in the night. "You'll need your strength tomorrow."

"Another day like today, huh?"

"Maybe worse."

Mari sighed, wondering what "worse" could be. "Thanks for being here, Kira."

"It's an honor and a pleasure, Lady."

"The honor and the pleasure are mine, sister."

Mari watched another ballista projectile trace a fiery path across the sky and slam down in the buildings below. The night was at least half gone.

She must have passed out from exhaustion after that. The next thing she knew, she was being shaken awake as breakfast rations were passed out.

* * *

They attacked at dawn, ballistae firing volleys of projectiles, clouds of crossbow bolts filling the air, and endless waves of legionaries and scaling ladders trying to surmount the battlement.

Alain destroyed another siege tower.

Mari helped Sergeant Kira wipe out another attempt to place a Mechanic bomb at the gate.

Her rifle became useless when the operating rod cracked, probably due to the haste with which they were being manufactured. Mari drew her pistol and used that as legionaries fought to gain a toehold on the battlement.

The defenders fought off one assault, then a second, then a third.

Mari stared up at the thickening overcast, guessing that it was nearly noon. Alain, weary from casting spells and using his knife in hand-to-hand fighting, slumped beside her.

She hadn't heard any rifle fire from the battlement to the right since the second assault, and guessed that the last Tiae rifle was dead.

The portion of the battlement defended by the Third Regiment had shrunk as more and more soldiers were killed or wounded. It felt like an awful lottery, Mari thought, one where chance alone decided who lived and who died.

Sergeant Kira knelt behind the battlement beside Mari. Kira had been next to her all day, once killing a legionary who had reached the battlement and, unseen by Mari, had leveled a crossbow at her. Alain had told her of that. Now Kira rested her head against the stone like one driven beyond endurance.

Mari kneeled beside her. "Are you all right?"

Sergeant Kira nodded, reloading the rifle, then looked at her. "Lady Mari. I wish to say again that it has been an honor fighting alongside you. Thank you."

"Thank you," Mari said. She suddenly realized how much she had come to like Kira in a very short but very intense time. "Call me Mari when we're alone."

"You honor me…Mari," Kira paused, her eyes looking at something invisible to Mari. "You will tell your children of me?"

"Of course. I said I would."

Sergeant Kira smiled at her. "I'm not afraid. Tell my brother I fought well." The Imperial brass horns called the legions to the attack again, and Kira came to her feet, resting her rifle on the parapet, taking careful aim again.

An instant later she jerked backward, falling loosely onto her back, eyes open and staring up sightlessly at the sky. Mari stared at the crossbow bolt protruding from Sergeant Kira's forehead. With one trembling hand, Mari reached to touch Kira's face. Neither the woman's face nor eyes moved. Reaching higher, Mari's fingers closed Kira's unresisting eyelids.

Too much. Too much. The long fights on the first wall and the second wall and now the third wall. The retreats. The death, the killing, the dying, the city burning and being smashed around them. And now Sergeant Kira dead as well.

Mari heard someone sobbing, loud gasps of pain and sorrow, and only gradually realized it was her. Her entire body was shaking, tears streaming down her face to splash onto the dusty stone beneath.

She heard the latest Imperial assault hit the wall.

As if acting on its own, one of Mari's arms reached out, grabbing the rifle and pulling it gently from Sergeant Kira's unresisting grasp. In a convulsive motion, Mari lunged up and forward, bringing the rifle down on the parapet. Setting the sights on an Imperial crossbow wielder, Mari fired, seeing the figure jerk and fall. She couldn't feel anything, couldn't hear anything even though she was dimly aware of bullets and crossbow bolts tearing past or striking the wall near her. The world seemed to have gone gray, all of the colors pale and washed out, only the figures of the Imperial soldiers clear in her sight.

She aimed carefully at another crossbow carrying soldier, her mind numb, fired, shifted aim again to an Imperial centurion urging legionaries forward, fired, shifted aim again to a Mechanic with a rifle, fired...

"Mari!" Alain must be yelling, but his voice sounded faint and far away. A hand seized her and pulled her back and down. Alain shook her. "Mari! Your weapon is no longer working!"

She looked down, seeing that she was still pulling the trigger but without result. The ammunition clip was empty. Still acting in a daze, Mari ejected the empty clip, dug in her pocket for a full one, slammed it home, then shrugged off Alain's hands and reared up to level the rifle at the Imperials once more.

The rifle leaped in her arms, slamming back against her shoulder, as she aimed and pulled the trigger again and again, blinking as tears momentarily obscured the Imperial soldiers in her sights.

Rock dust sprayed her as a bullet struck very close. Mari rubbed her eyes, trying to see well enough to aim, then Alain's hands had her once more and were pulling her down.

"Mari! Please!"

She shoved Alain away with a snarl as the top of a scaling ladder thudded against the battlement nearby. The rifle was empty again. Mari yanked out her pistol, flipped off the safety, pointed it at the ladder and fired as a legionary pulled himself up.

Knocked off the ladder by the impact of Mari's bullet, the Imperial soldier fell downward with a despairing cry. Ignoring the projectiles still aimed at her, Mari leaned up and over to fire down at more soldiers climbing the ladder. They fell, too. Something fired at her sliced across one cheek and left a bloody gash in its wake, but she kept shooting at the endless stream of soldiers until the slide on the pistol stayed back, indicating the clip on that was empty, too.

Alain was setting fire to another ladder just to the side. Mari glanced around, still numb inside, and grabbed the empty rifle. Setting the butt against the top of the Imperial ladder, she shoved with more force than she would have guessed possible for her. The ladder toppled backwards, soldiers leaping off of it as it fell, crashing down among the attackers.

Mari flipped the rifle around, loaded another clip, and emptied it into another group of soldiers trying to raise a different ladder.

For the moment, there were no enemies coming up the wall near them. Mari fell to her knees, exhausted and stunned, next to Sergeant Kira's body. She couldn't see any other defenders on the battlement near her and in a vague way wondered why.

"Mari." Alain was beside her again, though his voice still seemed to come from far away. "They have broken through to the left and right. Orders have come to fall back to the next wall. I told the others to leave. We must also leave now."

"No. I won't leave Kira."

"She fought to save this city, Mari. Dying uselessly will betray what she fought for. She is no longer here. She has gone to the next dream. What you see is only what she has left behind. She would not want you to die here. We must leave now!"

Mari glared at Alain, shivering with reaction, then nodded wordlessly. He pulled Mari to her feet, but Mari broke away to grab the rifle and the remaining packs of ammunition before running toward the stairs.

Feelings were returning to her, foremost among them fear as Mari realized there weren't any living Confederation soldiers visible amidst the smoke and dust around them. As they reached street level an Imperial soldier appeared, charging toward them from the left, sword held ready. Mari felt another surge of rage, giving her extra strength as she swung the rifle like a long club, slamming the legionary to the side. An explosion erupted in the front ranks of more legionaries coming after the first, Alain staggering beside her from the effort he had just expended.

As if a switch had been thrown, the world came fully alive around Mari again, the rattle of crossbow bolts fired by legionaries who had gained the battlement striking the pavement around her, the clash of metal on metal, screams of rage and pain, blood bright red on weapons and bodies. Her arms hurt and she was desperately tired. And more legionaries were rushing toward them.

Mari put one shoulder under Alain's, taking most of his weight, and ran. Part of her marveled that she still had the strength to help Alain, and part of her wondered what price she would later pay for expending her strength so recklessly. The street seemed endless, the buildings on either side crumbling in flames.

She could hear the hoarse shouts of the Imperials coming on behind. Her legs began to falter, the last dregs of her energy draining out.

Alain pulled himself away from her, lessening her burden. But as she ran alongside him, her heart pounding, her legs quivered with that deep weakness that meant they wouldn't keep moving much longer no matter how badly Mari needed them to.

But they were finally in the open area before the fourth wall, and the safety of the main gate was in sight, and Mari kept going, she and Alain side by side, each moving as fast as possible so the other would have to keep up.

She made out a line of cavalry stretched in front of the gate. It wasn't a long line. The soldiers sat astride their horses, lances pointed skyward, as defenders streamed between them to safety. Over the cavalry a green and gold banner waved.

Mari heard a triumphant roar behind her. She could not afford to turn her head to look, knowing that if she did so she would surely stumble and fall, but she knew without seeing what the roar meant. Legionaries were pouring into the open area as well, running down laggard defenders. They had seen Mari and Alain, a Mechanic and a Mage together, knew who the two must be and that the daughter and her Mage were almost within their grasp.

She tried to run faster, cursing her lungs and her legs as they betrayed her.

Was it fear or fatigue that caused the world to slow down? Everything began happening at a snail-like pace, the exultant cries of the legionaries drawn out, her motion over the ground as sluggish as if she were running through waist-deep water, every detail of the waiting cavalry clear.

They were the rest of those sent by Queen Sien, the Tiae soldiers who had not received rifles and whose only weapons were lance and sword. They sat in their saddles, side by side, a single row forty-six cavalry wide. Mari saw the heads of their horses tossing in slow motion, the mist of the horses' breath spreading in the air like syrup, the lances of the cavalry coming down to level position with the ponderous pace of mighty trees toppling.

As she and Alain ran between two of the cavalry, she saw Major Danel look down at her gravely, one hand to his helm in salute, before the hand swept down faster and faster to grasp his sword and draw it as the world began moving at a normal pace again.

"For Tiae!"

Mari reached the gate and staggered to a halt, lungs burning, turning to see the small force of cavalry charging the overwhelming numbers of legionaries swarming toward the gate. "No."

If the legionaries had been in formation, shields locked and spears forming a bristling barricade, the small number of cavalry would have been brushed aside. But the hasty Imperial advance had left units strung out and broken up. The legionaries attacking the gate were more of a mob than an organized force at the moment the cavalry charged, the weight of human and horse and their reckless pace giving the cavalry far greater force than their numbers alone could have produced.

The legionaries knew it. Some fell back, others stopped to form small pockets of defense, and a few tried to stand against the charge on their own.

The cavalry of Tiae hit and rolled them back, turning the Imperial assault into chaos.

"Lady, please!"

Mari looked to see other defenders urging her to get farther inside the gate. She stumbled back, seeing the gates beginning to swing shut as the cavalry rode back inside.

What was left of it.

Less than half as many cavalry rode back as had charged, accompanied by a few riderless mounts staying with the other horses.

Mari couldn't see Major Danel among them.

The gate thudded shut and the massive bars were lowered to seal it. Defenders stood around it, leaning on the gate, breathing heavily, worn out.

She could hear the legionaries shouting again, faintly hear orders being called on the other side of the wall.

A mare with a sword wound on one flank ran past her, eyes wide and white with fear.

That sight shocked her mind into motion again. "Get up on the wall!" Mari shouted. "Get up there and stop them! They're going to be putting up ladders! Move!"

Defenders bolted into action, most racing up the stairs, others gathering as the ground reserve. Mari, who a moment before had thought herself incapable of taking another step, joined the movement up the stairs until she reached the battlements and clung to a stone crenellation.

She stared at the rifle she was holding, trying to remember how she had come to reclaim it, memory of Sergeant Kira's death nearly overwhelming her again. On the heels of that, her last sight of Major Danel came back to her. Mari's hands shook badly as she ejected the empty clip, pulled the pack loaded with more ammunition off her back, loaded a fresh clip, and swung herself about to look down at the attackers.

An officer near the wall was gesturing, directing legionaries carrying ladders.

Mari aimed and fired, her hands steady now, and the officer jerked and fell.

She caught sight of Mechanics carrying a heavy object through the disorganized mass of attackers, the dark jackets easy to spot amid the Imperial uniforms and armor. Mari killed three of them with rapid shots, and as the others fled she called to Alain. "Another bomb. Get it."

He nodded, braced himself against the battlement, and sent his heat at the object.

The explosion tore through the Imperials.

A bullet pinged off the battlement near Mari.

She saw another dark jacket, someone kneeling to fire. A Mechanics Guild assassin. The assassin fired again, the bullet striking a bit beneath Mari this time, as she steadied her rifle on the battlement, aimed, and fired.

The assassin jolted from the impact of her shot and dropped to lie unmoving.

There were attempts by the legionaries to raise ladders, but only a few had been brought forward from the third wall, and the defenders were making free use of the fresh supply of rocks and bricks stockpiled on the battlements of the fourth wall, hurling them with deadly effect. The legionaries, disordered and exhausted, fell away.

Mari slumped down behind the battlement, staring at nothing, Alain by her side.

Sergeant Kira was dead.

Major Danel probably was, too.

She had no idea how long she had sat there when a few old soldiers came along the battlement, carrying buckets of water and bottles as well as boxes of crackers and jerky.

Mari saw a bottle thrust at her. Her throat felt choked with dust. She took the bottle and drank.

The liquid scorched a trail down her throat. The dust was gone, but it felt as though the lining of her throat had been burnt out as well. Hastily lowering the bottle, Mari coughed and gasped for breath.

Alain, alarmed, checked the bottle. "This is brandy," he told Mari. "Not water."

"I guessed that already," Mari managed to reply in a hoarse whisper.

A dipper of water was held out this time, and she drank gratefully, still shuddering from the unexpected shock of the alcohol. Mari grabbed a piece of jerky. "Thank you," she whispered.

She sat there, holding the jerky, unable to focus any thoughts until Alain spoke gently. "You must eat."

Bending her head, Mari began chewing the hard jerky, noticing neither taste nor texture. She kept chewing and swallowing until it was gone, leaning back against the battlement. One of her hands, resting on her legs before her, kept twitching and jerking, but as she sat the shivers slowly decreased.

"Lady."

Mari roused herself from a fog of sorrow and fatigue to see Lieutenant Bruno crouched down before her. "Yes."

"Everyone is amazed, Lady. The way that you and Sir Mage Alain held that part of the third wall, all by yourselves, and then made it through to this wall. You held up the legions along here enough to ensure they didn't get any footholds on the fourth wall."

Mari gazed at the lieutenant, trying to understand his words. "How are we doing?"

Bruno hesitated. "Field Marshal Klaus is checking on the left, but he says it could be worse."

"We've lost three walls in four days."

"Four walls remain, Lady."

"Yeah." Mari tilted her head back and breathed deeply. The overcast filled the sky now, heavy clouds threatening rain. *This time of year we usually have storms that we say come in easy and slow, then hit hard and fast.* "Sergeant Kira died," she told Lieutenant Bruno. "I think her platoon has been wiped out."

"I'm sorry," Bruno said. "Lieutenant Kaede is also dead. The field marshal will assign another unit for your protection."

"No. Having to stay close to me is too hazardous." She realized what that meant for Alain and looked at him, but he only gazed back without any sign of worry. "Does the field marshal need to see me in person?" There might be candid appraisals of their situation that he wouldn't want to risk sharing with others.

"No, Lady," Bruno said. "He's making certain that all the necessary supplies get to the troops on the wall and that they're sorted out into their units so they can fight better when the Imperials come at us again."

Mari nodded, feeling incredibly tired. "All right. If he needs anything from me, tell me." She looked around, realizing that something was missing. "We left my banner at the third wall. I have to let everyone know I'm here. Alain, can you help me up?"

It took Bruno stepping in to get them both on their feet. Mari grimaced, cleared her expression, then looked to the right. "Thank you, Lieutenant. They need to see me."

"It would mean a lot to everyone," Bruno agreed.

"Let's walk, Alain."

She headed down the battlement, pausing when she saw a captain. "Is Colonel Teodor down this way? Commander of the Third Regiment?"

The captain, haggard with fatigue, shook his head. "No, Lady. Colonel Teodor…Colonel Teodor died on the third wall. As far as I know, I am now the commander of the Third Regiment. We've…we've lost a lot of our number."

Mari paused to gather her strength. "What's your name?"

"Captain Niklas, Lady."

She gripped his shoulder. "You and I will have to do our best, then."

Niklas roused himself, nodding. "Yes, Lady. We all will."

Three walls in four days. The Imperial horns were sounding their triumph again. She had no idea how far away her army still was.

CHAPTER TEN

THEY HELD THE fourth wall for most of the next day, throwing back repeated attacks by fresh legions. Alain stayed close to Mari, concerned by the fatalism with which she fought, as if death was now inevitable and she no longer wished to run from it. But she took no insane chances, just dangerous ones, and after a certain point every choice they faced was dangerous.

Late in the afternoon, word came down the battlement that a secondary gate had been forced. There were no longer enough reserves on the ground to seal the breach, so they fell back again, through the flaming ruins of the buildings between the fourth and fifth walls, most of the surviving Confederation cavalry hurling themselves at the pursuing legions to buy time for the footsore defenders to make it to the safety of the fifth wall.

Mari led Alain up to stand near the main gate again, but the legions did not move against it while light remained.

Field Marshal Klaus came by, his eyes dark, and spoke in quiet tones with Mari as they stood on the battlement. When they were done, he saluted her and went back to what was left of his headquarters staff, all but the most essential having been sent to combat units to replace a few of the losses.

Alain watched the Imperials occupying the city between the fourth and fifth walls, looking for any indication that the Mage Guild was returning to the fight. But his sense of other Mages still showed them far from the fight. "Their numbers may be lessening," he told Mari. "I cannot tell for certain. They are too far away."

"Too bad the legions' numbers aren't lessening," Mari muttered.

He could not tell when the sun set, only when the gloom of the overcast darkened even more.

It was some time later when the clouds which had been piling up in ever thicker, darker masses finally had enough of watching humans slaughter each other. As he and Mari huddled against the battlement of the fifth wall, light suddenly flared nearby, illuminating everyone brightly. The lighting bolt struck the top of a bartizan a hundred lances down the wall, followed by an immense crash of thunder that shook the world. More lightning stabbed downward in jagged patterns, flaying the highest points in the city, and the roll of thunder grew until it seemed as if the sky had unleashed artillery far more powerful than humans had ever created.

Mari pressed herself against him. "We shouldn't be so high in a lightning storm," she gasped.

"We could get hurt," Alain said.

Her laughter held a note of frenzy to it. "You're right. We should be more careful. You know, the Senior Mechanics suppressed a lot of knowledge and technology, but at least they were smart enough to retain lightning rods. Those are the metal poles sticking up from the highest points. They attract the lightning so it doesn't hit anything else."

Even after days of horrible fighting, even when teetering on the edge of collapse, Mari kept trying to explain Mechanic things to him. Alain held her close, loving who she was and fearing for her.

He stared at the bartizan, memory tugging at him.

It was the one where he had once taken his farewell of Mari, she to go south on orders of the Mechanics Guild and he to go north by command of the Mage Guild. The place where he had seen the vision of the two of them fighting on a wall of Dorcastle amid a great battle.

That moment, perhaps two years gone, felt like an eternity ago.

He could not help wondering again why his only vision of the future beyond this had been one of Mari lying badly injured. Nothing after that.

There must be something after that, Alain vowed to himself. "I love you," he said to Mari.

"I love you," she whispered in reply, her head buried against him.

Rain did not simply begin. It fell in abrupt, heavy torrents as if endless buckets had been upended. Mari and Alain held each other as the storm raged, pressing against the battlement that offered some small protection from the winds driving the sheets of rain.

So tired that he fell asleep even when being pummeled by rain, Alain felt himself awaken. It was still very dark. He did not move, holding Mari and feeling the rain still pelting them though not as badly as earlier, trying to make sense of a vague feeling that something was about to happen.

More thunder rolled through the air, but something about it sounded different.

Mari jerked her head up, staring into the rain-driven darkness.

"What is it?" Alain asked, sensing alarm in her.

"Some of that thunder...that last crash." Mari got to her feet, crouched against the rain, peering to the right. "Do you hear shouts?"

He could not over the rain and occasional thunder, but before Alain could answer, Confederation trumpets began blowing signals.

"Fall back!" the nearest officers bellowed over the storm. "The Imperials have breached the wall! Fall back!"

"The Mechanics Guild must have used the storm as cover to get a large explosive charge next to the wall and detonate it by surprise," Mari yelled to Alain.

Imperial horns began sounding a call Alain knew all too well. "The legions have been told to advance. All-out attack," he told Mari.

"I can hear!"

"We can't hold!" a messenger yelled, racing down the battlement toward them. "The hole in the wall is too large! The Imperials are coming through fast! Get back to the next wall!"

"Can you run?" Alain asked Mari.

"Yeah." She gripped her rifle, made sure she had her pack of remaining ammunition, then led him down the steps off the wall as fast as the dark and the rain-slick stone permitted. Soldiers were fleeing all around them. They reached the ground, where soldiers were running south, abandoning small stockpiles of supplies behind the wall as all semblance of organization vanished in the chaos born of darkness, the raging storm, and near-panic.

Alain followed Mari to an intersection where an officer was waving soldiers off. "Back! Not this way! The Imperials already have this area. The last reserves are holding them! Go around!"

Mari dodged down a side street, Alain sticking with her like a shadow just as he had every moment. Part of a building, weakened by fire and battered by the storm, crumbled as they ran past, blocking part of the street.

By the time they had scrambled over the debris, no one was else was visible in the extremely small range of vision offered by the night and the storm. "This way, right?" Mari asked Alain.

"Yes." The training of a Mage acolyte, often cruel and brutal, had left Alain with an ability to concentrate even under the worst circumstances. He was certain that south still lay in the direction that Mari had pointed.

They had to run around more debris, but as they reached the open street again they found themselves in the midst of a large group of soldiers hurrying south. Alain's sense of relief died as he realized that his foresight was nearly screaming a warning of danger.

He peered closely at the nearest soldiers, then grabbed Mari and put his lips close to her ear. "Mari! These are Imperials!"

Mari's intake of breath was so loud that Alain feared she had attracted their attention. How could they break contact with the Imperials, who were rushing toward one of the same gates that the retreating defenders were trying to reach? As Alain tried to think of an answer, he knew that the most important thing was to avoid being noticed—

Mari's yell pierced the night. "Halt! Who is in charge of this unit? Halt!"

The tones of a Mechanic being as arrogant as a Mechanic could be worked on legionaries drilled to obedience. The Imperials stumbled to a halt.

One came shoving his way through the ranks toward Mari and Alain. Alain saw that Mari had crossed her arms in such a way that one hand covered her armband of the New Day, and he quickly did the same, stepping back so that he could not be clearly seen in the murk of the night and the storm.

"Who the blazes gave that order!" the Imperial roared.

"I did!" Mari roared back. "Who the blazes are you? What unit is this?"

For centuries, commons had been forced to obey Mechanics. For centuries, Imperial soldiers of the legions had been trained to respond to authority with obedience. In the middle of the dark, rain-lashed street, the legionary commander reacted in the only way the product of that history could. "Centurion Markel, First Cohort, Twentieth Legion."

"Why are you running in the wrong direction?" Mari demanded, still maintaining her angry, arrogant Mechanic attitude. "The next wall is that way!" She pointed down a large intersecting side street just visible through the gloom.

"That way? But, Honored Mechanic—"

"You got turned around in the dark!" Mari shouted at him. She held up her far-talker. "This tells me the way to the gate and it is *that* way. This part of the city is designed to trick invaders by leading them in circles. Didn't you get briefed on that? The gate is that way! Hurry! Tell any other units you encounter who are running the wrong way!"

Better men than the centurion would have been fooled by Mari's performance and the brandishing of a mysterious Mechanic device, Alain thought. The centurion hastily saluted. "This way! Fast!" The Imperials took off through the storm down the side road.

Mari watched until the last legionary had passed, then reached to grab Alain. They ran.

"It might not take them long to realize I sent them down a road that runs parallel to the walls," Mari gasped. "But at least we slowed them down."

"You are amazing," Alain said, resolving again to learn what "parallel" meant.

"No, I'm just scared out of my mind."

The quality of the rain and the wind and the darkness changed, telling them that they had run out into the open area before the sixth wall. More figures loomed ahead out of the rain. "What unit?" Alain called, wanting to know before they got among the soldiers this time.

The reply came in the welcome accents of the Confederation. "Elements of the Third, Sixth and Seventh Regiments. Friend or foe?"

"Friends!" Mari shouted in reply.

"What unit are you from?"

"None of them! I'm in charge!"

They reached the friendly soldiers, who were moving back toward the sixth wall while trying to maintain a defensive line facing north. "It's the daughter! How did you get through the Imperials?"

"I told them to go away," Mari said, her breathing rapid. "This includes the Third Regiment? Is Captain Niklas here?"

The reply took a moment. "Lady, we lost Captain Niklas part of the way back. Imperials came charging at us. He took command of a rear guard and told the rest of us to run." The woman speaking hesitated, her voice breaking. "They couldn't have made it. None of them. They held off the Imperials for us."

"All…all right," Mari said. "We honor their sacrifice by continuing the fight."

They reached the gate in the sixth wall and rushed inside. Alain tried to see how many soldiers were with them. Elements of three regiments, someone had said. That should be a few thousand soldiers. But he could see only a few hundred.

The soldiers at the gate turned to Mari. "Lady? Should we shut the gate?"

"What?"

"You are in command," Alain reminded her in a low voice that barely carried over the sounds of the storm.

Mari did not answer him but ran to the gate, looking out into the dark, the rain drumming on the rock pavement and wall. "Is there anybody else out there?" Mari asked, her voice tight.

"We…we don't know, Lady. Maybe."

Alain stood beside her, looking and listening.

A single figure in Confederation uniform wavered out of the gloom, staggering through the gate. "Is there anybody behind you?" one of the soldiers demanded of him.

"We got hit. Imperials everywhere. I couldn't tell. I…" The lone soldier's voice trailed off.

"Lady?" the soldiers at the gate asked with increasing urgency.

Alain wondered if he was hearing the rhythmic pounding of the boots of soldiers in formation growing closer. Those would have to be Imperials. Did he hear them? Or was it his imagination creating an illusion of imminent danger?

A half-dozen cavalry rode of out the storm, their worn-out mounts blowing clouds of breath through the wet air. "I think we're the last," one said. "I don't know. It's a mess out there. I don't know."

The foot soldiers looked to Mari for orders.

"Close the gate!" Mari said, walking backwards. Alain touched her shoulder and felt tension making the muscles rigid. "Close it!"

Alain stood with Mari as the gate swung ponderously closed and the soldiers fastened the locking bars across it one by one. "There was probably no one left outside," he told Mari.

"We don't know that," she said in a toneless voice. "We don't know how many I might have just locked out and left to the Imperials." Mari turned again, slowly. "You," she ordered a soldier. "Find Field Marshal Klaus. Tell him this gate is closed, and that Mage Alain and I are here."

"Yes, Lady." The soldier trotted off into the storm, wavering from exhaustion.

Alain looked around at the troops who had made it from the

prior wall, seeing them standing about. "Find your commanders," he ordered. "The senior survivor in each regiment. Get organized."

"I want one regiment to stay down here to hold the gate," Mari said. "The Sixth. The Third and the Seventh get up on the wall with me."

"Yes, Lady." Given clear instructions, the soldiers got into motion, dividing into their units.

"Shall we go up?" Alain asked Mari.

"Does it still matter?" she said almost too low to hear.

"Yes. Are you hurt?"

"Not yet. Let's go. Thanks for helping me with those orders. I'm a...little worn out."

They scrambled up the rain-slick steps, the storm continuing to pelt them. Alain helped Mari across the worst stretches until at last they reached the battlement and stared out into the night for signs of the Imperials.

Lieutenant Bruno came down the battlement, gasping with relief when he saw Mari. "All gates are secure, Lady, though it was close getting them shut before some of the Imperials reached them. Field Marshal Klaus is feeding in the last reserves. The Imperials haven't made any attempt to assault this wall yet. They'll probably wait for daylight."

"Thank you," Mari said.

Alain was not surprised that she said nothing about her role in confusing and delaying the Imperials. Respecting her wishes in the matter, he also stayed silent.

Bruno left, and Mari sat down heavily. Alain helped her against the battlement and sat with her, their backs against the stone of the sixth wall. As he slowly recovered from the strain of the most recent escape, Alain noticed something about Mari that caused him increasing concern. She sat next to him, their shoulders touching, her rifle between her legs, one end resting on the stone and the other slanted upwards toward the enemy. She had her hand cupped over the open end to keep rain from getting in. Her breathing was calming, but

Mari did not say anything, instead staring straight ahead. Even in the darkness with the rain still falling, Alain could tell that her expression was oddly lacking in feeling.

Alain had never forgotten his first impressions of Mari, how the open intensity of her emotions had been almost painful to someone used to dealing with other Mages, who hid any feelings that still existed inside. Mari was acting oddly Mage-like now, though, her face offering no clue to any emotions.

"Mari?"

"Yes." Her voice, too, lacked feeling. It came out listless, not just tired but as if every emotion had been wrung from it.

"Are you all right?"

"I'm not hurt. I told you that." The words carried no force and were swiftly absorbed in the drum of the rain as it fell on the stone around them.

"What is wrong?" Alain pressed, striving to put as much worry as he could into his own voice. "You had to give that order. You had to close the gate."

"I know."

"If you had not diverted that cohort, the Imperials might have fallen on the defenders here before they could close the gate."

"I guess." She turned her head, her eyes searching him but the darkness hiding any feelings. "I'm just…not sad. Just tired. Sorry it's over."

"What is over?" He gestured over his shoulder to where they could hear the muffled sounds of the Imperials reaching the area before this wall in growing numbers. "Hopefully the rain will hinder the legions enough that they will not try again before dawn."

"I hope we still win, Alain." Mari leaned her head back so the rain was falling on her face, dripping off like a torrent of tears. "But I won't make it. It's over for me."

He felt cold inside. "Why do you say that? My vision did not guarantee such a thing. The elder said as long as I remained with you there was hope. I am here. There is hope."

She shook her head slightly, looking past him. "I can feel it. A person gets born with just so much luck, Alain. I must have born with an ocean of it to get this far." Mari sounded a tiny bit wistful, but otherwise emotionally numb. "So many others have died. But not me. And it's gone. I can feel it." She inhaled deeply, closing her eyes against the rain falling on them. "Maybe tonight, maybe tomorrow. I'm sorry."

"Mari," Alain said through growing desperation, "you will not die. Do not speak that way."

"Too much, Alain. Too much hatred, too much fighting…death…I can't—" She stopped speaking for a moment. "Do you remember the land north and west of Pacta? That spot not far from the ocean?"

"Yes," Alain said, hoping that Mari was about to speak of a more hopeful subject.

"That would be a nice place to live. I know you would like it there. When this is all over, you should go there, and build a nice house, and listen to the ocean. When you hear it, think of me." Her voice sounded listless again, devoid of hope or fear or anything else but acceptance of fate.

He could not reply for a moment, distress blocking his throat, but managed to get some words out. "I will think of you there, because both of us will be there. I will see you and I will think of you."

She shook her head slightly again, keeping her eyes closed. "We've only got a little time left together. Let's not argue."

Thunder rumbled again off to the left, lightning flaring inside the low clouds.

"I will not accept that it is hopeless," Alain said. "I will save you, or I will die trying."

"No, you mustn't do that."

"I will not leave this place alive unless you are with me," Alain said.

"No!' Mari's voice was regaining some feeling. "Stop being unfair."

"I will not leave you behind," Alain said, knowing that she would hear her own vow not to leave others behind echoed in that.

"I'm not leaving by choice, Alain," she said, her voice breaking slightly. "Why does everyone think I can do this? How could anyone keep trying? Don't push me. I can't handle it anymore. Let's get some sleep. Stay close."

He did not think she actually slept, and he could not sleep, his shoulder touching hers, trying to will confidence back into her. Why could he not do that? Why would such a spell not work? Why would no spell work on Mari? She was real. He was as certain of that as he was of his own reality. Why could he not use the power of the illusion to help her?

He feared that he might have only a very short time left to try to learn the answer.

* * *

At dawn the Imperials came again.

During the night, as the rain kept falling and occasional growls of thunder rolled across the beleaguered city, Mari had felt her despairing acceptance of her fate shifting to something else. She still didn't feel that her survival was likely, or even possible, but her determination to win, to ensure that her job was done no matter the cost, had grown to dominate her again. Yes, she might well die. Very likely would die. But she would not stop trying to win, because those she fought deserved to lose, *had* to lose, if the world was to have any hope of avoiding the Storm. If the sacrifices of those who had already died were to mean something more than a failed effort.

The rain still impeded her view, and the clouds allowed only a glimpse of the dawn's light. But Mari could see enough. The numbers of the enemy had been much diminished, but the attacking legions still filled the area before the sixth wall. To either side of her, the battlements were still occupied by defenders, but their ranks were thin in places. Behind them, on the ground, only small formations remained as reserves to reinforce threatened sections of the wall or deal with Imperial penetrations of any gates.

The Imperials had begun rolling forward a ram to use against the gate nearest Mari and Alain.

Alain stood watching it for so long that Mari wondered if something was wrong. Nearby Confederation soldiers were watching him anxiously.

The ram burst into flame as Alain loosed his spell, legionaries abandoning the burning wreck in a spot where its death throes helped block further Imperial attempts against that gate.

Imperial ballistae had been moved forward to fire directly at the battlement. One erupted into flame as Alain struck.

Mari took careful aim and dropped another Mechanic, then a centurion, wondering if he might be the same one she had bluffed the night before..

She didn't have much ammunition left.

As a soldier near her staggered and fell from the sword blow of a legionary trying to climb onto the battlement, Mari picked up a pike and shoved it into the legionary and onward to overbalance the ladder he had ridden up to the parapet.

The Imperials gained a toehold on the battlement to the left, only to have it wiped out by frantic defenders. They broke a gate to the right, only to have a few surviving Confederation ballistae slaughter the wave of attackers by launching projectiles directly into them.

The defenders threw back the first assault. Then the second.

They couldn't hold the third.

Mari wasn't sure if the retreat this time qualified as a rout. The only thing that saved the defenders, that allowed them to reach the seventh wall and close the gates, was that the Imperials didn't chase them as quickly as in the past. "They are tired, too," Alain gasped. "They have taken awful losses."

"We're more tired than they are," Mari said, leaning on the battlement, "and our losses have been awful as well."

Alain didn't deny that truth. But he did grasp her hand. "Live."

"I'll try."

Mari thought it was past noon, but night was still far off. Before the seventh wall the legions were gathering to take the final barrier defending Dorcastle. Behind the seventh wall lay the rest of the city and the uplands leading to Danalee, now packed with refugees, and the heart of the Confederation, with Tiae beyond.

Mari sat once again with her back against the parapet, a tight feeling of despair filling her, hearing crossbow bolts and occasional bullets striking the wall, staring upward and outward at the looming overcast that had finally ceased to spill rain but still blocked the sun.

Her pack was empty. She had one clip of ammunition left in her rifle and one clip in her pistol.

Lieutenant Bruno came up the nearest set of steps, limping but still moving, his face set in lines of endurance. He saw Mari and dropped lower to come close to the battlement but out of sight of Imperial crossbows firing at anything that showed. "Lady Mari, Field Marshal Klaus has been wounded. He told me to tell you that everything we have left is on this wall. There are no more commands left to give except stand and die."

"All right," Mari said, not knowing how else to reply to such a thing. She looked down the parapet on either side of her, seeing the defenders huddled there, trying to protect themselves while gathering strength. The seventh wall was the shortest of all, and only that allowed the remaining defenders to occupy its length. They hadn't been beaten yet, but they weren't far from that point. They had fought wall by wall, watching their comrades die in ones and twos and dozens and scores until further fighting seemed useless. On the other side of the wall Mari could hear the legions marshalling, preparing to assault this last bastion. The Imperials knew this was the last wall. They could surely feel victory waiting for them. They only had to take this wall and then their sacrifices would have meaning and be crowned with the greatest success in the history of the Empire.

And the Great Guilds would be that much closer to defeating the only chance the world had against the Storm that threatened to wipe away everything. Just so that they could maintain their power for a little longer.

"We'll stand then," she told Bruno, finding the strength to make her voice sound confident. "We'll hold here until my army arrives. It must be close by now."

"We will fight to the last," the lieutenant said. "But you, Lady: Field Marshal Klaus told me to inform you that…that your courage and commitment are unquestioned, and that you need not remain on the battlement any longer." Bruno gestured to a place behind the wall. "Most of the cavalry we could still gather and mount are there, along with two horses for you and your Mage."

Mari frowned at Bruno, trying to understand what he was saying. "Field Marshal Klaus wants me to lead a charge?"

"No, Lady, you can get away." Lieutenant Bruno pointed south. "You and your Mage. Get clear of Dorcastle and make it to Dana-lee, where you can organize another line of resistance to the Imperial attack."

"Me? And my Mage? What about everybody else? What about you and all of the other defenders?"

"We'll hold them as long as we can to give you the best chance of getting away."

She felt hot anger rising inside, burning away the apathy of despair that had once filled her. "What?"

Lieutenant Bruno, apparently used to having to explain things more than once to superior officers, began saying the same thing again.

"No," Mari interrupted. "I'm not going anywhere."

"But, Lady, the daughter's struggle—"

"It's not *my* struggle!" Her voice was rising, catching the attention of other defenders who looked toward her. "It's everyone's struggle!"

Bruno shook his head, momentarily letting his extreme weariness show. "Lady, ask anyone. You are the daughter of Jules. We can all see it in you. We've watched you and heard you and we all know it's true. No one else can do it. You have to stay alive no matter what, because we can't do this. We spent centuries waiting for you because we're not strong enough to do it alone. You have to leave us here so you can—"

"NO!" Mari struggled to her feet, glaring at the hapless lieutenant. "This isn't about me. Don't you understand? All of you!" she shouted as loudly as she could, her voice carrying along the battlement. "I am the one who can't do this alone! I am the one who needs you! They've lied to you! They've told you that you're inferior! They've kept you in chains! But you, each and every one of you, are the equal of anyone in this world!"

She was exposed to enemy fire, and heard crossbow bolts rattling off the battlement near her as the Imperials took their opportunity, as well as the occasional crash of a rifle shot and the snap of the bullets tearing past. But she stayed on her feet, raising one fist skyward as if defying even the low, leaden overcast. "I cannot win freedom for you! Only you can do that! Only you can win it, and only you can hold it! I will lead you! I will stand here and lead the defense of Dorcastle until the last breath of life leaves me! Because I will not leave you! I will not leave this wall! We will hold here, we will hold, we will save Dorcastle, we will save this world! Together!"

She kept her fist raised but swung up her other arm to point toward the Imperials. "They want to keep this world in chains! The Great Guilds and the Imperials who do their will! But we will not let them! We will be free! Our children will be free! Yours and mine! Because we held this wall, because we held this city, because we refused to allow ourselves to be beaten!" The harsh blare of Imperial horns sounding the attack came from below. "Stand up! Stand up and fight! So that our children will be free! Freedom!"

A roar erupted along the battlements that drowned out the battle cries of the Imperials hurling themselves at the last defense standing between them and victory. The defenders rose to their feet, unleashing a furious bombardment on the attackers, the air filling with shouts of "Freedom and the daughter!"

The front ranks of the Imperial assault shattered under a hail of rocks, spears, and crossbow bolts. Startled by the vigorous defense put up by an enemy they had thought tottering on the edge of defeat, the Imperial attack faltered, but only for a moment. Their officers screaming commands and brandishing swords to threaten their own soldiers as much as the enemy, the legions surged against the wall again.

Mari heard the fire aimed at her, but she felt no fear. She was beyond that, in a place where nothing mattered any more but continuing the fight. She brought up her rifle, standing in almost full view of the enemy, and began firing. An Imperial officer fell. Legionaries at the head of scaling leaders dropped. Mari aimed and fired, the weapon bucking against her shoulder with each shot, knowing that the last clip for the rifle would soon be empty.

Alain stood beside her, his long knife in one hand. A ram exploded into flame as it approached the nearest gate, then another ball of heat exploded among the Imperial ranks.

Two Mechanics reeled away from the explosion. Mari shot both of them before leaning out enough to pump shots into the legionaries trying to hold scaling ladders against the wall.

The slide on the rifle jerked back and stayed there. Out of ammunition. Setting the rifle aside, Mari methodically drew her pistol, knowing that her last clip for that weapon was already partially used. She took a firing stance, extending her arm forward and down toward the enemy and began firing once again with slow deliberation, aiming carefully between each shot. One shot, two shots, three...

An Imperial came up a ladder just to Mari's left, clashing swords with the nearest defender. Mari shot the legionary, seeing the slide on her pistol staying back, too. She bent down to grab a dropped sword as Alain dashed past her, using his long knife with deadly skill to kill the next two legionaries coming up the ladder. In the brief pause afforded by his blows, Alain and the Confederation soldier shoved the scaling ladder to the side so that it toppled and fell.

All along the wall the Imperial wave hit and hung there, striving desperately to surmount the last obstacle in its path. The legionaries had spent day after day charging to the attack, suffering horrendous losses as their commanders flung them forward time and again. The worn-out, wounded legions pushed against the exhausted, decimated defenders of Dorcastle. The strident blare of the Imperial horns bellowed the call to attack, while the defenders of the last wall screamed their defiance. "Freedom and the daughter!"

Beneath Mari, a sally gate was forced, but the small force of cavalry gathered to escort her to safety charged the Imperials coming through and drove them back until the broken gate could be shoved closed again and barricaded.

The Imperial assault clung to the wall, reaching for the top, running into an unyielding line of defenders. The legions pushed, and halted, then slowly, step by step, began falling back like a tide which has reached its highest point and now must recede.

Mari held her empty pistol in one hand and the sword in the other, looking for any attackers still trying to come up the wall, seeing none. All along the battlement, defenders were cheering and waving their weapons at the legionaries who had fallen back. The Imperial soldiers were staggering with weariness, not even yelling back to match the defiance of the defenders. They just stared upward while their officers bellowed and beat at them with the flats of their swords, slowly reforming the Imperial units.

Reforming them for another attack.

Lieutenant Bruno stood nearby, radiating joy, awe, and pride as he looked at Mari. "We held them. Lady, we held them!"

Mari, her burst of anger-fueled energy spent, looked down the battlement and saw how many of the defenders had fallen while hurling back the latest attack. Saw how few defenders remained. How the piles of rocks and spears were gone, used up in repelling the last assault. Her own weapons were empty of ammunition, nothing more than clubs. She held a sword she barely knew how to use.

There was nothing left. Mari glanced at Alain, saw the grimness in his eyes, and knew he understood the same thing. They had held the legions this time, but the legions were already regrouping. They would come again. Only another miracle could stop them, and miracles didn't come in twos.

She heard the sweep of huge feathers overhead and felt a rush of wind.

Mari jerked her head up, staring in disbelief as a Roc glided low overhead, flying beneath the overcast despite the risk of Imperial projectiles. She could see the Mage who had created the bird, riding where the neck joined the body. Behind the Mage was a Mechanic, waving down at the defenders.

"Mari? Mari?" The words didn't come from either side, but from one pocket of her jacket.

Still gazing upwards, Mari dropped the sword, holstered her pistol, and fumbled out the far-talker, her hands trembling as she found and pushed the transmit button. "Here. This is Mari. Calu?"

"You got it! Big as life and twice as ugly! We thought we wouldn't get here in time. Part of your army is entering the city and coming on fast."

"Where have you— Why didn't you—" Mari saw more Rocs flying in just beneath the clouds, all carrying both a Mage and a Mechanic. Some of the Mechanics tossed objects down toward the Imperials, the objects exploding as they hit the ground. The "grenades" Alli had been working on, Mari realized as she tried to grasp what was happening.

She saw soldiers in the blue uniforms of her army running up the stairs to her left, all of them armed with rifles, lining the battlement and beginning to fire a barrage into the legionaries below, the rattle of gunfire forming a continuous roar that drowned out the calls of the Imperials.

More soldiers in blue came up onto the battlements to her right.

Young cavalry soldier Bete from her army dashed up the stairs nearest to Mari and Alain, carrying the banner of the New Day, and breathlessly planted the flag next to Mari.

The roar of fire from scores of rifles, then hundreds of rifles, echoed through the city.

The Imperial officers who had been beating their soldiers into another attack had stopped when the Rocs began swooping overhead. The Imperials were all staring upwards as the rifles of Mari's army began filling the air with lead and thunder. The legions had never faced that kind of punishment. No one had, in all the world. With the last wall standing strong, with fresh forces appearing before them bearing overwhelming firepower, the legions wavered.

They started running.

Legionaries, their officers, the few Mechanics with them near the front line. They all ran, down through the ruins of the city toward the harbor where the Imperial fleet was now being bombarded by some of Mari's Mechanics tossing firebombs from the backs of Mage-created Rocs.

"Mari?" Calu's voice came again. "How are you doing? Are you all right?" Mari raised the far-talker to her lips again. "Yeah. I'm…I'm all right." That was all she could get out. She stood there, dazed, gazing with disbelief on the retreating enemy. An occasional enemy figure was still turning to loose a crossbow bolt or fire a Mechanic rifle in their direction, but the rest were running. "We actually did it, Alain," she told him. "We held them. We saved Dorcastle. We beat the Great Guilds."

She didn't see the Mechanic assassin, one of the few still alive, who stopped long enough to aim and fire his last bullet.

Mari began turning to look at Alain, just having time to realize that he was staring not at the retreating legions, or at the Rocs overhead, or even at her, but at the stones beneath her feet as if they told of something horrible.

He began lunging toward her.

Too late.

Something slammed into her upper body as if a heavy hammer had struck her. Mari felt and saw the world spin wildly as her body fell, the pain almost lost in the shock of the moment. The spinning stopped as she came to rest on her back, staring up at the gray sky, unable to move.

Alain's face came into her field of vision, his expression openly terrified. "Mari! No!"

She could hear other voices, sounding as from a great distance, calling faintly and frantically. "She's been shot! The daughter has been shot!" Mari could hear the words, but couldn't understand what they meant.

The rock was hard beneath her. Something wet was all over her shirt and back. People were pushing at her, shoving her body around, but she was only vaguely aware of the pressure.

Darkness gathered around her, clouding her eyesight. She tried to focus on Alain as her vision faded. "Goodbye, love." Mari didn't know if she had actually been able to say that. The darkness covered her and filled her, leaving only a lingering sense of regret.

CHAPTER ELEVEN

ALAIN, ON A short bench against one wall, sat outside the room where Mari lay. Inside, behind a sealed door guarded by two grim-looking sentries, healers were working to save Mari's life in the small emergency hospital built into the back of the seventh wall.

Beside him sat Mechanic Calu, and on the other side Mage Asha. Both had rushed to join him as Mari was carried into the hospital, Calu looking ready to cry and even Asha revealing shock that anyone could see. Everyone else had been kept away.

Alain could not forget his last sight of Mari. Her shirt and jacket had been soaked with her own blood, her breathing shallow and labored, her mouth hanging open, death hovering very near. Just as in the awful vision he had first seen a year ago.

"I did not look in time," he whispered. "We retreated to the last wall. The Imperials came after us. We repelled the enemy attack. I did not think to look. I did not see that the stones beneath our feet were the same as in my foresight."

"It's not your fault," Calu said, his voice cracking with grief.

"You were beside her," Asha said. "You did what you could."

"It was not enough, it— You can sense her, Asha. What do you sense?"

Asha shook her head. "The fire of her inner self still burns, but it is weak and grows dimmer. It fades as she does. It feels...as if it will soon cease."

"It...cannot." Alain looked down at his hands, the hands that had just started to pull Mari down when the enemy bullet struck her. The hands that now felt useless. "The elder said that as long as I stayed with her, hope would remain. I stayed with her. Why did hope flee? Why is there nothing left?"

"She's hurt really bad," Calu said. "Nobody is stronger than Mari when it comes to spirit, but even she can't will itself out of this."

Asha grabbed Alain's arm so tightly that it hurt him. "Mage Alain. What did the elder say? About hope?"

"She said that if I stayed beside Mari that hope would remain."

"You are not beside her."

Calu jumped up. "Asha's right. Mari's still alive and you're out here!"

Alain felt a sudden shock of anger and fear, realizing that they were right, that in his dismay over Mari's injury he had forgotten what the elder's words might mean. "There must still be something that I can do."

They were all on their feet, Asha and Calu somehow beating Alain to the door and pushing aside the startled guards before they could protest. Alain slammed open the door, staring past the shocked faces of healers and their assistants to see Mari lying on a table nearby.

Some moved as if to block him, but Alain shoved his way through with all the speed he had. He had the impression of voices raised, but the words meant nothing to him. It was just noise.

Mari lay on the table, not moving. Her injury had been bandaged. Someone else lay nearby, a tube showing where blood was being sent from that person to Mari. But he could see that was not enough. Not nearly enough. Mari's eyes were still closed, her mouth open and slack. She gave no sign of awareness of him or anyone else.

A hand reached for him, but Alain threw it off violently. "No! No! This shall not happen while life is in me!" He seized Mari's limp hand in both of his, staring at her.

In that moment, he didn't see Mari lying before him. He saw the young Mechanic appearing out of the dust as the caravan to Ringhmon was attacked, Mari as he had first seen her. He saw her in the dungeon of Ringhmon, he saw her in Marandur, in the office where they got married, in the tower of the librarians on Altis, on the *Gray Lady*, leading the charge into Minut, aboard the *Terror*, standing on the last wall of Dorcastle and rallying the nearly beaten to one last effort. In an instant, he saw her in every way and form he had known Mari, and in that instant there was nothing else but her.

He saw her in Altis, both of them trapped, hopeless—and power suddenly coming to him from somewhere, from Mari, he had always believed, who had sworn to die before she allowed the assassins to reach him, thinking not of herself but only of him.

That was the answer. He finally understood, now, when it might be too late.

What happened then? He felt an odd jolt inside himself, knowing not just that she was real, that the Mage Guild elders had lied when they claimed Mari was only a shadow born of Alain's own imagination. For the first time Alain felt nothing of himself. His own reality, the sense of himself being here, had vanished. He felt no urge for self-preservation, no need to protect himself, no ambitions or thoughts or desires. Except one. That Mari should live.

The power of the world illusion could provide him strength to use. But no Mage had ever been able to directly affect another person, because Mages thought only themselves were real. If he completely forgot himself, if he thought only of Mari, he could direct his Mage power into her. He could become for a few moments part of the illusion, not real. He could become the spell.

The spell to change, to give power, to what was real. To do something no one ever could before. To save Mari.

Her body knew how to heal itself. It just needed the power to do so.

His mind worked as if during a spell to change the world illusion, summoning a vision of a different illusion, but it felt as if everything was happening in reverse. Nothing changed outside of him. Strength surged into him from the Mage power available here, but instead of funneling it into something to alter the illusion Alain funneled it into Mari. It was as if a hole had opened in him, a place where his hands met Mari's hand. The power of this area drained to nothing and Alain drew more strength from the core of himself, pouring everything into the almost empty basin which he felt still held a lingering spark of Mari's spirit. Was it still there? He no longer knew. It no longer mattered.

Alain felt an odd trance overlay his vision, as if he could see inside Mari's body, see it soaking up the power and using it to greatly speed up its own processes of healing. He saw breaks closing in a flash in the large vessels that carried her blood, flesh filling in gaps, shattered bone reforming, more blood surging through her.

His head spun with weakness and disorientation. How long had he been doing this? Alain had lost all sense of anything outside of himself and Mari, and his feel for his own condition was fading quickly as he focused only on her. Drained of almost everything, he kept offering all he could to Mari.

But his strength failed at last and with it went the link through which he had poured the spell to save Mari. A grayness filled Alain's mind and an emptiness dwelt inside him.

He no longer felt or knew anything, except for a vague sense of falling.

He fell.

And fell.

Into something dark and bottomless that had opened beneath him.

* * *

Alain had no idea how long he fell. He gradually became aware of bright arcs of light swinging through the darkness above him. The arcs slowed, grew shorter, and after an eternity settled into the brilliance of stars he had never seen, arrayed in strange constellations.

He realized that he had stopped falling, but was still moving. Not walking, but gliding along as if he were a puff of smoke on a breeze. Alain drifted down long paths shadowed by huge, ancient trees that watched him with unseen eyes. He found himself in an endless corridor lined with closed doors, occasional windows revealing an outside world with impossibly bright colors. Somehow, he was in a ballroom of immense size filled with innumerable faces. Most seemed unaware of him, though a few glanced his way with eyes that held secrets beyond his grasp. He saw a man and a woman smiling at him, and fought to stop his movement. Could they be—?

But they waved him on. He could not turn or stop, only continue his slow drift. He became aware of voices whispering to him, but the words meant nothing. *What is all this?* Alain cried wordlessly into the dark. *What does it mean?*

And just for a moment he understood the whispers. Only two words, seemingly an answer to the questions he could not speak.

Not yet.

He fell again. Alain felt no fear, no worries for when he might strike whatever lay beneath him. Falling was all there was. But after a time he could not measure, Alain felt his headlong plummet slowing. It was as if he were sinking slowly into a deep pile of the softest down.

He was lying down.

All he could see were reddish patches that swam and shifted constantly before him.

Alain became aware that he was awake. His eyelids were closed. That was the source of the shifting reddish patches. There must be light wherever he was.

A slow beat in his ears became his pulse, then he felt air going in and out as he breathed. He could hear a distant murmuring, or perhaps it was a breeze blowing somewhere.

He thought about moving, and realized that he felt incredibly weary. Even the effort of breathing shallowly was taking every bit of strength he had.

It was a bed, Alain decided. He was lying in a bed. On his back. What an odd end to his visions. Why would one enter a new dream, the one beyond death, by waking up in a bed?

He could open his eyes and find out.

But that would take a lot of effort. Alain had to wait and gather his strength. Finally he managed to open his eyes, wondering what he would see.

If this was a new dream, another world to which the dead passed, it seemed very much like the old. The ceiling overhead was white plaster, light dancing on it from the reflection of sunlight on water somewhere nearby. Alain watched the light for a long time, too exhausted by the effort of opening his eyes to do more, fascinated by the ever-changing patterns of the reflection.

"Alain?"

It was a whisper. Saying his name.

He knew the voice, and felt sudden hope that bought him enough strength to move his head. The simple gesture required immense effort, but Alain managed to roll his head toward where the voice had come from, to his right, seeing the top of a window, then a view through that window of a blue sky flecked with clouds, then the top of a bedstead next to his own bed and a water pitcher that must be the source of the reflection on the ceiling.

Then, as his head flopped sideways onto his pillow, he saw Mari on the other bed. She lay on her back, her head resting on a pillow, her face thin and drawn. She was watching him with eyes that were open and aware and desperately worried.

She was alive.

Alain managed to get one whispered word out of his throat. "Mari."

"What...did you...do?"

He had to think about that, trying to remember, his mind fuzzy with fatigue and a strange sense of dislocation. "Gave...you...all...I... had."

"How?"

That took some more thought. "Made...myself...the spell."

"Mage Alain." Asha walked to a spot where he could see. She leaned over to study him intently. "You made yourself the spell? All know that you must have saved Mari, but no one knew how. It nearly killed you, Mage Alain. I must tell the healers that you have awoken."

He heard a door open and close, but kept his eyes on Mari, feeling physically awful but emotionally wonderful. "You...are...all right."

"Sort of." She managed a smile for him. "Thanks. Don't ever... again."

Before he could try to tell her that was still a promise he would never make, Alain heard the door open and people crowding quickly into the room. Several came beside his bed, looking at him and touching his forehead and wrist.

"Sir Mage Alain?" a woman healer asked, her eyes on his. "Can you hear me?"

"Yes."

A ripple of noise went through those who had entered. "What happened to you?" the healer asked. "We couldn't find anything wrong with you. No injuries to your body at all. It was if you suddenly became so exhausted that for a little while your body had no strength to keep even the heart and mind going."

Alain couldn't move his head, but he did move his eyes slightly to indicate Mari. "Gave her...mine."

The healer shook her head, exchanging glances with her comrades. "Sir Mage," she told Alain, "the most critical injuries suffered by Lady Mari seemed to heal almost instantaneously, leaving scar tissue that looks like it's from an old injury. But whatever caused that had some other impact on her body, some major stress that was like a combination of shock and exposure, that she barely managed to overcome. Can you tell us anything about that?"

Alain, to his own surprise, managed to shake his head a tiny bit. "I...gave...strength...her...body...used it."

"Mage work," one of the healers commented. "I've never actually seen it before."

"It has never been seen before," Asha said, startling the healers. "No Mage has ever done such a thing. Will Mage Alain be well?"

"Yes, Lady Mage," the woman healer said. "His body is suffering from the results of severe stress which...I think...is a side-effect of what he did. There is no reason to think he will not recover quickly now."

"And Master Mechanic Mari? She is still weak."

"She, uh, went through a lot, Lady Mage. Even though the wound healed so remarkably quickly, or maybe because it did, her body seems to have a memory of the injury that is taking time to, well, heal."

"Thank you," Asha said, further shocking the healers.

As they left, Alain heard the healers conversing excitedly. One of them used the phrase "a new day" just before the door closed.

Asha leaned down to Alain again. "Sleep, Mage Alain, wisest of the wise. Either Mechanic Calu or I will always be here watching you and Mari." She turned. "You as well, Mari. Your fire burns again, but must grow stronger."

"Asha," Mari whispered. "Dav. How is…Dav?"

"My uncle Mage Dav is well," Asha said. "He who will soon be my promised husband, Mechanic Dav, can yet only walk with great difficulty, and so stayed at Pacta, but gains strength by the day."

"I'm…sorry," Mari said.

"It is only his hip," Asha said. "You saved the rest of him. Now sleep."

Alain, worn out, closed his eyes, too, somehow knowing that he would have no more dreams for a while.

* * *

The next time that Mari awoke she saw a familiar face in the room and felt a rush of happiness. "Calu?" Her voice, still weak, broke on the name.

"That's right." Calu stood up from the chair by the door, his old grin fading as he looked at Mari. "You look like you got pressed through a hydraulic ram."

"Thanks. I feel like that, too."

"Do you remember me calling you? On the last day of the battle?"

"Yeah." Mari tried to smile reassuringly. "Not much after that, though. Why didn't you call sooner…instead of waiting until you were flying over me?"

Calu waved upward. "Because the river valley surrounding Dorcastle has pressure layers in the air above it that you can almost bounce rocks off. You can talk to someone else inside the city all right, but far-talker signals can't get in or out most of the time. I discovered that the long-distance far-talker at the Mechanics Guild Hall runs underground wires out to antennas on top of the cliffs to get around the problem."

"You'd think somebody would talk about that," Mari said. "I guess it was a Guild secret, as far as the Senior Mechanics were concerned." She tried to pace her words, feeling a curious mix of being stronger along with a sense that her endurance was still very weak.

"Yeah. They probably didn't have a clue about it so they said it had to be kept secret. Stars above, Mari, don't try to sit up!" Calu sat down again in a chair next to her bed, shaking his head. "I'll never forget how it felt, sitting outside the healers' room with Alain and Asha, then breaking in there once we realized he needed to be beside you, and—"

"You broke in?" Mari had wondered if she would ever feel like laughing again, but she heard herself and it sounded breathless but good. "Why didn't I expect that? What's going on? Outside?"

"How much have they told you? Nothing? Typical." Calu squinted in thought. "Uh, in order of importance, the Imperials and the Great Guilds ran all the way to the harbor and kept going. The entire city is safe, though it's pretty beat up. Pacta also held. Alli couldn't join your army when we went past because they were worried about the Syndaris trying again, but from what she told me Syndar got a major butt-kicking. Queen Sien went through them like a sword through butter. And it looks a whole lot like the Mechanics Guild is collapsing."

"What?" Mari stared at Calu, unable to believe that she had heard right.

"When the Imperials ran," Calu said, "the Senior Mechanics at the Guild Hall here in Dorcastle joined them, along with maybe a quarter of the other Mechanics there. The rest sort of surrendered. That is, they claimed the peace of the daughter, which is what everybody is calling your demand that any Mechanics willing to accept the New Day be protected from any retaliation or attacks by commons. Hey, two of the Mechanics at the Guild Hall are Tyron and Inira. Do you remember them from Caer Lyn? Anyway, the Mechanics who stayed used the long-distance far-talker at the Guild Hall to spread the word about what happened here. The Senior Mechanics and the Guild Master in Palandur weren't too happy with that and told them to shut up, of course. Too late, and the local Mechanics have stopped listening to them anyway. The Mechanics here have heard from other Guild Halls now, and a lot are breaking free of the Guild. Not in the Empire, but everywhere else."

"I didn't think it could happen this quickly," Mari said.

"It wasn't all that quick," he corrected. "You called it right. The Guild has been developing stress cracks for a long time, patching them when they got too big. For the last couple of years you've brought major pressure to bear on the Guild by introducing new technology and giving the commons hope and Mechanics an alternative to the Guild and, well, just by surviving. The Guild might have fallen apart eventually anyway without you, but without you it would have been awful when everything broke. The way you've done it offers hope for a soft crack-up that won't hurt too many people."

Calu scratched his head, looking at Mari. "A big reason we're hearing from the rebelling Guild Halls is that they can see change happening. They want to be part of it and not run over by it. But they all want you to promise that they and their families will be protected if they go along with the New Day thing."

She gasped another weak laugh. "Calu, my word has force in Tiae, but not anywhere else. The leaders of the Confederation and the Alliance and the Free Cities need to give that promise."

He eyed her skeptically. "Are you all right? Um…I mean…I know you're not all right. You got shot and died and all, but if you don't think what the daughter says matters—"

"What did you say?" Mari ran the words past her memory. He hadn't really said that, had he? "I got shot and *almost* died."

Calu didn't answer for a long moment, looking steadily at Mari. "Here's what I heard and saw, Mari. Alain burst in the room while Asha and I got the guards out of the way, he ran over to where you were lying, pushing healers aside right and left, grabbed your hand, and maybe a couple of seconds later, collapsed. And while he was doing that, some of the healers told me *it's too late, we lost her, the daughter has died*, and some of them were already crying, and then as the nearest people grabbed Alain to keep him from hitting the ground you coughed and started breathing hard and the healers looked at you like they were seeing a ghost. Somebody said *she was dead*, and they all raced back to you and started doing their healer things again."

Mari stared back at him, unable to speak for a while. "I…I didn't die. That's ridiculous."

He spread his hands, uncomfortable but unyielding. "That's what they said."

"They were wrong. I'd know if I had died." She paused, uncertain. "Wouldn't I?"

Calu shook his head. "How does it feel to die? Nobody's ever been able to came back and explain it." He gave her a quick look, then shifted his eyes away.

"Calu, I didn't…I don't remember…I saw Alain's face after I got shot…it got dark, and I was cold, but then it got warm and…bright… and…" She tried to smile in self-mockery. "I thought I saw a locomotive. Can you believe that? The engineer and some apprentices were waving at me to join them in the cab, and I started to walk that way, but then—" She swallowed, finding it difficult. "I…I realized that Alain wasn't there. I couldn't find him, but I could feel him. I shook my head…and turned away to go look for him…and sometime later I woke up."

Calu smiled at her. "A locomotive? Seriously?"

"Yes." Mari felt herself smiling genuinely this time despite her inner turmoil. "How else should an engineer go somewhere?"

"You saw what your mind could understand," Alain said.

She looked that way too quickly, making herself a little dizzy. Alain had woken again and was watching them, his head still flat on the pillow. He looked a lot better, but then according to the healers he hadn't had much physically wrong with him and just needed to regain strength. "What do you mean?"

"The next dream is, we think, very different," Alain said. "When we see it with our minds that know this dream, this illusion, we see the next dream in ways that are familiar to us."

"What did you see, Alain?" Calu asked.

"Many things. But I was not welcomed. I was not allowed to stay."

"You wanted to stay?" Mari asked, knowing that she sounded sad.

He managed a small smile at her. "No. I wanted to be where you were. I had to find you, just as you sought me."

Mari smiled back. "So you know I didn't die before you…did that."

Alain shook his head slightly. "I do not know. I know you were still within my reach. If you had left, you still retained a grasp on this life, a grasp on your body."

"Oh." Mari looked up at the ceiling, feeling weird inside. "So I wasn't really dead. Not *completely* dead. Maybe my body needed help getting started again, but I must have still been there. Right? At least… Calu, how many people have heard about that? What the healers said? It's a secret, right?"

"Uh, no, it's been heard by a lot of people," Calu said with obvious reluctance. "Just about everybody. By the time I got outside again everyone was talking about it. The daughter died and her Mage brought her back. I'm sure the Emperor has heard that by now."

"No! Stars above, how can I ever…" Mari screwed her eyes shut, imagining how people would look at her. She opened them again, staring at Calu, trying to see something different in his own gaze on her.

"Ummm…" Calu looked around as if physically searching for some way to change the subject. "There's a Mage outside who's been waiting to see you or Alain. She's pretty old and not one of yours, Mari, but Asha says she's all right."

"An elder?" Alain asked. "From the Guild Hall in Dorcastle?"

"Yeah. Do you know her?"

"Yes. I sense her presence. I lacked the strength to notice earlier. I would like to speak with her."

Calu jumped up, relieved, and hastened out, returning in a short time with a Mage elder that Mari recognized. "Greetings, elder," Mari said, feeling weak again.

The elder, once more leaning on a cane, walked to the foot of Alain's bed, watching him, then turning her head to study Mari while Calu waited. "So. You have done this thing, Master of Mages."

"This one does not understand," Alain said.

"You are still weak, otherwise such lack of knowing would be inexcusable," the elder said. Her voice was almost toneless, but Mari could hear undercurrents of emotion. "But this one cannot criticize the wisdom of a Mage who has done what no other Mage has. You changed that one. You used your spell to alter her. You know this."

"I know this," Alain said. "This one had to. To save her."

"Many Mages have wished to save another, or harm another," the elder said. "None could. You found the wisdom. She is the proof. What is the secret?"

Alain hesitated. "She is real. The secret lay in understanding that she was the only real thing, the only thing that mattered. That I was nothing."

The elder nodded. Mari thought she saw the ghost of a smile on her lips. "The Mage Guild has always taught that wisdom required seeing all others as only shadows. That wisdom has never managed to advance, staying fixed in place. You have declared a wisdom which says the opposite. Wisdom lies in seeing others as real. That is the test, is it not, young Mage? Not to disregard others. Rather for each to be able to step outside of ourselves, to lose our selfish focus on ourselves, enough to see others as being as real as we are, as even more important than ourselves. Only then can we advance."

To Mari's amazement, Alain looked visibly embarrassed by the elder's words. "This one is not worthy of such praise."

"That one knows better," the elder said. "Do you not know the term Master of Mages? It is a rank of wisdom only rarely given. I declare you worthy of that. I know many others will agree, even though the council of elders no longer commands a Guild to enforce such a decree. Or to dispute it."

Instead of seeming abashed once more, Alain looked at Mari, then back at the elder. "The council of elders no longer commands a Guild?"

"No," the elder said as if that was a matter of no consequence. "There has been growing discontent, as you know, with many joining you in search of new wisdom. But two things have happened. One was the events in Danalee which you described to me. Word also came from Mages who reached the city after you and spoke to the elder who did not die. That the council of elders would order such a thing was against all wisdom as Mages understand it. Even before the failure of the Imperial invasion Mages were departing, refusing their orders from the council of elders. Then came this." The elder flicked a single forefinger toward Mari. "You, already declared to have lost all wisdom, who had told many of your emotions toward this other, did what no other Mage ever could. It was proof that the wisdom enforced by the Guild was false in important ways. The Mage Guild no longer exists. Each Guild Hall is gathering to it Mages who think in similar ways. Many seek new paths. Others cling to the old. But the Guild that once enforced its rule over Mage and shadows alike is gone."

A thought came to Mari then, but she was afraid to voice it.

Calu, though, didn't hesitate. "You did it, Mari." He grinned as widely as she had ever seen. "The Great Guilds have been overthrown. They don't rule the world any more."

"The prophecy is not yet fulfilled," the Mage elder said, her voice stern. "The daughter of Jules must also save the world. The chains that bound this world also held it together. The Great Guilds are gone. The old rules have vanished and new ones have not yet been found. The daughter of Jules must help the world survive these changes."

Mari, feeling as if someone had just massively rewritten her job scope, gave Alain an accusing look. "Have you seen that Storm vision lately?"

He pondered the question. "Last night, I saw something like but unlike the earlier visions given by foresight."

"And you didn't mention that until now?"

"You were sleeping." Alain paused again. "There were armies clashing, cities burning, but the mobs of commons could no longer be seen. No one sought to fight the light of the sun, but where that light shone the armies fell back and lowered their weapons."

"Which means?" Mari pressed, knowing she sounded upset.

The elder answered her, startling Mari. "You have power of your own, daughter." The Mage elder pointed her cane at Mari. "Use it."

"To stop wars from happening? How am I supposed to do that? I've got an army. It's been fighting a war. I wanted to be able to do this without any battles, but I couldn't, and look at…look at…" Mari, feeling sick, waved helplessly toward the outside, to the ruins of much of Dorcastle.

The elder walked closer to Mari's bed, looking down at her. "That young Mage saved you, daughter of Jules. It had never been done. Many had failed. But he tried. No one had ever overthrown the Great Guilds. But you tried. Wisdom does not lie in accepting what the illusion shows us. It lies in trying to change the illusion in favor of what is real. You have already cast your shadow wide and done what many said could not be."

"Isn't that enough?" Mari demanded.

"No." The Mage elder studied Mari again. "I see this in you. Would you ever be…what is the word?" she asked Alain. "For…something that…pleases."

"Happy," Alain said.

"Happy." The Mage elder nodded slowly, her eyes distant for a moment. "Yes. Would you be happy?" she asked Mari. "If there were no more challenges? Or if you saw ill events and could do nothing?"

"Yes," Mari insisted. "I'd be fine with it. Somebody else should have to worry about all that."

"Daughter of Jules," the elder said, poking at Mari with her cane, "did not this young Mage tell you not to attempt lies before those who can see through illusions? You came to this place in the face of foresight that showed a great possibility of your death."

"I had to," Mari said. "If I was the only one who could—" She clenched her teeth in exasperation. "You're saying that's still true. But I'm not special."

"No, you are not," the elder said. "It is what you can do that is special. The choice remains yours. Live with the illusion made by others, or change it as you can, if you can." She turned to go. "I am tired. Come see me, young Master of Mages, when your strength returns. You will be safe when visiting the Mage Hall." Without another word she walked out, leaning on the cane again.

Calu closed the door behind her. "Um, wow. Can I get you anything, Mari?"

She gazed up at the ceiling, feeling awful. "Red wine and chocolate."

"I don't think the healers will allow you to have—"

"I hate healers. And I hate the daughter and I hate this job and I hate not being able to just work as a Mechanic and I hate having anything to do with wars." Mari, out of breath, glared at Calu.

He nodded. "All right. Red wine and chocolate."

"Calu?" she added before he left. "Thanks. If not for my friends, I'd be lost. You...you guys are real."

He smiled again and closed the door behind him.

She turned her head slowly to look at Alain. "Did you have any idea the prophecy meant what that elder said?"

"No. Her interpretation does seem consistent with it, though." Alain did not, to her eyes, look nearly regretful enough when he said that.

"Fine!" Mari snapped. "Then you have to help me keep trying to save the world. I hope you're happy."

He gave her a weak smile. "I am, because I am with you."

"Oh, go to blazes." Mari looked away, wishing that she felt strong enough to get up and beat her head against the wall. "I'm sorry. I love you. I'm just waiting for life to get a little easier."

It looked like it would be a while before there was any hope of that, though.

"Mari?"

"I said I'm sorry. I shouldn't have said something mean to you."

"That is not it." She turned her head back to Alain, seeing him watching her. "You saw more, did you not? More than just the locomotive creature?"

Mari sighed, then nodded, grasping at already failing memories. "Just fragments of things. Weird stuff. I'm having trouble remembering it. What did it all mean, Alain? Do you understand?"

"No." He paused as if recalling something. "Not yet."

✷ ✷ ✷

"General." Mari, still in bed but propped up with pillows, smiled at the sight. "It's very good to see you."

General Flyn nodded, looking from her to Alain, then back at Mari. "I had to fight my way through a solid wall of healers to get in here. You look remarkable well for what I was told of your injury. I had heard it was a mortal wound."

"Alain…did something," Mari said. "I'm still weak inside. I hope you haven't heard any rumors about…"

"You dying?" Flyn asked. "All I know is that you're here and obviously very much alive." He sat down near the door, sighing. "It's been a tough few weeks, not that I'm asking for sympathy from either of you." Flyn pursed his mouth, looking like a man about to plead guilty to a crime. "We nearly came too late."

"No one has told me much," Mari said. "It's getting to be annoying."

Flyn smiled. "Now there is the Lady Mari I know! You must be feeling better. You realize, I hope, that we came as quickly as we could. I tried to use our Rocs to shuttle some small help to you, but when we attempted to fly them out we discovered that the Mage Guild had sent their own Rocs to keep ours grounded. They had those Mages who cast lightning riding them. Our Rocs wouldn't have stood a chance, so they had to stay close to our army where we could provide cover for them."

"Alain guessed that might be the reason," Mari said. "Because none of the lightning Mages were at Dorcastle."

Flynn nodded. "Then came that storm, which our Mages said nothing could fly in. As soon as I could when we neared the city and the storm let up I sent some Rocs forward, flying under the overcast so the Mage Guild's birds couldn't spot them."

He sighed again, looking toward the window. "We drove ourselves hard, Lady. At the end, your army was strung out all the way from Danalee to Dorcastle. What you saw, what came onto the battlements to hit back at the Imperials, was a small force I sent ahead using all the horses who could still move fast and including just about every rifle we had. The main force of the army was still close to a day's hard march behind. Fortunately, the rifles and the surprise of their appearance and the Mechanics riding on Mage Rocs were enough to convince the Imperials that they were beaten."

Flyn cocked an eyebrow at her. "Mind you, we couldn't have done that if you hadn't all but broken them before we got here. You won this victory, Lady, you and your Mage and the other defenders of Dorcastle. Stars above, I wish I had been there!"

Mari scoffed and shook her head. "No. You wouldn't wish for that. It was so awful. So close a thing."

"Many battles are a close thing and all of them are awful in their own ways," Flyn said. "I will tell you this. For many years to come this world will be divided into two groups. Those who held the last wall at Dorcastle alongside the daughter, and those who wish they had been there with her."

"General, I can't imagine *wanting* to have been there."

"It's only truth, Lady," Flyn insisted. "There are moments that decide everything that will come after, and that was such a moment. Then, once you'd held them, we broke the invasion force and hurled them back to the sea. The mightiest force that could be created by the combined strength of the Empire and the Great Guilds could not overcome you. Dorcastle was saved, the Confederation was saved, reborn Tiae was saved. That was one thing, and a big thing it was. And Pacta Servanda, with its schools and workshops in the land that is once again the Kingdom of Tiae, also held, against all that Syndar could throw at it. That was another thing. But then you lived when death had already called you. I am told that the Great Guilds have both fallen. The Empire is in total retreat. All the world, even those who doubted, now look at the daughter of the prophecy and knows she has in truth come at last and that she is invincible and indestructible."

Mari looked down at her thin hands and laughed again, feeling a momentary shiver at how frail that laughter sounded. "The world needs to get a good look at me. Right now a hot kiss and a cold meal would kill me."

"Seeing you wouldn't change their opinion," Flyn stated. "Because you are alive. But there is a…slight change to your appearance."

"What?"

"No one has…?"

Mari looked over at Alain. "What is he talking about?"

Alain gave her one of his Mage looks, meaning he was trying to avoid something by withdrawing into that state. "Nothing of importance. But if you wish to see, there is a hand mirror on that table."

"General?" Mari asked.

Looking wary, Flyn picked up the mirror and held it where Mari could see herself. Yes, as she expected, she looked absolutely awful. Her face was thin and drawn, her eyes reddened, her hair— "What is that? What is that in my hair?"

She reached up, lifting the strands above her right temple.

Just as she saw in the mirror, there was a streak of bright white amid her black hair, as if someone had taken a brush and painted every hair in that shock pure white from tip to root. "What is this?"

Flyn put down the mirror. "Lady, I have seen something similar on occasion in someone badly injured or frightened, where the hair loses color seemingly overnight."

"Like this?"

"Not exactly like that, no."

"It must be a side effect of the spell," Alain said. "I could not give you everything I had. That must show what I could not give."

"Do you sound regretful?" Mari asked. "Do you actually sound sorry? Because you saved my life and couldn't kill yourself in the process and so I ended up with a streak of white hair? Which everyone who looks at will know marks the fact that my husband literally nearly killed himself to save my life? You're sorry about that?"

Alain paused, thinking. "I am not supposed to be sorry?"

"No." She suddenly felt like crying again. It must be because of the stress and her weakness, she told herself. "Everybody is going to look at me funny now anyway. I can just pretend it's because of my hair. Which will always remind me of how wonderful you are, and how we won when it seemed impossible, and how many other men and women gave their lives for—"

Mari broke off, sobbing, tears running down her face. Flyn waited, patient, until she had regained control.

"There is no shame in it," Flyn told her. "I have seen many who endured less and displayed it more. I should tell you why I came today. Word has reached the Emperor of how badly his forces were defeated. I am told that the former Mechanics Guild Hall is using their far-talker to tell everyone, and the Mages who accompanied the Imperial attack surely used Mage means to send messages among themselves. A Mage came to us this morning to inform us that the Emperor has decreed an immediate halt to attacks and is sending a very high-ranking delegation to negotiate a permanent end to hostilities. We received the same message through the far-talker at the Mechanics Guild Hall."

"That's good." Mari sighed, relieved. "I guess I'll need to be involved in that."

"Yes, you certainly will. Perhaps I should clarify," Flyn added. "The Imperial delegation is coming to negotiate with you."

"Me?"

"Yes. The daughter."

Mari stared at the ceiling, then at Alain, then back at Flyn. "What about the leaders of the Bakre Confederation?"

Flyn's smile was thin and hard. "The Emperor appears to consider their wishes far less important than yours."

"I can't bind the Confederation to any peace agreement," Mari insisted.

"Yes, you can. The Bakre Confederation, the Western Alliance, the Free Cities, and most places not covered by those associations. That's because the people of those places, who have what seems to be a natural distrust of their own leaders even when they have selected them, have a huge amount of trust in you."

"That's wrong," Mari said. "I can't act like I'm in charge of all of these places. I'm not, and I shouldn't be."

Flyn eyed her. Was there something hidden behind his gaze? She couldn't tell. "Lady, I hope you hold to that. For now, representatives of the Western Alliance and the Free Cities are on their way to Dorcastle. The highest leaders of the Confederation should be here tomorrow. I would advise that you speak with them before the Imperial delegation arrives."

Mari wanted to scream with frustration. "I'm a Mechanic. An engineer. Not a diplomat. Not a politician. Why am I doing this?"

"Because you're the only one who can."

She glowered up at the ceiling. "Generals and Mage elders shouldn't be telling me the same thing. I want to talk to someone else before I meet with all the representatives. Confederation Vice President Jane and Confederation Vice President Eric. I need to see them."

"I'll ensure that is done, Lady," Flyn said, rising to his feet, coming to attention and saluting. "Lady, I hope I will always be honored to serve you."

After Flyn had left, Mari looked over at Alain. "Did you notice anything?"

"He was worried," Alain said. "As he looked at you and spoke with you."

"Worried for me?"

"Or worried about you," Alain said.

CHAPTER TWELVE

VICE PRESIDENT JANE'S right arm was completely encased in a cast, held steady by a sling around her neck. The right side of her face had a large bandage on it. "Will you be all right?" Mari asked, upset that she still wasn't strong enough to stand to greet her visitor. "Where's Eric?"

Jane sat down heavily. "I should recover, the healers say, though there may be problems with the arm for a long time. A break and some bad burns. I can't complain. Many suffered worse." She hesitated. "Like Eric. I regret to inform you that he died during the siege. It was during the retreat from the second wall to the third. We found his body among the others of the rear guard that must have been trapped by the Imperials." Jane closed her eyes, rubbing them with her good hand. "He died valiantly, I suppose. Eric told me that he wondered how he would respond if it came to that, if he would cower or hide. He didn't."

"I'm sorry," Mari said, not knowing what else to say.

"What did you want to speak to me about, Lady?"

Mari nodded outwards. "There's an Imperial delegation coming to negotiate the end of the war with me."

"I've been told that," Jane said.

"I would appreciate your thoughts and advice on it. I can't imagine the Bakre Confederation's government is happy about it."

Jane paused again before speaking. "The Confederation Vice President of State would say one thing. Jane of Danalee would say another."

"What would the vice president tell me?" Mari asked.

"To respect the rights and prerogatives of the Confederation government. To listen to their desires and expectations and honor them in your discussions with the Imperials."

"And Jane would say?"

She looked Mari in the eyes. "Jane of Danalee would tell you to honor the sacrifices of those who died to defend Dorcastle, and not to let their sacrifices be tarnished by using them for purposes that are not for the profit and benefit of all."

"I will remember that," Mari said. "I promise you that I will."

"I've learned what your promises are worth, Lady, that they stand firmer than the walls of this city. I have no doubt you will honor your words to me."

"Call me Mari."

Jane smiled slightly. "Thank you, Mari. The Confederation President of State will want to know why you sought to speak with me. What should I tell him?"

"Tell him I wanted to express my condolences for the death of Vice President Eric to one who risked herself alongside us," Mari said.

Jane's smile changed, taking on a hard aspect. "I imagine that will forestall any other questions he has in mind." She got to her feet with a little difficulty. "The next soldier I hear sneering about diplomats being in a safe profession is going to get my cast upside his or her head."

"I'm sorry that you got hurt," Mari said.

"It's not like I got run over by a wagon while going to get groceries," Jane said. "I was fighting for a great cause. I suspect my arm will heal a lot faster than what's in here," she added, tapping her chest. "That's the way of it, isn't it? Figuring out how to live on when so many others died."

"They won't be forgotten, Jane," Mari said. "Not what they did, and not who they were."

"No. I'm sure they won't. Thank you, Mari." Jane half-bowed toward Mari before leaving.

* * *

The next day high-ranking dignitaries from the Confederation, the Western Alliance, Tiae, and the Free Cities arrived. Mari was called to what was described only as "a very important conference" with them. She and Alain were both still too weak to handle flights of stairs and long hallways, so they were carriedto the meeting in chairs that had poles fastened to the sides. Mari felt ridiculous, as well as uneasy on the stairs when her chair tilted, but thought it an easier thing to endure than many other things she had been through.

They went out through the streets, where Mari stared at her surroundings. She had been told her hospital was beyond the seventh wall, in the part of the city that had received little damage, but it was still strange to see intact structures when her memory of Dorcastle was filled with entire blocks of buildings burning and collapsing.

Men and women began shouting as they saw Mari and Alain, a crowd rapidly gathering to watch them pass, chants of "freedom and the daughter" making it hard for Mari to maintain her composure. She smiled and waved despite her lingering weakness, trying to focus on what had been achieved and not the human cost.

They reached the site of the meeting, a grand inn serving as a temporary government building while repairs were made to others still intact enough to be salvaged.

Guards, half of them wearing Bakre Confederation uniforms and the rest the uniforms of Mari's army, stood before wide double doors leading into a ballroom. The Confederation soldiers were armed with short spears and swords, while Mari's soldiers carried rifles. She suspected that General Flyn had deliberately ensured that her soldiers were much better armed than their Confederation counterparts.

Those carrying Mari and Alain's chairs set them down in the front of the room, then left. Mari and Alain faced ranks of comfortable chairs, all holding men and women in the dress of high-ranking officials or military officers. One of them was General Flynn. Some junior officers and officials filed out with the chair carriers, and then the door was firmly sealed.

Mari recognized one of the officials who remained, the older woman who led the city government of Julesport. Before she could say a greeting, the woman rose to her feet and began applauding.

The other officials jumped to their feet as well, with what seemed to be varying degrees of enthusiasm, and joined in the applause.

When everyone had seated themselves again, a man in the center of the front row stood up. Mari recognized him from Jane's description as her boss, the Confederation President of State. "Lady, this meeting was supposed to be with you alone."

"My Mage goes where I go," Mari said. "I told your people that I would not come to this meeting if he was not brought as well. He has been my partner in all things, and can claim an equal credit with me for any achievements thus far."

The President of State hesitated only a moment. "Of course. I did not mean to imply Sir Mage Alain was not welcome. Let me begin by saying that we are honored to meet with you following the great victory won by Confederation forces at Dorcastle!"

"I had heard that a substantial role in that victory was played by the army of the daughter," a woman seated near him remarked.

"And Tiae contributed forces!" another insisted. "That must not be forgotten!"

"Of course," the President of State quickly agreed. "That is why Tiae has a seat at this conference." He waved toward the back, where Mari finally spotted Colonel Hasna. Why had Queen Sien sent Hasna, of all people?

"Thank you," Mari said to stop the debate over credit for the victory, which she found a little distasteful coming from those who hadn't fought. "What exactly do you want to talk about?"

"The negotiations with the Imperial delegation must include

representatives of the Confederation government," the President of State declared.

"Any agreement made would have to be approved by your government, of course," Mari agreed. "But if the Emperor has given his delegation orders only to meet with me, they won't yield on that. You know how Imperials are."

"The Empire is at its weakest," a woman announced, her northern accent revealing she was from the Free Cities. "We have at our disposal weapons such as this world has never seen. This opportunity will not repeat itself. The Free City of Cristane believes that we need to make sure the Empire pays for what it has done."

A murmur of agreement sounded among those present, though Mari noticed some did not take part.

Alain spoke, his dispassionate Mage voice ensuring attention to his words. "I know that many bodies of Confederation fighters have been removed from the streets of Dorcastle. Their bravery ensured that many more Imperials died in the attempt. Can anyone believe that the Empire has not paid dearly already?"

The woman from Cristane appeared rattled, but pressed on. "Umburan. If the Imperials are forced to yield Umburan and the lands around it—"

"Exactly what did the Free Cities do during this battle to earn such a prize?" the Confederation President of State demanded.

"The Sharr Isles are far more important," a man in a fine suit declared. "The Western Alliance is willing to lead an expedition to expel the Imperials and establish a forward presence—"

"The Western Alliance will not have the Sharr Isles!"

"Landfall should be demanded, to ensure the Imperials are unable to once again threaten the West!"

"The Empire should be broken up—"

Angry words flew back and forth, many now speaking at once.

Mari, trying to control her own temper, looked at Alain.

Alain spoke one word. "Listen."

The Great Guilds might have been recently toppled, but when a

Mage gave a command in that curiously dead voice only they could achieve, commons still paid attention. Quiet fell.

Mari spoke into the resulting silence, knowing that she sounded angry. "I want one thing to be clearly understood. I did not raise an army, help bring about the overthrow of the Great Guilds, and help defend Dorcastle, in order for anyone to launch a larger, unnecessary war. If any of you are thinking of using my army and its weapons to conquer territory, they can forget it now."

"As her general," Flyn said, nodding to Mari, "I will affirm that I will answer only to orders from Lady Mari."

"Then what do you intend to do with the power you have?" asked a woman wearing a pin showing the rampant horse symbol of Ihris.

Mari tried to moderate her tone, speaking forcefully but calmly. "I will demand an end to Imperial aggression. I will demand that the Sharr Isles be freed from Imperial domination. But that's it. You! From Cristane. You want Umburan? Suppose the Empire yielded the city and its population and the lands around it to the Free Cities. How many soldiers would the Free Cities have to use to garrison that city and those lands? To keep control over a population which does not welcome them or wish to be a part of them? How much would Umburan cost you, a bleeding wound that never healed? Why would the Free Cities want to swallow that kind of poison?"

Mari paused to catch her breath, annoyed that she was still having difficulty speaking.

Alain filled the silence. "Have you seen Marandur? No? I, a Mage who felt nothing, was horrified by it. A city ground to wreckage, filled with death. Do you believe the recent siege at Dorcastle was an awful thing? Marandur was far worse. Yes, the legions are weak and broken by their attack here. But if you invade the Empire, if you strike at their homes and their families, those same legions will find their heart again. They will turn every place you seek to conquer into a ruin like Marandur, dying amid the rubble, as will your soldiers in uncounted numbers. Is that what you wish for the men and women of your lands? That they die by the thousands to claim the ruins of Imperial possessions?"

"The Confederation has suffered far more than any others," the President of State said. "We have a right to demand full compensation for our losses."

"Compensation?" Mari asked. "You want the Empire to pay you money? For the men and women who died defending Dorcastle?"

"For the destruction! We must rebuild! And families will need payments to make up for the loss of their loved ones. Reparations are justified!"

A finely-dressed woman snorted in derision. "No soldier of the Western Alliance will die to help fill the coffers of the Bakre Confederation."

"No soldier of the Western Alliance died to help defend Dorcastle!"

"That's not true," Mari said, before another outburst could erupt. "I have among my army volunteers from the Western Alliance. And from the Free Cities, and from the Confederation, and from independent cities. Some of the volunteers died here and at Pacta Servanda. This was a victory for everyone."

"We admire you and your accomplishments," another woman began, "but I am the minister of the northern reaches of the Western Alliance, and these others here have similar authority and responsibilities. You are after all only a low-level Mechanic. We are dealing with issues far beyond—"

"Master Mechanic," Mari said, annoyed that the old issue of her professional status was once again a problem.

"If you wish to lie about having admiration regarding Master Mechanic Mari," Alain added to the minister, "it would be wise not to do so where a Mage can see and hear."

"So, those stories of Mages' ability to read truth and lies are accurate?" the older woman from Julesport commented with a sharp glance at the others present. "What a useful skill to have in a gathering of politicians!"

"Not all of us fear that," a man leaning back in his seat said. "Lady Mari, you have said that you will negotiate nothing except an end to the war and freedom for the Sharr Isles. That is so?"

"An end to the war," Mari said, "an agreement for the Empire to leave the Sharr Isles and hopefully for *everyone* to guarantee the neutrality of the Isles, and an agreement by the Empire to not conduct any future aggression against other countries or cities."

"Can you exempt Ringhmon from that non-aggression agreement?" a woman asked. "They'd benefit from Imperial overlords, and they deserve them."

Mari couldn't help smiling. "I agree, but I think I have to be impartial and careful about making exceptions."

"What about Syndar?"

"They'll sue for peace," said the man who had earlier spoken frankly. "I have had word from an agent in Syndar. Their losses at Pacta Servanda were massive. There is much sorrow in Syndar, and at least one ruler has already been deposed by an angry populace. Syndar will not be in a position to fight for some time. They will ask for peace, they'll probably ask for your protection against vengeance from Tiae, and as part of that they should be forced to agree to not allow any more piracy or other aggression."

"And allow pursuit of pirates into their waters!" someone else added.

"We can discuss that," Mari said. "The only place directly attacked by Syndar this time was Tiae. What does Tiae want?"

Colonel Hasna stood. "Tiae desires a treaty binding Syndar not to attack or permit attacks. In all else, Queen Sien expresses every confidence in the ability of the daughter of Jules to respect and protect the rights of all."

"Queen Sien?" someone said in a very low voice, the tone mocking.

A diplomat from the Western Alliance looked around and spoke before Mari could. "Whoever said that, I have met with Queen Sien. If you're thinking that she's another warlord or pretender, think again. Tiae is a kingdom once more, and its leader is not to be underestimated. What was said earlier is true. The entire League of Syndar is scared to death that Queen Sien is going to ride through their islands with fire and sword to avenge the attack on Pacta Servanda."

"Do you trust her word?" Mari asked, pleased that someone else had defended Sien.

"Yes."

A woman stood up. "As the Confederation President of the Senate, I must take heed of the mood of our people. Tiae sent aid to Dorcastle. Tiae's soldiers died alongside our own in this fight. Everything I'm hearing from the people of the Confederation is that to them, Tiae has gone from being a frightening land of chaos to being a loyal and welcome friend. We can't run roughshod over Tiae's interests or our own people will make us regret it."

"And," a Confederation admiral commented, "Queen Sien is probably more popular in the Confederation than anyone in this room, with two notable exceptions." He nodded toward Mari and Alain.

"What about the Mechanics?" the woman from Cristane asked. "It seems every Guild Hall is claiming the peace of the daughter, like that means something."

"Ask the people of your cities if it means something," a man near her grumbled.

"This woman cannot dictate what we do!"

"You think so? Go against the wishes of the daughter and see how long your government lasts."

Mari, not happy with the turn the conversation had taken, broke in. "You need Mechanics. You all know I've got schools down at Pacta Servanda that teach basic Mechanic skills to commons. But if you want to keep using the technology you already have, you need Mechanics to do the work. And now that those Mechanics are freed from the need to follow orders that nothing ever change, they can do better work and build better things and more of those things, and compete with each other to build new things that cost less. I've got access to technology that will create wonders on this world. It will be shared with everyone. But we have to advance by stages—"

"Why?"

"For the same reason you can't suddenly create a building out of thin air! You need to get the materials and the design, lay the foundation, build the walls level by level, and everything else." Mari held up her far-talker. "These will be available for everyone now. But they're hard to build. And better ones will require making better tools to make them with. And some of the processes used to make these new things are themselves hazardous. If you don't handle them right, a lot of people could be killed or hurt. If you want your cities and countries to be able to make use of the new technology, to not fall behind other cities and countries, to be able to build these new things safely, then you will accept Mechanics are a part of the New Day."

"But they won't tell us what to do anymore!"

"That's right. I've told them that in no uncertain terms. Any who feel otherwise can go to the remnants of the Mechanics Guild inside the Empire's borders."

"I can't speak for others," the diplomat from the Western Alliance said in a thoughtful voice, "but the peace of the daughter seems to me to offer a perfect solution for dealing with those who want revenge and retaliation. The daughter says we shouldn't do that! If you don't like it, talk to her. The daughter is probably the only person with the popular authority to make that work. It's ironic that she turned out to be a Mechanic herself."

"If she wasn't," the woman from Ihris said, "the other Mechanics wouldn't trust her."

"I suppose not. And the Mages? What of them?"

Alain answered. "The Mages will no longer dictate to commons. But with the collapse of the Mage Guild's authority, there will no longer be any rules that each Guild Hall must follow. Some Mages will change, as I have. Others will cling to old ways."

"They're dangerous."

"Some are," Alain agreed. "It must be made clear to them that they must now abide by the laws others have made. That can only be done by Mages such as myself who see a new wisdom and can speak to such Mages in ways that will cause them to listen."

"Some Mages are not dangerous anymore," Mari said. "They have important skills and insights. And many more of the Mages can learn to be more considerate of others, to be…human again. What they were taught, that people like you and me are only shadows who have no importance at all, has been proven wrong, and many are listening to that. Mages can change, can be good people once more. Colonel Hasna can testify that many Mages in Tiae have changed."

"Sir Mage, what happened with Lady Mari, can you do that to anyone?" the Confederation admiral asked. "Bring them back from the dead?"

Mari was relieved when Alain answered as she had hoped.

"Mari was not fully dead when I was able to help her body repair itself," he said. "I do not know how well it can be taught. It requires a Mage to be totally dedicated to the life of the person he or she wishes to help. But perhaps we will learn other ways to do it. I will tell anyone who asks what I know."

The Western Alliance diplomat who had met Queen Sien spoke up. "I can also confirm what Lady Mari says. There are good Mages in Tiae. I mean it. They weren't nice, but you could talk to them and they'd talk to you. And even though we're hearing that some of the things Mages could supposedly do were never true, there's no doubt they can do some amazing things. If there are still going to be bad Mages running around, I think it would be very useful to have good Mages at hand."

"This is all very well," the Confederation President of State remarked in acidic tones, "but it does not resolve the issue of this Mechanic's authority. Or rather, the lack of it. If we accept that only she is allowed to negotiate with the Imperial delegation, then we are ceding to her power that we are obligated to retain for the elected leaders of our people!"

The old woman from Julesport stood up. "Lady Master Mechanic Mari said nothing but the truth when she spoke of the Imperials. The Emperor is sending them to speak with her. It's not a matter of us allowing it. We weren't asked by the Emperor."

"That is not—"

"I am not finished," the woman from Julesport said. Seeing the looks that passed between her and the Confederation President of State, Mari could tell that some old rivalry divided them. "It is foolish to make demands. Have you seen the army that answers to her? Have you seen their weapons? Most importantly, have you paid no attention to the feelings of those we represent toward this woman, the woman who freed them and who is the daughter in spirit and perhaps in blood of Jules who founded our Confederation? If she had ill intent, she could become ruler of the Confederation with a word, and we could do nothing but flee. Nor can we threaten the Empire, weak as it is at the moment, because our own losses here at Dorcastle were so great we could not launch an attack without leaving our lands completely defenseless."

The First President of the Confederation, who had been quiet prior to this, silenced the President of State before he could say more and nodded to the woman. "What would you recommend?"

"The daughter of Jules is no enemy to us. Neither will someone with the spirit of Jules be dictated to by us. Or by anyone." The old woman nodded toward Mari. "She has died and returned. She commands an army loyal to her which is superior to any other. What can you threaten her with? But even now she does not issue orders when we all know that she could. She listens, while we argue. Trust her, I say."

"The Free Cities will not be ruled by the whims of a Mechanic!" the woman from Cristane insisted.

"You do not speak for every city!" declared the man who had previously argued with her. "Alexdria has not forgotten our debt to the daughter and her Mage."

"The Western Alliance is very concerned," one of those representatives said cautiously. "But recognizes that for now we must wait to see what actions may be necessary in the future."

Alain leaned over to murmur to Mari. "There is something hidden behind those words. The leaders of the Western Alliance still seek some gain in the long run."

"They all do," Mari grumbled under her breath.

"What about all of the once-banned technology?" the Confederation First President asked Mari. "When will we get it?"

"Copies of some of it have already been sent to you," Mari said.

"The rest is being copied. It will take a while because the copies have to be exact."

"They're in Pacta Servanda?" the President of State pressed. "Are we permitted to send representatives to view them?"

"Yes," Mari said, nettled by the tone of the question. "Though since Pacta is on the territory of Tiae it would be courteous to inform Queen Sien of your intentions."

"They shouldn't be under your control. They should be someplace neutral," the President of State continued.

"Someplace neutral?" the Western Alliance diplomat asked. "Such as? What place on Dematr is neutral in this matter?"

"The Western Continent," the man from Alexdria suggested wryly.

It went on that way for some time, until the meeting ended with courteous expressions of mutual respect that did not sound to Mari all that sincere.

General Flyn smiled and saluted her as he watched Mari being carried out, but some worry still shadowed his eyes.

Mari said nothing until she and Alain had been left alone in their room again. "What was going in there? I mean, aside from the obvious power grabs that some of them were attempting."

"They were testing you," Alain said. "As an acolyte is tested by Mage elders to see if they can provoke the acolyte into failure, and to see what the acolyte will do when confronted. Some pushed to see what they could get from you, some sought to diminish you, others watched to see how you would react. Did you notice that there was no one in the room who was not of high rank?"

"Yes," Mari said. "Colonel Hasna was the most junior there. I think they only let her in because she's the sole official representative of Tiae. I guess they didn't want anyone of lower rank knowing what was being said."

"In that, they failed. When we left I could sense the feelings of those waiting outside. It was clear they had found means to hear what was said inside, and that they were unhappy. The unhappiness was not aimed at you."

Just how unhappy they were was obvious the next morning. "Lady, will you come listen to us?" Lieutenant Bruno looked worried, but determined.

"Who is us?" Mari asked.

"The people whose freedom you have won."

She and Alain were carried down via chair seats again, but this time into a large room in a building connected to the hospital. Mari stared out across the crowd, seeing many uniforms from many places, none of high rank except for some of those from her army. Mechanics and Mages were also in attendance. This time her chair and Alain's were placed on a raised platform before the others, so that she looked down on everyone.

That bothered her. Positioned like this, her chair felt entirely too much like—

"A throne," Alain murmured.

"What are we doing up here?" Mari demanded, speaking to everyone. She felt suddenly naked without her Mechanics jacket to bolster her confidence.

"Use mine," a familiar voice said.

Mari turned to see Alli standing next to her, taking off her own Mechanics jacket so she could drape it over Mari's shoulders. "Alli! How did you know I'd want— Wait. When did you get here?"

"A little while ago. Since you messed up your own jacket, you can borrow mine for this."

"My jacket has a big hole in it and was soaked with dried blood, Alli, and when I wanted to get it cleaned and repaired everybody freaked out so now I have to get a new one. What is this? What's the matter?"

Alli looked at Mari. "Nothing, I hope."

"Is that Professor S'san? And Master Mechanic Lukas? And I see Mage Dav and Mage Hiro and— That's Master Mechanic Lo!"

"Yeah, just like old times." Alli touched Mari on the shoulder. "Do the right thing."

"What's the right thing?" Mari asked, surprised that Alli, of all people, was being so solemn.

"I don't know," Alli said. "I hope you do."

"What is going on?" Mari hissed to Alain as Alli walked off the platform and joined the other Mechanics.

"What you have feared," Alain said. "I am certain of it. Remember what you asked me on our way to Marandur the first time? When I said that some might want an empress?"

She remembered. Hiding from the Imperial patrols. Worrying about what might happen. The words were clear in her memory. *"Can you see me on a throne?"* she had asked Alain, mocking the idea.

Mari looked again at her raised chair, then stared out at the crowd, wishing that she had the strength to stand and walk away.

"Lady." It was Lieutenant Bruno again, standing out from the crowd. "Lady Mari, daughter of Jules. We have asked you here in the hopes that you would accept our petition."

Mari forced a smile. "Petition? Shouldn't that be presented to your own leaders?"

"Our own leaders don't care about us. They seek more power and wealth for themselves and their friends. They did nothing while the Great Guilds made our lives miserable, and did little to aid you when you began your campaign against the oppression. They let Tiae suffer, they suppressed riots instead of dealing with the causes, they cooperated with the Great Guilds in keeping us enslaved. But you care. You stood beside us. You freed us. We represent many, many more people who feel as we do. Please accept our plea to govern us."

"Govern you." It really was happening. They actually were asking that of her. "You have governments. All of you. You have leaders that you elected," Mari protested.

"Leaders who have betrayed us. Who have worked only for themselves!" someone called.

Master Mechanic Lo spoke loudly. "Which leader is going to protect us? We have none. The Senior Mechanics never cared about us, but used us to protect themselves. Now we're alone, in a world full of people who have long-standing, and I will admit justified, grievances against us."

"Where is the path of wisdom?" asked a Mage Mari did not recognize. "Where do we turn? All know that you led the Master of Mages to wisdom. Show us the same. All know you have treated well the Mages who have journeyed to follow you. Show us the same."

A woman in the uniform of the Western Alliance spoke up. "We need you to protect those who will be forgotten as our leaders fight each other over who will profit most from the new day. Who will look out for the weak and the small? We know that you will!"

Mari felt her resolve wavering. They were right that someone needed to watch over the least, and that too many of those with the most—the people she had met with the day before—seemed to pay little attention to that. If she had the power to ensure that things were fair, the power to tell those squabbling self-important people in fine suits that their interests were not the only things that mattered, if she could prevent the wars that she had heard the leaders of the West arguing over just yesterday…

The elder had told her that she still had an important role to play. As little as she liked it, how could she ignore the real concerns of these people?

How could she sit back and watch new wars blossom in the light of the new day that she had done so much to bring about? How many would die during those wars if she refused to accept responsibility for what only she might be able to do?

CHAPTER THIRTEEN

MARI LOOKED AT Alain, desperate for his opinion.

He gazed back at her with calm confidence. "Freedom."

Freedom. Mari inhaled as deeply as she could, the scar tissue in her chest protesting the effort. "We're all used to being told what to do," she said to the crowd. "We've been told that was the only way to protect ourselves and the people we cared about. To have someone in charge who can give orders that must be obeyed. That is what the Great Guilds told all of us. Yes, even the Mechanics and the Mages, because our Senior Mechanics and the Mage elders insisted on obedience to their rules, their orders. But the commons here are from places where you can select the people in charge. Even Tiae. I see you, Colonel Hasna. Even in Tiae, Queen Sien has said she will rule only with the consent of her people. What I said on the battlements was true. You are all the equals of anyone. Make sure your leaders know they are no better than you. Demand that they serve you well. But that is your task, not something that you should give away to someone like me. Do not immediately surrender the freedom you have just won."

She felt the wave of disappointment from the crowd. "Lady, you are needed!"

Alain spoke, his voice Mage calm, but not void of feeling this time. "You wish Lady Mari to become your ruler. She would be Empress of the West in all but name, with a wider realm than that ruled by the Emperor in the east. Let me ask this. If Lady Mari is all that you believe, if she can be everything you hope for, what will happen when she is here no longer?"

The crowd stirred wordlessly.

"I will do all I can to keep her alive," Alain said. "I have proven that. But sooner or later she will pass on to the next dream. You will have made her empress, and become dependent on an empress to control and to order and to dictate. Who will be the next empress? What orders will that empress give?"

"We wouldn't get to choose the next empress, would we?" Professor S'san asked.

"You could choose her. Or him," someone in the crowd suggested.

"Who?" Mari asked. "You say you trust me. Fine. I don't think I'm worthy of that, but fine. Say you are right. Who else do you trust? If I'm gone, who else would you accept in that position?"

"If the daughter's army continues to exist for years to come, and whoever it is has command of the daughter's army," General Flyn said, "everyone else would have to accept that person's rule, no matter who he or she is."

"Which Mechanic?" Mari asked. "Which Mage? Which common? Who would you *all* accept? Who would you all trust? You don't need a system dependent on me. You need a system that depends on you to select worthy leaders and does not take that obligation and that responsibility out of your hands."

Lieutenant Bruno spread his hands helplessly. "But Lady, you are needed."

"You are needed," Master Mechanic Lo agreed loudly.

She looked at Alain again, hoping he would have another answer.

"I understand little of Mechanic devices," Alain said. "But I have heard the words *safety valve* and *governor* as things which prevent devices from hurting people. They do not rule the device, but they keep it from exploding."

Mari frowned at Alain, trying to understand.

Mage Dav spoke up. "You speak of Lady Mari as being such a thing in the larger illusion of the world? Someone who would not rule the west, but would protect those in it?"

"Oh," Mari gasped. She smiled at Alain. "Oh. I get it." Two Mages had realized what she could not. She remembered the meeting yesterday, the competing men and women in their various factions, and how she had worked as a brake on the arguments sometimes without even intending to. "I'd help look out for everyone, I'd help resolve problems, but I wouldn't be in charge. I'd keep things from flying out of control."

"Anyone who needed your help could ask for it," S'san said.

"But if she has no title and no army—" Lieutenant Bruno began.

"You don't understand!" Colonel Hasna called, pointing at Mari. "She has given me back a country and a queen. She has given us all our freedom. Her power lies not in a title or the authority to coerce. Her power lies in the willingness of others to follow, and in her willingness to listen. Do not require her to keep an army that answers only to her. It betrays what the daughter has done and would be an endless temptation to whoever comes after her."

Master Mechanic Lo spoke forcefully. "Will you enforce the peace of the daughter by your words and actions? Will you call out those who act unfairly?"

"Yes," Mari said, though she wasn't yet sure exactly how that would work. "Anyone who tries to mistreat you will be my enemy, and I will tell everyone that."

"Then you need no other title or army. I've been listening to the commons. Your words have more power behind them than a decree of the Emperor."

She didn't like hearing that, but most of the others in the room seemed happy with it.

"Will you always be fair?" a woman called. "Will you favor Tiae?"

"I will favor no land," Mari promised. "We are all one people. Look at my army. If we can fight side-by-side, Mechanics, Mages, commons from Tiae, the Confederation, the Western Alliance, the Free Cities, and other places, then we can build a new day side-by-side."

"With you as the governor," Professor S'san said.

"Only in the Mechanic sense of the word," Mari said.

There were more words, more requests for reassurance, but the crowd began to discuss the new day among themselves rather than demand answers from Mari, who gradually began to relax.

"If you're not going to be empress, can I have my jacket back?" Alli asked, getting back up on the platform.

"Go ahead! I would have kept it if I'd become ruler of everything," Mari threatened. "I still need a new one, though. You would think somebody who was offered an empress-ship…is that a word? A chance to be an empress. You'd think she could get a new jacket!" Mari glared at Alli. "Did you know what this was going to be about?"

"Yeah." Alli stood next to her chair, looking down and smiling. "Mari, none of us knew what the right answer was. We could see the problems, but not the solution. We hoped you would. And you did."

"Alain came up with the solution!" Mari insisted.

"Well, yeah, but you always listen to Alain. You're a team. We knew getting you meant getting him, too."

Mari shook her head in disbelief. "I help overthrow the Great Guilds, which is what so many people have wanted for so long, and the first thing everyone wants to do is give total power to a Mechanic and a Mage. What is the matter with you?"

"Maybe we need somebody to keep us from flying out of control," Alli said, grinning.

"You've always needed that, Alli," Mari said.

"Yeah, but I've got Calu to help with that. Hey, I hear you blew up the rail yard. It sounds like I'm rubbing off on you."

"Yeah," Mari said. "I blew up the rail yard. Could you check on Betsy? She was there and—"

"I already heard," Alli said. "Betsy got a little beat up, but she's salvageable. By the way, what's with the fashion statement, your daughterness?" She pointed to the white streak in Mari's hair.

"It's not a fashion statement. It's…something that happened when

Alain…saved my life." Mari sighed. "I thought maybe it would grow in black again, but those hairs are staying pure white from tip to root. And stop calling me that. For once I'd like to not be the one everybody looks to and asks *now what do we do?*"

"Sure," Alli scoffed. "You say that now, but in any group you'll take charge without realizing it. You can't help it."

"I'll prove you wrong! —Professor!" she added as S'san came to the edge of the platform, looking up slightly at Mari. "Thank you for backing me up, but why didn't you warn me?"

"I didn't really have time," S'san admitted. "I did have confidence in you. You have a tendency to search for and find unorthodox solutions, and that is what the world needed on this occasion."

"I've had good teachers," Mari said, looking over at General Flyn as he came up and saluted her, the concern no longer present in his eyes. She finally understood what that worry had been. "You wouldn't have stayed, would you?"

"If you had become Empress of the West?" Flyn asked. "No. I could not serve an empress. But my sword will always be at the service of Lady Mari, daughter of Jules."

"Oh, yeah, just one more regular, everyday Master Mechanic and daughter of Jules," Mari said. "All of you! Never do this to me again. I mean it."

"What's the worst that could have happened?" Alli asked. "You've already been dead once."

"I didn't die!" Mari's next words caught in her throat as she saw another person standing behind Alli. "Father?"

Marc of Caer Lyn nodded brusquely, his lips pressed tightly together. He looked…self-conscious. "Mari…Lady Mari—"

"Don't you dare call me Lady, Father. I'm always Mari to you."

Her father paused, then nodded, smiling slightly. "I arrived with these others, and…I'm sorry. I should have known that my daughter would be…you." He looked at Alain, speaking stiffly. "Sir Mage, I apologize to you. If not for you, I would not have had the chance to tell my daughter how proud I am of her."

Alain nodded in reply. "To my father-in-law, I should be only Alain, not Sir Mage."

"It will take a while to get used to that."

"We will hopefully have many years to do so."

"Where are mother and Kath?" Mari asked.

"Safe in Pacta, since an old fool never acted on his threats to leave there," Marc said. "I'll send them a letter letting them know I saw you and that…that you are everything everyone says."

"We're going to talk more, Father," Mari said, smiling through tears at him, "but you can reach them much faster than a letter. Mage Dav? Can you help my father get a message sent by Mage means?" Her father didn't look thrilled at the chance, but the sooner he got used to being around Mages the better.

She looked out across the room, seeing how many people still wanted to talk to her and Alain. It looked like it would be another long day in Dorcastle.

"Stay beside me," she said to Alain, grasping his hand.

"Always," he replied.

* * *

Only a few days later the healers allowed Alain and Mari to move into something called an apartment but whose size and comfort seemed more in keeping with a suite in a mansion. As uncomfortable as she was with the rooms, Mari agreed to stay because there was literally nothing else available in Dorcastle with citizens returning to the ruins of their homes and every other possible place to live packed to capacity.

Alain went to the door, grateful to be walking again, in response to a hail from one of the guards on duty. He found Vice President Jane waiting, still wearing the same cast but a fresh bandage on her face. "I have news for Lady Mari."

"Jane," Mari greeted her, standing briefly before falling back into her chair. "Sorry. Standing is still a little difficult. I haven't seen you since before the meeting."

"Which meeting was that?" Jane asked. "The one with my boss, or the one where you decided you wouldn't be my new boss?"

"Both," Mari said. "Does everybody know about those meetings?"

"They do. This is a business call, so I will be formal, Lady Mari." Vice President Jane bowed toward her. "We have received notice that the Imperial delegation will arrive tomorrow. The Emperor sent Camber of Dunlan to lead the delegation."

Mari shook her head angrily. "Somebody with no Imperial rank or title? Why would the Emperor try to insult everyone here that way?"

Jane shook her head in turn. "You don't understand. Camber is… Camber. Only people at the highest levels of diplomacy know of him. He doesn't need any title or rank. Camber is as close to the Emperor as a brother. No one in the Empire has more influence or power short of the Emperor himself. Sending Camber here to speak with you is huge. It's an acknowledgement by the Emperor that he is dealing with a peer, someone equal to himself, and no Emperor or Empress has ever done that before."

"Oh," Mari said. "Now I feel like an idiot for having gotten upset. So, this is a very good thing."

"Yes." Jane looked at Alain. "Camber is famously inscrutable. You will have your Mage with you when you speak with him?"

"Of course I will." Mari studied Jane. "How are your bosses feeling about me these days? I saw the First President of the Confederation yesterday and he was happy and cheerful and respectful and looking at me like I was a poisonous snake. I guessed then that he'd heard about the second meeting."

"They are all scared of you," Jane said. "I am hearing that, as they consider the outcome of that second meeting, they are also all coming to realize that if you were what they feared, they'd already be gone. They still worry about the power and influence you have over their people, though."

"I'm keeping my promises, Jane. All of them."

"Thank you, Mari."

* * *

That night Alain roused to see Mari sitting in a chair, the room dark, gazing out a window at the stars. "Are you well?"

She nodded. "I was just remembering."

"Sergeant Kira?" he asked, already knowing the answer.

"Yes. Her, and others. Are you sure there's a next dream, Alain?"

"I am certain," Alain said.

"I think I'm always going to be on that battlement, Alain," Mari said. "Some part of me, forever standing on the third wall with Sergeant Kira."

"But also forever with me," Alain said.

"Well, yeah, that goes without saying." He sat by her and they watched the stars until Mari fell asleep, breathing peacefully. He carried her to bed, hoping there would be no nightmares to torment her sleep later.

* * *

The next day Alain sat next to Mari, beside a fine table slightly scarred from the recent battle. There was one other chair on the far side of the table. The room they were in was not very large, but big enough to feel comfortable. There were no windows that might have provided someone with a means to eavesdrop on the words spoken within. The walls were bare except for lamps that burned oil. On the table lay a map of Dematr.

The door opened and Mari struggled to her feet with Alain's help as the head of the Imperial delegation entered alone. Camber was tall, thin, his hair very short and graying except where it had turned white at his temples. His suit was of fine quality but in no way flashy or attention-grabbing. Alain watched him, noticing that as Vice President Jane had warned, Camber had a remarkable ability to hide his feelings.

Camber walked up to the table and nodded politely to Mari.

Mari sat again with obvious relief. "You'll have to forgive me for not standing longer."

"Not at all," Camber said, taking his seat. Alain noticed that his voice also displayed noteworthy control. "I am honored that you stood for me, given your recent experiences. How do you wish to be addressed?"

"Lady Mari is fine. Or Master Mechanic Mari if you prefer. This is Master of Mages Alain."

"Master of Mages Alain's name and reputation are well known," Camber said, resting both of his hands on the surface of the table and looking steadily at Mari. "I am Camber of Dunlan, representative of the Emperor. It is the Emperor's wish that our differences be resolved as quickly and effectively as possible."

"If the Emperor wants peace, that shouldn't be a problem," Mari said.

"And in exchange?" Camber asked.

"Not much. The Sharr Isles need to have their independence restored, and all Imperial forces withdrawn."

Camber eyed her. "The Emperor knows how well the Sharr Isles would serve as a base for attacks on the Empire."

"The treaty can guarantee the neutrality of the Sharr Isles, with all parties enforcing that," Mari said, glancing at Alain to make sure she had said it right. "No military bases there for anyone. I know that's what the people of the Sharr Isles want."

Camber pondered that for a moment. "Done."

"And I would like a non-aggression agreement," Mari continued. "Everyone promising not to attack the others."

Camber's gaze on her was intent. "You wish to bind not just the Empire but also the powers of the West to not launch wars of aggression?"

"Yes."

"Lady Mari, I know you are aware that the Empire is temporarily in a weakened position. I know that there are those in the West who would like to take advantage of that. I have seen your army. It is more than impressive. You have power and opportunity."

Mari shrugged, wincing slightly as the motion tugged at her chest. "I also have common sense, and a desire to avoid useless wars." She gestured toward Alain. "And a husband who gives good advice. You know how the Great Guilds remained in power as long as they did. It was only partly because of the Mages' ability to use spells and the Mechanics' control of technology. They leveraged that power, by getting common cities and states to do their bidding."

Camber watched her without saying anything for a moment. "As the Empire recently did? I assure you that the Empire had larger goals."

"I'm sure that the Empire did," Mari said. "For centuries everyone has had larger goals, and the Great Guilds have played them against each other, getting one city or state to attack another to further the goals of the Great Guilds. But if the Empire and the states of the West agree not to conduct offensive wars, what remains of the Great Guilds will be denied that tool. There will be little chance of them sowing further chaos in this world."

Camber glanced at Alain, then back at Mari. "You include yourself in that? As one whose power could be used for others' ends? And therefore would vow not to use the army of the daughter against the Empire?"

"Yes. Not for a war of aggression. As long as the Empire promises not to attack anyone else and abides by its promises."

"The Empire would retain the right to self-defense?"

"Yes."

"And the other powers of the West would also agree to this?"

Mari nodded. "Yes."

Camber paused. "You are giving the Emperor what he most wished to have, and at little cost. Why?"

"Because I know what would happen if any part of the West attacked any part of the Empire," Mari said. "Any victories won by the West would be temporary and very costly. Further war would serve only the interests of what remains of the Mechanics Guild. And because I know that everyone involved in the treaty would be more likely to abide by it if it serves their own best interests."

Camber looked at Alain again. "Master of Mages, you have seen that the leaders of the West will follow such a treaty?"

"Yes," Alain said. "Some see the wisdom in it, but all know they must abide by its terms. Lady Mari will condemn any attack in violation of such an agreement if it is made."

"Done," Camber told Mari. "You do not demand actions against the leaders of the Mechanics Guild?"

"I suspect," Mari said, "that things aren't going so well for them already. They no longer have a monopoly on technology. They're much weaker. And their only remaining refuge is within the Empire's protection. What could I demand that would be worse than what they are already going to suffer?"

"You could demand their deaths. Others in your place would."

Mari shook her head. "The people I have fought think nothing of ordering the deaths of others. I will not become like them just because I might have the power to demand such measures."

Camber studied her. "And if those leaders of the Mechanics Guild continue to threaten you and those you love?"

"Then I will reconsider what steps may be necessary," Mari said. "I think I have proven that I make a good friend and a dangerous enemy."

"You have." Camber smiled slightly. "Your information regarding the leaders of the Mechanics Guild is accurate. The Mechanics Guild will from now on be bound by what the Emperor decrees. They will receive orders, not give them, and obedience will be demanded. Their change in status will not be a pleasant thing for those former masters of the world. The Emperor asked me to inform you that he will not tolerate actions by them against a friend such as you."

Mari raised her eyebrows at Camber. "Friend?"

"As you said, Lady Mari, you have proven that you are not an enemy anyone should want. The Emperor hopes that our future relations will be based on mutual friendship and respect."

Mari gave Alain another glance. He nodded to let her know that Camber was not lying, though it was not easy for Alain to tell with this man. "The Emperor respects strength," Alain said.

"He does," Camber replied. "But not strength alone. Strength wisely employed."

"Then we've addressed the biggest things," Mari said. "The issues on which we need agreement from leaders in the West. The details can be worked out, but if the Emperor will accept those terms in a binding treaty, we've done the heavy lifting."

"You are a poor diplomat, Lady Mari," Camber commented. "A good one would have drawn out this discussion for many days and demanded many more concessions, and in the process achieved far less."

"I've got my priorities straight," Mari said. "And I don't play games when the lives of other people are involved. There are two issues of personal interest to me that I want to also discuss, though. The Mechanics Guild has a prison at Longfalls, in Imperial territory. Would the Emperor agree to taking over that prison, and freeing everyone locked up there, letting them go wherever they choose?"

"The Emperor has promised protection for the Mechanics Guild within Imperial borders," Camber noted.

Alain spoke. "Will the Emperor permit the Mechanics Guild to retain places within the Emperor's domain that the Guild alone controls?"

"No." Camber nodded once to Alain. "The Emperor has already resolved to do the thing you asked," he told Mari. "But he will do it because he must, in order to protect all within his lands. There may be Imperial citizens within that prison. All will be released."

"Good," Mari said. She hesitated, finally drawing out a document that Alain knew. "There's another matter, pertaining to Marandur."

"Ah, yes, Marandur." Camber smiled slightly once more. "You know that there is no means for the Emperor to pardon the offense of going to Marandur? That any who go there must die?"

"Why does that amuse you?" Alain asked.

"Because the Emperor has already decreed that both incidents where you," he gestured toward Mari and then Alain, "went into and left Marandur, never occurred. If the ban was not violated, no punishment is called for."

Mari eyed Camber skeptically. "What about those who were with me?"

"Who were with you in incidents that did not happen?" Camber said. "Imperial records are being changed to reflect that reports of your entering and leaving Marandur were false. Officially, your offenses never took place. It is still on record that you and certain companions entered Imperial territory without permission, but that offense is a minor one and easily pardoned." He produced a document sealed with wax. "Such a pardon has already been signed, for you and all others involved."

Mari gave Alain a questioning glance and turned back to Camber. "What about all of those stories the Empire kept spreading about me being the Dark One, and that was why I came out of Marandur?"

"Those rumors actually started spontaneously among the Empire's citizens, who have long entertained and frightened themselves with stories of Mara the Undying. Encouraging those rumors and fears seemed like a clever way of dealing with your actions," Camber said. "We didn't realize how hard neutralizing you would actually be. If neutralizing you is possible at all. But then you not only won here, but rose from the dead." He gave Alain a longer glance. "With assistance from a Mage. Those events are too close to the stories about Mara the Undying for anyone's comfort. I assume that you do not wish to be seen by others as Mara herself, lusting after power and the blood of young men? I did not think so. Regaining control of that narrative will not be easy, but we will try. It does not benefit the Emperor to have his subjects worried that the Dark One is loose and might some-day return to share his throne."

"I assure you that I have no interest in that," Mari said. "I've already got the only man I want. So the Empire will actively discourage any stories linking me to the Dark One?"

"That will happen, but the citizens of the Empire may be hard to convince. If you had stayed dead it would have been easier to persuade them that Mari and Mara were not the same, but I understand why you and your Mage did not wish to have that happen."

"I didn't die," Mari said. Alain had noticed that she always said that when the subject came up. He did not know for certain that she was wrong, so he never contradicted her. Although he would not have contradicted her on that matter even if he had known she was wrong.

Camber showed little reaction, but to Alain's eyes appeared unconvinced by Mari's denial.

Mari laid the document she held on the table between her and Camber. "As I started to say, the second personal item is related to Marandur. I would like the Emperor to view this petition from some of his subjects."

The Imperial representative did not pick it up, instead giving Mari a curious look. "Why would subjects of the Emperor have to send a petition through you?"

"Because the petition is from the inhabitants of the Imperial University of Marandur."

Camber was surprised enough to show it, staring at the document. "The university still exists? How is that possible?"

"The masters of the university, who are the descendents of the original masters, told us the rebels didn't occupy it during the siege," Mari explained. "They had no idea why it was spared, but it meant the university wasn't damaged much during the battle. Because the university had a smaller wall around it, they have been able to hold out all this time, though with great difficulty."

Reaching out, Camber tapped the petition with his forefinger. "Why did the university's inhabitants not leave when ordered to by Emperor Palan?"

"Their oaths obligated them to remain at the university," Mari said. "They honestly thought they weren't supposed to leave, until it was too late."

Camber sat looking at the petition, his feelings guarded so well that Alain could not guess at them. He began to suspect something about the Imperial, but decided not to bring it up yet.

Finally, Camber spoke again. "This is a difficult matter. You surely know one reason why. Anyone inside the city is officially dead, and the Emperor cannot consider petitions from the dead. There is also the hard fact that the ban on entering or leaving Marandur has been ironclad since the reign of Emperor Palan. Making any exception to it now might signal weakness at a time when only strength must be shown. There are already many changes taking place. To add this…"

"Loyalty is important to the Emperor," Alain said.

"It is," Camber agreed.

Alain indicated the petition. "The inhabitants of the university have renewed their oaths of loyalty to whoever was the reigning Emperor or Empress every year since Marandur was sealed off from the outside world, even though they did not know who that person was. Their loyalty has never wavered, even as decades passed, as their numbers dwindled from hardship, as any hope of a change to their situation faded. They have remained steadfast through all that, with no hope or expectation of reward. It is a very powerful example of selfless loyalty."

Camber eyed Alain narrowly, then nodded once again. "A very powerful example. Such loyalty through adversity long sustained is too rarely seen."

"The Emperor," Alain said, "can grant relief to those loyal subjects, now that he has learned of their need, proving that nothing is more important to him than the welfare of his people. And that loyalty is always eventually rewarded."

The small smile was back on Camber's lips as he looked at Alain. "I see that reports of your wisdom have not been exaggerated. Are there any other benefits that you could foresee if the Emperor took this action?"

"Yes," Alain said, pleased that he had spotted Camber's suppressed surprise at the answer. "Marandur is a terrible monument to the cost of war. Why keep it sealed? Those who advocate war should see the city. Those who doubt what the Empire will do to those who attack it should see Marandur."

"Open the city to visitors?" Camber smiled openly. "Wisdom indeed. I have viewed the ruins from the guard towers. That was close enough for me. Others, from within the Empire and from the West, might benefit from walking the haunted streets of Marandur."

"They're not exactly easy to walk," Mari said.

"How bad is it inside the city?" Camber asked.

"Very, very bad."

"Unsettling, even to one whose emotions are strongly controlled," Alain added.

Camber finally picked up the petition, reading it. "You brought this with you from there, through those streets, through every danger?"

"Yes," Mari said. "I promised them that I would try to get the Emperor to view their petition."

"Promises mean much to you." Camber made it a statement, not a question. "I will tell you something which should not be shared with others. The Emperor is not a cruel man. He will do what is necessary, no matter how hard, but he takes no joy in needless suffering. Before our attention was focused on Marandur, it was assumed by the Imperial court that only a few scattered barbarians remained trapped within the city. No more than a handful. But as we investigated…your travels through Imperial territory…we discovered from the legion which has traditionally guarded the city that there may be larger numbers of people living in barbaric conditions inside Marandur. Not a large number, but more than we had thought. Hundreds, perhaps. Trapped within a dead city.

"This caused the Emperor distress." Camber looked from Mari to Alain as if expecting them to challenge that assertion. "But there seemed to be no means to help them that would not cause too many difficulties." He held up the petition. "This offers a means. Not just for those in the university, but all inside the city."

"Are you serious?" Mari asked, smiling in disbelief. She looked at Alain for confirmation of Camber's sincerity, and he nodded in reply.

"Many of those barbarians might die fighting you," Alain said. "But their children would have hope."

"Some in the bureaucracy might question the cost of rooting out all of the barbarians, but the alternative is maintaining the full quarantine, which is an expense that the Imperial government needs now less than ever." Camber folded the petition neatly and slid it into a inner pocket of his dress coat. "This matter need not be part of any formal agreement. I give you my word that the Emperor will see this petition, and I believe that he will look upon it favorably."

"Thank you," Mari said. "You will meet with representatives of the Bakre Confederation?"

"Those who came with me will," Camber said.

Mari flicked a glance at Alain, in which he read her rueful agreement that Jane of Danalee had been right. Camber had come only to talk with her. "I have no doubt those representatives will approve of the three main issues we discussed, but they will want to discuss other matters."

Camber rubbed his forehead lightly. "I saw the state of the city. I cannot deny much of it lies in ruins because of the Empire's actions. I know many of those defending the city died."

"You'll consider reparations? If you can't reach agreement I can help work things out."

"We will consider reparations within limits," Camber said. "There are many, many families in the Empire who must also receive death payments for the fathers and mothers, sons and daughters, who will never return home. But the Empire will soon come into a very large extra source of money which should offer the means to fairly compensate all of those who deserve it."

Mari gave Camber an intent look. "A very large extra source of money? I thought you said the Emperor guaranteed protection for what's left of the Mechanics Guild."

"He did. But the Emperor made no guarantees regarding the property of the Mechanics Guild." Camber spread his hands slightly in a gesture of regret that was obviously insincere. "In their eagerness to gain sanctuary, the leaders of what remains of the Mechanics Guild apparently overlooked that. We have strong reason to believe that the vaults in the Guild headquarters have substantial amounts of silver and gold which should be put to better use. And if the leaders of the Guild do not cooperate, we have, thanks to the daughter of Jules, learned of a means to get into those vaults with the help of Mages."

"That's not all that's in those vaults," Mari said, her voice gaining force even though she did not speak louder. "You know, don't you?"

Camber nodded. "Copies of the same once-banned technology texts that you hold at Pacta Servanda."

"You know those texts, my copies, would have been made available to the Empire."

"Surely you understand," Camber said, "why the Emperor would want to have control over the copies that exist inside his lands."

"I do understand," Mari said. She spoke with great care. "It's hard to explain everything that is in those texts. But if someone tries to rush building new devices, if someone skips over important stages or neglects warnings or doesn't prepare properly, the information in those texts could cause a lot of damage. Maybe something as sudden as explosions, big explosions that could ravage a city, or something as long-lasting as rivers and land becoming poisoned. Some of the by-products—gases—can choke to death anyone who breathes them and could slay every living thing in a city. One of the things we are going to try to do in the West is to add new technology at a rate that doesn't result in that kind of damage, and to pay careful attention to all the warnings and cautions in the texts about certain aspects of production and other issues."

Camber nodded again. "I have heard this from the messages you sent to the Emperor. I assure you that he takes your warnings seriously. We will have control of the Mechanics Guilds leaders. Do you question their competency to do the same as you will?"

"Yes," Mari said. "The leaders are administrators who got promoted to be bosses by saying yes to their bosses every time. Plus they're not going to be happy with the Emperor because of their change in status. You can't trust them."

"What about you?" Camber asked.

"I hope you know that you can trust me."

"But in this matter. If the Emperor sends emissaries to you asking for your advice and arguments on aspects of the new technology, would you give him the same answers and appraisals that you give to those in the West?" Camber asked. "Not seeking to hold back the Empire in order to give advantage to the West?"

"Yes, I will do that," Mari said. "Because if the West gets too far ahead of the Empire, that would be a dangerously unstable situation. And if the Empire races ahead on something that ought to be done with careful deliberation, it might inspire some in the West to do the same, with possible big problems everywhere."

"It is in your self-interest to do it?" Camber gave her that small smile again. "Like you, Lady Mari, I prefer agreements based on such grounds. You will commit to that? If so, I will advise the Emperor to accept your offer."

"I will commit to it," Mari said.

Camber looked at Alain. "And you, Sir Master of Mages, will you share your wisdom? The Emperor is keenly interested in your accomplishments and wishes to know more of them for himself and for those Mages who remain in Imperial service."

Alain nodded once, purposely mimicking Camber. "I will share what I have with all who come."

"At what price?"

"Wisdom has no price."

That very nearly got a laugh out of Camber. "Certainly those who sell it seem to have less wisdom the more they charge for it. Then this need not be negotiated or put into writing?"

"You will not accept the word of a Mage?" Alain asked.

Camber's smile was wider. "You tell jokes?"

"It is a skill that takes some time to relearn, does it not?" Alain asked him.

The smile was replaced by a keen look. "You figured it out? No one else ever has."

"What did you figure out, Alain?" Mari asked.

"Camber was once a Mage," Alain explained, drawing a surprised look from Mari.

"Yes," Camber said. "Taken to be an acolyte, many years before you were, and forced to endure the training. I learned enough to be granted Mage status, though my spells were only small things because hidden within me was a desire to escape. When I was finally able to leave the Mage Guild Hall alone, I left for good, finding a place where I could hide and slowly regain the humanity driven from me by the Mage elders. I lost what few powers I had in the process. Eventually I was able to be among commons and even other Mages without them knowing who I had been. It was a secret, until now."

"I will not divulge it," Alain said.

"You kept your power," Camber said. "I would not have brought this up if you had not seen it in me, but now I ask if we could speak. I have always wondered whether I could have retained some of those skills."

Alain inclined his head respectfully toward Camber. "This one would speak with you."

"Tomorrow? I will send a messenger when I can." Camber stood up, extending his hand to Mari. "I wish that I had met you two before this war began. My advice to the Emperor would have been very different. Will you answer a question for me?"

"What is it?" Mari asked, grasping Camber's offered hand for a moment.

"Since arriving in the city, I have learned that you were given an opportunity few ever have, and that you gave a response that perhaps no one ever has. You could have ruled all of these lands. But you said no. You rejected the chance to hold such power. Why?"

Mari shrugged. "I didn't think I was a good fit for the job, and frankly I didn't think the job should exist."

"I cannot pass judgment on either of those things," Camber said. "But you could have been far more than a Mechanic."

"All I ever wanted to be was a Mechanic," Mari said.

Camber nodded, stepping back. "Yet you were willing to be the daughter when called upon. The world suffers from those whose ambition drives them to be more and more. But it needs those willing to be more than they wish when they are needed. I will tell the Emperor he need not fear you."

Mari nodded in return. "I hope you don't mind me saying that I'll be keeping my eye on the Emperor. He and I might not see eye to eye on what's necessary."

"I would expect nothing less."

Camber had no sooner left than an official stuck his head in the room, looking worried. "Lady, the Syndaris are here."

CHAPTER FOURTEEN

"THEY'RE NOT ATTACKING, are they?" Mari demanded.

"No, Lady! I'm sorry. It's a delegation from Syndar. They urgently request a meeting with you."

Mari rubbed her forehead, sighing. "Do they look scared?"

"We ensured that they came past your army encampments on the way in, so, yes, they are probably very worried, Lady."

"Let's get this over with."

Three Syndaris entered, two women and a man, all dressed in the bright, colorful garb of the highest-ranking officials of the Syndar Islands. The woman in the lead bowed stiffly toward Mari. "There has been an unfortunate misunderstanding."

Alain answered. "Is *unfortunate misunderstanding* the term used in Syndar for a surprise attack?"

The woman paused. "We were lied to, told that you intended to attack us and that we must strike first if we were to have any chance. The lies were inexcusable, but surely you, in your mercy and your wisdom, will understand why we acted in self-defense."

"It is difficult when someone lies about such important matters," Alain said, knowing that Mari would understand that he was telling her the Syndari emissary was lying. "Lies inspire neither mercy nor wisdom."

Mari leaned forward slightly, her expression hardening. "As my

Mage says, I'm not feeling particularly merciful. You struck at Pacta Servanda and shipping in the Umbari without warning."

"The Empire did the same at Dorcastle!"

"The Empire just sued for peace," Mari said, her voice cold. "You come in here and claim that you're victims."

"We have full reports of the losses you suffered at Pacta Servanda," Alain added. "We know how dangerously weak the remaining forces of Syndar are, and how poorly they would fight if attacked now in the wake of such an awful defeat. And we have heard that the Queen of Tiae is full of wrath at your attack. It would be best not to give her cause to act on that wrath."

The three from Syndar exchanged looks. "What do you want?" the leader asked Mari.

Mari relaxed a bit. "I don't want Syndar. Neither does anyone else. But we'll all act if we have to. What we want are some solid assurances that Syndar will not pose further threats to us."

"You are speaking on behalf of the Bakre Confederation? And of Tiae?"

"Yes."

"If you wish the heads of those responsible," the Syndari woman said, "you already have them. They all accompanied the attack, and all died."

Alain nodded to Mari to let her know that this time the Syndari had spoken the truth.

"What I wish," Mari said, "is measures to ensure that Syndar's neighbors are safe from attack, and that no one can use the Syndari Islands as a safe haven for threatening others."

"What are your demands, daughter of Jules?"

"Nothing you shouldn't be able to live with."

Getting those terms spelled out in ways that the other countries involved would accept took quite a while longer. After that, Alain found himself and Mari called in to help resolve the reparations issue between the Empire and the Confederation. Alain's sympathy for the Confederation was tested by what he thought unseemly haggling over what appeared to be small sums compared to what the Empire had already agreed to, but he could not feel sympathy for the Empire given how many had died defending Dorcastle.

He could tell that Mari was feeling the same, but she maintained an outwardly evenhanded approach, trying to get past the stumbling blocks, until her low endurance betrayed her. As Mari slumped in her seat, Alain turned to the stubborn negotiators eyeing her with wary concern. "Is it not enough?" he asked in a toneless voice.

The Empire yielded on one point, the Confederation on two others, and the agreement could proceed.

After Mari and Alain got back to their room and a belated dinner, Mari sighed heavily. "You know what, Alain? At one point in that room I started thinking fondly about the good old days when people were chasing you and me and trying to kill us. That felt like a much happier time than being locked up in a room with a lot of people arguing endlessly over fine points of grammar."

"We could still be trapped in Marandur," Alain said.

"Don't make me choose," Mari said. She smiled, looking out the window, which faced east. "We kept our promises to the students, Alain, and to Professor Wren. They'll have a chance at life outside Marandur."

"And those masters of the university who refused their help to us will be proven wrong," Alain added.

Mari's smile took on a wicked cast. "Really? I hadn't thought of that at all."

* * *

Thirty days after the victory at the last wall of Dorcastle, the anniversary was marked by a special ceremony to honor the defenders.

Mari sat in a chair placed on the edge of a field outside of Dorcastle. She could walk again, though weakness still stood at her elbow, and a lingering tightness in one side of her chest reminded her constantly of the sharpshooter's bullet that had almost ended her life.

Field Marshal Klaus marched up, a healing scar running down one side of his face and neck. With him was Lieutenant Bruno. If the field marshal knew of Bruno's part in the move to offer Mari control of the west, he gave no sign of it, whether of approval or disapproval. Klaus should have had an additional lieutenant accompanying him, but he had left that position vacant to honor the memory of Lieutenant Kaede, who had died during the battle.

Klaus saluted. "Lady, though I commanded the details of the defense of Dorcastle, you were our leader. It is no exaggeration to say that we all followed you in that fight." He turned to face the open area where ranks of soldiers were drawn up. The soldiers who had fought to defend Dorcastle and not been too badly injured to stand in ranks this day.

Behind the open area units representing Mari's own army stood at attention, their banners dipped in respect toward the ranks of the defenders.

Mari gazed at the neat formations, seeing how small most of them were. The gaps that should have been in them, the places so many fallen comrades would have occupied, couldn't be seen because the ranks had been closed. But that meant that units which should have covered much more area instead showed much smaller numbers. In some places only a single rank of soldiers stood, some of them obviously still recovering from wounds suffered during the battle, their colors waving both proudly and forlornly before the survivors.

Her eyes sought out the Third Regiment. Sergeant Kira's unit. It was one of those with only two ranks left, a lieutenant the senior-most survivor. The sight forcefully reminded Mari that Colonel Teodor had died at almost the same time as Kira. "I'm going to walk." Mari used her arms to push herself up from her chair, shaking her head to fend away offers to help. "If they can stand in ranks, I can walk."

"Of course, Lady," Klaus said. "If you will follow." The field marshal led the way, Mari and Alain walking behind him, Lieutenant Bruno following.

Fighting back tears at the losses these soldiers had suffered to defend their homes, Mari forced her legs to carry her along the ranks of those she had fought beside. Her vision got fuzzy at one point, but she leaned on Alain, breathed deeply and kept going, returning the salutes offered her, pausing to speak thanks as she passed each unit, giving a wave or salute to any of the individual officers or soldiers that she recognized.

The new Mechanics jacket she wore still felt stiff and a bit unfamiliar. Mari wondered if she should take it off in deference to these common folk who had won their freedom from the Great Guilds. But she had worn a jacket like it in the battle, and everyone seemed to be pleased to see her wearing one again. Mari kept it on.

She almost broke down when she reached the tiny line of cavalry that represented all the survivors of the soldiers who had escorted her and Alain from Tiae. Sixty-one, counting Major Danel, had ridden north with her. Seven sat their horses this day, all that remained. Danel had indeed died in the charge at the fourth wall.

As Mari paused before the cavalry, striving for words, Colonel Hasna stepped forward. "With the permission of the daughter, I will read a message from Queen Sien."

Mari nodded.

Hasna unfolded a paper and read, her voice carrying easily across the field. "By command of Queen Sien, by the grace of birth and her people's choice the ruler of Tiae, those who formed the escort for the daughter and who fought with such bravery and skill at Dorcastle will form the core of a unit henceforth to be known as the Queen's Own Lancers. It will be a unit whose mission is to defend all who need their aid, and to commemorate the sacrifices of those who gave all they had to help free the world. The memory of those who died will forever be honored, and those who lived will always be among the first in Tiae."

"Thank you," Mari said to Hasna, then looked at the seven remaining and said it again. "Thank you." The words were woefully inadequate, but there were no words strong enough or good enough, so they would have to do.

Major Sten stood with the survivors of a Confederation cavalry unit, his face marked with new cuts but otherwise unharmed. "You're the lucky one, aren't you?" Mari told him. "I'm glad."

When they finally reached the two ranks made up of the Third Regiment's surviving members, the lieutenant who was the senior surviving officer saluted Mari. She halted, looking down the ranks and seeing not only those here, but all of those who had fallen. Mari turned to Field Marshal Klaus. "I'll never forget any of those who fought here, but the Third Regiment will always have a special place in my heart."

Klaus nodded. "Soldiers of the Third Regiment, by request of Lady Mari your unit is to henceforth provide her honor guard whenever she visits the Bakre Confederation."

When she had walked down the last line of soldiers, her steps increasingly weak, Mari finally allowed herself to be fully supported by Alain, leaning heavily on him. "Thank you," she called across the field. "No one will ever be more honored than I am to have fought beside you all. May your deeds, and those of the many who do not stand here now, never be forgotten. From this day, outside of formal settings I am only Mari to you all, because we will always be equal as comrades who stood side by side on the walls of Dorcastle. The new day has just begun! Thanks to you, our world will see new wonders and our children will see freedom!" She was going to cry. She knew it.

As Mari was being supported from the field by Alain a lone voice called out from the ranks. "Freedom and the daughter!" Others picked it up, chanting the phrase, until the field rang with it so loudly it was if the voices of the fallen had joined in.

Mari did cry, not trying to hide the tears, as Alain helped her off the field.

* * *

Her mother Eirene and little sister Kath had arrived in time to witness the ceremony, joining Mari afterwards when she had regained her composure. Kath, having witnessed the bloody aftermath of the battle at Pacta, had lost her earlier enthusiasm for joining Mari's army. She ran to Mari, hugging her and crying. "Please don't die again," Kath begged.

"I didn't die," Mari reassured her, but neither her mother nor Kath seemed to believe her. They both looked at the white streak in Mari's hair and then at Alain, who also got a hug and a tearful thank-you from Kath.

"Is it all over?" Eirene asked. "Can you just be Mari again as you wanted?"

"I may never be just Mari again," Mari admitted. "I've got some long-term commitments. Short term, there is one very important thing left to do. It shouldn't be dangerous. We've sent for someone to see if we can get that done."

Coleen, the head of the Librarians of Altis, arrived the next day on the back of Mage Alera's Roc. After dismounting from the giant bird and following them into their private rooms, Coleen inclined her head respectfully towards Mari and Alain. "You could have made this decision yourself, you know. We couldn't have denied you."

"You librarians have spent centuries protecting that information," Mari told her. "Only you have the right to decide if it is time for the world to know about it, and about you."

Coleen smiled. "We have decided. The librarians agree that it is time to let the world know about us, and to open the valley to those who wish to see what we have protected all this time."

"Good. I'm going to arrange a high-ranking delegation to go there. We have a piece of equipment to test." Mari gave Coleen a level look. "I do have another important question. What's at Pacta Servanda?"

"Pacta Servanda?" Coleen spoke as if unfamiliar with the name.

"You are seeking not to say something," Alain said.

"I am baffled by the question, Sir Mage. Why are you asking me about Pacta Servanda?" Coleen said.

Mari studied Coleen before answering. "I'm asking because the royal family of Tiae was secretly tasked with protecting that town, a tasking that seems to have taken place centuries ago. It doesn't appear to be in any way a special town. So why does that obligation rest with the kings and queens of Tiae?"

The librarian gazed back at her for a few moments without answering, then shook her head. "There are things we do not know. Why did Queen Sien say her family was required to protect that town?"

"She doesn't know. That knowledge vanished somewhere along the way, maybe when Tiae fell apart a couple of decades ago. The librarians don't know what's special about Pacta Servanda?" Mari pressed.

"I cannot tell you anything about Pacta Servanda that you don't already know," Coleen replied.

Alain, watching the librarian closely, gave Mari a nod. Apparently, she was telling the truth.

This was one mystery that wasn't going to be resolved right away.

* * *

Reaching agreement on all the details, getting approval from everyone who needed to approve, and setting up the trip to Altis took another month. Fortunately, many of the world leaders Mari wanted to see the things at Altis had gathered at Dorcastle, making it easier to rope them into the expedition.

Mari and Alain rode the *Gray Lady* north, retracing their flight from Altis over a year ago. This time the *Pride* sailed along as escort, carrying some of those Mari had wanted along for the trip.

The captain of the *Gray Lady* was not the piratical old sailor who had gotten them safely to the Umbari Ocean. He had died helping to repel the attack on Pacta. His former first mate commanded the *Lady* now with the same air of outward legitimacy and barely hidden opportunism. "Don't feel sad for him, Lady," she told Mari. "He wanted to die on the water, under sail, not in some waterfront tavern living away his last years with nothing but memories of the sea. What more can an old sailor hope for?"

Mari and Alain arrived once more on the island of Altis, not sneaking ashore using false papers this time but escorted into the harbor as part of a small fleet of warships that carried a large group of Mechanics, a smaller group of Mages, and those dignitaries representing most places in the world.

"Why didn't Syndar send anybody?" Alli asked Mari as they stood on a pier watching equipment being offloaded.

"They apparently thought it was some kind of trick to lure people here for some nefarious purpose, but I think they really were afraid they'd run into you again," Mari said. "The she-demon Mechanic who blows up entire armies with a glance."

Alli grinned. "There are worse reputations for a girl to have. Is it true that Ringhmon wouldn't send anyone unless they were rewarded with a big payment just for showing up?"

"Yeah." Mari shook her head. "No one cared enough to pay them to come, but they probably could have gotten some money by demanding ransom *not* to show up."

"Lady." A large delegation from Altis stood beaming at Mari. "We regret not being able to greet you properly the last time you visited our island."

"To be honest," Mari said, "I didn't think you'd be thrilled to have me and Alain back after what happened to Altis last time."

The grand mayor of Altis smiled. "Once the fires were put out and the smoke cleared, the damage wasn't as bad as feared. And the aid you arranged to be sent us over the last six months was most appreciated. Our finest hotel awaits you and your party."

Alain pointed toward the mountains. "We will be staying inland."

"Inland? There is nothing inland but rocks."

"We'll take the road," Mari said.

"The road?" The leaders of Altis exchanged baffled looks. "There's a road inland?"

Mage Alera had been at work, her huge Roc appearing on the waterfront. "We'll see you there!" Mari called. "Tell Coleen we're on our way!" Swift spread his wings and the mighty bird leaped skyward.

"Too bad she couldn't haul this on her Roc," Master Mechanic Lukas grumbled as he supervised the loading of equipment on mules.

"What is it?" the First President of the Bakre Confederation asked.

"A disassembled hydro-electric generator," Mari said. "The tower of the librarians has been losing power slowly, so we're going to install some new capacity for them."

"The librarians. I'm still trying to understand exactly what librarians are and why they would need power?"

"Librarians," Mari said, "are one of the greatest things on Altis." She turned to the leaders of the island. "You have hosted and protected them without ever knowing they were there. But now the world will know, and many will come to Altis to see them and the knowledge they have kept safe at great sacrifice."

One of the librarians who had come to Pacta to copy the tech manuals Mari and Alain had rescued from Marandur helped point out the hidden entrance to the road inland, astounding the people who had lived on Altis and never known such a thing existed.

The procession headed inland along the concealed road through tortuous mountain terrain. After a few days traveling through the harsh, often barren landscape, it was obvious that if not for the undeniable fact that the road existed, most of those traveling with Mari and Alain wouldn't have believed there was anything of significance at the end of it. But then the view opened out onto the mountain valley where the great tower stood.

Coleen and many others waited at the small bridge spanning a stream, this time smiling in welcome rather than trying to bar entry to the valley. While Master Mechanic Lukas led a team to the waterfall to install the generator, Coleen guided the others into the tower.

Mari pulled Alain to the side as they entered the large underground room where numerous pieces of equipment from the ship that had come from Urth had been kept safe. "We need to give them time to absorb this," she told him.

The Mechanics, the Mages, the leaders of the world, looked around in amazement at devices far beyond the technology they knew, at the map of the far-distant world known as Urth and the diagram of the great ship named *Demeter* that had brought people to this world.

"I would not have believed it," Camber eventually told Mari. "Can these items now be freed? Be put to use?"

"They no longer work," Coleen told him.

"None of them?" S'san asked, looking closely at the equipment in the cases.

"No," Coleen said. "Our records say they all ceased working soon after being left here for safekeeping by those who founded the Mechanics Guild."

"According to the tech manuals, devices such as this should have kept working for a long time. They should have been very reliable." S'san gave Mari a sharp look. "The manuals say that these pieces of equipment all contain tiny versions of our Calculating and Analysis Devices, and all use something like our thinking ciphers to operate. Do you remember what you encountered at Ringhmon?"

Mari nodded in understanding. "A contagion that kept the CAD there from working. Do you think these devices were all infected with contagions?"

"Very likely. The tech manuals call such things viruses." S'san tapped the protective cover over the instruments. "The founders of the Mechanics Guild wanted these things available if they ever needed them, but wouldn't have wanted anyone else using them. How better to ensure that than by sabotaging the devices?"

"And if they did need them, they could cure the contagions, since they knew what they were." Mari shook her head. "How long ago do you think the Mechanics Guild's leaders lost knowledge of the contagions?"

"Hard to say, since eventually they forgot this place even existed." Professor S'san looked at Coleen. "The librarians had no Mechanics among their numbers?"

"No," Coleen said. "None of the crew with such knowledge was allowed to join us. Those who stayed here could operate these devices, but not repair them if something went wrong."

"Do you think we can get them working again?" Mari asked Professor S'san.

"After so long? It's hard to say if they can still be repaired. Even if it is physically possible, it is almost certainly practically impossible. You're one of our finest minds on contagions, Mari, and whatever was done to these must be far beyond your skills." S'san looked around the room. "Perhaps it is better that way. Unleashing all of this on our world could be incredibly disrupting. And we can't replace any of it, not until we've worked for generations. Imagine becoming dependent on devices such as this, only to have them fail."

"I must agree," Camber said. "Can study of them yield anything of importance?"

"I'm sure it would," S'san said. "But will that study be permitted?" she asked Coleen.

"Yes," Coleen said. "That's why they were kept safe, so that someday they could benefit the world again. We will be happy to host those who want to try to learn some of their secrets."

"There are no weapons," the man from Alexdria commented.

"No," Coleen said. "No weapons were left with us."

"Maybe that's better," said the diplomat from the Western Alliance. "Can you imagine what sort of weapons they could have had?"

"I wish at least one thing still worked," Alli commented.

"One thing does," Mari said. "We think, anyway." She pointed at the bulk of the Feynman unit. "That is supposed to be a far-talker with enough range to reach Urth."

"You're kidding." Everyone rushed to crowd around the unit, while taking care not to touch it.

"That's one of the reasons we're here," Mari said. "Once Lukas figures out how to hook up that extra generator, we're going to see if that device still works, and we're going to try to call Urth."

"You like doing that, don't you?" Calu said to her. "Just suddenly dropping a conversational bomb in a room and watching everybody else freak out."

"She does," Alain said.

"Do you think you have room to talk, Alain? The guy who suddenly told me 'By the way, you're the daughter of Jules'?" Mari scoffed.

"How are the Mages taking this, Alain?" Calu asked.

"They are mostly content to observe. I have told them that, as far as is known, Urth does not have those capable of Mage talents. This news was welcome to them."

"Huh," Calu said. "You know what? It's welcome to me, too. This is all pretty intimidating to a Mechanic. We can't match it. Not for a long time. If our world has something that Urth can't match, it makes me feel better."

The lights suddenly brightened noticeably. "Lukas must have figured out how to hook up the new generator," S'san commented.

Master Mechanic Lukas arrived soon afterward to confirm that guess. "The tech manual for this tower showed how to do the hook-up, but I thought we'd have to do some manual adjustments. Instead, as soon as the power was flowing, whatever governs the tower's power distribution handled it all automatically." Lukas shook his head. "This is so far ahead of us. I feel like a common looking at a far-talker for the first time."

"If we have the power," Coleen asked eagerly, "should we try the device?"

Mari looked over the bulk of the Feynman unit. "Who's going to do it?"

"You are, Mari," S'san said. "Go ahead."

"Me?" Mari looked around at everyone. "Shouldn't someone else—"

"We talked this over while waiting for the power hook-up. We're here because of you," S'san said.

"This wouldn't be happening without you, your daughterness," Alli pointed out. "You're the one who changed the world."

Mari shook her head at Alli. "And yet I can't stop you from using that term."

"Everyone agreed," said the First President of the Bakre Confederation. "It may be the first and the last thing in this world that everyone agrees on, but all believe you have earned the right to do this."

"Besides which," Camber said, deadpan, "we would never agree on any other person to have the honor."

There obviously wasn't any sense in arguing, and Mari knew how badly she did want to do it. She walked through the crowd, faced the transmitter, and looked over at Alain. "I can't believe how nervous I am."

Everyone was waiting. "Can you tell what to do?" Master Mechanic Lukas asked, not in a challenging way, but as one Mechanic to another when faced with a strange device.

"There's a button here, under a protective cover," Mari said. "It has the universal sign for an on/off switch."

"I guess we finally know where that universal sign came from," Lukas said. "Push the blasted thing!"

"Yes, honored Master Mechanic." Mari reached out to flip up the protective cover. It protested the movement, but finally gave way. Mari took a deep breath and pushed the button.

A low humming began coming from the device. Two large panels that looked somewhat like glass suddenly lit up and words began to appear on them, drawing gasps from everyone who saw, others crowding to get a look. Mari began reading some of the words out loud. "*System initializing…diagnostics running…*there's a long list here of what I guess are components. It's like when one of our Calculating and Analysis Devices boots up, loading its thinking ciphers. *Permanent memory OK.* What does Oh-Kay mean? The same thing is showing up next to everything else."

"Maybe that's some sort of shorthand for *it's working*," Calu suggested.

"Maybe. What if that's Zero K? What could that signify? Um… proceed with set-up? It's asking me. There are two tabs under the question saying yes and no."

Calu was close enough to squint and study the image. "I don't see anything you're supposed to flip or push to say one or the other."

"There have to be some controls," S'san insisted.

"Maybe there's some little arrow on those tabs that points to a control, something that we can't see," Mari said, raising one finger to rub at the tab labeled "yes."

To her shock, the tab glowed at her touch and new words appeared. "Set-up proceeding. All I did was touch this surface! That's the control!"

"How in blazes—?" Lukas began, shaking his head.

"We'll learn," S'san replied.

Words flew across the screens faster than Mari could read until one of the screens settled down to display a few items. "Universal Time. It's showing seconds, minutes, hours, days, months, and a year. Nothing like our date and time. Here's another. Local time. That must be here."

Calu nodded. "The time fits, but whatever it's using for day, month, and year don't. I wonder if that's something the great ship was supposed to use but the founders of the Mechanics Guild deliberately changed?"

"Use Universal or Local Time?" Mari read, looking to the others again for guidance.

The non-Mechanics looked to the Mechanics, who all shrugged. "Local?" Alli suggested.

Mari reached out cautiously and touched the Local tab under the question, gasping as the device once again accepted the input. "Verifying location. Establishing links. Verifying access. Ready."

She drew one hand back through her hair, staring at the screen. "This one says *ready to receive*, and this other says *transmit*. At least we understand what those words mean."

Calu scratched his head. "Since this seems to be a sort of far-talker, it might be a good idea to see if anybody is saying anything before we break in."

"Yes," S'san agreed. "That's good far-talker etiquette as we understand it. Let's try *receive* first."

Mari touched that tab.

A voice filled the room, speaking in a strange accent that was still understandable, the tone that of someone doing something routine. "—government of Sinharat province on Mars has proposed new adjustments to planetary weather patterns which are under consideration.

That completes Sol update. Colony update begins. For Amaterasu, request you provide more detailed information on local crop ailment so possible genetic modifications can be proposed. Please include as much research and environmental data relevant to the crop as possible. For Brahma, in response to your question, request you continue relaying these transmissions to Demeter in case any survivors of the colony exist who can receive over a damaged Feynman unit but cannot transmit."

"Demeter!" Coleen cried. "That is us!"

A murmur of excited comment nearly drowned out the next words from the speaker. "This is ERIS, Earth Relay and Interstellar Signals center, sending the daily update from Sol system to all colonies. Latest update will be repeated in one hour universal time."

"Urth," one of the librarians breathed, tears coming. "The home of our ancestors still lives."

"And they still worry about us," Coleen added, wiping at her own eyes.

S'san gestured peremptorily at Mari. "Well? Go ahead! Answer them!"

CHAPTER FIFTEEN

SHE DIDN'T FEEL worthy of the honor, but everyone else was clearly set on it. Mari reached one hand to hold onto Alain's. "We're doing this together," she whispered to him.

She used her free hand to touch the transmit tab, which hesitated only a moment before a glowing "ready" appeared next to it. There was a far-talker 'phone attached to the transmitter by an armored cable. Mari took it, seeing the illuminated button labeled PUSH TO TALK. "They really did try to idiot-proof this when they designed it," she told the others, trying to quell her nervousness.

Everyone was waiting. Everyone was watching. Mari pressed the button with her thumb and spoke slowly and clearly. "Urth, this is Lady Master Mechanic Mari of Caer Lyn calling from the world of Dematr. I repeat, this call is from Dematr. I am here with my promised husband, Sir Master of Mages Alain of Ihris, along with many other Mechanics, and Mages, and leading common folk of this world. We have suffered a very difficult period and lost many things. But after a great struggle we have regained our freedom and the ability to speak with you again. We extend our hands in peace to our distant brothers and sisters, who we did not even know existed until a short time ago. Please respond. This is Master Mechanic Mari on Dematr, over."

She released the button, looking and listening expectantly.

Some new words appeared on one screen. "Estimated time to reply," Mari read, feeling disappointed, "six hours, fourteen minutes."

"That must mean whatever form of transmission this uses will take that long for a signal to get to Urth and get back here," Calu said.

"You don't think it uses far-talker tech?" Lukas asked him.

"There are some sections in the advanced tech manuals that talk about far-talker signals, what they call rah-dio, taking a lot of years to travel from one star to another, so if we're going to get a reply in six hours, it has to be something else."

"Such as what?" S'san said.

Calu scratched his head as he thought. "One of the manuals referenced SAD Signaling as being a whole lot faster than far-talker waves. Maybe that's it."

"SAD?"

"The manual said," Calu replied, looking embarrassed, "SAD stood for Spooky Action at a Distance. I've got no idea whether that's some weird tech joke or if it sounds serious to people from Urth."

"So six hours is really fast?" Mari asked.

"I think so."

"It will work, right?" Coleen asked. "You can tell? They could hear us?"

"They will hear us," Calu said. "I think."

"There's no real way to tell," S'san said. "Not until we either get a reply or…never hear back."

"It ran all of those tests and diagnostics," Mari said. "Everything was, uh, OK."

"Which might mean that it sort of works in a minimal way! Or has a high failure rate. We don't know." S'san looked around at the anxious faces. "If the device is working properly, then in a little over six hours we will hear back. Maybe not from Urth. Maybe that's how long it will take the nearest place to answer us, whatever that place is."

The group around the Feynman unit broke up. Some went to eat or rest, others continued pestering the librarians with questions. Everyone made their way back into the room well before the time was up, but as Mari stood nervously by the transmitter she saw the words change. "It just went from saying fourteen minutes remaining to saying thirty-three minutes remaining!"

"It did say estimated," Calu pointed out.

"It's like dealing with a bureaucracy," Camber commented.

"An automated bureaucracy," Lukas said. "Can you imagine? Maybe some things we shouldn't be too eager to get built again."

Everybody, Mari noticed, was avoiding saying that the device might not have worked, that her speech might have gone nowhere, heard by no one.

But before anyone else could say anything, the numbers Mari was looking at abruptly went to zero and another voice filled the air. It was someone different from the first speaker. The unusual accent was nearly the same, but the tone of the voice was now filled with joy and excitement. "Demeter, Demeter, we copy your transmission! This is Earth Relay and Interstellar Signals acknowledging the message from Demeter. You can't imagine how much excitement there was here when your call came through. We have heard nothing from your world for centuries. Not since two standard months after the arrival of the colony ship. We feared the colony might have been totally wiped out. Your brothers and sisters are very happy to hear from you. We regret that your colony has experienced major difficulties and would appreciate a detailed description of those problems as soon as possible.

"Lady Master Mechanic Mari, if you are still there please provide a description of what your title means. We are uncertain of the title you gave for your husband and its meaning as well. We would like to know as much as possible about your society and the history of Demeter since we lost contact."

"Please respond. Your Feynman unit is using a transmit setting dedicated to Demeter, so speak as long as you want and tell us as much as possible. You won't be interfering with anyone else, and I promise you that nearly everyone on three planets and several moons in the solar system plus those on the colonies orbiting other suns will want to know everything you can tell us. This is ERIS, Earth Relay and Interstellar Signals center, responding to the transmission from Demeter from Lady Master Mechanic Mari."

Mari realized that she was staring at the Feynman unit, her mouth hanging open, overwhelmed by the moment. As she stood there, unable to think, Alli suddenly grabbed her in a hug.

"Good job, Mechanic!" Alli yelled.

Then it seemed everyone wanted to do the same, the room erupting into bedlam as it sank in that it was all real, that Urth was real and that they were once more part of a vast community of people on worlds that none of them had known existed. Even the Mages were partially caught up in the euphoria. Calu replaced Alli hugging Mari, then Professor S'san was there, Professor S'san was *crying* and embracing Mari, and even stoic Master Mechanic Lucas slapped her back with a broad grin that seemed likely to crack his stern, old face. Head Librarian Coleen forced her way through to Mari for another hug, then Alain was there, Alain was smiling, and Mari held him so tightly no one else could break in, realizing that she was laughing and couldn't stop herself.

Because in this room, where history had long been kept safe, new history had just been made. This victory marked the final end of the Mechanics Guild and its control of the world. No matter what happened after this, Dematr would never again be isolated from the rest of humanity.

* * *

The visitors left in groups over the next week, trudging back along the hidden road, most of them talking enthusiastically about what they had seen and learned from the librarians. Altis would soon have a steady stream of visitors heading inland where few had ever ventured.

Alain and Mari led their mounts a bit ahead of the rest of their group, the two walking side by side and the mountain ponies ambling behind them. The healers back in Dorcastle, still baffled by the healing she had undergone and the resulting shock to Mari's body, had alternated between stressing the need for Mari to get exercise and the need for her to get enough rest and not overexert. As far as Alain could tell, Mari had stopped listening to them on that topic and was instead stubbornly doing whatever felt right to her.

Physically she seemed to be doing a lot better, which made Alain a lot happier. Emotionally, though… He had noticed a moodiness ever since they had left the valley. She was finally perking up a bit. "It's so hard to leave all that," she finally explained to Alain. "I mean, it was amazing to see that stuff, but it also made it clear how much we had lost and how long it would take to recover that level of technology. Still, we look at it and think about how we're going to get back there. And we're going to, Alain. The damage done by the Mechanics Guild will take a long time to repair, but we'll learn what we have to learn." She turned an inquisitive glance his way. "What do you think is the most important thing you learned in the last couple of years?"

"That no one can ever win an argument with the woman they love," Alain said. "Every form of apparent victory is just another type of defeat."

"You have learned wisdom," Mari said, grinning. "I learned how big a difference one person can make, both in the lives of those closest to them, and to many others. I'm talking about you, by the way."

Alain nodded. Ahead the road dipped beneath a concealing over-hang. The shade would be welcome, with the winds nearly calm and the mountains around them hot from the midday sun. "Never doubt that your words also apply to you. I do not feel wise. So many Mages wish to speak with me about the new wisdom. I tell them what I know, but that is too little."

"At least they're not coming to you to work out compromises to avoid another war." Mari tilted her head to one side as she studied him. "The threat of the Storm never entirely goes away, does it? I went into this thinking, all right, we'll stop the Storm and things will be fine. But even though we stopped that storm, others will always threaten. Am I right?"

Reluctantly, Alain nodded. "I have been speaking with the other

Mages, who agree with what the elder and I have seen. Our foresight was dominated by the storm of chaos that you stopped—"

"That *we* stopped."

"Yes. But we continue to see occasional warnings. Not as frequent, not as urgent, but with the sense of something to be ever on guard against."

"At least I have job security," Mari commented. "Somewhere along the line we have to figure out a way for the world to do things without having me as a governor for the machinery of human interactions, but that's likely to be a long-term project. In the near term, you and I need to make sure we get some time for ourselves. I think we've earned that." Mari gave him a smile. "Are you still all right with settling near Pacta, like we talked about during the battle? It will give us a better chance to maybe figure out what's strange about Pacta, but I'd like to live there anyway."

Alain let his surprise show, remembering that despairing night on the sixth wall of Dorcastle as the rain fell. "That was a difficult conversation. You can smile when speaking of it?"

"Yes, because we're both going to live there. You were right."

"I will treasure being told I was right," Alain said. "There is something else?" he asked, seeing that she was eager to say more.

"I was thinking," Mari said, looking ahead, "we've got a lot of things to worry about, but the number of people trying to kill us shouldn't be nearly as high anymore, and if I do my job right we shouldn't have any more big wars for a while. We'll have to wait two or three years for things to settle down enough, but we could try starting a family then."

He felt that same pleasant jolt inside that he had experienced the first time Mari had mentioned such a thing in the Northern Ramparts. "I would like that. Perhaps we would have a daughter who was like you."

She laughed. "You don't want that, Alain. Trust me. The last thing we want is to have a daughter who takes after me. If you think I was difficult when we first met, you should have seen me a few years earlier!" Mari paused, her expression growing wistful. "Can we name her Kira? If we have a daughter, I'd really like to name her Kira."

"Kira would be a proud name for her to carry," Alain said, then blinked in surprise at the vision that appeared after he spoke those words.

"Did you just have foresight?" Mari questioned, her voice growing anxious.

"Yes," Alain said. "It was odd."

"Not scary? Odd?"

"I saw before me the map of the world of Urth that the librarians have in their tower. The map was the size of a mountain. We stood before it, you and I and a third person between us who I could not see clearly. Flame and dark smoke burst from part of the map, but the other half glowed with light."

Mari gave an exasperated sigh. "What could that possibly mean?"

"It means there is something from that world, something from Urth, that will offer great danger, and great promise," Alain said. "We will face it someday, along with that other, whoever she—" He paused again. "Yes. The person with us was a woman…or a girl."

Mari stared at him. "Our daughter?"

"I think so. The vision came as soon as we named her."

"You saw yourself. So that's a vision, an allegory, of something that might happen to us? The three of us, facing something together? Something that originates on Urth?"

"Yes, but…" Alain met Mari's eyes. "There was to the girl also a sense of promise, and of danger."

To his surprise, Mari laughed again. "Isn't that true of every daughter and every son? All right. So our daughter might be a handful. I expected nothing less, and I'm sure my mother thinks I deserve nothing less. I guess our adventures aren't over."

"I would hate to be bored," Alain said. "The vision showed danger but also hope. Thank you."

"For?"

"You never gave up. Not on me, and not on the world. The day we met I told you that happiness was an illusion, as I had been taught by the Mage Guild elders. You have shown me that happiness does exist."

She grinned. "I bet you say that to all the Master Mechanics who decide not to shoot you on sight." Mari came a little closer and grasped his hand tightly. "You're welcome. I still think I got the better end of the deal. Thank you for not giving up, even when our chances of reaching this day seemed like an illusion, even when it seemed there was no hope left. It looks like we have some more challenges to face someday, but I won't mind dealing with them as long as you're beside me."

Alain looked ahead, where the road ran onward to where it would reach the city of Altis, and along many paths through the city and to the port, where ships would continue the road across the water to countless other roads. Sometimes you could see where the road was going, but other times you could only guess. Like life, the road took on different aspects, and might wander down strange and unexpected ways.

But it never really ended.

FOR NEWS ABOUT JABBERWOCKY BOOKS AND AUTHORS

Sign up for our newsletter*: http://eepurl.com/b84tDz
visit our website: awfulagent.com/ebooks
or follow us on twitter: @awfulagent

THANKS FOR READING!

CPSIA information can be obtained
at www.ICGtesting.com
Printed in the USA
LVOW12s0042090118
562346LV00001B/177/P